W9-AML-967

PASSION'S CAPTIVE

Tonight, as Tanya lay on the mat watching Panther, she shivered, a shiver that had nothing to do with fear of being hurt, but everything to do with her fear of losing herself to him entirely.

He was a beautiful male animal; tall, bronze, graceful, with a power representative of his namesake. Panther lay down and gathered her trembling body close. Gazing deeply into her golden eyes, he felt his own body begin to throb with passion. His lips lowered to cover hers, claiming their sweetness as his alone, his tongue delving deeply into her mouth.

Tanya had told herself she would not respond to Panther's lovemaking this night, but the minute his mouth claimed hers, she was lost to reason. As his wandering hands charted her body, she began to tremble violently beneath his touch. His lips moved over hers, melting them like hot wax, boldly staking his claim.

Tanya arched against his body involuntarily. He was murmuring meaningless phrases, encouraging her touch. Her hands were spread out against his smooth chest, warding him off, but now they seemed to have a life of their own. Slowly, tentatively, they began to explore, measuring his shoulders, feeling the muscles contract beneath her palms, working their way gradually up into his thick ebony hair. White hot flashes of passion seared through her, making her cry out in longing—for what, she wasn't sure . . .

OTHER LEISURE BOOKS BY CATHERINE HART:

FIRE AND ICE
ASHES AND ECSTASY
SATIN AND STEEL
SUMMER STORM
FOREVER GOLD
NIGHT FLAME
FALLEN ANGEL
SWEET FURY

CATHERINE
HART

LEISURE BOOKS  NEW YORK CITY

A LEISURE BOOK®

July 1990

Published by

Dorchester Publishing Co., Inc.
276 Fifth Avenue
New York, NY 10001

Copyright© MCMLXXXV by Diane Tidd

All rights reserved. No part of this book may be reproduced or transmitted in any form or by any electronic or mechanical means, including photocopying, recording, or by any information storage and retrieval system, without the written permission of the Publisher, except where permitted by law.

The name "Leisure Books" and the stylized "L" with design are trademarks of Dorchester Publishing Co., Inc.

Printed in the United States of America.

A PANTHER STALKS

A panther stalks the forest deep
And roams the mountain high;
A silent form so dark and sleek
Till shrill screams split the sky.

On padded feet he stalks his prey,
Eyes gleaming in the dark.
The sight of his great tensile strength
Strikes terror in the heart.

A shadow in the moonlit night,
He fears not beast nor man.
By day he sleeps and keeps from sight;
By night he prowls the land.

His mate he'll take as his alone,
And fight to keep her safe.
He rules his kingdom from his throne,
Proud and strong and brave.

Take care if you should wander
through
His empire on your walks,
For nature will provide his due
As the mighty panther stalks.

Chapter 1

SILENT AS ghosts and nearly as invisible, the Indians watched the white women bathing in the river. Only their onyx eyes gave any sign of life, sparkling with lust as they spied on the scantily clad pale skin so near at hand. One young brave nudged his companion and pointed to a particularly lovely girl. In her chemise and pantalets, wet and clinging and nearly transparent, she was a vision of budding womanhood. Her breasts were high, firm and full, her waist so small his hands could span it, and her hips gently rounded.

As they watched, she lifted her head, and her face was fully revealed. Her forehead was high over delicately arched mink-brown brows. Below a small, straight nose, her lips gleamed a rose pink, perfectly formed to tempt a man's, the lower lip slightly more full with just a suggestion of a pout. It was her eyes, however, that made him draw in a sharp, silent breath of surprise. They were a gleaming golden hue, too light to be brown, yet definitely not yellow; a shade that made him think of the eyes of a lioness on the prowl. The comparison was reinforced by the tawny color of her long, gently waving hair. It was an unusual combination of sun-streaked light brown and golden blonde, with just a hint of a few strands of strawberry through it.

The brave motioned to his friend, and they retreated as noislessly as they had advanced. In all, there were ten young Cheyenne in the group that met where they had left their ponies. Quickly, their eyes gleaming with excitement, they laid their plans. The leader made it clear to the others that he desired the woman with the golden eyes and mane of the lioness. She would be his before his heart could beat a thousand times more.

Heedless of the approaching danger, the women cavorted in the cool water. It felt so good to be clean again! There were six of them in the stream, all young except one.

Tanya Martin shook back her heavy wet hair from her golden eyes and reached for the scented soap her sister Julie was handing her.

"I'm going back to the wagon now," Julie informed the others as she hastily dried herself and pulled on a loose dress over her wet underwear. "I can't wait to slip into clean, dry clothes."

The others waved her on, not yet ready to give up the cool luxury of the stream. They had traveled a long way, and the journey's end was nearly in sight for some. The Martin girls and their parents had traveled all the way from Philadelphia, going from there to St. Louis by rail, and from St. Louis on by wagon train, following the Santa Fe Trail through Kansas and now into the Colorado Territory. It had been rough going through the April rains this spring of 1866, but they had endured.

There were sixteen wagons in their group, bearing an odd mixture of people all traveling west for a variety of reasons. There were farmers looking for more fertile lands; ex-soldiers from both sides of the Mason-Dixon line seeking their fortunes and trying to forget the horrors of the recently ended war; war-torn families hoping to relocate and recoup their losses in a new land. There were young men looking for excitement and old ones looking for peace. There were young women seeking husbands and older ones wearily following theirs across these vast miles of wilderness.

Tanya looked around her at the other women. In the shallows near the bank Rosemary Walters, older than the others at thirty-six, was washing her husband's blue shirt, a pile of children's clothing yet to clean. The Walters, all seven of them, were looking for good cheap farm land. Harry was the youngest of his family in Kentucky, and had no desire to share the skimpy profits from the tiny, crop-weary farm with his brothers. With his four growing sons, his wife, and small daughter he expected better success on his own.

Pretty Nancy Owen, at the tender age of fifteen, was relocating with her father, mother, and younger brother to New Mexico. Mrs. Owen's doctor had recommended the change of climate for the lady's lung condition.

Red-haired, sassy Suellen Haverick was the spoiled brat of the entire wagon train, beating out even the fractious Julie in Tanya's estimation. The daughter of a prominent eastern lawyer, she was used to demanding anything and everything and expecting results immediately. When disappointed, she voiced her displeasure loud and long in a voice that resembled fingernails scraping across a chalkboard. For this reason, among others, Tanya was glad the trip was almost done and the Havericks would continue on to California. If only Suellen had not been prone to *mal de mer* they could have sailed instead and spared the others her presence these past two months.

Last, there was Melissa Anderson. A petite blonde with eyes as blue as cornflowers, Melissa as an orphan at fourteen. She was traveling with the Wells family, also heading for California, to live with a distant cousin she'd never met, her only other living relative.

Tanya and her family were headed for Pueblo, just two days away. Edward Martin's brother George and his wife Elizabeth had come west during the gold rush of 1859, settling in Pueblo. Uncle George now ran a mercantile and a small lumber yard.

When Aunt Elizabeth had visited back east last year, she had traveled with a handsome cavalryman by the name of Jeffrey Young. Once the dashing Jeffrey was introduced to Tanya, he courted her with undaunted spirit and boundless energy until she finally promised to marry him. He returned to Fort Lyon where he was stationed, and now awaited her arrival in Pueblo, where he had been transferred and promoted to lieutenant.

Tanya's family was to stay with Aunt Elizabeth and Uncle George, vacationing awhile after the wedding. Uncle George was determined to convince his brother Edward to stay and help him in his business. Edward and Sarah Martin were willing to entertain the possibility, as their eldest daughter would now be residing there, but they would not commit themselves without first seeing the town and territory. Julie, two years younger than Tanya's sixteen, was not happy about the whole idea, loathe to leave her friends and comforts back home. To hear her tell it, they had nearly walked across the continent barefoot and ragged. She complained every step of the way, until Tanya was ready to slap her.

Now they were almost there. They had survived rain and boiling sun that had baked the mud into cracked ruts. They had learned to combat bugs, snakes, and all manner of creatures, to cook over hastily built campfires, and to sleep and travel in the crowded confines of the wagon. Quickly they learned how to pull together as neighbors, repair wagon wheels and broken harness, take advantage of safe streams for washing, and put up with the dust and grit good-naturedly when they must.

Only a few of the original travelers had not survived the trip. Old Elmer Jones had a heart attack and died trying to help push a stuck wagon out of a mudhole. Tom Travis had died of snakebite, but Helen Wells had survived one. Iris Miller's baby was stillborn, and ten-year-old Joey Cord had died of a fever. That had nearly thrown the entire group into a panic as they thought it was cholera, but no one else had become sick, so they considered themselves lucky. A couple of oxen had eaten some kind of poisonous weed and died, and a couple of others had died of pure exhaustion, but no other ills had befallen the travellers. Luckily, they had encountered no Indians. There had been signs of them along the way, and once they had seen what looked like a family band traveling in the distance, but they had not had any problems or attacks to counter.

Four days past they had stopped at Fort Lyon, a combination trading post and fort, where they had met William Bent and his Indian wife Yellow Woman. Mr. Bent had told them that the Indian bands always rejoined their tribes in the spring, coming together to perform spring rituals, exchange news, and unite against the threat of warring tribes. The soldiers confirmed that all had been quiet so far. Little was heard of Roman Nose and his band of Cheyenne for months now, though he was prone to attack along the western Kansas border when the mood struck. Black Kettle, the chief of the Southern Cheyenne, was peaceable and more apt to negotiate than fight, but he was in his sixties and getting rather old for war. Black Kettle's brother had been killed in the Sand Creek Massacre of 1864, and things had been touch and go for a while, but as long as Black Kettle could keep his young buck of a nephew, A Panther Stalks, under control, there shouldn't be any trouble. Red Cloud and his band of Sioux were quiet, and Sitting Bull, chief of the Sioux, was in treaty with the government for once.

The wagon train had left Bent's Fort on its next ninety mile trek to Pueblo with only six added soldiers as escorts, who were being exchanged for half a dozen new recruits from Pueblo. Things were too quiet to warrant more, and no trouble was brewing that they knew of.

Tanya dove under the crystal clear water, swam to where Melissa stood in her underslip, and surfaced next to her.

"Where'd you learn to swim like that back in Philadelphia?" Melissa wanted to know, her blue eyes big and earnest as always.

Tanya laughed and tossed back her streaming hair. "We're right along the Delaware River, Missy, and summers Daddy would rent a cottage outside of town along a sandy stretch. Mother could get away from the city heat that way. Daddy paid a couple of boys from a neighboring cottage to teach Julie and me to swim so Mother wouldn't have to worry so about us. I took to it right away, but Julie couldn't stand to get muck between her delicate toes and never did learn."

Melissa nodded her understanding. "I hope for her sake Pueblo is a nice place. The trip has been rough on her."

"Oh, pooh!" Tanya retorted. "Julie isn't happy unless she has something to complain about."

Melissa smiled one of her rare smiles. "You haven't complained much. I'll bet you've been too busy dreaming about what's-his-name . . . Jeffrey?"

A dreamy look of anticipation crept over Tanya's face. "Yes, Jeffrey. I can't wait to see him again. It seems like forever since we've been together," she sighed. "Just think, in less than two weeks we'll be married and I'll be Mrs. Jeffrey Young."

Melissa cast her a wistful look. "I envy you, Tanya. I really do. I wish I had that to look forward to."

Tanya was instantly contrite. "Oh, Missy! You will! Just wait and see! You are going to love California, and you are so pretty, all the boys will be lined up knocking on your cousin's door and begging for your hand. You'll be breaking hearts left and right just trying to decide who to accept."

Melissa laughed outright at the picture Tanya painted for her. Suddenly the laughter broke off in midstream and her smile froze on her face, becoming more of a grimace.

Before Tanya had more than a second to wonder about it, she heard splashing in the water behind her. Her gaze fell on Rosemary at the water's edge, her mouth open in a soundless scream, but as Tanya turned to see what was happening, something caught and tugged hard at her hair. As she stumbled backward, she was seized hard about her chest and under her arms, and the next she knew she was being lifted out of the water. As her startled thoughts registered the feel of a horse beneath her, a hand was clamped down on her mouth, stopping the reflexive scream in her throat.

In a matter of seconds they were out of the water on the opposite side of the river and thundering through the trees. The attack had come before any of them could scream for help. Until someone wondered why they were taking so long and went to investigate, no one would realize they were in trouble. By then it would probably be too late. Somewhere in the back of her mind, Tanya reasoned that the wagon train itself had not been attacked. There had been no sounds of alarm or fighting before, during, or right after the abduction at the river. The Indians had arrived swiftly, silently snatched up their hapless victims, and departed. Tanya doubted anyone else had been taken but the five of them.

All these thoughts were racing through her mind as Tanya struggled to release her captor's hold. Desperately she squirmed and wriggled and kicked, considering a fall from the horse a small matter compared to what was in store for her if she failed to escape. She freed her arms and flailed at the bronze thigh resting so close to hers; clawed at the arms and hands binding her to him.

She felt his hold slacken slightly, and just when she thought she might be making some headway, he brought his arm up tightly about her ribs under her breasts until all the breath left her lungs and she could draw no more. Her head began to spin, then a grey mist with brilliant yellow spots rose up before her eyes. Struggle as she might, the mist was swallowing her, and she felt her limbs going limp, useless. Her last conscious thought was, "This has to be a dream, a nightmare! Oh, God, don't let this be real!"

Consciousness returned all too soon. Her first sense was of the steady rhythm of the horse beneath her. There was a warmth along her right side, a drumming in her ear. Tanya stiffened as she remembered what it was all about and realized the warmth came from the Indian's body as she lay against him, her head against his chest. The pounding was the beating of his heart in her ear. Screwing up her courage, she opened her eyes for her first glimpse of her captor.

She looked straight up into the darkest eyes she'd ever seen in her life. They were as black as night, so much so that she could not tell where the iris left off and the pupil began. Tanya could see her reflection perfectly. Not able to hold his gaze, she let her own wander to his high forehead beneath the decorated headband, the blue-black hair hanging in braids across his shoulders, and the two eagle feathers dangling on one side. Her eyes traveled from his high cheekbones along his well-defined jawline, then skipped to the straight, sculptured nose and down to the firm, unyielding shape of his lips. Feeling his eyes still upon her as she studied him, she jerked her gaze back to his and thought she caught a glimmer of humor in his eyes before they again became unreadable mirrors.

His shoulder was solid beneath her, his arm corded with muscles, his hands long-fingered and strong. His stomach was flat, his hips—as far as she could estimate—were slim, and his chest broad, deep, and hairless. His skin was a bronzed copper shade, and she noticed that he was clean, smelling of leather, wood and smoke, not at all repellent but very masculine. As she searched her brain for a word to describe him, she was shocked to find the only words to come to mind were *handsome, noble male.*

"I must be out of my mind!" she thought in bewilderment.

Tearing her gaze from him, she struggled to sit up

straight, and was surprised when he aided her attempt, though she noted he remained alert to her every move lest she became unruly again. Glancing about, she saw they were traveling across the plains, heading for the foothills and mountains to the west. The sun was setting. Darkness would be on them soon, and surely they would be lost to rescue then. By craning her neck about and peering over his shoulder, she could see the other Indians and their captives. She counted ten Indians and horses in all, and only four other women besides herself as captives. Behind them she could see no sign of a rescue party.

Her gaze reviewed their group. Rosemary rode before a tall, stern-looking Indian a bit older than the others. Still in shock, her eyes had a fixed, glazed look, as if she was not aware of a single thing that was happening. Nancy was sitting in a crumpled heap across her brave's lap. Her chemise was undone and her straight brown hair straggled down across her bared breasts. The coppery hand of the brave rested intimately on her thigh.

If the situation had not been so serious, Tanya could almost have laughed at Suellen's predicament. As it was, a smile flirted at the corners of her mouth for the smallest of seconds. The snooty Suellen's nose wasn't up in the air now. As a matter of fact, it was just the opposite. She was riding slung stomach down across the Indian pony's back. Her head and arms dangled down on one side, her legs on the other, and her rear in the air. Every time she attempted to protest this position in her piercing voice, her captor administered a smart slap to her posterior.

Poor little Melissa drew all of Tanya's compassion. She sat in tears before one of the ugliest, most repulsive human beings that Tanya had ever seen. She sat stiffly, a look of abject terror on her face. There was a vivid, rapidly darkening bruise on her cheek. Her petticoat was torn half off, revealing the entire upper portion of her body, the cloth lying limply in her lap. Her captor was taking pleasure in tormenting her by squeezing her breasts, cruelly twisting the already red, swollen nipples between his fat, stubby fingers. Down his three chins saliva dripped, and Tanya could almost smell the stench of his fat body from where she rode. Tanya shivered involuntarily and drew a curious look from her captor.

As she studied the remaining Indians, Tanya reluctantly admitted that though they were a fearsome lot, they seemed a proud people. It showed in the way they carried themselves, even on horseback. For the most part they were tall, fit, and well-muscled. The long, slim bone structure of their faces was cleanly defined with high cheekbones and straight noses, and Tanya was thankful they were not decorated in hideous war paints.

One young brave came abreast of them and said something in a deep guttural tongue to her captor. Since he glanced at her as he spoke, she assumed his remark had to do with her. Her captor answered in the same language.

Although the young man was no more of a menace than the man on whose big black horse Tanya rode, she unconsciously shifted closer to her captor for protection. It may have been her imagination, or did his hold tighten on her waist?

Night fell and they rode on into the darkness. Lulled by the monotonous movement of the horse and the length of the ride, Tanya finally gave up the struggle to keep her eyelids open. She slept, once again supported by that broad bronze chest.

She opened her eyes to a darkness so black she was at once disoriented. The only reality was the hard wall of muscle behind her, the iron band about her middle, and the warmth of the black horse beneath her travel-weary bottom. As her eyes adjusted, she could make out the shadows of trees on either side of the trail they were on. They seemed to be climbing, so she guessed they were across the plain and into the foothills she had seen.

Tanya sighed and twisted about, trying to find a more comfortable position. The brave assisted her, grunting something unintelligible near her ear. She supposed he was telling her to sit still. Were they never going to stop to rest or eat? Tanya's tongue felt like cotton, and her stomach was surely touching her backbone. The attack had come in late afternoon after the wagon train had camped for the evening, and Tanya was regretting her missed supper. It seemed a trifling thing to worry about under the circumstances, but she was bone-weary, and dreadfully hungry and thirsty. To top it all, she was sure to disgrace herself unless they stopped soon. She just had to find a place to relieve herself before her bladder burst.

When they finally did stop at a clearing in the dense trees, Tanya's muscles were unprepared. Her brave lowered her to the ground, and before her limbs had adjusted to her weight, he pushed her roughly toward where the other women were being dumped. He grunted a terse order in his deep voice, which she interpreted as a directive to stay put, and went to tend to his horse. The other men did the same, leaving the women in a trembling and frightened huddle in the center of the clearing. Adversely, Tanya now wished they had not stopped, for as long as they were riding she felt somewhat safe. Now a feeling of dread was creeping up her backbone.

Looking at the pathetic group about her, Tanya's fright grew. Rosemary was still in her fright-induced trance, staring stupidly ahead at nothing. The other three, Suellen included, were weeping softly. In an odd way Tanya felt removed from them, neither crying nor hidden from reality in a stupor. Admittedly, she was scared, unsure whether her limbs were shaking from fright or weariness, but an icy calm was setting in. Dread of facing an unknown, inevitable fate made her eyes huge golden orbs in her face, but a fierce will to survive whatever was in store was holding the tears at bay.

Moved by compassion, Tanya wrapped the trembling Melissa in her arms. Melissa clung to her, sobbing. With words so soft and shaky that Tanya could barely understand her, she whimpered, "Oh, Lord, Tanya, I'm so scared! What is going to happen to us?"

Tanya patted the blond head ineffectually. "I don't know, Missy," she answered. "It all depends on them." She glanced at the approaching Indians.

Her own tall captor clamped a hand around her upper arm and led her off toward the trees. Quaking inwardly, she stumbled, half running to keep up with his long strides. Just inside the treeline he stopped, and with a few brief hand signals made her understand she was to relieve herself here.

She stared at him dumbly for a moment. Modesty overcoming her fear, she motioned for him to turn around. Folding his arms across his chest, he continued to watch her steadily, making no move to honor her request.

Mad enough to spit, she frowned at him. "Oh, for heaven's sake!" she complained. "It's too dark in these woods to see two feet in front of me. I wouldn't get a yard away before you heard me!" She thrust out her chin and requested primly, "A little privacy would be appreciated, if you please."

She knew he hadn't understood a word, but his lips quirked suspiciously, as if he were holding back a smile. "Indians aren't supposed to smile, are they?" she wondered to herself.

Whatever, the result was that he gave her a level, warning look, then turned his back to her. Knowing her chances of escape were nil, she quickly and thankfully used her few seconds of privacy to empty her aching bladder.

He led her back into the clearing, and Tanya immediately wished he hadn't. The scene before her was right out of the halls of hell. She stopped so abruptly that she caused her captor to walk right into her rigid back. He grumbled what amounted to a curse, but she was beyond noticing. Mesmerized by the horrifying scene before her, she was at once revolted, but unable to turn away.

One of the Indians had built a small, smokeless fire that illuminated the area well enough that Tanya could not help but see what was happening, and if ever she had prayed to go deaf it was now.

Not one of her friends had a stitch of clothing on, and each was being raped by a different savage. Not a sound came from Rosemary as a grunting, sweating savage rutted over her. Nancy was sobbing loudly and crying out, and Suellen was screaming at the top of her limitless lungs and cursing with words she should have never known.

Tanya's eyes zeroed in on Melissa, struggling

beneath her grotesque captor. The ugly beast was thrusting himself into Melissa's tender flesh with a malicious vengeance, while he kneaded and bit at her bruised breasts. Melissa's wild shrieks of agony ripped the air.

"Oh, God!" Tanya muttered before she bent and vomited violently on the ground before her.

Her captor gave her little time to recover herself as he dragged her close to the fire and shoved her to the ground. Fully expecting to have to defend herself, Tanya was surprised when he seated himself beside her, dug into a leather bag, and handed her a strip of dried meat. Eyeing him warily, she watched as he took out another container, shook out some dried grain and berries into his palm and mixed it with water. Cupping her hands before her, he dumped the mixture into her palms, motioning for her to eat it. Then he prepared more for himself.

Over her initial shock but still revolted, Tanya tried not to notice when other braves replaced the first attackers over the prone bodies of her friends. Feeling guilty that she was the only one not violated so far, she was also honest enough with herself to feel grateful, knowing she did not wish to trade places with any of them, not even to spare them. It was selfish, she knew, and she felt badly about it, but she could not help them by wishing ill on herself. Accepting this, she chewed morosely on her food, willing her stomach to accept the needed nourishment. She took the water he gave her and drank greedily, then sat quietly and waited to see what would happen next.

After a while, he rose. Motioning for her to stay there, he stalked off toward where the horses were staked. He was gone only seconds before Tanya was grabbed roughly from behind. Thrown onto her back, she looked up into the horrid, beefy face of the beast who had attacked Melissa so vindictively.

Momentarily too stunned to do more than emit a startled squawk, Tanya's survival instinct suddenly erupted full force. If she were going to be violated, it would not be by this animal if she could avoid it, even if it meant her life! A low, vicious snarl issued from deep in her throat, startling both herself and her attacker. Then Tanya was a blur of flailing arms and legs as she fought him. He threw himself onto her, trying to subdue her with his weight, aiming blows at her body and face. She successfully deflected the worst of his blows with her arms, scratching and biting. Then one of her kicking legs landed a knee hard in his groin. The fat, blubbery savage roared in pain and struck her hard on the chin with his fist.

Stars of pain blurred Tanya's vision and swirled in a gathering mist as she fought to stay conscious. When she felt his stubby fingers hook in her chemise, ripping the material to expose her breasts, she rallied. With a furious shriek that rivaled that of a mountain lioness defending her cubs, she lunged at him, unaware of the crowd of onlookers they had attracted. Her teeth connected with the lobe of his ear and she bit down hard. He howled in agony and hit at her, trying to shake her loose, but she clung like a dog to a chunk of raw meat. She felt the flesh give way under the pressure of her teeth until her jaws met. Her attacker pulled loose, leaving his earlobe still between her clamped teeth, and leveled a blow to her head that nearly cracked her jaw.

Several things happened at once. The ugly savage's weight was lifted from her, and Tanya recognized her original captor. He had a hold on the fat Indian's shoulder, whom he lifted and propelled away from her. Her mouth full of blood and part of the Indian's ear, Tanya rolled over and retched violently for the second time that evening. Pulling herself to elbows and knees, she willed herself not to faint as she concentrated on the events going on nearby. Her tall, bronze captor had subdued her attacker and was issuing what sounded like terse commands. From the angry tone of his voice and various gestures at her, she gathered he was making it clear to all that she was his alone, at least for the time being. She hoped this was what he was saying, though what the difference was between being ravished by one savage or another, she couldn't have said.

Her captor yanked her up and propelled her to a spot he had picked out. Throwing some blankets at her, he directed her to spread them out on the ground. Afterward, he lay down, motioning for her to do the same. She did so warily.

He lay on his back, his arms folded beneath his head, eyes closed. After a few minutes of listening to her fuss and squirm trying to adjust her torn chemise and rid her mouth of its acid taste, he sighed and sat up. Handing her the water flask to rinse her mouth, he pulled a strip of leather from one of his braids. This he handed to her to lace her bodice back together. Taking another thong, he tied it about her right wrist and tethered it to his left one. Once again he lay down to sleep, leaving her to do as she wished, as far as her leash allowed.

She sat for a while studying her situation, reviewing the events of the day. However, she was exhausted, and it wasn't long before she eased herself down on her blanket, as far from his body as she could reach, and went to sleep.

* * *

The sky wasn't even light when she was shaken awake. She lifted sleep-heavy eyelids to find her head nestled on a bronze shoulder and her face just inches away from that of her captor. Her arm was thrown across his chest and her leg rested intimately between his. During the night she must have gravitated toward the heat his body had offered.

Tanya was mortified. Talk about embracing your enemy . . . literally! He gave her a level, measuring look, awaiting her reaction, which was not long in coming.

First she turned a delightful shade of bright pink and immediately tried to push herself away from him. With his arm clasped about her shoulder and her leg caught between his, he held her easily, watching her struggle for a few seconds. Then she quieted, and he could see her thinking the problem over in her mind, her straight pearly teeth worrying her lower lip. He nearly laughed aloud as she very gingerly tried to untangle her limbs from his, her small white hand grazing his thigh as she tried to get him to move his leg without actually touching him. His chest shook with repressed laughter as she finally gave up.

Resting her forehead on his shoulder, she sighed in defeat. "Will you please let me up, you big bronze brute?"

He hid a smile and lifted her chin in his palm, tilting her face to his. With a look that said he knew he had her at his mercy and could do with her whatever he wished, he released her. He severed the thong that bound her to him and led her into the trees for her morning nature call, politely turning his back. Then he threw her some more dried meal and meat for breakfast and indicated she was to retrieve the blankets and follow him.

When his big black horse had been tended to, he gave Tanya her ration of water and they mounted. The rest of the band followed suit.

A quick look around at the other women made Tanya realize how fortunate she had been thus far. Suellen, Melissa and Nancy all looked half dead. Surprisingly, Rosemary was starting to rally. Having survived the previous night, she was coming out of her stupor and seemed more aware of what was going on around her.

An hour into their ride, the sun was up, and Tanya was trying to get her bearings. Now that darkness did not cover the landscape, she saw that they were indeed in the foothills. The sun was behind them; the mountains ahead. On the top of a rise, Tanya twisted about, trying to memorize landmarks and mark the direction of their travel in relationship to the probable location of the wagon train. A smart slap on her thigh brought her attention to her captor's face. He glared at her in disapproval, fully aware of what she was thinking. A sharp, negative shake of his head told her to forget all ideas of escape.

Chapter 2

THEY REACHED the Indian encampment just before dusk. In the fading light, Tanya saw what looked like a city of tents spread out in the secluded mountain valley.

At the edge of the encampment, Tanya's captor halted his party of braves. Looping a length of leather about Tanya's neck to fashion a collar and leash, he pushed her from his horse to fall to the ground at his mount's hooves. With a tug at his end, he urged her to her feet.

Fear and anger warred in her golden eyes, making them blaze. He felt them shooting darts into his straight bronze back as he turned from her and rode proudly through the maze of *tipis*, his leonine captive in tow.

Never would Tanya forget the humiliation of that trip through the avenue of *tipis* to the center of the village. Forced to trot to keep up with the pace of his horse, it was difficult to maintain her dignity. As they wound their way past the skin-covered conical structures, a crowd gathered about them to welcome the returning braves and torment their victims.

Tanya stiffened when the first red-brown hands reached out to touch her pale skin. Vaguely she heard Nancy, behind her whimper, and Melissa cry out in alarm. More hands reached out, pulling at her arms, pinching, tugging at her tangled hair. Jostled and pushed about, Tanya struggled to keep her balance. Hands struck out at her; feet deliberately thrust into her path, threatened to trip her. A sea of taunting faces loomed closer.

An inner strength she never knew she had stiffened her spine and held the tears at bay. Staring straight before her, Tanya refused to look to either side. Compressing her lips tightly together, she called upon her fierce pride to school her features into rigid planes, refusing to show her growing fear and panic. Stoically she bore the taunts and blows, ignoring the pain, willing herself not to cry out.

Once she lost her footing and fell headlong in the dirt. The leather thong cut into her neck, cutting off her air, choking her. Amidst the throng of bronze limbs thrust at her, she fought her way to her feet, stumbling after her captor's horse. Scraped, scratched, and bleeding, she clawed at the noose until she could once more draw a ragged breath. Hatred and pride rescued her flagging composure.

In a clearing at the center of the camp, they stopped. The captives were herded together to one side as the returning braves dismounted and were greeted by their fellow warriors. Out of the largest and most ornate of the decorated *tipis* emerged a tall, gray-haired Indian. His proud stance proclaimed him a man of importance in his tribe. He spoke to Tanya's captor, his deep commanding voice carrying to where Tanya waited with her fellow captives. A silence fell over the crowd when he spoke. Tanya's captor responded, and together with several other men, they went into the ornate *tipi*.

This seemed to signal a return to camp activity.

Standing with her friends, Tanya watched as two Indian women lit the huge fire in the center of the clearing. As the flames drove away the encroaching darkness, so did it drive away all hope of escape. Glancing about her, Tanya winced at the number of tents surrounding them. Should they somehow manage to slip unnoticed to the edge of the camp, they would have to cross an open expanse of field separating them from the forest's edge. For the moment the Indians seemed content to ignore them, but Tanya sensed their every move was being monitored.

Most of the crowd had dispersed. The women had dragged the curious children away. Tanya wondered if they were now inside their skin-covered homes eating supper and sharing conversation the way white people did. Many of the men had stayed and were sitting about the fire talking, now and then throwing a glance at the captive women.

Bone-weary and sore, Tanya tentatively lowered herself to sit on the dew-dampened ground. Seeing no reaction from their guards, the other women followed suit. Too tired and scared to talk, they huddled silently together, a tense, pathetic group. The aroma of cooking food caused their empty stomachs to cramp painfully, especially as they watched Indian wives carrying bowls of food to their husbands around the fire. No one came to give them food or water or blankets to ward off the evening chill.

Every so often a few of the Indians would wander off, only to return after having painted his face and chest, and sometimes his arms and legs, with strange, frightening designs. Soon they were all decorated in bright, greasy paints, and the hostages shivered, wondering if this was a prelude to their torture or death. It certainly appeared as if they were preparing for some sort of celebration or ceremony.

Tanya's nerves were stretched taut. Huddled with her trembling, terror-filled fellow captives, she strove desperately to keep her own panic at bay. Her heart had lodged somewhere in her throat and was pounding at a frightening pace. She jumped involuntarily when Melissa slumped against her. Melissa had found a temporary escape from her terror, whether in sleep or a fright-induced faint Tanya wasn't sure. She shifted Melissa so that the girl's head lay in her lap, absently stroking the bright hair. The soothing action brought her a measure of calm.

Tanya barely recognized her captor when he finally re-emerged from the large tipi. He, too, had painted his face and chest. Across both cheeks he wore what resembled huge black claws, and one wide stripe of black followed the straight line of his nose. On his broad, hairless chest was the caricature of a snarling panther. At another time perhaps the artistry of the design would have fascinated Tanya, but at the moment she was frozen with fear, unable to do more than stare.

With the arrival of the old chief and his entourage, the evening's activities picked up. Seated about the fire, the men talked, their women taking up places behind them to hear the news. As Tanya and the others awaited their fate, drums began to sound, echoing their frantic heartbeats. A weathered, stooped old man began to chant, shaking a rattle as he sang. Soon others picked up the chant, and the eerie tones wafted on the evening breeze, sending shivers along Tanya's spine. Several of their captors got up and mimed the story of how they had captured the white women.

Even Tanya had no trouble interpreting some of their actions. She frowned as one of the braves mimicked how she had bitten the squat captor's ear. Would this earn her additional torture . . . more pain . . . a longer, slower death? Many of the Indians seemed to appreciate this part of the skit, guffawing loudly at the ugly man's disfigurement. Several pairs of dark eyes turned toward Tanya, assessing the white girl who had done this to one of their own. Tanya steeled herself not to cringe beneath their stares, returning their looks steadily with her own golden gaze.

The night and the noise seemed to go on and on. At one point there seemed to be an argument between Tanya's captor and the fat, gruesome creature whose ear she had bitten. The ugly one shouted and gestured wildly to Tanya and then to his deformed ear, addressing himself to the gray-haired man Tanya assumed was their chief. Icy fingers danced along Tanya's spine. Then her captor spoke, firmly stating in quiet, angry tones what he had to say. The old chief nodded, spoke a few clipped words, and Tanya's captor sat down, evidently satisfied, while the other stomped angrily back to his place in the circle. What this meant, Tanya could not tell, but she hoped she would not be turned over to the ugly warrior.

The evening's activities seemed to be building up to a climax. The very air seemed to tingle with excitement. Finally, at a word from the chief, several women approached the captives. The white women were led to their original captors; Tanya's leash was placed in her captor's hands.

Melissa nearly fainted again, and Nancy broke out in a series of ear-piercing shrieks. From the corner of her eye, Tanya could see Suellen struggling against her captor's hold. Rosemary was sobbing quietly and muttering what sounded like a prayer. Tanya felt frozen, unable to react in any way.

The girls were led toward the fire, and for one heart-stopping moment Tanya was sure they were to be burned alive. Brought up short by a tug on her leash, she stopped. She watched, holding her breath, as Rosemary was led forward. At the fire's edge her captor held her as an Indian woman reached out and took a burning twig from the fire. The tattered edges of Rosemary's skirt threatened to catch fire as the glowing end of the stick was brought to her thigh. Bile rose up in Tanya's throat as she watched, horrified. Rosemary's screams tore the night air as her leg was seared. She slumped against her captor as he led her away.

By this time the other girls realized what was in store for them. Nancy, next in line, was screaming and pleading, to no avail. Suellen had renewed her struggles, twisting and clawing in her bid for freedom, her strident voice even more piercing in her terror. Melissa's eyes looked like two large blue-glazed dinner plates in her otherwise colorless face. Her mouth opened and shut soundlessly.

The smell of singed flesh filled Tanya's nostrils, making them flare. Her heart was beating so fast she thought it would fly out of her mouth. Her eyes huge, she swallowed hard, trying desperately not to be sick.

She felt hard, lean fingers on her chin, tilting her face up to that of her captor. As her ears received the sounds of Nancy's agony, her eyes saw his narrow in warning, and his hand tightened on her jaw as he shook his head. He pushed her ahead of him, forcing her to watch as Melissa was held for branding. The petite blonde fainted in mid-scream. Tanya felt his fingers pressing into her upper arms, forcing her shoulders back, straightening her stance. As Suellen was led forward, bucking and kicking, he again forced her to face him and shook his head.

Tanya stared up into his ebony eyes, realizing this bronze savage was telling her to bear this bravely; proudly. Strangely, his gaze lent her strength, as if his own strength were flowing into her.

Mutely she reached up and removed his hands from her arms. He released her without comment, his gaze locked with hers. Tanya's chin came up proudly, and she squared her shoulders and walked calmly ahead of him to the fire's edge. Outwardly she was regal; inside she was quivering and afraid. With shaky fingers she reached down and tore away the lower length of her pantalets, not wanting the material seared into her wound.

The Indians watched her in surprised approval. If there was one thing they respected, it was bravery. Tanya saw her captor gesture to one particular stick in the flames. When it was removed from the fire, she understood why. It was fashioned in the same design as the one he bore on his chest; that of a snarling panther. She was to be branded as his, with his distinctive mark.

Swallowing convulsively, she turned to face him, presenting her thigh to the woman holding the glowing brand. His hands came up to grasp her wrists, and hers automatically closed about his, seeking something to hold on to. Gritting her teeth and holding her breath, Tanya braced herself, staring up into his jet black eyes.

The pain was worse than anything she could recall. The stench of her own burnt flesh made her stomach lurch. If not for the support of his hands holding her up, her knees would have buckled beneath her. Her hands clenched spasmodically, digging her fingernails into the flesh of his wrists. Tanya's eyes closed as if to shut out the pain, and her head fell back, but the only sound to escape between her tightly clamped teeth was a long, loud hiss.

When it was done, he gave her a moment to recover herself, then led her away, into a nearby tipi. After seating her on a mat, he took down a bag from a pole and a bowl from near the fire. Gently he washed her wound with water and applied a salve from the pouch.

As he worked over her leg, an older woman entered the tipi. She stood silently watching, and when he had finished, he said something to her in that gruff language Tanya was becoming used to. With gestures he told Tanya to sleep. Then he turned and left the lodge.

The woman repeated his gesture for Tanya to sleep and settled herself by the fire. For a while Tanya lay staring up at the top of the tipi, mentally blocking out the searing pain in her thigh. As the pain lessened, she began to take note of her surroundings. The inside of the tipi was larger than she'd expected, easily twenty feet across. Long poles formed the supporting skeletal structure. Crossing near the top and tied together, they formed a cone, large at the base, smaller toward the top, leaving a hole at the top for the smoke to rise through. Animal skins were sewn together and laid across the pole supports, creating the walls. Now Tanya recalled that many of the lodges had brightly painted designs on the outsides. Tanya wondered whose tipi this was. Was it her captor's or the old woman's?

She was lying on some kind of woven mat, like the one the woman was seated on. Nearby was a pile of furs. From the lodge poles various leather bags and pouches hung, also what appeared to be articles of clothing. On the floor near the fire was a stack of bowls and pots, and a tripod that may have been used for cooking over the fire. Near the entrance hung a collection of braided leather straps like the one that her captor used as a bridle on his horse. What caught Tanya's eye was the hatchet that hung with them, and the feather-decorated lance leaning close by. With weapons she might escape and survive.

Tanya glanced at the old woman, discomfited to find the black eyes watching her intently. She sighed tiredly and closed her eyes. Now was not the time.

Her opportunity came sooner than she would have guessed. Tanya woke to a pain in her leg. In her sleep she had rolled over onto her branded thigh, and the pain had jerked her out of a sound sleep. Hesitantly, she glanced about. The fire had burned low, but she could see by the glow of the coals that she was alone. Her captor had not returned, and the woman must have left once she was sure Tanya slept, not expecting the weary girl to awaken so soon. Sounds of the revelry outside told her the ceremony was still going on.

Slowly Tanya rolled to her feet, careful not to touch the raw red wound on her thigh. She removed the hated leash and flung it to the ground. Stealthily she crept to the flap-covered opening and peeked out. Not thirty feet away, the Indians were celebrating around the central fire, but all seemed quiet away from the fire.

Ducking back inside, Tanya longed for the time to search out food and water, but dared not spare precious moments that might mean the difference between escaping or not. She grabbed up the lance and hatchet and crawled out the opening. Quickly she dashed around to the darkened side of the tipi. Keeping to the shadows, ever wary, she wound her way past lodge after lodge on silent bare feet. With the lance as a crutch, she worked her way to the edge of the encampment.

Once free of the village, she dashed headlong across the open field, intent on the cover of the forest, determinedly ignoring the pain in her leg. Her breath was coming in short gasps, and her heart was pounding so loudly in her ears she was surprised the whole village hadn't heard it. She wished she could have stolen a horse, but she hadn't known where they were kept, and hadn't passed any along her way.

So intent was she on her flight, Tanya failed to see or hear the person following her. Reaching the treeline, she stopped to catch her breath, leaning against a tree trunk for support. As she straightened up to go on, a hand clamped itself down over her mouth as another snatched the hatchet and lance from her. She felt herself hauled back and dragged into the moonlit field to face none other than her captor of two days ago. Tears of frustration welled up in her eyes, but she blinked them back furiously.

Once more she found herself marched back past the circling pattern of tipis. Upon reaching that of her captor, he threw her through the opening to sprawl on the dirt floor inside. Before she could scramble to her feet, he took one of the braided leather strands from its place on the wall. She watched in horror as he approached her, his dark eyes flashing in anger.

Instinctively, her arms came up to shield herself from the first blow. She rolled to her stomach, trying to get her legs under her to stand, but the blows were landing furiously on her back and buttocks, making it impossible for her to rise. Through a haze of pain, she knew she was crying. Tears coursed down her face, blinding her as she huddled into a ball. She tasted the metallic flavor of blood and realized she was biting her bottom lip to keep from screaming. By the time the blows had stopped, she was moaning and begging for mercy.

Tanya's humiliation was complete when he stripped her camisole and pantalets from her. Completely naked, her tawny hair streaming wildly over her shoulders, Tanya stared at him with eyes wide with pain and fear. With her last remaining spark of false courage she spat, "Don't you touch me!"

Her coppery captor loomed over her, naked himself except for his breechcloth and moccasins. He slapped her hard across the cheek, then picked her up as easily as he would have a child and tossed her onto the mat.

Sprawled in the most undignified manner, Tanya quaked before his smoldering midnight gaze. His dark eyes raked her exposed body, and she felt violated before he'd even touched her. Then, to her profound surprise, he turned, collected her torn clothes and anything she might use for a weapon or to cover herself, and abruptly left.

A long sigh of relief escaped her lips. For long moments she lay unmoving, quivering and crying silently. Finally her mind prodded her to review her situation. Her captor had indeed been wise. With nothing to cover her nakedness and no weapons, he had no need to tie her up or post a guard. She could not expose herself nude in another escape attempt.

Aching, her body thoroughly bruised, she turned onto her side. Her back and bottom felt on fire, and her right thigh pained her even more now. Slow, hot tears slipped from her closed eyes as hopelessness overwhelmed her. Exhaustion finally took its toll and she slept.

Tanya never flickered an eyelash, so deeply asleep was she when A-Panther-Stalks returned to his tipi. For a long time he sat watching her sleep. Taking a strand of her honey-colored hair, he let it slip through his roughened fingers. It was a beautiful color; so soft and silky. Tomorrow he would see that she was bathed, and the tangles brushed from her hair.

With gentle fingers he examined her back, glad to see he had not badly damaged her in his anger. Tanya's back and buttocks were striped with welts, but only in one or two places was the skin broken.

A-Panther-Stalks had been on many raids in his twenty-five winters, and had taken many captives, but never before had he kept one for himself. Always he had given or sold them to another warrior or woman. This was the first time he had deliberately earmarked one for himself, but never had one struck him as being so beautiful before. Her hair and her eyes fascinated him. Her face was perfection, even to the stubborn tilt of her chin, and her figure was alluring.

A-Panther-Stalks felt himself becoming aroused as he studied her, and quickly schooled his thoughts in another direction. He would have to handle her with care, and exercise patience and wisdom in order not to break her proud spirit. He admired her courage too much to see her end up broken and witless, a spineless slave, as so many others did.

The next week or two would be crucial. So much depended on Tanya's ability to adapt and learn the ways of his people. She must learn to accept him as her master and obey him willingly, without questions or hesitation. She must forget her foolish thoughts of home and escape, and accept her life here among his people. She must begin to learn the Cheyenne language, and how to do all the tasks that are required of a Cheyenne warrior's woman.

He had no doubt it would be hard for her, but she was quick and intelligent. She would first have to come to terms with her new life here. Once she had resolved herself to it, he was sure she would learn quickly. His one problem would be to teach her acceptance and obedience without breaking her spirit.

He smiled as he recalled the way she had fought Ugly Otter. "Poor little wildcat," he thought. "You are about to have your claws trimmed. You are going to fight against it, I know, but there is little you can do to change it. You will strain against the leash, and spit and snarl, but I will bring you to heel with a gentle hand. Do not fight me too hard, little wildcat, for you will only harm yourself. I mean to have you. You will be mine until I decide otherwise, and the sooner you accept that, the easier things will be."

Tanya awoke stiff, sore, and thoroughly chilled in the early morning. She huddled into a ball, trying to generate some body heat. What she would give right now for a blanket!

After ascertaining that she had the tipi all to herself, she crept closer to the fire. With a short stick she poked at the fire, trying to stir the coals to life, though what she would use for fuel she couldn't guess.

The flap that covered the entrance to the tipi was opened, and bright sunlight spilled in. Tanya shrank back, vainly trying to hide her nakedness as her captor entered, followed by the old woman who had guarded her the previous evening. The woman dumped an armload of wood onto the floor, shooting Tanya a disapproving look that said without words how displeased she was that Tanya had made her look bad by attempting to escape.

Tanya's captor claimed her attention by capturing her chin in his hand. Pointing to himself, he said, "*Meshepesha Tsi.*" He repeated the gesture and phrase. Then he pointed to Tanya and waited. Once more he went through his actions, and it dawned on Tanya he was telling her his name and asking hers.

Tanya pointed to herself and said, "Tanya."

The warrior nodded. "Tan-Yah." He pointed at her, and then to himself. "*Meshepesha Tsi.*" He pronounced his name slowly and distinctly, then urged her to repeat it.

She did so hesitantly, but he made her repeat it until she got it right.

Then he pointed at Tanya once more and shook his head negatively. "*Mattah* Tan-Yah." Jabbing her with his finger, he said, "*Peshewa Matchsquathi.*"

Tanya shook her head. "No, Tanya. Tanya," she insisted.

He shook his head vigorously. "*Peshewa Matchsquathi,*" he corrected.

For a moment he thought she would weep as she gave him a pitiful look. "I don't want to be *Peshewa Matchsquathi,*" she said, pronouncing the name perfectly. "I want to be Tanya!"

"*Mattah.*" He shook his head at her.

"That, I take it, means 'no,' " she muttered.

Again he jabbed her and waited. With a sigh she capitulated. "All right, I'll be *Peshewa Matchsquathi*, whatever that means."

On a piece of bark he drew a picture of a panther stalking his prey, and repeated his name, and she finally understood the meaning of his name. *Mesh-*

epesha Tsi was A-Panther-Stalks. The name rang a bell, and she remembered the soldiers saying that the nephew of the Cheyenne chief, Black Kettle, was called A-Panther-Stalks. Thus she concluded they were captives of the Cheyenne. Later she would discover the meaning of her own name—Little Wildcat.

The remainder of the morning was a language lesson for Tanya. A-Panther-Stalks introduced her to Walks-Like-A-Duck, and the old woman took over from there. While Panther sat repairing a bridle, Walks-Like-A-Duck taught Tanya how to start the fire and cook the morning meal, diligently drumming into Tanya's head the words for each item she touched.

Acutely conscious of her nudity, Tanya had to force herself to concentrate, particularly since Panther seemed disinclined to leave. Both he and Walks-Like-A-Duck blithely ignored her unclothed state however, and Tanya was forced to do the same, though her color remained high the entire time. Never had she appreciated privacy more than now, when she lacked it completely.

Tanya learned the Cheyenne words for face, arms, head, legs, mouth, nose, hair. Later Panther would teach her the words for the more intimate parts of her body, but ignorant of this for now, Tanya struggled to wrap her tongue around the strange, guttural syllables. She did not stop to ask herself why she bothered to learn; she just did it.

Besides picking up a few basic words and phrases, Tanya learned to fix the morning meal. Then she learned, much to her dismay, that after cooking it, she had to wait for Panther to eat first. The women were required to either busy themselves at something else or sit quietly until the man was finished, when they and the children could eat.

After breakfast, A-Panther-Stalks gave her a blanket to cover herself, wrapping it about her and tucking the loose end between her breasts. Tanya blushed to the roots of her hair. Looping the hated leash about her neck, he led her to a nearby stream. There he left her in Walks-Like-A-Duck's charge, to be scrubbed clean with cold mountain water and sand until her skin glowed and her hair outshone the sun.

Gowned in a deerskin sheath that pulled on over her head and reached past mid-calf, Tanya at last felt decently covered. The dress was sleeveless and plain, with a drawstring neckline and a strip of leather for a belt, but it could have been a satin ballgown, so grateful was she for it. Clean, fed, dressed, and with soft moccasins on her feet, Tanya felt almost normal again, but she cringed inwardly as Panther slipped the leash about her slim neck once more.

Before returning her to his tipi, Panther led her about the encampment. When several young boys would have taunted her, a few sharp words from him turned them away. Embarrassed and ashamed, she hung her head, looking at the ground as she walked. He stopped and with firm hands, straightened her posture, throwing her shoulders back and her chin up. From then on, she walked behind him, her head high and her back straight.

Tanya's natural curiosity soon took over, and she looked about her eagerly. Though constructed the same, each tipi was decorated differently. Panther's, she knew, had elaborate replicas of fierce panthers painted on it. The chief's was black and had a bright yellow sun rising over a mountain. Some had moons and stars; some had pictures of animals; but each was individual. The largest and more elaborate were toward the center of the village, the others fanning out in gradually widening circles toward the edge of the camp.

Some tipis had small awnings constructed over the entrance, and many had fires outside as well as in. Tanya noticed that all the entrances faced east, toward the rising sun. In front of many tipis, women were busy at work. No one approached or spoke to Tanya, but every few feet a warrior or woman greeted Panther.

Toward the end of their tour, Panther led her to a staked-off area where the horses were kept. A young brave was trying to tame a wild pony. The pony was tied to a central stake by a long rope, and each time the brave attempted to approach, the horse would rear and shy away. With infinite patience, the man would wait until the horse settled down and try again. Panther and Tanya watched a long time as the brave talked softly, crooning to the frightened beast, until it finally let him come close enough for the warrior to hold out his hand for the animal to smell. The horse would not let the man touch him, but stood quivering and wary, nostrils flared as he inhaled the Indian's scent.

Panther led her back to his tipi. There he tied her to a longer rope and left her in Walks-Like-A-Duck's charge. Throughout the long afternoon she learned to grind dried corn into a fine powder with a bowl and pestle. Huge blisters rose and broke on her tender fingers. Panther returned and flung two dead rabbits at her feet, and much to her disgust, she then learned to skin and cook them. As the rabbits stewed in the pot, Walks-Like-A-Duck showed her how to prepare the rabbit hides for tanning.

Weary beyond belief, Tanya watched sleepily as Panther ate the meal she and Walks-Like-A-Duck had prepared. Almost too tired to eat, she forced herself through her own meal. When Walks-Like-A-Duck left for the evening, she took with her Tanya's dress, leaving the girl bereft, frightened, and naked once again. With no one to see or care, Tanya had cried herself to sleep on her pallet long before Panther returned.

Chapter 3

TANYA'S DAYS took up a pattern after that first one. Each morning she would arise early, and as Panther sat chanting his prayer outside the tent entrance, she would start the fire and prepare their morning meal. Walks-Like-A-Duck would arrive with Tanya's beloved dress, and they would make a trip, leash and all, to the stream to bathe and gather water. After straightening the tipi and washing the bowls, the day would truly begin.

It was spring in the mountains, and soon the Cheyenne would leave their winter camp to follow the buffalo herds across the vast plains, but first there were preparations to make. Men sharpened their weapons, restrung their bows, trained their ponies, and checked their equipment. Braves, young and old, trained for war, practicing for many hours.

The women were equally busy. While the sun was yet gentle, they gathered in the fields, hoeing and planting the new crop. The food would be planted and left to nature, since they were a wandering tribe, and perhaps in the late fall they would return to their winter camp and harvest what they could for winter. They planted corn and beans, pumpkins and melons, and cultivated wild wheat and potatoes. In the autumn they would find wild squash, onions, carrots, and turnips to add to the fare, as well as fall berries, apples, nuts, grapes and honey.

When the sun rose higher, they would take to the woods, gathering wild strawberries and spring berries. They plucked strange plants Tanya had never seen before, some for stewing, some for seasoning, and some for their medicinal value, and they gathered firewood along the way. Even the flowers had a use other than their fragrant beauty. Finally they would all trudge home to prepare what they had found.

Sometimes the roots and plants and berries were cooked (boiled or stewed) and mashed, then dried and ground to a powder. Others were strung and dried as they were. Walks-Like-A-Duck patiently and thoroughly led Tanya through all the intricacies of the preparations. In addition to this, she taught Tanya how to skin, bone, and prepare the fish and meat Panther brought in. Nothing, it seemed, was wasted. Some of the fish they smoked and dried; others they ate. The bones were saved and fashioned into needles. Oil was extracted from glands and carefully hoarded in waterproof pouches, as was the fat from ducks and geese. The eggs from the fowl they ate and relished. Turtles were a feast, their eggs a delicacy, and crayfish a delight.

Every scrap of meat from an animal was either eaten or smoked and dried. Every bone and sinew found a use in the preparation of food, clothing, or weapons. Each hide was carefully prepared and treated to become a household article or item of clothing. Every gland had a use of some sort, whether for its vitamin content, its medicinal value, or its lubricating qualities. Tanya had never seen a more thrifty, ingenious, and industrious people. They took from the land only what they needed to survive, replaced what they could, and used everything totally and wisely. Anything else they might need or want . . . coffee, sugar, flour, blankets . . . they traded for with their government agent, Major Edward Wynkoop at Ft. Lyon or Ft. Larned.

Tanya was learning the Cheyenne language by leaps and bounds. Panther, Walks-Like-A-Duck, and the other women constantly pointed out new things and taught her their Indian names. Even the children would help her learn and pronounce the strange words. They directed her in her work and corrected her pronunciation, and had in no way mistreated her since that first day, but neither were they open and welcoming. Tanya was both white and a slave, and only Panther's protection prevented them from taunting and beating her as they often did the other captives.

Tanya saw her friends nearly every day, but was not allowed to communicate with them. The first time she had tried, the result was disastrous. When she attempted to speak to one of them, she was drawn up short on her leash, the words choking in her throat, but this was mild compared to the punishment the other girls received if they tried to speak. Their captor's wives, or the women set to guard them, would immediately beat them. They hit and kicked and pinched and pulled at their already battered victims, sometimes beating them with sticks or lashes until they fell bleeding to the ground. The girls soon learned to ignore each other's presence, painful though it was, for it was far more painful not to do so.

Tanya was appalled at the condition of the other girls. Melissa was the worst, her swollen face barely recognizable beneath the lumps and bruises. Still clad, if you could call it that, in her tattered petticoat, she was a mass of bruises and dirt. Her once-bright hair hung in dirty, tangled strands, her blue eyes glazed with pain and misery. She hobbled along, sore and weary, every shred of pride stripped from her.

Nancy fared little better, and though Rosemary now wore a grimy, grease-stained deerskin dress to cover her bony body, she had a gap where one of her front teeth used to be. Suellen also sported an old, dirty deerskin dress, her glorious red hair matted and tangled, her fingernails broken and grimy, but she had fewer bruises than the others.

Tanya was almost embarrassed to appear before them clean and whole, her tawny hair brushed and shining, her dress clean and mended. She felt ashamed to think she had bemoaned her fate, when the others had fared so much worse. Compared to them, she was being treated as a pampered princess! So far Panther had not raped her. He had not beaten her since her attempted escape. Other than the humiliation of the leash and having to expose her nakedness to him each evening, he had not treated her badly at all. He had even introduced her to a lovely young Indian woman, Shy Deer, with whom she was becoming friends.

At some time during her busy day, Panther took her for a walk through the village, always on her dreaded leash. She grew to hate the leash and all it symbolized, but she put up with it so as not to forfeit her precious walks. Always, they ended their walk by stopping a while to watch the young brave training his spotted pony. His progress was slow, but steady. The first day, the horse finally sniffed at his hand. The second, the Cheyenne could stroke his head and muzzle. By the end of the third day, he was stroking the pony's back and whithers almost anywhere he wished.

If Tanya's days were busy, her nights were tense.

After her first full day at the camp, she had fallen into an exhausted sleep, only to awaken later when Panther had returned. The first she sensed his presence was when he had lowered himself onto a pallet next to hers. He had removed his moccasins and breechcloth, and lay in naked splendor next to her. He had stopped her with a hand about her wrist when she tried to move away from him, but otherwise he had not touched her. All he required was that she lay quietly next to him.

The following night he had insisted that she share his pallet, holding her closely to him, their naked bodies touching. His embrace was warm, and once she was assured he wanted nothing more, she found his arms strangely comforting. She awoke the next morning to find her head pillowed on his chest, their limbs entangled.

The third night had been more disquieting. Settled on their pallet, Panther had drawn her close to him. Then he had commenced stroking her hair and face. His long bronze fingers followed the planes of her face, tracing her eyes, her nose, the shape of her lips as they quivered under his touch. Briefly he had let his hands discover the contours of her body, lingering for a moment over her thighs and breasts. Just when Tanya was starting to panic, he ceased his explorations, cuddled her close, and went to sleep. It took Tanya much longer to gain her rest that night as she lay awake reviewing this new advance. It confused her to admit his touch had not been repugnant.

Now, as she sat at the edge of the stream with Shy Deer and Walks-Like-A-Duck, she wondered at her reactions. Dread and anticipation mixed equally within her as she sat laundering Panther's clothes. Panther would be coming to get her soon for their walk. One part of her looked forward to his arrival, and another pleaded for more time before he came.

The brave was making progress with his wild, spotted pony. In the last six days he had gotten the animal to come to him for treats, then to come when called, and then to accept a halter. Now he was able to lead him about on a lead line. Yesterday the pony had accepted a blanket across his back, and this afternoon, the weight of the brave half-laying across his back.

Tanya was making progress of her own. She had been in the Cheyenne village nine days now. She had learned a great deal and worked hard. Her muscles were becoming more accustomed to her labors; her hands no longer bled. Her back and bottom no longer smarted from her lashing, and the scab on her thigh had finally fallen off, leaving only shiny, bright pink flesh to mark her branding. Where her skin was exposed to the sun and wind, she was now tanned a light gold. Her command of the Cheyenne language was rapidly improving to the point that she could now form simple sentences and understand many things said to her if the words were basic and spoken slowly.

When Panther was not occupying her time or thoughts, Tanya worried about her family and fiancé. Had they figured out what had happened to her and the others? Had they searched for the missing women? Was rescue possible in the next few days, or had the Cheyenne covered their tracks too well? Would they give the women up for dead and stop looking?

Where was her family now? she wondered. Had they gone on to Pueblo or returned to Ft. Lyon? Had Jeffrey been notified, and Aunt Elizabeth and Uncle George? Did they have any inkling that A-Panther-Stalks was behind the abduction? Did Julie realize what a narrow escape she'd had? Did everyone miss her as much as she did them? Was Jeffrey distraught? How were her mother and father coping with this disaster?

Tanya's one prayer was that rescue would come soon, before she became too accustomed to this life. With her fierce will to survive and excel, she was well aware of how quickly she was adjusting. Young and flexible, her ear and tongue were picking up the language rapidly, and her body was beginning to respond to Panther's caresses in the long, dark nights.

Each night for more than a week now she had shared his mat. Panther had progressed from stroking her lightly to long periods of stroking and kissing and whispering to her in the amber glow of the tipi. Each night she fell more under his hypnotic spell. Beneath his burning black gaze, she felt her resolve melting. With his warm lips molded to hers, his tongue searching out the hidden recesses of her mouth and tangling with hers, her senses would take over and her mind spin out of control. At first she had been too frightened to respond, determined to ignore the first tentative stirrings of her body, but as his hands worked their magic across her skin she was weakening.

Now, over a week later, Tanya was more confused than ever. Just the night before, she had found herself responding hotly to his caresses and returning them with her own. Tonight, as she lay on the mat watching Panther undress, she shivered, a shiver that had nothing to do with fear of being hurt, but everything to do with her fear of losing herself to him entirely.

He was a beautiful male animal; tall, bronze, graceful, with a power representative of his namesake. Panther lay down and gathered her trembling body close. Gazing deeply into her golden eyes, he felt his own body begin to throb with passion. Now thoroughly familiar with her silken skin, his hands took their own course, memorizing her curves and contours. His lips lowered to cover hers, claiming their sweetness as his alone, his tongue delving deeply into her mouth.

Tanya had told herself she would not respond to Panther's lovemaking this night, but the minute his mouth claimed hers, she was lost to reason. As his wandering hands charted her body, she began to tremble violently beneath his touch. His lips moved over hers, melting them like hot wax, boldly staking his claim. One hand caught her hair and held her head still for his kisses, while the other moved upward along her ribcage, seeking and finding one swollen breast. Slim, agile fingers sought her rosy nipple, teasing it erect, creating an aching throb in her loins.

Leaving her lips, his mouth mapped a course across her face, placing delicate kisses along her brow, her nose, her eyes, her jaw, finding its way to her ear and making her shiver as he traced its contours with his tongue. On down her neck his teeth nipped and his tongue soothed until he found the sensual curve of her shoulder. His loosened hair caressed her breasts and shoulders.

The combination of his hand teasing her breast and his mouth playing along her shoulder was too much, and Tanya arched against his body involuntarily. He was murmuring meaningless phrases, encouraging her touch. Her hands were spread out against his smooth chest, warding him off, but now they seemed to have a life of their own. Slowly, tentatively, they began to explore, measuring his shoulders, feeling the muscles contract beneath her palms. Her questing fingers stroked his arms and shoulders, working their way gradually up into his thick ebony hair.

Panther's velvet lips at last found her breast, scorching her with their heat. His teeth worried her throbbing, swollen nipple, and his tongue laved it. White hot flashes of passion seared through her, making her cry out in longing—for what, she wasn't sure. She clutched at his head, pressing him closer in her need.

As his mouth worshipped her breasts, his hand slid to her thighs, caressing and then parting them. Tanya gasped, and Panther's mouth immediately came up to cover hers in a hot, passionate kiss that increased her desire. Her own hands searched along his back, feeling the corded muscle and sinew beneath smooth, sun-kissed skin, tapering to the trim waist, the compact buttocks, the powerful thighs.

Panther groaned, sweat breaking out on his skin as he strove to control himself. His hand nestled itself between her legs, his long, sensitive fingers evoking pleasures Tanya had never imagined existed. Tanya quivered and thrashed beneath him, her breasts straining against his chest as Panther ignited an inferno throughout her body. He heard her shocked gasp as his fingers slipped inside her warmth, stroking the moist velvet there, his thumb continuing its arousal of her sensitive feminine core.

Tanya's incoherent cries were lost in Panther's mouth as she gasped for breath and cried out in amazement. Her whole body tensed in expectation and then seemed to explode in a million tiny fragments as he brought her to fulfillment. Spasms shook her from head to toe and she collapsed in quivering wonder, too stunned to do more than whimper. Gathering her close, Panther held her until she finally calmed and slept. His own body aching still, he forced himself to be patient. This night it was Panther who lay awake for hours.

Tanya was filled with self-loathing the next morning. How could her body and mind betray her in such a manner! My God, the man was a savage! Yet her body throbbed at the memory of his caresses, and Tanya found herself studying his hands and lips as he ate. She blushed furiously and turned quickly away as he caught her gaze.

Panther smiled to himself. Yes, she was ready. He could have taken her last night, but he'd wanted to show her something of what to expect before he mated with her. He wanted her to be prepared, and he wanted her willing and eager. Today she would think about it, anticipate the evening, and be ready for him when the time came.

All day long Tanya fumed and fussed, trying to sort out her feelings. In all honesty, she was not repelled by him, though she felt she ought to be. Until a few days ago she was preparing to marry Jeffrey. Now she was panting after, of all things, a Cheyenne warrior! She felt drawn to him; had since that first day. She admired his quiet dignity, his noble pride. Part of the reason she tried so hard to adapt and learn the ways of his people was to earn his approval, his praise.

Panther satisfied her senses. He was magnificent to watch; tall, proud, handsome. His deep voice grated pleasantly on her ears. As she lay against him at night, her fingers adored the smooth texture of his skin, and she was becoming addicted to the musky male scent of him. Even the salty taste of his skin appealed to her, and the taste of tobacco on his tongue when he kissed her.

Still Tanya hesitated. She feared the time when he would make her wholly his. She didn't want to desire him; yearn for him, for she felt certain that once that barrier was crossed there would be no turning back. Once she fully accepted him and life among his people, she would have no wish to leave.

Later that day, Tanya knew what she would see before it happened. The young brave finally rode his spotted horse. As he cantered proudly about the meadow, Panther and Tanya watched, each with their own thoughts. Then Panther turned to her. Holding her gaze with his own, he silently reached out and removed her leash, throwing it on the ground at his feet. Tanya eyed the leash, then Panther, and finally turned to watch the proud brave on his pony. Her mind struggled to sort out the jumble of thoughts rushing through it. Each day Panther had brought her here to watch the warrior gentle his horse. He did so with patience, and each day the horse responded a bit more to his touch and his voice. It struck her that Panther had done the same thing with her, in correlation with the progress made by the young brave.

It also occurred to her that Panther wanted her to realize this; had more or less said so by his action of throwing away the hated leash. Today the warrior had realized his goal and ridden his horse. Tanya's eyes grew huge as she realized the significance of this. Panther was letting her know that tonight he expected to realize his goal. Tonight he would make her his completely and bind her to him with bonds stronger than any chain or fetter.

Panther eyed Tanya warily, intent on her reaction. He saw the confusion in her face, then the humiliation and anger of her wounded pride. Not really expecting her to accept this calmly, he was not surprised by her reaction.

Tanya turned on him with eyes spitting golden flames. Quietly but vehemently, she fumed, "If you think I'm going to take this calmly, like a sheep led to slaughter, then think again!" she spoke in English, too upset to try to find the words in his language. Tears of frustration welled in her eyes, making them glitter brilliantly, but she blinked them back. She stood facing him defiantly, her hands clenched into two tight fists at her sides.

"I'm not a mare to be gentled and mounted! I'm a human being with feelings of my own! Isn't it enough that you've taken me away from my family and friends? Isn't it enough that you've made me your slave, to fetch and carry and wait on you hand and foot? Need you humiliate me at every turn?"

Panther did not touch her. He stared down at her with those stern, dark eyes and spoke firmly. "Speak to me in my own tongue, Little Wildcat."

"I haven't the words to say it in your tongue," she told him, and then in English she continued, "how could I tell you in any language how I fear you?"

At his concentrated frown, she turned her back to him. "How can I explain this feeling I have that if I'm not rescued soon it will be too late for me? You have stolen another man's woman. Do you know that? I was to be married today. I pray each night that he will come and rescue me in time. Now you have made it plain that my time has run out."

Tears finally spilled over and ran silently down her cheeks as the utter futility of her situation overwhelmed her. "How could he still want me after you have had me?" she choked out.

Panther's hand on her arm wheeled her about. His

face was a hard mask of anger held barely in check. "Come," he ordered. "You have yet to prepare my meal. There is no time for your womanly tears of self-pity. They are wasted on me and will change nothing."

The tension in their lodge that evening was so thick you could slice it with a knife. Walks-Like-A-Duck had escaped even before the food had finished cooking. This time she had not taken with her Tanya's dress, and for that at least Tanya was grateful. Tanya sat stiffly across the fire from Panther as he ate his fill, but could not manage a bite of her own portion. While Tanya straightened up after the meal, Panther re-worked the form of a new bow he was making. A heavy silence hung like a pall in the air.

Finally Panther lay the bow aside. "Bank the fire, Little Wildcat, and go to the mat." His face gave nothing away, and Tanya could not read his mood. Outwardly passive, she dutifully saw to the fire, her heart thundering in her ears all the while. Panther was still sitting between her and the only avenue of escape, and she knew any attempt would be futile.

Slowly she walked to the mat and sat upon it, her head down to hide the tears from his avid gaze. His approach was silent, as always, but now he stood before her.

"Remove my moccasins from my feet," he commanded her.

Tanya's head snapped up as if on a puppeteer's string, her mouth open in amazement. He had never asked this of her before. As he balanced first on one foot and then the other, she complied without comment.

"Now remove my breechcloth," he ordered tersely.

Tanya's face flamed and her hands shook as she

reached out for the ties of his garment. Then her hands fell limply to her lap, and her lips and voice quivered as she whispered, "I cannot. Please do not make me do this."

"You will obey me. Do it," he answered relentlessly, his tone of voice indicating his impatience.

Once more her icy fingers reached out, and this time she completed her task, though she refused to look at him. The breechcloth fell to the floor between them. Silently he leaned down and removed her dress, then sat facing her on the mat, his onyx eyes pinning her in place.

"Unbind my braids, woman," he directed, his voice now as soft as velvet. She did as he bid her, gently untwining the raven strands and combing them with her fingers. Tanya could feel his eyes upon her face, but would not meet his look. Instead, she concentrated on her task, but even that had its perils. His hair sliding between her fingers felt like thick, smooth satin, awakening every nerve in her fingers, sliding sensuously across her palms.

Her fingers were still entwined in his hair as he pressed her gently down upon the mat. She looked up into his dark eyes, now so filled with naked desire that she shivered in response. His mouth descended to cover her quivering lips, warming them with his own. His firm white teeth tugged gently at her lower lip until she parted them to his questing tongue. Warm, calloused hands cupped her breasts tenderly, as if they were priceless treasures, feeling them swell to his touch, his long fingers searching out the sensitive tips and teasing them to life.

Tanya felt her fear and anger ebbing away, being replaced by a growing desire she could not control, and found she had no wish to. Her body arched into his with a will of its own, pleading without words for his touch.

His mouth left hers, finding its way across her face to her ear, her throat, and along her shoulder, searching out each sensitive spot along the way to her breasts. As his questing lips captured her nipple, a sigh quivered from her throat. Her hands slipped from his hair to clutch at his shoulders, her lips finding the sensitive cord along his neck, her teeth teasing at it.

Panther's hands traveled the curves of her body; down across the flat of her stomach, the bend of her hip, his fingers trailing up the inside of her thighs until they met their goal. There they lingered to tease and tantalize until Tanya was mindlessly arching to meet his touch, shamelessly calling out his name against his shoulder, raking his back with her nails.

He brought his mouth back to hers as he settled his body over her, parting her thighs with his own, and she felt the heat of his passion throbbing against her. "Tell me you want me," he whispered against her lips.

She understood and answered in kind. "I want you, Panther. Please, I want you now."

There was a moment of pain as he entered her, making her his own, but he cut off her surprised gasp with a searing kiss that set her senses reeling. His mouth devoured hers and his hands excited her as he introduced her to a world of sensuous pleasure. As she surrendered herself to him completely, his thrusts became faster and deeper until her passion flared into an all-consuming desire, and she met his thrusts with her own. Her body was aflame, consumed and fed by his, and his needs became her own. Together they climbed from one plateau of passion to another, even higher, until at last the sky broke open and they soared on wings of ecstasy to the stars. Ripples of rapture shuddered through them as they clung together, savoring the delight of their mutual release.

He held her close to him afterward, stroking her and murmuring to her in words she could not comprehend. But one thing she knew. She now belonged to him totally, body and soul. There was no turning back after this; there would never be any escape for her now.

For a week afterward Tanya found it hard to meet Panther's gaze. She felt unaccountably shy around him, and the slightest move on his part could set her blushing furiously. During the day she worked with the other women, diligently applying herself to her tasks and improving her language skills.

Tanya now had full responsibility for Panther's tipi. Walks-Like-A-Duck no longer came to the lodge, except to instruct Tanya in some new skill. Dutifully, Tanya cleaned the lodge, cooked Panther's meals, and sewed and cleaned his clothes. Each night she shared his sleeping mat, and only there did her painful shyness melt away under the flame of shared passion.

Never again did Panther place the detested leash about her neck. Now she was free to come and go from the tipi as she pleased. The new freedom was exhilarating, but Tanya was not so much a fool as to think she was not watched.

The possibility of escape was remote at best, but Tanya found herself barely even entertaining the idea these days. She worked long and hard, but was content at the end of the day, especially when she could look forward to a long night enfolded in Panther's embrace. And she did look forward to the nights, as much as she tried to berate herself for it. A part of her grieved for a while over her lost way of life, but another part openly and willingly accepted and adapted to her new life, gradually overshadowing any residual sadness with a blossoming joy.

Sometimes she wondered at her growing happiness, failing to understand how she could possibily enjoy her life here. She was a slave, Panther's woman. He had but to command, and she obeyed without question. She cooked and cleaned, tanned and sewed, and satisfied his desires—but he also met her desires.

As the days wore on, Tanya finally stopped warring with herself and admitted to herself that she was in love with Panther. He was everything she desired and admired in a man, Cheyenne warrior or not. He was brave, wise, noble, extremely handsome, and strong enough to be tender when the situation warranted.

Her brain warned her that she was merely his slave, and that he could at any time decide to trade or sell her, or take a wife who might mistreat her and have her beaten every day of her life, but her heart refused to be discouraged. Tanya now loved him irrevocably, and she would take him on any terms. Her pride was humbled before this devastating love.

Panther's first clue to all this was when he entered his tipi one day to find Tanya plaiting her usually unbound hair Indian fashion into two long braids across her shoulders. Neither of them commented on the fact, but he caught the shy smile she threw in his direction.

"She is no longer fighting her fate," he reasoned, greatly pleased by the thought and her gesture.

Later that day he presented her with a beautifully decorated headband. It was his first true gift to her, and her delighted smile lit up her face. She sat there looking so captivatingly lovely that Panther's breath caught in his throat. "I would bring you gifts each day if you would smile upon me each time as you do now," he teased her, enjoying the way she blushed at his comment.

"I shall smile for you if you bring me no gifts at all," she answered shyly.

As he absorbed her words, he asked, "Are you happy here now, Little Wildcat? Do you no longer desire to escape or pray for rescue?"

His heart nearly stopped at the spark of love in her eyes as she met his questioning gaze. "I have no wish to leave here, Panther," she admitted softly. "My life is with you, as long as you wish it."

One more thing he had to know. "Do you not grieve for your lost love?"

Momentarily startled by his question, she wondered how he knew about that, but she pondered it only for a second. "I belong to you now, Panther. It is you I love. You hold my heart in your hands." Her face held a solemn promise.

"Then I must treat such a treasure gently," he responded tenderly, as he gathered her into his arms. Never had Tanya seen such a magnificent, victorious smile as Panther's. Then his lips claimed hers in a kiss that branded her his forever; the Panther's mate, his Wildcat.

Chapter 4

TWO DAYS later the tribe moved. The tipis were pulled down, packed and loaded on pack horses and travois. Robes, rugs, mats, and parfleches loaded with household and personal items were secured alongside the burdened beasts.

Tanya was amazed at how swiftly and easily everything was accomplished. These people were used to being on the move and had developed a rhythm and economy of motion that allowed them to prepare to relocate with very little fuss and bother.

One last time Tanya checked the knots, making sure the bundles were properly tied for the journey ahead. It was early morning, and the sun hadn't yet burned the dew off the grass. A slight breeze brought the freshness of spring to her nostrils, and the sun shone gently, warming her upturned face.

She turned as she heard Panther approaching astride his big black horse. Panther's cousin, Winter Bear, rode beside him, leading a buckskin horse behind. Tanya liked Winter Bear. A mere inch shorter than Panther, he was a handsome young man with a friendly, ready smile. He and Panther were very close in age, and had grown up together. More like brothers than cousins, they liked and respected one another, and either would lay down his life for the other if need be. They had spent their boyhoods playing and working side by side, became warriors at the same time, went on raids and war parties together, and shared joy and sorrow throughout the years.

There was a slight family resemblance between the two men, but their attitudes were often different. Panther was much more arrogant, Tanya thought. Winter Bear was less volatile, more calm and quiet, with an inner serenity that shone in his dark eyes. Though Tanya preferred Panther, with his flashes of anger and passion, she found Winter Bear pleasant to have around. It seemed to her that the two men complemented one another; Winter Bear with his calm and thoughtful ways, and Panther with his quick intelligence and vitality.

Tanya smiled as the two men approached. "Is everything ready?" Panther asked, looking about.

"All is packed, Panther, unless you have something else for me to do," Tanya answered softly.

"Good. Now come, Little Wildcat, it is time to mount."

As she walked to the side of his horse, preparing to mount behind him, he shook his head and smiled. "No, Wildcat, you shall not ride with me this time." He gestured to the beautiful buckskin mare, complete with saddle and bridle. "You shall have your own horse from now on. Do you like her?"

Tanya looked from the mare to Panther and back again, her golden eyes mirroring her delight. "Panther! Is she truly mine, to keep always?"

"For as long as she pleases you," he nodded.

"Oh, she pleases me, Panther. She is beautiful! Is she already trained?"

"Little Wildcat, I would not place your life in danger by presenting you with an unbroken mount,"

Panther admonished with a frown. "She is trained by my own hand."

Her eyes shining like twin suns, Tanya looked up at him. "Thank you, Panther, for such a wonderful gift! I will take good care of her."

Panther dismounted in one lithe motion. "Come," he said, approaching the mare. "Come let her smell you. Let her get your scent into her nostrils and feel your hand upon her. You must learn to guide her with your knees, as a Cheyenne does, and not hurt her. She was gently broken, and you must treat her with care. Do this and she will always give her best for you."

Tanya ran her hand along the long, smooth neck of the mare. "I will not mistreat her, Panther. I know it would displease you, and I have never mistreated an animal in my life."

Panther cupped his hands and boosted Tanya into the saddle. "Ride beside me and I will teach you how to ride like a Cheyenne brave," he teased with a broad grin and a chuckle.

Winter Bear gave a gruff laugh. "Cousin, if you can no longer tell a woman from a brave, you are beyond help!" He gave Tanya a sly wink and she giggled.

Panther scowled at him. "Winter Bear, when I need your advice, I'll ask for it. You would do better to direct your energies toward your own courtship with Shy Deer. I've noticed how she follows you with those doe eyes of hers."

Winter Bear laughed. "There is nothing wrong with my eyesight, Panther. I've noticed that and a lot more."

They travelled north for eight days, stopping each night to set up a temporary camp. Tanya had learned that they were journeying to a meeting spot where they would join many other bands and tribes, both Cheyenne and Arapahoe. There the tribes would celebrate their spring festival and hold ceremonial rites, the most important being the Sun Dance.

Mid-morning of the eighth day, they reached their destination. Hundreds of tipis had already been erected. Dogs and children swarmed everywhere and chaos seemed the order of the day, but Tanya knew that under all the confusion, the women had everything under control.

Quickly and efficiently, with help from Walks-Like-A-Duck and Shy Deer, Tanya erected Panther's tipi, taking care to face it east. Then she began to unload the pack horse. She collected fresh water and firewood, and started meat boiling in the pot.

Finally she had time to tend to her horse. Tanya had just fed and watered Panther's horse, Shadow, and her own, which she called Wheat. Intent on combing the burrs from Wheat's mane, she was shocked to hear the hiss of a whip, followed by a blinding, searing pain across her back. Stunned and gasping for breath, she stumbled against the mare. When she found her balance, she whirled about to face her attacker.

Before her stood a beautiful Indian girl Tanya had never seen before. She probably belonged to another tribe. About Tanya's own age and size, her dark eyes sparkled with arrogance, her manner haughty and overbearing. "Get away from that horse, slave," she ordered as she brandished the whip again. "Were you trying to escape?" Her voice was almost drowned out by the whine of the whip as it lashed toward Tanya once more.

The leather wound itself about Tanya's arm and

back, cutting into her tender flesh. With a hiss of pain, Tanya grabbed the thong and held it firmly. "Stop this!" she screamed. "The horse is mine!"

Her tormentor's face hardened with hatred. "Ha! You lie! I know that mare. She belongs to A-Panther-Stalks." The girl tried to retrieve the whip, but Tanya held on, swiftly lessening the distance between them.

"The horse used to belong to Panther, as I do. He gave her to me," Tanya managed to say.

Now the two girls were face to face. The Indian girl launched herself at Tanya, arms flailing. "You lie! You were going to steal his horse and escape! Only a fool would give a horse to a slave!"

"Panther is no fool, but *you* certainly are!" Tanya grated out. Warding off blows right and left, her temper finally snapped. "Enough is enough!" she shrieked, and threw her full weight against her slim opponent. Down they both went, wrestling and rolling in the tall grass, shrieking like banshees. For several minutes they fought, until Tanya managed to gain the advantage. Straddling the other girl, one knee firmly against her breastbone, Tanya held her to the ground, pinning her arms alongside her head.

Heaving with the effort of their battle, Tanya repeated, "The horse is mine!" Her golden eyes flamed with anger.

The Indian girl tried to buck her off and failed, her own dark eyes snapping. "You lie, white face!" she spat out.

"Hardly ever, mud face!" Tanya retorted heatedly.

"I'll see you beaten for this," came the threat.

"I belong to Panther and am under his protection. No one beats me but him!"

"I will tell him of this and he will give me permission," the girl avowed.

"You can try," Tanya countered. Her captive had calmed by now, and Tanya slowly released her and stood.

The young girl rose and launched herself at Tanya once again.

"Oh, for pity's sake!" Tanya grumbled, throwing the girl face-down on the ground and sitting on her. "Look, I am very busy. I don't have time for this nonsense! I have a lot of work to do, and Panther will be expecting his meal. Surely you can find something better to do than harass me!"

Whatever answer the girl was about to make was cut short as both spied a pair of moccasinned feet before them. Tanya's startled gaze travelled up firm, dark legs, past the loincloth and broad chest to a familiar bronze face.

Panther barely managed to hide a smile as he beheld Tanya's bedraggled state. "What is the meaning of this, Wildcat?" he demanded calmly.

Tanya remained seated on her victim's back. "This girl refuses to believe me when I tell her you gave me the mare."

"So you decided to sit on her?" Panther's look was incredulous.

"No," Tanya began, but now her silent combatant found her tongue and started squealing accusations non-stop, appealing her case to Panther.

With a sigh, Tanya reluctantly released her. The girl immediately threw herself, weeping, into Panther's arms. Deciding she didn't stand a chance of getting a word in edgewise, Tanya turned and headed back to her tethered horse.

"Wildcat!" Panther's authoritative command halted her in her tracks.

Tanya turned, and could scarcely believe the anger

she saw blazing in his ebony eyes. She waited silently.

"Who put the whip to your back?" he roared.

"Your little friend there." Tanya nodded at the girl in his arms.

Panther pushed the girl from him. "Mountain Flower, who gave you permission to lash my woman?" he demanded.

The girl's lips quivered and her eyes widened in disbelief. "She is a slave! She was about to steal your horse and escape!"

Panther's eyes narrowed. "Did she not tell you I gave the mare to her?"

"Yes, but I knew she lied."

"You would not hear the truth," he insisted. "The horse is hers, and Wildcat is my woman. No one touches my woman or my horse unless I give permission."

Mountain Flower stiffened. "How was I to know you would take a white woman into your tipi?" Her face showed her distaste.

"You know now. Do not let it happen again."

"Your woman is very arrogant, Panther. You should teach her better behavior," she shot back.

"This tops it," Tanya muttered, bending to retrieve the forgotten whip. Stalking up to Mountain Flower, she stretched the leather against the girl's throat. "I'll tell you one thing, honey pot, you ever come near me again with this whip, and I'll take it away from you and strangle you with it, with or without permission from anyone!" she threatened.

Mountain Flower sputtered and looked at Panther for help. Panther merely smiled and said, "That is why I call her Wildcat. Take heed, Mountain Flower, I think she means it. After your attack on her today, she probably feels you'd deserve it, and so do I. I will not stop her if you harm her again."

Turning to Tanya, he said, "If you are done here, I suggest you return to the tipi." At her hurt look, he continued softly, "Your wounds need tending to, my little spitting kitten."

"Oh," she said, blushing, "I thought you wanted your meal."

Panther shot her a definitely suggestive look. "I do not believe I will starve, but that is not what I had in mind after I soothe your injuries."

Tanya blushed even deeper and docilely followed Panther to the tipi.

By that evening, word of Panther's woman had spread through other bands. No matter whose version was told, the end result was the same. It was clearly understood that Panther would brook no interference with his woman. Her status was not clear, but Wildcat was no mere slave.

Had it not been for Shy Deer and Walks-Like-A-Duck, Tanya would have been very lonely for female companionship throughout the next weeks. Though Panther's own tribe accepted her presence and doubtful status with their chief's nephew, the women did not socialize with her as they would a member of the tribe. Tanya was in her own no-man's-land, neither slave nor Cheyenne, and she was thankful for Shy Deer's and the old woman's company.

Curiosity brought many women from the other tribes past Panther's lodge, to catch a glimpse of the daring Little Wildcat. Stories of her capture and her courage had spread rapidly, growing with each retelling of the accounts, and they were eager to see the white woman who inspired the tales. None were willing to extend a hand in friendship yet, however, and certainly none wished to incite Panther's anger by taunting this woman with the hair, eyes and purported temperament of the cougar.

To Tanya's delight, the children were not so shy. Their avid curosity overcame any lingering timidity, and soon she felt like the Pied Piper of the village. Once they were assured she meant them no harm, they followed her everywhere, at first Tanya thought they came to taunt and tease, but soon realized they were merely drawn by curiosity, and a kind word and a smile wrought wonders.

It helped that she could communicate with them in their own tongue, and because of their constant chatter, her own language skills broadened daily. Before long, she found herself responding easily to their many questions, and was surprised one day to find herself thinking in Cheyenne, rather than first in English and having to translate her thoughts.

Panther was not unaware of Tanya's attraction to the children, or theirs for her. Whenever he neared his tipi he would hear the laughter and the ringing of young voices. The little girls would sit about her and watch her tan or sew, sorting beads or cutting fringe for her, listening to the tales she wove for them as she worked. Sometimes she translated children's songs for them. The boys gathered around to hear her tales too, but more often they showed up while she was cooking, hoping this would be the day Wildcat would make a batch of candy or sweetened cakes for them. They would help her gather firewood or haul water from the river, or tend the horses. Sometimes they fished or hunted for berries, each learning something from the other.

On one occasion, Panther found the boys teaching Tanya how to shoot their bows and arrows. He bit back a laugh at the look of intense concentration on her face as she took aim at her target. Her straight white teeth caught at her bottom lip, and her eyes narrowed as she sighted down the shaft. Out of sight, he watched for several minutes. With excellent instruction from her tutors, she did not do badly, especially considering neither the bow nor arrows were of a proper size and weight for her.

A few days later, Panther presented her with a bow and a quiver of arrows of her own. She had seen him working on them, but had no idea they were for her.

"These are the proper size and weight for you, Little Wildcat," he told her. "The curve and tension of the bow and string are important, and the arrows must be straight; the feathering just so, for accuracy. The bow must be balanced, and the arrows also. I will show you how to hold the bow and draw the bowstring properly; the correct way to nock the arrow; the position your arms and shoulders should take. Then you must practice, and when you are proficient enough, I shall take you hunting."

"You saw me practicing with the boys," Tanya guessed with a rueful smile.

"Yes."

"I will practice with these until I can hit my target every time," she vowed, stroking the bow lovingly.

Then she threw herself into Panther's arms, tears glistening in her golden eyes. "You are so good to me, Panther! I shall do everything in my power to make you happy!"

Panther stroked her bright head. "You do that now, Wildcat. You please me in more ways each day. Your eagerness to learn Cheyenne ways, the joy of discovery on your face, your delight in a new accomplishment, your willingness and your courage, and your loving attitude all please me and add joy to my days. Your eager caresses and kisses, your open and willing sharing when I join with you each evening, bring pleasure to my days and delight to my nights."

He raised her glowing face to his, and lowered his lips to hers. "You are becoming as necessary as air to breathe and water to drink," he whispered.

"And you are the food of my heart," she replied softly as their lips met in mutual desire.

Tanya was appalled when Shy Deer explained the Sun Dance to her. "It's barbaric!" she exclaimed.

Shy Deer merely shrugged and smiled. "It is our way," she said simply.

"But for young men and boys to purposely subject their bodies to such torture!" Tanya still could not believe it. She shuddered as she recalled the matching scars on either side of Panther's upper chest. She had never asked him how he had gotten them, and he had never volunteered the information, but she had often wondered about it. Now she knew. He had received them during the Sun Dance.

Two days previously, the men had ridden out in search of just the right tree for the center ceremonial pole of the Sun Dance. They had brought it back and erected it, and the head shaman had blessed it with mystical chants. Long rawhide ropes were connected to the top of the pole. To these lines, the skewers would be attached that would be laced into the chests of the young men.

"The skewers are laced through skin and muscle, one on each side of the chest; or sometimes only one in the center of the chest, but when this is done often the breast bone breaks during the dance," Shy Deer explained calmly. "The skewers are attached to lines from the ceremonial pole, and the men are hoisted to dangle several feet off the ground, held only by the skewers in their chests. The weight of their bodies, combined with their agitated movements, causes the skewers to cut through their flesh. When the flesh is cut through, they fall. Many times the men decide to re-attach the skewers and dance again, but once is enough for most."

"How do they stand the pain?" Tanya wanted to know, aghast.

"They prepare themselves for days before the ceremony. The young men who elect to participate, and often their families as well, fast. They pray alone or with the shaman in secret ceremonies, they sweat the impurities from their bodies in the sweat lodge, and smoke the ceremonial pipes, sometimes with the powders from the peyote buttons. They stay in the ceremonial lodge and have no contact with women during their preparations."

Here Shy Deer gave Tanya a friendly wink. "Thank goodness most men only participate once in their lives, usually as young men about to become warriors. However, they may elect to participate again if they are seeking a personal quest or vision, or revenge, or for several other reasons. All the men usually take part in the ceremony in some way, whether they are going to dance in the air with the spirits or not. They fast, pray, smoke, and sweat together. They review their medicine bundles, seek visions, purify their bodies, chant, and go through other phases of the ceremonies in brotherhood with the chosen young men. It is a time of review and renewal for all of them; a time of thanks and a quest for courage and victory in battle and the hunt. The entire ceremony lasts for days, but only on the last day does the actual Sun Dance take place. The entire village turns out to watch.

"Afterward, the men's wounds are tended and bound, and in a day or two the tribes split into groups and we move to the plains to follow the buffalo."

Tanya listened closely to all Shy Deer told her. Hesitantly, she asked, "Do the women have a ceremony where they must prove their courage?"

Shy Deer laughed. "No. As long as we tend their horses, their lodges, and their children, and are good wives, that is all they expect. If any of us exhibits courage, it is an added benefit. True, we are supposed to be loyal during an enemy attack or in times of trouble, but being women, they do not expect us to be daring and brave in the ways of a warrior."

"That's good!" Tanya heaved a sigh of relief, and both women laughed.

Then Shy Deer sobered. "*You* have courage, Little Wildcat. That is part of what makes you so special, I think."

"I am not special," Tanya denied.

Shy Deer disagreed. "Panther has waited a long time to choose a woman. I think he was waiting to find someone like you. A man such as he needs a woman of courage. How could a great warrior like Panther settle for less?"

Panther was thinking along the same lines. In fact, at that moment he was in the middle of a private conversation with his uncle, Chief Black Kettle.

"I want to make Little Wildcat my wife," he informed his uncle.

Black Kettle shook his hed in dismay. "You know what happened with your father, my brother. Once he had taken your mother as his wife, he was never the same. She cast her spell over him, and when she could no longer stand the Cheyenne way of life, he had to let her go. He took her back to her white family and you went with her. Also she took with her a vital part of White Antelope's soul."

"My mother's family were Spaniards, Uncle, from Mexico," Panther corrected, "not *gringos*."

Black Kettle ignored the interruption. "You were an infant at the time, and White Antelope felt your place was with your mother. It tore his heart out to part with the two of you. It was years before he married again, and even then his heart was not in it. He did it to please our father and to have more children. White Antelope lived for the summers when your mother would send you back to us. Each fall he died another death when you returned to the white world for your education. He was a great chief among our people, always working for peace with the whites, as I do. It is a great irony that he met his death at their hands when his heart lived among them from the day your mother left."

Panther leaned forward, his face a portrait of sincerity. "My mother loved him, Black Kettle. She never married again. Always she had been faithful to my father, and grieved terribly upon his death. She just could not adjust to the Cheyenne life."

"That is my point, Panther. Now you are asking to walk the same path your father trod. Have you learned nothing from his mistake?"

"Little Wildcat is different. Already she speaks our tongue. She never weeps for her lost life or the family she will never see again. She does not beg for her freedom. I have given her a horse and allow her to come and go about the village at will, yet she does not flee. She goes out of her way to learn our ways, she works well and hard and does not complain. Always, she is asking questions, thirsting for knowledge, wanting to learn new things. Her brain, her tongue, and her hands are quick to learn, and she has the courage to endure."

Black Kettle sighed. "If you were any other warrior, it might not matter so much, but you are my nephew. As such, you will be a chief soon, and you have an obligation to our people. You are a great warrior, Panther. You have great courage. Already you are a leader. Men follow your lead without question. They trust you and believe in you."

"Yes, but they follow Winter Bear also. He, too, is your nephew and will be a chief one day," Panther pointed out.

"True," Black Kettle conceded, "but I will hesitate to bless a union between you and Little Wildcat. Is it because of your white blood that you are attracted to her, I wonder? Why not keep her as your woman, but marry within the tribe? Marry a Cheyenne woman."

"I cannot, Uncle. I do not know what draws me to her. It is as if the spirits led me to the river where she was bathing that day. I have never seen a woman so beautiful. One look at that magnificent hair and golden eyes, and I saw a wildcat; a she-cat; a lioness. I had to have her. She is the mirror of my soul; my soul-mate. My heart recognized her immediately."

"That is fine, Panther, but must she be your only wife? First take a Cheyenne bride, and let the white girl become your second wife. In many ways you fit your namesake. You are swift and silent on the attack, and move with the peculiar grace of a great cat. Like the panther, you stalk your prey, and he rarely eludes you. You emerge from battle victorious over your foes, and many fear just the mention of your name. The panther mates with many she-cats. He does not limit himself to one."

"That is where the big cat and I differ, then. I have chosen my mate, and want no other. It is Little Wildcat I wish for the mother of my children, and I want no bastards. Even now she could be carrying my child."

"How would she feel about this if she does bear you a child, Panther? You have told me how she is adjusting, but you've said nothing of what she feels. Has she told you of her thoughts and emotions?"

"We have spoken of this, Uncle. She wishes to stay among our people and with me. She has told me of her love for me. When I brought her to my tipi, she was untouched. She has known no man but me. She is not a whore.

"I have seen her with the children of the tribe. She is good with them, and they adore her. She would make a good mother for my children, and she will love them because they are a product of our love."

"Would she not wish to raise them in the white man's way, as your mother did?" Black Kettle questioned.

Panther shook his head. "She would raise them to be good Cheyenne because I ask it. Her pride is great, but above all else she is obedient to my every wish. Her dignity and courage are remarkable, and these traits would be strong in our children."

Black Kettle contemplated Panther's words. At last he spoke again. "There is but one way I would sanction the marriage. Little Wildcat must first prove herself to be worthy of being called Cheyenne. I would then adopt her as my own daughter, but first she must pass certain tests of loyalty, skill, and courage, much as our young braves do. Only then will I bless your marriage. When she has proven herself, and I am satisfied, she will become a daughter of the tribe and you will have your Cheyenne bride. It is the only way our tribe will accept it."

Panther nodded in agreement. "I accept your edict as my chief. Little Wildcat will not fail you."

"One more thing," the old chief added. "As her first test, I require her presence at my side during the final day of the Sun Dance. It will interest me to see her reaction. Most whites who have ever viewed it, your mother included, have thought it cruel and inhuman."

Panther clenched his teeth at his uncle's craftiness. "If it is explained to her properly, I am sure she will understand its significance. She may not like it, but she will not shame any of us by discrediting its meaning to our people," he assured Black Kettle. "Neither will she flee from it, for my woman is brave of spirit. She is not cowardly or faint-hearted."

"You are very sure," Black Kettle commented.

"I know her as well as I know the lines of my own hand."

"For both your sakes, I hope you are right," Black Kettle relented. "I know I am being hard on you both, but I must be assured. I do not wish to see history repeat itself. I only wish to save you the pain your father endured. If she is truly the woman you claim, it will be proven, and I will proudly proclaim her as my daughter."

Much later, Panther entered his own tipi to find Tanya waiting for him. He had said nothing to her about approaching Chief Black Kettle on the subject of marriage. Hesitant over his uncle's reaction, Panther had not wanted to build Tanya's hopes, only to have them cruelly crushed.

The tests his uncle had laid out were difficult, but a woman of Wildcat's courage and defiance stood a strong chance of passing them. At least Black Kettle had not dismissed the idea entirely. Now Panther had the chore of outlining the plan to Tanya, and convincing her that she had the strength, with his guidance, to see it through.

Chapter 5

"IT'S IMPOSSIBLE!" Tanya exclaimed. "Panther, the list of tests you just reeled off are as long as your arm! There is no way I could pass them all!"

Panther eyed her calmly. "Do you wish to be my wife or not?"

"Of course I do!" Tanya was pacing the floor of the tipi. "I love you more than life itself!"

Panther sat on the mat watching her. "Then set your mind to the task before you, Wildcat. You are a strong, stubborn woman. You can meet the challenge. I will help you, as will Shy Deer, Walks-Like-A-Duck, and Winter Bear. We will get one of the elders to instruct you in our religion, our history, customs and ceremonies. The old medicine woman will help you learn the herbs and ways of healing. Already you know the language and nearly all the work required of a woman."

Tanya gave a rueful laugh. "That is not the part that bothers me. I admit, with practice I may be able to shoot an animal and clean it myself. I can tan the hide and sew it into clothing. Erecting and dismantling the tipi will be easy, as will preparing a meal for the chief, but how on earth can I be expected to learn the religion and history, and the customs and rites that took you years to absorb? I'll be an old woman before we can marry!"

"You don't give your intelligence enough credit," Panther said. "Learning our language was the hardest part, and you picked it up easily. The Cheyenne tongue is one of the most difficult of the Indian languages, and you have mastered it in weeks."

"Fine," she acknowledged, "but what about the rest of it? According to Black Kettle, I must learn to ride and shoot and hunt as well as one of your braves. What about the part where I must learn to track an animal or man, and avoid being tracked in turn? That must take months to learn, at least!"

"I will teach you the ways of the forest and plains, Wildcat, and you could ask for no better teacher," he told her.

"It is not your abilities I question, Panther," she conceded. "It is my own. If I succeed in learning all this, I still have to learn to fight as a brave would. How can a woman fight a man and win?"

"I will see that you are matched with a young brave of your own size so the contest will be evenly matched," he assured her, "and I will teach you how to defeat him. We will practice until you can throw me on my back and keep me there, and you will be able to defeat your opponent with ease. It is not so much a matter of size and strength as how you use your weight to your best advantage, and use moves your foe does not expect."

"That's just great," she grumbled, "but I still have to count coup on an enemy and survive a full week in the wilds on my own. Isn't that a bit much to ask of a mere woman?"

"You are no mere woman," he reminded her, his

dark eyes glowing as they traced her slim form. "You are *my* woman, and you will be my wife."

Tanya stopped pacing and went to kneel before him. Taking his face gently between her two small hands, she said earnestly, "You have such great faith in me, Panther. How can I ever hope to live up to what you and your uncle expect of me?"

Panther enfolded her in his arms, her head in the hollow beneath his chin. "You need the same faith in yourself, Little Wildcat. We will work hard, and you will surprise even yourself. Is the prize not worth the effort?"

She raised her face to his. "You are right, my love, as always. I will succeed in this if it kills me, for I want nothing so much as to call you husband."

Tanya sat stiffly next to the old chief on the last and most important day of the Sun Dance ceremony. She had made herself a new outfit for the occasion, for she refused to sit next to the proud chief in a less than perfectly sewn doeskin dress and moccasins. Her hair hung in two long, tawny braids across her shoulders, and about her head was the beautifully beaded headband Panther had given her.

Stoically she watched as the skewers were driven through the young men's chests and attached to the ropes of the central pole. She willed herself not to wince as they were hoisted off the ground to dangle like macabre puppets. Feeling Black Kettle's eyes on her, she purposefully kept her face blank of all emotion.

"What do you think of it so far?" the chief asked her.

"It is unusual and impressive," she replied evenly, thankful that her voice did not waver. Panther and

Shy Deer had both explained the ceremony to her in great detail, and while she still didn't like it, she at least understood and accepted its importance to these people.

"Do you not find it cruel and inhuman?" Black Kettle persisted.

"Many things in this life seem harsh and cruel, but we must endure them," she answered. "I would not criticize something I do not fully comprehend. I know this is an important part of Cheyenne tradition, and I accept it as such."

Black Kettle nodded and declined further comment.

For hours Tanya sat with him in the hot sun and waited for the ceremony to end. The sun and the chanting were giving her a headache, and her back ached from her efforts to keep it straight. As she watched the Sun Dancers in their tormented agony, she sympathized with their pain, deliberately willing away the nausea that threatened her.

One by one the dancers dropped, sometimes breaking bones as they fell. Finally it was over.

"You did well, Little Wildcat." Black Kettle complimented her.

"Your respect and approval are important to me," she replied. "I will work hard to earn and deserve your esteem."

"The road ahead is hard. Make sure you choose the right path," he advised.

Tanya responded simply and sincerely, "All my paths lead to Panther."

The plains were a familiar, if unwelcome, sight to Tanya. She recalled the long, difficult trek with the wagon train. She much preferred the cool, green mountains, but wherever Panther decided to go, she would follow. The tall, thick buffalo grass was not as difficult to travel through on horseback as it had been by wagon, at least.

In the next months, they moved every few days, following the buffalo herds. Whenever the scouts reported a herd had been sighted, the men would form a hunting party and go after them on their specially trained buffalo ponies.

The women would follow at a distance and set up camp nearby. Then they would take their hatchets, knives, and scrapers, and start butchering the slain beasts. As in everything else, every part of the buffalo was put to use; nothing wasted. It was grueling work, and Tanya's respect for the Indian women grew even more.

Tanya was amazed at the size of the beasts. Personally, she thought them ugly creatures, but she was delighted at the thought of the warm robes their hides would make for the cold winter to come. The number of animals needed to provide meat and hides for the tribes astounded her, but she had heard the Cheyenne tell of long, cold winters with little to eat toward the end. February was known as 'the month the babies cry for food.'

For long hours under a merciless sun, Tanya toiled with the other women. After butchering and skinning the buffalo, the women spent days drying the meat and cutting it into strips. Sinew, bone and fat were processed. The hides were salted and scraped, wet, and stretched out to dry, rubbed with brains and oil, scraped again, and on and on until they were finally fit for use. Then another herd would be located, and the whole process would begin again.

Much of the time, Tanya would perform her tasks while listening to the elder whom Panther had enlisted to instruct her in Cheyenne theology. It was the only way she could fit her lessons into her busy day. When she was not learning from the elder, she was trying to absorb the information the medicine woman, wise in the arts of healing, imparted to her.

"If learning by absorption is possible," she thought wearily, "this just may work."

Whenever possible, she practiced with her bow and arrows. Panther was relentless about this, and she improved if only from constant repetition. He managed to take her hunting a few times, and the day Tanya killed her first rabbit was the proudest moment she could recall. A week later, she killed a doe. Winter Bear was along to confirm the kill, and using its soft, pale hide, she began to sew the outfit she would wear when adopted into the tribe. A few weeks later she had enough skins to complete the dress and soft moccasins.

Panther was an equally hard taskmaster when it came to her riding skills. "It is not enough merely to sit astride the animal and guide him with your knees," he told her.

Much to her dismay, she learned this was true. Tanya, like any young Cheyenne brave, was expected to become a living extension of her mount. She nearly broke her neck the first time she attempted to swing to the side of her horse, clinging only by her legs and feet, with one arm about the horse's neck.

"In this manner," Panther explained, "you can hide your entire body along the unexposed side of your horse, and shoot at your enemy from under the horse's neck."

"Easy for you to say," Tanya complained as she rubbed her bruised posterior.

Not only that, Panther insisted she learn to crouch on the horse's back and to stand as the animal galloped over the rough terrain. "You need to know this in order to leap onto an enemy's back or onto another horse, or to catch hold of an overhead tree limb and swing yourself onto it."

"A skill I'll need every day, I'm sure," she grumbled, shooting him a nasty look.

Panther merely grinned and made her try again.

If Tanya thought she was bruised and battered from this, it was nothing compared to the beating she received when Panther decided it was time she learned the fine art of fighting.

"You tricked me!" she howled, glowering at him as she picked herself up and dusted herself off for what seemed like the thousandth time.

"That's the general idea," he retorted calmly. "When you are fighting for your life, you don't stop to consider what is fair and what is not. You defeat your enemy in any way you can, and as swiftly as possible. You don't announce your intentions or give him a plan of your every move."

"Go ahead and laugh at me, you big brute! Just remember, loving and fighting are not compatible. Bruises and sore muscles are not conducive to love-making." Tanya glared at him, hands on her hips.

Panther laughed aloud. "I'll give you a massage and you'll be fine."

"Don't count on it," she warned.

In total disregard for her tortured body, Panther taught Tanya how to throw her weight into her opponent and use leverage to achieve her objective. He taught her to feint and surprise her foe with unexpected moves. Along with this, he made her realize how important it was to keep her face expressionless.

"Too many times it is easy to read in someone's face

or eyes what his next move will be. Do not give your enemies that advantage."

Too many weeks later to suit Tanya, she finally succeeded in throwing Panther to the ground and pinning him there. In triumph she sat upon him, her face a wreath of smiles. "Now, my brave warrior, what will you give me to let you up?" she crowed.

"What would you have?" he grinned up at her.

"The price of your release is three kisses," she announced.

"You shall have them as soon as we reach the tipi."

Tanya shook her head. "Oh, no! *Now*, Panther, or we shall sit out here all night."

"Wildcat, you know public displays of emotion are not the Cheyenne way."

"I am aware of that, Panther, but the victory is mine, and I have named my price," she insisted, wedging her knee into his ribs.

"Wildcat, you drive a hard bargain," he grunted.

"All is fair in love and war," she said smugly as she bent to receive her reward.

During all this time, Panther was systematically teaching Tanya to track. Periodically, he would take her out of the village, have her locate an animal's tracks and follow them. This was by far the most interesting of her studies, but often frustrating. She would lose the trail and have to backtrack, or sometimes the trail would disappear on rocky ground only to pick up later somewhere else.

Tanya learned to distinguish on sight which animal had made the tracks. Sometimes it was buffalo, elk, or deer; at others rabbit, a grouse, or a cougar. Panther taught her to examine the footprints and the spore, the paths they left in the tall grass, or the rubbings on the trees. She learned to tell how fresh or old the trail was. He taught her how to tell how many were in a group or herd, and how to tell if a horse was being led or ridden.

In addition, Panther was helping Tanya learn to put all her senses to use. At times he would blindfold her and make her tell him what she felt through her fingertips and on her skin; what she heard and smelled; what she tasted; and what her inner senses, her instincts, told her.

He taught her to walk softly, disturbing as little of her surroundings as possible as she passed, and how to cover her trail. She learned to sit and hide quietly for hours without moving. She learned to move swiftly and stealthily on silent feet. He drilled her constantly on this.

Twice he took her for short trips into the forest. There they practiced what she had learned, tracking not only animals, but Panther as well. He would go off and leave her, making her find him by following his trail. As she improved, he made it harder and harder.

In her turn, she would go off, doing her best to cover her trail so Panther could not find her. At first he did so with ease, but as Tanya's skills improved, she eluded him for longer and longer periods. At last came the day they both anticipated. Tanya evaded Panther for an entire day, and finally had to find *him*, since he could not seem to locate her.

That night, alone by their campfire, they celebrated her achievement. Snuggled in his arms, she sighed contentedly, and his arms tightened about her in response.

"Summer is nearly over, and you are almost ready for your testing, Little Wildcat. Soon you will be a true daughter of the Cheyenne and I can claim you as my bride." Pride registered in Panther's voice.

"It had better be soon," Tanya sighed softly.

"I know, my heart. I do not want our child to be harmed by the testing; but neither do I want you to have the heartache of bearing a bastard."

"How did you know? I have told no one, and my stomach is still flat!" Tanya was amazed.

"Do you think after all this time I do not know every inch of your body? I know it better than you do; better than my own. Blind, I would know it; every curve, each rib, every mark, the scent of you. These days your breasts are more full and sensitive, your skin holds a special glow, and your hair and eyes sparkle with the vitality of the new life you carry within you."

"I didn't want to tell you just yet and cause you worry," Tanya explained. "I took special care to hide my sickness in the mornings and those times when certain smells nauseate me."

Panther gave her a tender smile. "I have noticed, but I think no one else has. I love you, Wildcat, and I would not put your life or that of our child in danger. You are young and healthy, and the testing should not be a problem if it comes soon. To wait would increase the danger."

"I would walk through fire for you, Panther. I love you so much!" Tears glistened in her golden eyes.

"I am honored to have you for my woman," Panther declared huskily, drawing her closer.

He worshiped her with his lips and hands, making love to her more gently than ever before. One after another, he searched out the sensitive areas of her body, leaving no spot untouched, no part of her that was not yearning for him.

Caught up in a web of desire, Tanya drew him to her, arching her body into his. "Panther, Panther," she sighed his name. "You set my soul aflame!"

"Then I must quench the fire with my love," he whispered back, and proceeded to make tender, exquisite love to her until they were both consumed by the flames of their desire.

Later they talked softly. "Are you happy about the child, Wildcat?" he asked her.

"I cannot tell you what joy it gives me to know your child grows within me," she sighed, her face all aglow. "I find myself imagining a boy, a miniature of his handsome father, or a little girl with your huge, black eyes. Are you, too, pleased about the baby?"

"More than pleased, I am proud and thrilled. I shall eagerly await the arrival of the child of our love and passion."

"Would you be disappointed if it is a girl? I know how important a son is to a man."

"If it should be a girl, she will be beautiful and courageous like her mother. How could I regret that? But son or daughter, I hope it has your golden eyes, the eyes that first drew me to you. We should make beautiful children together, Wildcat. Brave, intelligent, proud."

"And if the first is a daughter, we can try again for a son. The trying is so very, *very* nice, Panther," Tanya whispered softly in his ear.

The day after their return to the village, Black Kettle set up Tanya's tests. During the morning, she would sit in Black Kettle's lodge and be examined orally on her knowledge of history, religion, customs, and medicine. In the afternoon, she would demonstrate her skills at riding, shooting, and fighting. She had already passed all her woman's skills before Black Kettle's wife, Woman-To-Be-Hereafter.

The usually placid Panther paced outside his uncle's tipi, unable to conceal his anxiety. Three hours later, Tanya emerged. Her face was set in calm lines; only her eyes were sparkling in delight. She gave Panther and Winter Bear a broad, saucy wink as she passed.

Panther was unable to follow Tanya as he would have wished, for just then Black Kettle emerged from his tipi and approached Panther and Winter Bear. "Your woman surprises me, Panther," he said. "She has the subtle tenacity of a spider's web. For one who appears so fragile, she clings stubbornly to her goals."

"Like the spider's web, she also wraps you gently in her grasp and holds you captive," Panther answered absently, his eyes following Tanya as she continued on her way.

"She does have great charm," Black Kettle admitted reluctantly.

"How did she do?" asked Winter Bear.

"Very well," Black Kettle told them. "I am beginning to think she may be a worthy mate for you, Panther. She has succeeded in grasping our beliefs and learning our tongue."

Here Black Kettle frowned thoughtfully at Panther. "In all the time she has been with us, I have rarely heard her speak English, and I have never heard either you or Winter Bear speak to her in her language, though you both have the knowledge. Have you said nothing to her of your ability to do so? Panther, does she not know of your Spanish mother and your up-bringing?"

"No, Uncle. I have not told her. If she had known I

could understand her words, she would not have felt the necessity of learning our tongue, and her progress would not have been as rapid."

"Will you tell her now?"

"The time is not right. I want her to accept me as I appear to be; as a Cheyenne warrior. I do not want her to see me as an extension of her white world, for I shall never return to it. I have chosen to live among my father's people, and Wildcat had to chose this life also, freely and totally, without reservation or doubt. I will tell her when I feel the time is right. Until then, I prefer she does not know."

"Are you having doubts about her?" Black Kettle questioned.

"No," Panther denied, "but if Wildcat knew I could pass easily into her white world, she might want me to take her to visit her parents. She still misses them, though she does not mention it, and she worries that they may think her dead or mistreated, especially now that she is with child."

"She is carrying your child?" Winter Bear exclaimed. "Then how can she carry on with the testing?"

Black Kettle's mouth set in firm lines. "I shall cancel the rest of the tests."

"No!" Panther's voice rang out loud and clear. "She wants to go on with it. We have discussed it and agree that Wildcat is strong and fit, and no harm will come to the child. Neither of us wishes our child to endure the pain of being born a bastard."

Winter Bear turned a concerned look on Black Kettle. "Uncle, is there no other way?"

Black Kettle sighed. "No, Winter Bear. As soon as I issued the ruling, the entire tribe learned of it. I cannot change it now."

"There is no need," Panther assured them both. "Wildcat has trained hard and learned well. She is ready and capable of proving herself not only to our chief, but to all our people. It is important that they accept her without reproach. As a chief's daughter and my wife, this will be possible. My pride and hers will accept nothing less."

Tanya had never been as nervous as she was this afternoon. Her future hinged on the result of all her intensive training. Panther, for once, was no help at all, for he was as edgy as she. By sheer will, she forced herself to forget about the child within her. To worry over its safety would make her less daring and more cautious, and could cost her a life with Panther. With one last, silent plea to both his God and hers, Tanya picked up her knife and her bow and arrows and headed for the edge of the camp.

Targets had been set up in various stops for her use. Taking her place where Black Kettle indicated, Tanya demonstrated her skill at throwing her knife. Time after time, her weapon hit the center of the target.

When Black Kettle was satisfied, Tanya then concentrated on doing the same with her bow and arrows. Again her aim was sure, so true that twice her arrows sliced through the shaft of a previously placed arrow to hit their mark.

Next she demonstrated her prowess on horseback. Galloping Wheat about the field, she aimed her shots from horseback, doing creditably well. In a simulated exercise, Tanya rescued a supposedly injured brave from his running mount; and attacked another by leaping upon him from her fast-moving mount and knocking him off his horse.

Finally came the test she dreaded. Her normally soft

mouth set in firm lines, she prepared to do battle with the young brave, Crooked Feather. To prevent injury to either party, they would fight hand-to-hand, without weapons.

Mentally reviewing all Panther had taught her, Tanya faced her opponent. Slowly they circled; each waiting for the other to move; each gauging the other, sizing him up; trying to read his intentions from his face.

Crooked Feather made the first move. Lunging at Tanya, he grabbed her arm and flipped her to the ground. Tanya rolled as Panther had coached her, bouncing immediately to her feet to face her opponent. When next he attacked, she pivoted neatly on one foot, catching his leg and arm simultaneously, tossing him flat on his back. Recalling Panther's instructions, Tanya yelled loudly as she made contact with the young brave. There was something about a good, strong shout that added impetus to the move and strength to the attack, but never in advance as a warning of your intentions.

Warily they circled again. Crooked Feather caught her by the arms and tried to throw her, but Panther had taught her to use leverage to her advantage. Failing this, he tried to force her to her knees, but could not. When he tried to trip her, she countered his move, butting her head solidly into his unprotected stomach.

They broke apart. Several times he threw her, but could not keep her down. Several times she tripped him up, but he was on his feet again before she could follow through. Once, he tossed her square on her bottom, and as he leaped upon her, she placed both feet flat in his stomach and tossed him over her head into the dirt.

For many minutes they fought, until both were dirt-smeared, tired, and panting. Neither had gained the advantage. In a surprise move, Crooked Feather threw himself at Tanya, grabbing her about the middle, both of them falling. As Tanya fell backward, she used their momentum to carry her and Crooked Feather into a neat backward flip, and when they finally came to rest, Crooked Feather was flat on his back, Tanya astride him. As he was flung onto his back, he loosed his grip, and Tanya quickly had his arms pinned to the ground, one under his own body. Her own long legs tangled in his, preventing him from flinging her off him. The force of the fall had knocked the wind from his lungs, and her sharp elbow in his chest kept it from returning. With the flat edge of her spare hand, she delivered a gentle blow to Crooked Feather's windpipe. Had she held a knife, his life would have ended there.

It was over. Tanya had won. She remained where she was until she heard confirmation from Black Kettle, then stumbled to her feet. With good grace, she held out a helping hand to Crooked Feather. For a moment she was afraid he would ignore the gesture. Then, with a wry grin, he caught her hand and let her help pull him to his feet.

Throughout all the contests Tanya had remained blank-faced, showing none of her emotions. At last she allowed a hint of a grin to tilt the corners of her mouth. "It was a good fight," she said to Crooked Feather.

He nodded. "It *was* a good fight," he agreed.

Black Kettle cleared his throat, but still his voice was husky as he spoke. "I, who have not been blessed with children of my own, may soon have a daughter." His eyes glinted with pride as he looked at Tanya.

"Tomorrow you will track one of our best warriors, and if you find him, you will then need to elude three of our finest trackers. That will leave only one final test, other than counting coup on one of our enemies. You will go into the mountains for seven suns and survive on your own, with only your knife, your hatchet, your bow, a flask of water and one of pemmican, and your horse."

"I will be ready," Tanya concurred.

Black Kettle eyed her seriously. "I wish you well, Little Wildcat. You have done well so far, and if you can continue to do so, I will be honored to call you Daughter."

A smile flirted at her rosy lips, and she couldn't resist saying, "Prepare the feast, then, for I do not intend to fail."

Black Kettle laughed aloud. "You have a great pride, Little Wildcat. You will make a fine Cheyenne if your actions match your words."

Tanya gave him a level look and nodded. Then, shoulders straight, she walked back to her tipi, exhausted but pleased.

Chapter 6

THE ATTACK came in the predawn light the next morning. Tanya was awake, dressed, and ready to begin preparing the morning meal, going over her day's strategy in her head. Panther was pulling on his moccasins, about to commence his morning prayers, when the first shrieks were heard. The short hairs on Tanya's nape stood straight up, and she stared in wonder at Panther.

"Ute war whoops," he answered her unstated question tersely. He grabbed for his quiver, bow, and lance, and loped for the tipi entrance. "I must get to the horses."

Breakfast forgotten, Tanya scooped up her bow and slipped the quiver of arrows over her shoulder. "I am coming with you," she announced as she hurried after him.

Over his shoulder, he shouted, "No, Wildcat! Stay and find Shy Deer. If we lose the battle, run south along the river and hide. I will find you." His voice was almost lost as he raced away on his stallion.

Checking that her knife was in its sheath at her waist, Tanya ran toward Shy Deer's tipi. Several tipis along the north edge of the village were in flames. The air was filled with sounds of battle and the shrieks of frightened women and children. Thick smoke hung in the air, and dogs and humans alike seemed to be running indiscriminately in every direction.

Tanya was thrust roughly aside as three braves on horseback raced by her. A Ute arrow whizzed past her head as she dodged and weaved her way into the fray near Shy Deer's lodge.

Rounding the lodge from the rear, she came abruptly upon a Ute warrior aiming his lance at Shy Deer's back as she fought off another Ute brave. Without hesitation, Tanya lined up her shot and let the arrow fly. It drove cleanly between the warrior's shoulder blades, and he fell from his horse, his lance still in his clenched fist. The brave attacking Shy Deer never knew what hit him, as Tanya's knife neatly severed his spinal cord at the base of his neck. He lay twitching on the ground as Tanya tried to lead Shy Deer away.

"Wait!" Shy Deer cried. "You killed him. You must take his scalp!"

Tanya gaped at her in astonishment. "He isn't even dead yet!"

Shy Deer's eyes were glazed with a strange light. "You must," she insisted. "It is the custom."

Tanya's throat muscles contracted as she stared at her friend. Finally she nodded, conceding that Shy Deer was right. She could ruin all chances of becoming Panther's wife if she faltered now.

Before she could dwell on it further, she quickly knelt, and with the razor-sharp knife, she lifted the scalp as easily as if she were slicing venison for steaks. Because he was still alive, the blood ran in a river between her fingers and onto the earth. Tanya closed her eyes and mind to what she was doing, and when she was done, she went on to the other warrior she had slain and did the same. This time there was less blood, for the warrior was dead, but the loud 'pop' as the top of his skull sucked loose from the rest of his head sickened her, and she was glad she hadn't had time for breakfast as her stomach lurched.

The attack was over almost as swiftly as it began. The Utes had surprised them, but had not caught as many of the Cheyenne asleep as they had hoped to. The Cheyenne warriors reacted quickly, and with a vengeance. Because most of them kept their horses near their tipis, they soon routed the raiding Utes and had them fleeing.

While a party of warriors chased the Utes across the plains, the rest of the villagers set about tending the wounded and assessing the damage.

Luckily, only two persons had been killed. One was a young boy who had been guarding the horses. His throat had been slit before he could sound the alarm. The other was an old woman who had been run down and trampled by a Ute warrior on horseback. Eight others had been wounded, two of them seriously. One warrior had taken a bullet in the chest, and another had a lance run through his shoulder. All the other wounds were slight and easily cared for.

Five tipis had been fired, and most of the women of the tribe donated goods from their own lodges to replace those that had burned. Tonight, several families would double up for shelter, but tomorrow the women would sew new lodge skins and gather lodge poles for five new tipis. Everyone would contribute something in either time, labor, or goods. It was the Cheyenne way to look after all members of the tribe, sharing the misfortunes as well as the good.

Tonight there would be ceremonies and mourning for those killed in the raid. Eight Utes had been killed so far. At least one Ute had been captured. More might be returning with the Cheyenne warriors later. This one had been knocked unconscious, but not seriously wounded. By dawn tomorrow he would be praying for death, for the Cheyenne would extract their vengeance in slow torture.

The morning was half gone when Black Kettle approached Tanya. She was sorting through some robes, trying to decide which to give to the families whose tipis had burned.

"Corn Crow awaits you, Little Wildcat," he informed her.

She looked up at him, confused. "I don't understand, my chief."

"You are to track him today. Surely you have not forgotten," the chief answered.

"I had not forgotten. I thought perhaps it would be put off for another day after all that has happened," Tanya commented. She stood to follow him.

"No, we will proceed while we are awaiting the return of our warriors. Corn Crow is not the brave I had originally chosen, but he is available and he will do. When you have found him, you will go on into the foothills and I will send the others to track you. If they have not found you by the time the sun rests over the top of the foothills, return to camp."

Black Kettle looked about at the destruction the Utes had caused. "Tonight there will be ceremonies for our dead and wounded, and then will be a war dance in preparation for our revenge on the Utes. Tomorrow our warriors will prepare themselves for war, and form a raiding party against the Ute camp. Repairs will be made to our own village, and while the raiding party rides out to seek revenge, the rest of the tribe will continue on to our winter grounds.

"While we spend our days at these things, you,

Little Wildcat, will finish your testing. Time grows short, and there is much to be done yet in preparation for winter. You must take advantage of this opportunity while you can, for Panther has told me of the babe you carry. Regardless of what you may think, I too prefer my first grandchild to be born properly, with his parents wed. Any risks to the child I wish to have behind us as soon as possible, so we can all settle down and await a healthy baby, preferably a boy."

Tanya laughed despite herself. "Naturally, I'll try my best, but often nature surprises us. My father also wanted sons, and got two daughters instead."

Black Kettle smiled with her. "A son is a man's immortality, but there is no shame in having a courageous daughter like you, Little Wildcat."

He eyed her belt. "Where are the scalps you took this morning?"

"They are in the tipi," she answered rather reluctantly.

Black Kettle gave her a sharp look. "You must prepare them properly to preserve them. You have counted coup on two of our enemy today, and saved the life of Shy Deer, who sings your praises. You have earned our gratitude; now go and earn your place in our tribe."

Even given a healthy head start, Corn Crow stood no chance against the excellent training Panther had put Tanya through. She cornered him in little over an hour. As he returned to a prearranged meeting place to inform her three waiting trackers, Tanya headed for the rocky foothills as Black Kettle had instructed her.

For a short while she followed a well-traveled track she stumbled across, mixing her horse's tracks with those of the deer. When she came across a river, she urged Wheat into the cool water, and followed it upstream for a few miles. Where she exited the water on the opposite bank, she dismounted and carefully covered her trail.

Some time later, she came across a rocky ledge. Here she dismounted, tied her pony, and explored the crevices. Hidden behind a huge boulder and a thick, bristly bush, she stumbled across a small, shallow cave. It was a tight squeeze, even for her, but she finally managed to get to it and carefully explored it for inhabitants. Luckily, there were no signs of any.

Climbing back down, she rode Wheat further into the trees, taking care not to ride her mare over rocks where her hooves would mark their surfaces. Eventually she found a thicket and led her horse into it and tied her. With a strip of leather, she fashioned a muzzle, hoping it would prevent her from whinnying should the trackers pass close by.

This done, she repaired the damage to the thicket and backtracked the way they had come, erasing the tracks as she went. When she reached the ledge, she wedged herself into the tiny cave and waited. The cave was set crosswise so that if she peeked out to her left, she could see the top of the foothills, and if she looked to her right and down, she could see for miles in the direction from which she had approached.

Tanya guessed she had been cramped into her cave about two hours or more when she thought she heard voices on the breeze. Hardly daring to move, she eased her head around and looked down to her right. There, far down the way, she spied two of her trackers. She recognized them as Towering Pine and Snail of her tribe.

As she watched, they looked up almost directly at her and waved. For a moment she thought they had spotted her, but almost instantly she realized they were signaling to someone above her.

"Drat!" she thought to herself. "Only another hour or so and I would have won!" If they had followed her this far, they were sure to find her soon.

Hooves rang out on the rocks not far above her, and soon the third rider came into her view. It was Clever Fox. He glanced her way, and Tanya dared not breathe, or even blink. Her eyes watered from the strain and her lungs begged for air. Finally he turned away and was soon hidden from her view. Cautiously she drew a much needed breath, thankful she had had the foresight to remove the colorful headband.

Snail and Towering Pine now split up, slowly going in opposite directions, obviously searching for signs. This told Tanya they had lost her trail, and she could only hope they didn't find it again.

Anxiously, Tanya sweated out her remaining time, her eyes and ears constantly alert for her trackers. Once more she thought she heard them far below her, but she could not spot them. At long last, the sun touched the peak of the foothills, and cramped as she was, Tanya made herself wait still longer to make sure they had really gone before she crept quietly from her hiding place.

She eased her rebelling muscles into a more comfortable stance, and rubbed and stretched them until she could once more move without painful needles shooting up her limbs and back. Then, on fleet, silent feet, she returned for her horse.

The stars had come out and the night sky was deepening from purple to black when she rode into the camp. She had stayed well behind the three braves on her return trip. Tanya rode directly up to Black Kettle's tipi, where the three trackers were in conference with Panther and the chief outside his lodge.

She arrived just in time to hear Snail saying, "There was no sign of her after a while. Perhaps she will not return, but will try to find her old family."

"I think not," Panther declared, catching sight of her as she neared. His smile nearly split his face. "Little Wildcat has returned!"

Five sets of dark eyes settled on her, but Tanya had eyes only for Panther. "It is well that you taught me so expertly, Panther, for they nearly found me," she said.

"Where?" Towering Pine wanted to know.

Tanya favored him with a smile. "Among the rocks near the long ledge, there is a small cave. When I saw you and Snail below me, I was sure you had located my trail, especially when Clever Fox rode almost directly over my head. You came so close I couldn't believe it when you didn't discover me after all."

Tanya dismounted wearily, and Panther was instantly at her side. "You are tired. Go to our lodge and rest. I will have someone look after your horse. I will send Walks-Like-A-Duck with food, and then you will sleep until I send for you."

Tanya started for the tipi, but Black Kettle's voice stopped her. "Little Wildcat, you are well?"

She glanced back to meet his concerned look. "Yes, my chief, I am quite well," she answered with a nod. "Just tired, very tired." As if to prove her point, her feet dragged every step of the way to her tipi, and her shoulders sagged, for once refusing to remain straight.

To Tanya it seemed only minutes after she'd closed her eyes that someone was shaking her awake. She opened sleep-heavy lids to see Walks-Like-A-Duck standing over her. "Panther says you are to join the ceremonies now."

Tanya sat up yawning. "I'd much rather sleep," she commented lamely as she started to dress.

Walks-Like-A-Duck watched silently as Tanya carefully re-plaited her hair and adjusted her headband. Then she reached out for Tanya's waistband. In her hand she held the two gruesome scalps Tanya had successfully pushed from her consciousness. Tanya reacted automatically, backing away abruptly.

Impatiently, Walks-Like-A-Duck held out the scalps. "You must wear these on your belt this evening, Little Wildcat. While you were gone today I scraped and dried them for you."

Grimacing inwardly, Tanya cautiously took them from her and hooked them to her belt, murmuring her thanks.

"Lord, the things I do for that man!" she thought to herself.

Bracing herself for the ordeal to come, she followed Walks-Like-A-Duck outside. The night sky was deceptively peaceful, bright and clear, as if to make up for the frightful events taking place beneath it. The moon was high, and Tanya judged it to be around midnight. She had slept for over three hours.

The entire tribe was gathered about the central fire, reminding Tanya of her first night in the Cheyenne village. For a minute she stood uncertainly, absorbing the sights and sounds around her. Once again, all the men wore their paints; colorful, fascinating, and gruesome. Tonight, it seemed, the women took an active part in the ceremonies. They were mourning their dead, and their shrieks and wails were heartrending. Tears sprang to Tanya's eyes as she saw them weeping and wailing, adorned in ashes, tearing at their clothes, and clawing at their skin and hair. Relatives of the dead had cut off their braids and slashed their bodies in an open display of their grief.

To one side of the central fire, two Ute braves were lashed to poles, their naked, sweat-slick bodies glistening in the flickering firelight. The Cheyenne warriors had captured the other when his horse had stumbled and fallen. This night the Cheyenne men would sit back and watch, as their women took their revenge on the unfortunate victims.

As Tanya looked from the Utes to the grieving women, she was torn between revulsion of what she knew was to happen and the knowledge that it was justified. Feeling the weight of the scalps at her belt, she only hoped she would not have to participate.

Her eyes travelled about the circle, finding Panther seated next to Black Kettle, Winter Bear on the chief's other side. Panther motioned to her to join him. When she reached him, he seated her next to him.

"Chief Black Kettle has demanded your presence for this evening."

Tanya nodded wearily. "I understand."

"You will be expected to participate later, when the Utes are turned over to the tender mercies of our women," he went on, his face a mask as he reached out to touch the scalps dangling from her belt.

"I know," she responded quietly.

"Shy Deer spoke of how you saved her life this morning. You showed great bravery." Still his face revealed nothing.

"I used the skills you taught me," Tanya told him, calmly meeting his look.

Still he fingered the scalps. "You hate these, don't you?"

Her answer was a simple "Yes."

"After tonight you will hang them on the lodge pole." Only his eyes reflected his understanding.

Tanya nodded stiffly, turning her attentions to the activities.

The tempo of the drums changed, announcing the change from grieving to vengeance. The men performed a lengthy war dance, and by the time it was the women's turn, the deep, steady throb of the drums seemed to have seeped into Tanya's bones, invading her being to commune with her soul. Without conscious volition, she was on her feet, joining the shrieking women, her knife flashing in her hand. Her own voice joined the others in their taunts and wild ravings.

As if in a trance, she approached the Utes, her golden eyes glowing. Caught up in the mood, it seemed that she stood aside and watched herself as her hand flashed out and her knife made a small, precise slice on the thigh of one of the captives. Her lips curled in a parody of a smile.

A small voice in a remote corner of her mind questioned her savage actions. Had she lost her mind? Was she suddenly possessed? Her pulse beat wildly in response to the drums, and her blood raced through her veins, obliterating her weariness. She felt wild and free, and exhilarated.

The sun had risen over the horizon when Tanya wiped the last of the captives' blood from her knife blade. The drums ceased as the last, shuddering breath eased from the Utes. Their lifeless forms hung from the poles, barely resembling human beings. Thousands of small cuts laced their blood-streaked bodies; pools of blood congealed at the base of the poles. Their ears, noses, lips, fingers, toes, and privates had been severed from their bodies. Empty sockets gaped where their eyes had once been.

Tanya took one last, long look, shuddered violently, and stumbled wearily off to her tipi.

She slept deeply until noon, never stirring when Panther gently stripped her clothing from her and covered her with the blanket. When she arose, it was to a lethargic feeling, as if she'd been drugged. She blanched beneath her golden tan as she recalled her actions of the night before. She had acted like a savage! But as she attempted to drag her conscience to the fore, the feelings of guilt she thought she ought to have dissolved. She tried and failed to dredge up feelings of remorse.

With one last fatalistic shrug of her shoulders, she muttered, "What is done is done and best left to rest. They were our enemies and would have done the same or worse to any of us." Still, she grimaced at the traces of blood on her hands and arms. Unbinding her hair, she headed for the stream.

The entire female population of the village seemed to have the same idea. Worn out from the previous evening's activities, they too had slept unusually late and were just starting the day.

With none of her old self-consciousness, Tanya slipped out of her dress and moccasins and waded into the cool, clear water. Intent on her bathing, she was unaware of Suellen's presence beside her until the girl's strident voice sounded loudly next to her.

"What do you think your parents and fiancé would say about the way you acted last night?"

Tanya spun to glare at her. Nancy was standing behind Suellen, frowning. Full of spite, Suellen continued boldly, "You're a born whore, Tanya! You like that tall, copper stallion between your legs. Unlike the rest of us, you seem to thrive on this dreadful life."

Tanya closed the distance between them swiftly, her eyes shooting golden flames. "You jealous bitch!" With that, she swung back her arm and delivered a sharp slap across Suellen's face. The other girl lost her balance and plopped on her rear into the shallow water.

Nancy let out a gasp of dismay. "Oh, Tanya, I'm sure she didn't mean it! It's just that you are treated so much better than the rest of us."

Suellen struggled to her feet, dragging her wet hair out of her face. "Oh, I meant it, all right! Every word of it! Miss High and Mighty here wants to join the tribe. Well, she'll fit in perfectly with this bunch of savages! I guess breeding really does tell!"

Tanya gathered her dignity about her. In a deadly quiet voice, she said, "You have overstepped yourself, Suellen. I shall have to see that you are properly punished."

At this, Melissa, who had come up soon after the fracas began, cut in. "Oh, no, Tanya. Please!" She touched Tanya lightly on the arm.

"I would not allow her insolence to go unanswered if we were in the President's parlor, Missy, and I cannot allow it here."

A crowd of Indian women had gathered round. Quickly Tanya sought out Forest Fern, Suellen's mistress, and told her of Suellen's insults. "I realize I am not yet a member of the tribe, but I soon shall be. If it were left to me, I would flay the skin off her back, but she does not belong to me. I leave it to you whether she shall be punished or not, and to what extent."

That said, Tanya went back to her bathing. Melissa sidled up to her. "Is it true what Suellen said about you wanting to join the tribe?" she whispered.

"It is," Tanya answered stiffly.

"Don't be angry, Tanya," Melissa pleaded. "I just don't understand why."

"I want to marry Panther."

Melissa nodded sadly. "He certainly is handsome, and he treats you so nicely. Do you love him?"

Tanya's anger dissolved. "Yes, very much. We are to have a child in the spring."

"What about Jeffrey?" Melissa protested softly.

"This is quite different than what I felt for Jeffrey. If he came for me tomorrow, I would choose to stay with Panther."

Melissa sighed. "Well, I'm glad something good came out of all this. I'm not sure yet, but I suspect I may be with child too, though I'm not at all happy about it."

Tanya eyed her small friend sympathetically. "I'm sorry, Missy. If there was a way I could ease your problems, I would, but Ugly Otter hates me. You'd better not let his wife catch you talking to me."

Tears glistened in Melissa's huge blue eyes. "I know. You wouldn't believe the evil things that woman can think up."

Later that afternoon, as Tanya sat with Shy Deer and several other women sewing buffalo hides together for a tipi covering, she was surprised to be summoned by Forest Fern.

"I wish you to be present to witness the punishment of our slave for her insolence to you," the woman told her.

Tanya arrived before Forest Fern's tipi to find Suellen tied to a post before it, stripped to the waist.

Forest Fern turned to Tanya. "Please tell her in your tongue why she is being whipped. I wish her to know so she has no doubt why she is punished and knows not to repeat her offense."

Tanya walked around to face Suellen, no trace of remorse on her face for what the girl was about to endure. "Your mistress wishes me to inform you that you are to be whipped for your insolence this morning, Suellen. You would be wise to hold your tongue in the future."

Suellen glared at her, but said nothing.

Forest Fern did not wield the lash herself, nor offer the honor to Tanya. A boy of fourteen had been selected for the chore. Anxious to be off to better things, he did not dally. He applied the lash in hard, swift, evenly spaced strokes, and in a very short time it was done with. Unlike Panther, the boy had not cared whether or not he broke the skin, and Suellen had several bloody stripes amidst the other welts.

After the first few lashes, Suellen had fainted and ceased her screaming. Tanya wasted no time feeling sorry for her. Expressing her appreciation to Forest Fern for her actions, she returned to her work, only to be interrupted a second time, this time by a summons from Chief Black Kettle.

He instructed her to be ready to leave the village the next morning. "Our war party will be leaving at dawn. Panther will be among them. You will ride with them into the foothills and go on alone from there. Seven suns from tomorrow you will meet one of our braves at the spot where you leave them."

One last night in Panther's arms and then a week or more away from him. One last test to pass and then a lifetime within the circle of his love. These thoughts passed through Tanya's mind as she held him close that eening in the privacy of their tipi.

"In a week's time you could find your parents and pick up the threads of your old life." Panther's voice sounded distant, though his mouth rested close to her ear.

"Do you think me a fool, Panther? I know Black Kettle will be sending someone to spy on me."

"You could easily elude him with the tricks I have taught you," he pressed.

Tanya turned so she could see his face. "Have you so little faith in me, Panther? Do you doubt my love for you and your child within me?"

"There are ways to rid yourself of my child and be free of all traces of me."

Tanya spoke around the lump in her throat. "I would never do that, Panther! Even if I lost your child, you would remain forever in my heart, as my heart now rests within you."

He held her face between his palms, his fingers playing over her eyes. "Be sure, bright eyes," he whispered, "for once we have been joined as man and wife, only death will part us."

"I am sure, Panther, very sure. I shall miss you dreadfully just the short time we are to be separated."

"It will not be for long, Wildcat."

All talk between them ceased as Panther's mouth closed upon hers. He drew her tightly against him, as if to absorb her into himself. Tanya's lips parted beneath the pressure of his, and his tongue thrust deeply into her mouth, searching out the sweetness there, twining with her own.

His hands traveled the curves of her body, teasing her breasts until her nipples were tight buds standing erect upon her swollen breasts. His lips searched out her ear, her throat, her pulse pounding wildly there. His tongue traced the line of her neck down to her shoulder as she matched him move for move, her small white teeth nipping delicately along his shoulder and chest. They were like dancers, moving in perfect synchronization.

His mouth found her breast as his hand found her mound, teasing and pleasuring her there. Her own hands were no less busy tracing the lines of his body, finding and fondling him until he was hard and near to bursting.

She sensed Panther's need to master her and succumbed to him willingly. She made no protest when he locked her arms over her head and held them there, nor when he spread her legs wide and anchored them with the weight of his own. She felt the tip of his manhood near her entrance, yet he held off, his lips and teeth teasing along her shoulder and breasts until she was nearly wild for need of him, her body twisting and arching to his, until she finally understood what he was waiting for and would not say.

"Please, Panther," she begged. "Please. I need you so. I need you now. Please love me!"

At last he joined with her, his body driving wildly into hers with such a fierce need that she felt her desires burst at his first mighty thrust. A rainbow of colors exploded in her brain and melted into a kaleidoscope of changing shapes. Then her passions rose again to greater heights and burst anew, again and again until she lay exhausted and half-conscious beneath him.

Knowing they were soon to be parted, he woke her time and again that night, each time renewing her desire for him; each time taking her to a land of light and fire and love, where passion knew no bounds. The last time they made love, she lay quiet beneath him once more, fully sated and thoroughly loved; the dawn was not far away.

"I shall think of you every minute and dream of you each night," she vowed.

"I shall will the time to pass quickly so I may claim you as my bride."

"Come back safely from your raid, Panther. Our child needs his father."

"I will return, Wildcat. Do not worry. Just take good care of yourself and our child." His dark eyes glowed into hers. "I love you, Little Wildcat, woman of my heart."

"As I do you, my beloved Panther."

Chapter 7

TANYA DIDN'T need to turn around to know that she was being followed. She could literally feel her shadow's eyes upon her, yet she knew that if she yielded to the temptation to look back, she would see nothing. He had trailed her all afternoon, ever since she had parted from Panther and the war party. She did not know which of the braves it was. Panther could tell her nothing more than to assure her that it would not be Ugly Otter, for the gruesome warrior was included in the war party headed for Ute territory.

They were high into the foothills now. The September sun dappling through the trees was warm, but the higher they climbed the cooler the air became. The slight breeze was crisp and clean, and Tanya breathed deeply, filling her lungs with the tangy smell of pine and moist earth. She was enjoying her trek into this virgin territory where few feet had trod. It was almost as if she had the world to herself, alone with nature at its finest.

The last lingering light was fast fading in the western sky when Tanya halted Wheat in a tiny glade and set up her camp. Building a small, smokeless fire to warm herself and ward off predators, Tanya watered and rubbed down her mare before she fed herself. Tonight she would fare on pemmican and water. Tomorrow she would search out a permanent camp, and hunt. With her knife in her belt and her bow within hand's reach, Tanya wrapped herself into her blanket and slept.

Early the next morning she woke, ate, and was on her way with the dawn. Midmorning, she found a sweet mountain stream, stopped for a while to refresh herself and her horse, and went on.

It was late afternoon when she stumbled onto the secluded clearing. Surrounded by mountain forests on three sides and a river on the east, it was a peaceful, welcoming place. Beyond the river, the land dropped off steeply, giving way to a magnificent view of the valley far below and a small mountain range in the distance. There were no signs of anyone having been here recently, if ever, and Tanya judged it a safe, defendable, beautiful hideaway.

When she had thoroughly scouted the area, noting the lush grass for her mare, she staked her horse, then dug a pit and started a small fire, surrounding it with rocks from the river. Cutting green limbs, she formed a spit, and then decided to go ahead and prepare a drying rack for meat. She came across a good sized rock that, over the ages, had somehow had its center eroded, forming a large bowl. Gleefully she lugged it up to her campfire. It would make a perfect cooking pot.

The sun was dipping low when Tanya collected her bow and quiver and headed for the woods. A short time later, she cut a well-traveled deer trail and soon had herself concealed and waiting. It wasn't long before two does wandered by, but Tanya let them go, having already noted the larger, heavier tracks of a buck. A short quarter-hour behind them, sure enough, the buck appeared. He was a beauty! Gracefully he balanced a wide, fourteen point rack high above his head.

Cautiously drawing back her bowstring, Tanya lined up her arrow, patiently waiting for the buck to reach the right spot for a perfect shot. As he did so, she let the arrow fly. The big buck stopped, startled, then took two leaps forward and fell as his knees buckled.

Within minutes Tanya had slit his throat. She field-gutted him, burying the remains in a shallow pit. Lashing her rope about his legs, she half-carried, half-dragged him the short distance to her camp. There she hoisted him from a limb on the edge of the clearing and left him to bleed out, slicing off only two small steaks for her supper.

For a long while that evening Tanya lay on her bed of pine needles, gazing at the bright stars and thinking of Panther. She wished he was here to share this lovely place with her, and fell asleep thinking of him.

Tanya awoke to overcast skies. During the night clouds had moved in, and the breeze had freshened. Before the day was out, there would be rain. That meant Tanya had a busy day ahead of her. Her primary concern was shelter. Scouting about the edge of the clearing, she found a suitable spot at the western side. Here she located a stand of saplings perfect for her needs. With the help of her horse and a few strips of raw deerhide, she bent the saplings over one another and lashed them together to form a leaf-covered bower. Closed on three sides, she purposely left the opening to the east, as Indian tradition dictated. Crude as it was, it would keep her dry and allow for a tiny, carefully tended fire for warmth.

This done, she set up a similar structure nearby. Then she set to work on the buck. After skinning it, she cut the meat into strips and placed them on the rack to dry, starting a stew for her dinner at the same time. Staking the skin out, she scraped it well, then removed it to the second small hut and staked it out to dry safe from the threatening rain. The meat rack she carted into her own small lodge to finish drying over the fire. Tying Wheat in the lee of her shelter, she snuggled down just as the first huge raindrops began to fall.

Tanya ventured out long enough to collect some wild onions she had spotted near the river's edge. These she added to her venison. Later she tended the small fire in the shelter where the buckskin was staked. Using the fat and brains she had reserved, she worked these into the hide, then rolled it up for better absorption.

It rained far into the night, but cleared by dawn. Tanya's private world lay sparkling before her, wet grass and leaves glistening like jewels in the morning sunlight. Once more she staked the deer hide outside in the sun. She wet it and scrubbed it with sand to make it supple, then left it to dry.

Deciding to supplement her diet with berries or nuts, if she could find some, Tanya automatically collected her weapons and headed into the woods. With her she took a leather pouch and her blanket to hold her discoveries.

She wandered far from her base in her search. Finally, her pouch full of berries and her blanket carrying a fair collection of nuts, she turned back. She wasn't sure if it was a sound she heard or something she only sensed, but Tanya suddenly halted stock-still and listened. She heard nothing. Frowning, she thought to herself, "It is only the warrior."

Several paces further she stopped once more. Now she was positive she had heard something behind her.

Flinging down her bundles, she slipped her bow from her shoulder and drew an arrow from her quiver as she turned. Her eyes scanned the trees and bushes, but could detect nothing.

Suddenly, from the side of her eye, she caught a flash of movement. She brought up her bow, drawn and ready. Her mind just had time to register the fact of the cougar launching itself at her. She let the arrow fly and threw herself to one side. The tawny panther screamed as the missile found its mark. One huge paw reached out and clawed Tanya's shoulder, rending the doeskin and drawing four long lines of blood as Tanya fell to the ground.

The animal shrieked in pain and rage, and with supreme effort, drew itself to its feet and lunged at Tanya's supine form. Tanya's knife flashed in a stray ray of sunlight as she brought it up and drove it straight into the panther's heart. The magnificent creature's golden eyes blazed into hers for a long moment, and then with a shudder, it collapsed.

Tanya lay for some time without moving; stunned, shocked, regretting. Tears of remorse stung her eyes. When Panther had years before gone in search of his vision, he had taken the name and identity of the panther. In doing so, he assumed a protective attitude toward the animal whose name he now bore, and an affinity with it. Never would he harm one of the big cats unless it was a matter of necessity.

Bitterly Tanya recalled the many times he had compared her to a cougar; her coloring, her actions. He had explained that he called her Wildcat because of that, not in reference to the smaller spotted cat, but as a small, wild she-panther.

Now Tanya had been forced to slay one of his beloved panthers. She knew deep in her soul she'd had no choice, and she prayed Panther would understand and not despise her for it.

She knelt beside it, stroking its tawny fur, so like the color of her own hair. The glowing eyes had almost mirrored the color of hers. Then she noticed what depressed her further. This was a she-cat, and from the looks of her she'd given birth sometime in the last few weeks, for her teat-milk was not yet fully dried up.

Tanya shook her head and sighed. Heaving herself to her feet, she carefully examined the smarting, bloody welts left by the cougar's claw. They were not deep, thank goodness.

Having determined the extent of her injuries, she retrieved her bow, arrows, and knife. Then she set off in search of the missing cubs. Surely she had come close, intruding on the cougar's territory, and this is what had upset the mother. Tanya searched diligently throughout the afternoon, with no success. Finally she admitted temporary defeat, knowing she would have to head for camp now if she hoped to reach it by dark. Tomorrow she would come again and try to find the babies.

Dumping the nuts, she managed to tuck the blanket under the mountain lion and tie it around. The animal weighed almost as much as she did and was approximately five feet long; a good eight feet if you counted the tail. Huffing and puffing all the way, she nevertheless managed to drag the cougar back to her camp.

Conscious of her need to provide nourishment for her body and her unborn babe, Tanya took time to eat as soon as she had cleaned her wounds. Then, by the light of the fire, she skinned the mountain cat. With the aid of a torch, she went a fair distance from her camp, dug a hole with her tomahawk and buried the cougar meat. Under no circumstances could she bring herself to eat it.

Back at camp, she worked late into the night scraping and cleaning the panther hide. Then she staked it next to the deerskin and crawled wearily off to bed.

Early the next morning she again worked both hides. Then she packed some dried meat, saddled Wheat, and rode back to the area in which she had encountered the cat. Try as she might, she could not locate the cubs.

Late in the afternoon she finally gave up hope. Returning once more to her base, she oiled and scrubbed and softened the hides once more. The deerskin was nearly done, soft and pliable, and she'd made a good start on the cougar skin. This, she had decided, she would leave the fur on and sew a hooded coat for Panther for winter. She hoped he would accept it, along with her apologies for having to kill the marvelous creature.

Just before sunset, Tanya went down to the river and speared a trout for supper. After cleaning it, she set it on a spit over a low, smoky fire and went back down to the stream. Aware of her warrior-spy, she hid herself behind a large boulder to undress. Wading into the cool, clear water, she bathed and washed her hair, then scrubbed her dress clean of the stains they had collected over the last couple of days. Carefully wrapped in her clean blanket, she went back to her fire and her dinner.

The fifth and the last full day she would be there, Tanya smoked the deerskin in the smaller shelter, then finished curing the cougar hide. She smoked the cathide to rid it of any lingering vermin, then treated it with grease and sand, washed it thoroughly, and staked it to dry.

When the deerskin was finished, she fashioned waterproof drawstring pouches from it and packed her dried meat away in them.

That evening she shot a rabbit and made a stew with some onions and nuts. Tomorrow she would start down the mountain again. Satisfied by both her meal and her contented thoughts, she fell asleep quickly.

In the middle of the night Tanya woke abruptly, her senses instantly alert and alarmed. She knew what had awakened her. It was a soft whinny from Wheat. Quickly, without benefit of light, she dressed. Her eyes were adjusted to the dark, and her movements were swift and sure as she located her bow.

"Hallo! Anybody there?" came the greeting in English.

Her sharp ears counted the hooves of three horses. Adjusting her quiver, she stepped out of the shelter. There was no sense hiding and being trapped like a bird in a cage.

Two men had entered her clearing, leading a pack mule. They looked to be traders or miners. Whichever, they had a rough, shifty appearance to them. Both sported shaggy hair and unkempt beards. Their clothing was so dirty Tanya was sure one good washing would leave them in shreds. Both had their rifles in hand and ready, though not aimed as yet.

Had they not spotted her immediately, Tanya might have tried to make a run for it and get away on Wheat, but they were looking directly at her as she stepped into the open.

"Ho! What we got here?" the one with the red hair and beard said.

"What do you want?" Tanya asked in English.

"Why, it's a white squaw, Zeke! How d'ya like that?" Red commented lazily. "Where's yer man, honey?"

"He and my brother went hunting this morning," Tanya lied. "At first I thought that's who you were. I expect them any time." She had been going to say he was in the lodge, but they would have soon found out that she was alone, so she thought it best to let them believe someone was due soon.

"You here all alone, darlin'?" Red persisted.

"Not for long," Tanya said. "I wouldn't get off that horse if I were you," she warned, bringing up her bow as Red made to dismount.

"Now, that ain't a friendly way t' be," Red complained. "Me an' Zeke here don't mean ya no harm. Do we Zeke?"

"Shucks, no!" It was the first Zeke had spoken. "Why, if we was up t' no good, we'd a shot ya by now. There's two o' us." He nodded his greasy blond head at his partner.

"Just be on your way, then," Tanya suggested.

"We been travelin' a long spell," Red said. "We ain't ate in quite a while. Wouldn't mind havin' a bite o' somthin' if ya could spare it." He eyed her still-simmering stew in plain sight over the fire.

"Take some and go," Tanya offered, "but don't get off your horses to do it."

"Well, I was gonna ask if we could warm up a bit by yer fire. It's mighty chilly ridin' t'night, an' our horses could use a rest. You ain't afraid o' us, now are ya?"

"No, but I'm not a fool, either," she answered.

"Sure wish you'd quit pointin' that thing, gal," Zeke commented, eyeing her bow and arrow. "Makes me nervous like."

"Tell ya what," Red interrupted. "I'll jest git a bit o'

that stew while ole Zeke here waters the horses at the stream. That O.K. with you?"

Tanya nodded reluctantly. Maybe they would leave peaceably after that. She didn't like the idea of being confronted with two men with rifles and pistols. The odds were not in her favor.

"All right, but be quick about it, and keep your hands in plain sight."

Red dismounted. As he did so, he gave his horse a sharp slap on the flank, and the animal charged straight for Tanya, blocking her view of the two men. By the time the horse had passed, the men were upon her. Tanya reached for her knife and realized she'd left it in the shelter, grabbing only her bow as she'd dressed.

One man Tanya could have handled, but two burly beasts were too much. They quickly had her subdued, one holding her arms pinned behind her back. The other, Zeke, stood before her, his eyes gleaming with lust.

"Looks like we got us a feisty little white squaw, Red. She sure as hell ain't no white man's woman dressed like that!"

Red agreed. "I hear tell them Injuns teach their squaws all kind o' tricks, an' you an' me is gonna find out. Laws! It's been so long since I had me a woman I'm about t' burst my britches right now!"

Zeke reached out to fondle Tanya's breast, and she let out a loud shriek of protest. "Lord, where is that fool warrior who's supposed to be guarding me?" she wondered. "What good is he if I can't depend on him? There's been enough commotion here to wake the dead!" Obviously he had been sent to observe, not interfere, or he would have helped her when the cougar attacked. Tanya was on her own.

She changed her tactics as Red forced her to the ground. "Please don't do this," she pleaded, turning huge, wounded eyes on him. "You don't know what it's been like!"

Red frowned. "Then why didn't ya run for it when yer Injun left ya alone?" he asked.

"Where could I go?" she countered, crocodile tears creeping down her cheeks. "I don't know my way out of these hills. Besides, my family's all been killed, and I don't know anyone even if I could find a town. Who would help me?" She could see his face softening.

"Me an' Zeke could take ya along with us if ya was t' treat us right. You do right by us, an' we'll see ya git t' town an' git settled. Won't we, Zeke?"

Zeke grinned lewdly as Tanya's gaze switched to him. "Sure thing, honey gal. Why, me an' Red are two o' the nicest guys ya'd ever want t' meet."

"Yeah," Red agreed. "Now, let's seal the bargain here an' now."

Tanya stiffened as his hand went to his belt buckle, then she forced herself to relax. "Gentlemen," she said with a sigh, "I was gently raised before I was so brutally kidnapped. Would it be too much to ask for a bit of privacy?"

Red's face instantly became suspicious. "What kind o' tricks ya up to, woman? I ain't ready t' let ya out o' my sight."

"No tricks. I'll stick by the bargain, but I'd rather it be one at a time, with no one looking on, if you don't mind. I may not be as innocent as I once was, but one's modesty does not simply disappear."

Red and Zeke grinned sheepishly at one another, and Red said, "Yeah, well, I guess I see yer point. Some things ain't meant t' be shared, an' there ain't no point in feelin' rushed."

Tanya nodded. "Precisely."

Red helped her to her feet and headed her in the direction of the shelter. "You take care o' the horses, Zeke, an' git some grub goin'. The way I'm feelin', this ain't gonna take long."

Tanya entered the lodge ahead of him. She bent, swiftly locating her knife, her hand closing over the hilt. She'd stopped so suddenly that Red stumbled into her and fell headlong onto the floor of the hut. Instantly her knife drove through his back. He was dead before he could call out for help.

Zeke was unsaddling the horses when she crept up on him. He had both hands on the saddle and was just lifting it from the horse's back when he felt the sharp edge of her knife kiss his throat. Immediately he froze.

"This is for my unborn child, who you and your partner would have killed if you had raped me," she hissed near his ear just before her blade sliced cleanly through his throat. The saddle fell from his lifeless hands and blood gurgled through his severed windpipe as he sank slowly to the ground at her feet.

Sleep being impossible, Tanya strung the two dead men up on the same limb she'd bled the deer from. Then she sat quietly outside her shelter, watching for the dawn. When the sun rose at last, she went to the river to bathe the scent and the touch of the men from her body.

One final time, she softened and stretched the cat skin. At last she lay down on the lush, sun-sweet grass and slept.

At midday, she packed her things and went through the two men's belongings. There wasn't much. Each had possessed a rifle, a handgun, a knife, and a horse and saddle. They had only a few dollars between them. Their saddle bags held one change of clothes each, a bit of tobacco and jerky, and a few rounds of ammunition. The pack mule carried a bit more ammunition, plus some salt, flour and coffee, a battered coffeepot, an old skillet, a kettle, and a few utensils. Tanya also found an axe, a shovel, a pick, two extra blankets, two heavy winter coats, and a small bundle of beaver pelts, either gotten in trade or stolen.

Tanya saddled the horses. She cut the bodies down, draped them over the backs of the horses, and tied them there. She would take the bodies back to the Cheyenne village with her, along with their horses and goods.

Tanya rode all that day and early evening. The next morning she reached the spot where she was to meet the warrior. For a couple of hours she waited, and almost began to think he was not coming, when he finally appeared. It was Dancing Horse, and he made no comment about the bodies or the extra horses.

Together they traveled all that day and most of the next to reach the old winter camp where Tanya had first come to know the Cheyenne life. In the early evening, they rode into the village.

The war party had returned, and Panther was there with Black Kettle to greet her. Black Kettle spoke to Dancing Horse first. "Has she fulfilled the requirements of her test?"

"Yes, my chief." Dancing Horse added seriously, "There were times I thought she would fail, and others when I felt she might need my help for her safety's sake, but she did not. She managed on her own through trials we could not have foretold."

Panther could contain himself no longer. "What is all this?" He gestured to the dead men and their horses.

Tanya answered him simply. "These men rode into

my camp on the fifth night. They meant to harm me and our child. I killed them."

The old chief nodded, his shrewd gaze travelling over her. "Did they harm you? Is that how your dress was torn?"

"I killed them before they could harm me in any way. The dress is another matter." To Panther she said, "Panther, I must ask for forgiveness. I have slain one of your sacred mountain lions. I must have gone too close to her den, and she attacked me. I had no choice but to kill her or be killed. I searched for her cubs, but failed to find them." Her eyes searched his dark face. "Does this harden your heart toward me? Do you now wish to withdraw your offer of marriage?"

Panther's answer was softly spoken, but clear. "It saddens my heart to hear of this, Little Wildcat, but it could not be helped. To have it otherwise would have meant your death, and that of our child. I still desire you for my bride as soon as Chief Black Kettle can arrange it."

Tanya smiled at last, and Black Kettle stated authoritatively, "Tomorrow we shall have a feast, and Little Wildcat will become my daughter. Then we will discuss the dowry and the bride price. As soon as the terms are met, we will arrange the marriage."

To Tanya he said, "Go now, and eat and rest. My grandchild must not come to harm. Your horse and baggage will be taken care of."

As Tanya turned to go, he added, "You will stay in the lodge of Walks-Like-A-Duck for tonight. She will bring what you need from Panther's tipi." At her dismayed look, he stated firmly, "I have spoken."

Tanya gave Panther a grieved, longing-filled look, but knew better than to argue.

* * *

Tanya slept through until morning. Walks-Like-A-Duck had brought her clothes from Panther's lodge, and Tanya slipped off to the stream to bathe and don fresh garments. She spent part of the day with the other women, helping to harvest ripe vegetables and gather fruits for winter. It felt good to be back. The afternoon hours she used to measure and cut the cougar hide for Panther. Tanya managed to sew the two front sections to the back before it was time to stop and prepare for the evening's activities. By careful measuring, and because the cat had been so long, she had enough material to fashion a hip-length hooded coat for Panther, using the tail for the belt. There was just enough hide left over to make a purse for herself, one that would hang from her waist. The claws she would string into matching necklaces for herself and Panther. One of the old men of the tribe who specialized in such things would preserve the head for Panther to display on his lodge pole.

Tanya dressed in the decorative doeskin dress she had made for this occasion, and took extra pains with her hair. Just as she was about to join the others, Walks-Like-A-Duck approached her, carrying two familiar scalps; one red and one mousy blonde. This time Tanya took them from her without hesitation, hooking them at her waist. Then she walked proudly through the camp to her place beside Black Kettle.

The atmosphere was festive and charged with excitement. It wasn't every day a chief adopted a daughter, and a white woman at that. Black Kettle was attired in his most ornate garments this evening; a full headdress adorning his head.

When everyone had gathered, he stood, regal and proud, and gained their attention. His deep, commanding voice rang out. "This night we accept a new member into our tribe. Tonight I gain a daughter to gladden my heart."

He gestured to Tanya, seated next to him. "Little Wildcat has come to us only recently, but she has proven herself to be brave of heart and courageous of spirit. No longer will we look upon her as a white-eyes, for she has the soul of a Cheyenne. She has earned the right to be called Cheyenne and claim the title of daughter of a chief. From this day forward, she is due the honor and respect of her position."

He motioned for her to stand and for his wife, Woman-To-Be-Hereafter, to come forward. Black Kettle took an ornate necklace with a pendant in the shape of a large silver disc, and placed it about Tanya's neck. In an unusual display of affection, he placed his cheek, next to hers. "Welcome, daughter."

To his wife he said, "Woman, I present your daughter."

The elderly, but still regal, woman approached Tanya. With great ceremony she placed upon Tanya's upper arms two decorative silver armbands to match the necklace. Then she, too, placed her cheek against Tanya's. With tears glistening in her eyes, she said, "My heart overflows with joy this day. Finally I have a child."

Tanya kissed the weathered cheek. "I am honored to be the daughter of two such wonderful parents."

This concluded the ceremony, but the festivities had just begun. The drums beat out the news to the tribal world that Black Kettle had a daughter. A great feast had been prepared to honor the occasion, and the games, contests, dancing and revelry went long into the night.

Tanya was overjoyed at having achieved her goal.

Next she would become Panther's wife and the mother of his child, but in the interim she would be lodging with her new parents. She hoped the preparations for her marriage would be accomplished quickly, for to see Panther and be near him, and not be able to touch him, was agony.

Chapter 8

THE NEXT couple of days Tanya was as nervous as a long-tailed cat in a room full of rocking chairs. First thing the following morning, Panther met with Black Kettle to discuss Tanya's bride price. Black Kettle accepted Panther's offer of thirty ponies. Now preparations were underway for the marriage ceremony.

Woman-To-Be-Hereafter was putting the finishing touches on an elaborately fringed, feather-soft cream-colored doeskin dress for Tanya. It was painstakingly decorated with intricate beadwork. Woman-To-Be-Hereafter had been working on it for weeks.

"It is better to be prepared, just in case," she told Tanya. "What if I had not started it? My daughter would not have a proper dress for her wedding."

"What if I had failed the tests?" Tanya asked.

Woman-To-Be-Hereafter shrugged. "You did not."

Black Kettle presented her with silver discs as decorations for her hair. Panther sent her a beautiful pair of copper earrings, and Woman-To-Be-Hereafter pierced Tanya's ears so she could wear them. Shy Deer gave her an intricately decorated headband she had made herself, and Walks-Like-A-Duck made her a new pair of beaded moccasins. Tanya sewed her panther-fur purse herself.

Panther, too, was to have a new outfit for his

wedding. Shy Deer and Walks-Like-A-Duck were sewing it for him. His shirt and leggings were to be heavily fringed, the shirt and moccasins decoratively beaded. His breechcloth would be elaborately painted. With it he would wear his finest headband and feathers, with silver discs dangling from his braids. He would wear a favorite necklace, armbands, and wristbands to complete the outfit.

Tanya finished the cougar-claw necklace, and sent it to him with the request that he wear it to their wedding, as she would hers. She also finished the cougar-fur coat, for she wished to give it to him as a wedding gift.

Tanya had given the utensils and foodstuff she had taken from her white attackers to Woman-To-Be-Hereafter. The tools, saddles, saddlebags and knives she gave to Black Kettle. She kept the mule, horses, beaver pelts, guns and ammunition for herself. Black Kettle and Woman-To-Be-Hereafter added household items to it; Tanya would be going to Panther a rich bride.

When Black Kettle asked Tanya what else she might want as a wedding gift from him and her mother, she asked that he try to buy Melissa from Ugly Otter. "He mistreats her so that I fear for her life," she told him.

Black Kettle frowned. "You are Cheyenne now. The white slaves are no longer your sisters. It is not right that you should sympathize with them."

"I would feel sorry for anyone under his hands," Tanya answered. "He is a cruel man. His own wife and children feel his lash and answer to his anger. Melissa is but a sweet, fragile child. Now she may be with child herself."

"If she carries Ugly Otter's child, he may not be willing to sell her," Black Kettle reasoned.

"It is not certain. Either way, is it necessary to tell him?" Tanya suggested. "I fear what his wife will do if she finds this out, and I don't see how Melissa or her child can survive many more beatings."

"What of the other white captives?" Black Kettle asked. "Have you plans for them also?"

"Do not misunderstand, Father," Tanya explained. "They did not ask to be brought here, but I can do nothing for them. Melissa I ask for because I truly fear for her life. If she belonged to another warrior who did not treat her so badly, I would not ask, but Ugly Otter is an animal; a brutal beast."

"This is true, but what will you do with the girl?"

"I will take her for a servant. She can help me in our lodge."

"She will not be much help to you when her stomach gets large and she is awkward and clumsy."

Tanya laughed. "Perhaps not, but four hands are always better than two, and it will not be for long."

Black Kettle gave her a thoughtful look. "How will you feel, daughter, when village gossip has this girl carrying Panther's child? For that is what they will think."

"I will know the truth, and so will Panther. That is all that matters."

Black Kettle nodded. "I am convinced that you do not sympathize with her just because she is white. Ugly Otter is criticized by many for the way he treats even his sons and horses. I will see what I can do."

"Thank you, Father. I would not ask it of you, but I know Ugly Otter would not sell her to Panther or to me. You are his chief, and if he does not know you intend to give her to me, he might let you have her."

"Knowing Ugly Otter, he will want someone to

replace her. Buffalo Grass just gifted me with a young Ute girl he captured. Perhaps he will take her in trade."

"I do not envy the Ute, but perhaps she can withstand Ugly Otter's brutality better than Melissa. Ugly Otter will kill Melissa soon if she stays with him."

It took three days for the wedding preparations to be completed. During that time, Tanya kept busy in the fields and preparing foodstuffs for winter.

On the day of her wedding, the women of the tribe took charge of Tanya. They took her to the river and scrubbed her skin and hair until they tingled, joking and giggling all the while. They dried and brushed her hair with a porcupine quill brush until it crackled and shone like burnished gold. With a pumice stone, they softened her roughened palms, feet, knees and elbows. Then they plucked the hair from her body and massaged her skin all over with scented oil. A few drops of the same wildflower-scented oil in her hair gave it a silky sheen, as well as making it delightfully fragrant. For the wedding, her hair would be left long and free, except for one thin braid falling in with the rest of her hair on each side. From these the silver discs would be hung.

Panther's hair would be left unbraided also, except for the braids from which his feathers and discs would hang. The warriors had taken him hunting, keeping him away from the village until it was time to prepare for the ceremony.

Finally the moment arrived. Panther was waiting with Black Kettle as the women led Tanya to him. He was magnificent in his ornate wedding attire, tall, proud and bold. His blue-black hair hung down over his shoulders and like a river of black satin; his midnight eyes gleamed with admiration as he watched her approach.

Tanya looked and felt beautiful. Her ankle-length dress had been tanned to the color of creamery butter, and elaborately decorated with beads and dyed porcupine quills and long, heavy fringe that swayed as she walked. Her unbound hair fell past her waist, shimmering like molten gold in the firelight; her eyes were like two shining stars in her radiant face.

Through a daze of impressions, Tanya noted that Panther had worn the cat's-claw necklace, as had she. Now she stood facing him before the ancient tribal shaman.

The old man inquired whether the bride price had been met. Black Kettle, in his role as the bride's father, stated the bride price of thirty horses for all to hear, and acknowledged the payment.

The shaman then determined that the dowry had been satisfactory. Winter Bear, acting as Panther's spokesman, agreed, and Tanya's dowry was listed aloud. All this time, Tanya had eyes only for Panther.

Tanya found herself and Panther kneeling before the shaman as he chanted a prayer for their happiness, fruitfulness, and long life, shaking his rattle and waving smoking embers in a bowl over their heads.

Once more they were standing, and the shaman reiterated all the things Tanya was promising in marriage to Panther.

"You shall follow wherever he goes, to make your home always with him; to attend to his meals, his comfort, his children; to honor him; to be ever faithful and obey without question his commands."

Tanya agreed.

In his turn, Panther affirmed his responsibilities

toward her. He was to provide for and protect her and their children, and accord her the honor of her title as his wife and daughter of a chief.

Panther's eyes glowed as he placed upon Tanya's wrists two gleaming copper wristbands, intricately engraved to match his own, symbolic of his ownership over her as her husband; delicate shackles that bound her to him for a lifetime.

The ceremony over, the time came for the newly-married couple to exchange gifts publicly. At a gesture from Panther, Winter Bear stepped forward with a blanket-covered basket. Holding it before Tanya, he watched as Panther lifted the cover.

Tanya was dumbfounded. There before her were two cougar cubs. Her hands reached out automatically to stroke the still-downy fur. Eyes glittering with tears of delight, her voice came out in a choked whisper, "Oh, Panther, they are adorable! Where? When? How?" Her tongue could not keep up with the questions in her mind.

He smiled at her confusion. "These are the cubs you searched for so diligently. Dancing Horse found and kept them, and when I would have met you that last day, he handed the kittens over to me and told me of all that had happened. It occurred to me that they would make a perfect wedding gift, so I brought them straight to camp, hid them, and waited for you here instead."

"They are a most unique and wonderful gift, Panther. Thank you. Now I have a gift for you."

Walks-Like-A-Duck handed it over to Tanya, and she placed the cougar-fur coat in Panther's hands. Slowly he unfolded it and held it up before him. "It is the most magnificent coat I have ever possessed. I will wear it proudly, Wildcat."

Tanya nodded, suddenly shy before his appreciation. "Grass Man is preserving the panther head for your lodge pole."

"I am honored," he said soberly.

"It is I who am honored, Panther, to be chosen as your wife."

The wedding celebration and attending feast lasted far into the night. At one point, Black Kettle spoke with them privately. "I have obtained the girl Melissa from Ugly Otter. Starting tomorrow she will serve you in your lodge." He had discussed the matter previously with Panther and made certain of his approval.

"Did you have to trade your Ute captive?" Tanya inquired.

"Yes. Ugly Otter would only release her if he could have a replacement."

Panther nodded and said, "I will try to bring you another on one of our raids, Uncle. It is only fair, since you had to give her up."

Finally a group of the women came for Tanya. They escorted her to Panther's tipi, helped her to undress, and left. It was ridiculous after all that had gone before, but Tanya waited for Panther as nervously as a young virgin on her wedding night.

Suddenly he was there before her, resplendent in his finery, gazing down on her nude, waiting form. Without a word, he removed his clothes, and if possible, was even more awesome as he stood naked over her. Tanya's golden gaze roamed over his bronze, muscled form, and she shivered with anticipation.

Panther lowered himself to her side, taking great handsful of her tawny hair and letting it slide like a shimmering river through his long fingers. "You are so beautiful," he told her softly.

"So are you," was her reverent reply as her hands

came up to stroke his shoulders. "You are everything I've ever dreamed of in a man, wanted in a husband. I am so fortunate to have found you! It is such a relief to have all the obstacles behind us, and to be able to call you 'husband' at last; to know that you are mine and I am yours."

"No one will ever part us, Wildcat. Never could I live with that. If anything ever separates us this side of the grave, I will move heaven and earth to regain you. You are part of my heart and my soul. You belong only and always to me."

"That is all I ask in this life, Panther; to belong to you and be with you. You are my life and my joy, and without you my life would be without meaning."

He enfolded her in the strong, protective circle of his arms, holding her tenderly as he began to make slow, delicious love to her. His lips found hers in a long, drugging kiss, as his hands mesmerized her body to his will. Their tongues danced and mated, and their lips clung together, as if drawing lifegiving nectar.

Her head spinning and her body breathless, Tanya gave herself wholly to his ministering hands and mouth. Capable of no thought but Panther, of pleasing and being pleased, she gave of herself completely.

His magic hands played her body as a master musician plays a lute. Her body was like dry tinder, igniting immediately to his welcome flame. Never had she felt so beautiful, so loved, so desirable, and Panther fed these feelings with words as well as caresses. All through their lovemaking, he whispered words of love and desire.

Her hands could not keep from reaching for him, stroking and caressing her tender, savage lover, pleasing him with her touch as he was doing to her.

With lips and teeth and tongue she traced his beloved form, now well-known, but ever exciting to her. Panther's mouth mapped a trail of fire across her body; her passion-swollen breasts, her quivering stomach, her yearning womanhood.

Finally neither could stand the excruciating tension a moment longer. He came into her with a long, smooth stroke, into her welcoming cave of moist, warm velvet, and her muscles clenched about him to hold him tightly. His tempo gradually increased, and she matched his pace, ever climbing toward that high mountain summit. At last, and too soon, they crested it to soar together in the bright sunlight of their love and passion, and floated gently down to a calmer valley.

All through the night he loved her, and she gloried in their mutual need; the need to hold and touch and love; to know that this joy was real and lasting, and properly claimed forevermore. That night their marriage was sealed, sacred, and consummated in glorious splendor; and they acknowledged it reverently, passionately, and thoroughly until both were replete and utterly exhausted.

Late the next morning, Melissa appeared hesitantly before Panther and Tanya. Her delicate cheekbones were still discolored and swollen, a split on her lip still healing, her arms marked with bruises and scratches. Her dirty, soiled clothing hung in tatters on her thin, childlike form, and the color of her once-bright hair was indistinguishable beneath the filth.

Panther took one look and ordered her from his tipi. Eyes wide with fear and brimming with tears, Melissa backed out and stood uncertainly, waiting.

Panther's anger and disgust showed only in his distended nostrils, as he turned to Tanya. "Take her to the river and see that she is thoroughly scrubbed, then get her something decent to wear. The camp dogs are cleaner than she is!"

Melissa's jaw quivered as she watched Panther stride off. Tanya took her arm and started for the river. "He is not angry with you, Missy," she assured the frightened girl.

As she helped Melissa to scrub away months of accumulated grime, she outlined the duties that would be expected of her. Most of them Melissa had been performing for Ugly Otter's wife already.

"Also, it is necessary that you speak to me in Cheyenne, not English, and call me 'Little Wildcat.' I am Cheyenne now, the chief's daughter and Panther's wife, and it is unseemly for me to speak English."

"I don't know the language very well, Little Wildcat," Melissa stumbled in Cheyenne.

"With practice you will learn. Life will be easier for you with us, Melissa. You will be decently fed and clothed, but I must warn you, you must follow orders and accord both Panther and me the respect due our positions in the tribe. It would be an embarrassment to me, and would anger Panther greatly if you did not."

Melissa nodded, and then stammered, "Will Panther expect . . . I mean . . . do I have to . . ."

"Have to what?" Tanya asked.

"You know . . ." Melissa blushed.

Tanya was incredulous. "Are you asking if you are to *sleep* with Panther?"

Melissa gave her a pained look and nodded.

Tanya hadn't even entertained the idea, but it was a normal happening in the tribe. Cheyenne wives were expected to look the other way and say nothing when their husbands bedded captives or decided to take a second or third wife. It was the way of things. Now Tanya had to face the fact that it was a very real possibility, as much as she knew Panther loved her and as much as she disliked the idea of Panther mating with another woman. Still, she doubted Panther would dally so soon after their wedding, especially since Melissa was possibly pregnant and so weak and battered.

Tanya answered the only way she could. "Panther is not an animal like Ugly Otter. I do not know his plans, but if he beds you, it will not be with violence and pain."

Now it was Melissa's turn to be astounded. "Doesn't it bother you, Tanya? What has happened to you?"

"I am Cheyenne. Whether it bothers me or not is not the issue. Panther is my husband. I bow to his wishes and look to his comforts." Then she smiled. "I really think you are worried about something that may not come to pass. Let's concentrate on making you well and comfortable. Your help will be welcome to me, especially as I become more ungainly. We can make life easier for each other."

A timid smile trembled over Melissa's lips, the first smile Tanya had seen from her since that fateful day they were captured. "I haven't thanked you, Tanya. No matter what comes, nothing can be as bad as belonging to Ugly Otter and his wife!"

Melissa became a part of their lives. Her bruises began to heal, her skin and hair were clean and more healthy, and the swelling in her face was disappearing. True to her word, Tanya had made sure she had nourishing food, clean and mended clothes, and shelter. On Melissa's part, she worked endlessly to relieve Tanya of her work load, but she was ever-cautious around Panther; always wary.

"It distresses me to see her cringe each time I enter my own lodge," Panther complained. "She is a bundle of nerves."

"These things take time," Tanya counseled. "Once she sees you are not going to ravish her or beat her senseless, she will calm down."

"You may assure her I will not drag her off to my bed," Panther said with a grin at Tanya. "She is much too skinny, and I am much too busy trying to keep my new bride satisfied."

"Melissa was once very pretty. With proper food and care, she will be again. Perhaps you may yet find her appealing," Tanya hinted.

"Perhaps," he mused without enthusiasm, "but you forget I saw her that first day. For many minutes we gazed upon all of you bathing in the river, and of all, I chose you for my own. If I had wanted Melissa, I would have chosen her then."

"I'm sorry to be so silly," Tanya explained. "I just don't like the thought of you bedding anyone else."

"As long as you give me no reason to, you have nothing to worry over."

"What about when I am heavy and awkward with your child? Will I not look ugly and misshapen to you?"

"My poor Little Wildcat, when you are heavy with my child, you will still be beautiful, and very special to me because you nurture our child inside you. Do you think me so weak that I cannot control the urges of my own body for a few weeks?"

"Forgive me, Panther. I do not mean to discredit you. I am being a foolish female."

"Your worries are natural and normal to your state, I suppose." He moved to draw her closer to him. "Just remember this. You are the woman of my heart, the light of my life."

Matters came to a head a few days later. Panther was preparing for a hunt, and asked Melissa to fetch his quiver from inside the tipi. In her hurry from the lodge, Melissa tripped. The quiver fell to the ground, scattering arrows in every direction. Expecting a violent reaction, Melissa immediately began to quake. She threw herself on the ground at Panther's feet, clutching her arms over her head in a protective gesture and began to wail.

"I'm sorry! I didn't mean it! It won't happen again! Please don't beat me! Please don't beat me! Please! Please don't!"

Tanya and Panther exchanged dismayed looks over her pathetic figure. As gently as he would a child, Panther drew her to her feet. Her eyes were wild with fear.

"Melissa! Melissa!" It took him several seconds to gain her attention. "It was an accident. No one blames you. No one is going to beat you."

Melissa's eyes flew from Panther's face to Tanya's for confirmation of his words.

"If it were deliberate, or done in spite, I would, indeed, beat you. Have no doubt of it. But as long as you try to please me; as long as you are respectful and obey my commands and those of your mistress quickly and willingly, you will not be ill-treated. You will not be punished for something you could not prevent."

Though still wary, Melissa calmed visibly.

Panther's voice was quiet and gentle. "Go now and collect my arrows, and try not to damage any of the feathers."

Melissa gathered all her courage to speak to him. "Are you really not angry?"

Panther smiled ruefully. "I am not overly pleased that my arrows took a beating, but I am not angry, Melissa." At her wondering look, he added, "With both you and Wildcat becoming clumsier by the day, I can see my patience will be tried to the limit in the coming months. Putting up with one pregnant female is trying enough, but two?"

His smile widened as he included both women in his teasing gaze. "War and raids will seem like child's play in comparison."

Melissa's smile lit up her face, rewarding Tanya and Panther for their tolerance. "Your husband is a just man," she told Tanya as she retrieved the scattered arrows. "You are a lucky woman."

"So I am," Tanya readily agreed.

Another adjustment to be made by the women was the idea of having a listening audience while Tanya and Panther made love. Tanya realized this was not unusual in tipis throughout the camp, and once she finally accepted it and overcame her embarrassment, she was able to relax and forget Melissa's presence.

"It's all in how you are raised and what you get used to, I guess," she thought.

Melissa, too, was embarrassed at first. Her natural instinct, after her brutal experiences with Ugly Otter, was to cringe in sympathy for her friend, until she at last realized that the moans and sighs reaching her ears were those of passion, not pain. She struggled to understand how anyone could find pleasure in the act. She, herself, would have been happy if no man ever touched her again, but if Tanya enjoyed it that was her business and Panther's.

The cougar cubs added another element of excitement to their lives. Never still a minute, the gamboling kittens were constantly into mischief. They playfully attacked anything that moved, especially bare feet, and adored anything with feathers or fringe. Tanya and Melissa were very careful to keep all clothing hung out of their reach, but not before the young cats had already demolished a fringed skirt of Tanya's and 'killed' one of Panther's feathered headbands.

Their favorite treat was honey, and this pouch had to be carefully guarded from the little darlings, who had a definite sweet tooth. They also showed a preference for Panther's tobacco and developed a taste for coffee. More than once Tanya had reached for her cup to find one of them had emptied it ahead of her. The women had to be very careful not to leave the stewpot unattended or an animal half-skinned.

After the second night in a row of being awakened by Tanya's hysterical giggling as one or the other of the cubs licked her ticklish bare feet, Panther decided they must be properly trained. Thereafter, Tanya and Panther would go out together, each with a cub on a leash, and Panther taught Tanya how to gently but firmly make them obey. In due time, once they had learned how to conduct themselves properly around the camp, they would be free to roam at will. They were smart little devils, and Panther ventured a guess that before too long they would learn what was acceptable and what was not.

Tanya, on a whimsical note, decided to name them Kit and Kat, explaining to Panther the English meaning of 'kitty cat.' The male, Kat, took an unmistakable shine to Panther, while Kit, the smaller she-kitten, obviously preferred Tanya. Both cubs learned to obey either their master or mistress, but both had a decided preference for one.

Tanya loved them, and though Panther would not come out and admit it, so did he. Melissa liked them, laughing over their antics, but she wasn't honestly crazy over them. Undoubtedly, they were adorable, soft and cuddly, with brown splotches in their tawny fur and black-ringed tails. Panther had said they would lose the spots and rings at about six months, but Tanya thought they were cute as they were. Cute or not, they were a trial at times, and Tanya began to doubt they would ever outgrow the kitten stage.

All in all, Tanya's life had changed drastically, and she was more contented than she'd ever dreamed she could be. Life with Panther was a constant joy, and she was forever learning from him. Here in the mountains, far from home and friends, she had found a new life. She had a new mother and father, the respect of the tribe, good friends, Melissa to help her, a baby on the way, and Panther—above all, Panther.

Chapter 9

WINTER CAME with a vengeance that year, but not before the Cheyenne warriors had launched several successful raids against the Utes, and a couple against white settlements. Tanya, in the company of the other wives, anxiously awaited her husband's safe return from each of these ventures. As October passed into November, and then December, her anxieties grew in direct proportion to her added girth.

Each time Panther set out, Tanya, like a dutiful wife, brought him his horse. She packed food and blankets, and stood by as he mounted his stallion. Then she quietly handed him his weapons and watched stoically as he rode from sight.

Before each parting, in the privacy of their tipi, Panther bid her farewell, kissed her and held her close to his heart. In public, they parted proudly and serenely, and after each departure Tanya would seclude herself in their lodge and weep sad tears and pray for his safety.

When the braves returned, there was always great rejoicing, and throughout the raids only one warrior was killed and four others slightly wounded. It was a season of triumph and honor for the Cheyenne.

Returning from one of their raids in December, Panther inadvertently sparked Tanya's temper. They had been gone a week longer than expected, and Tanya's nerves were frayed from the wait and the worry. As soon as the scouts had announced spotting the returning war party, Tanya rushed out to gather with the others to greet them.

Panther, on his great black stallion, and Winter Bear, were in the lead. In her joy at seeing her husband returning unharmed, Tanya did not at once notice anything different, but as he drew closer, the welcoming smile froze on her face. Her golden eyes flamed as she saw two pale, slender arms encircling Panther's waist.

When they reached the outskirts of the village, Panther shoved his captive from his horse and led her at the end of a thong to the center of the encampment, as did the others who had brought captives. All along their path, Cheyenne had gathered to taunt the captives, in the same manner as they had when Tanya had first arrived.

Tanya stood rooted in her place just outside Black Kettle's lodge. Her mind refused to believe what she was seeing, and her heart thudded heavily in her chest. As they neared, her eyes were drawn to the white girl Panther was leading. Even as tired and dirty as she was, her long brown hair in tangles about her shoulders, Tanya recognized her beauty. The girl raised her head and Tanya beheld the doleful hazel eyes and the clear ivory skin. She was of average height, but with a slim, well-rounded figure that immediately made Tanya feel fat and ungainly.

Only pride kept Tanya from fleeing as Panther rode directly to her and tossed the end of the leash into her hands. Tanya's nostrils flared in anger, and she knew she dared not look at Panther just yet, though she was sure her emotions did not register on her face. Without a word, she led the girl to where the women were herding the other captives, Ute and white alike. Then she busied herself caring for Panther's horse, and while he and the others reported to Black Kettle, she set about preparing his meal.

By this time a bleak numbness had settled like a huge rock in her chest. Unshed tears burned behind her eyes as she dressed in a soft doeskin skirt and top, adding her necklaces and armbands in preparation for the celebration to come. Her fingers fumbled endlessly as she rebraided her tawny hair, and her hands shook as she held them across her expanding stomach, trying to stop the trembling within.

It was the closest Tanya ever came to resenting her unborn child. Even as she sought to soothe the babe, she wondered if her burgeoning figure was becoming distasteful to Panther. Was this why he had come back with another woman?

Melissa gazed at Tanya with large, questioning eyes, wanting to comfort her friend. Tanya caught Melissa's sad look, and cringed at the sympathy she saw there. It was this that saved her from self-pity and held her pride intact. Resolutely, Tanya squared her shoulders, schooled her features into placid lines, and prepared Panther's paints and clothing.

Tanya's back was turned, but she felt his presence as soon as he entered the tipi. She felt his eyes upon her as she ladled his dinner into his bowl and placed it near the fire. Gritting her teeth, she sat back and stared into the flames, refusing to look at him.

For long minutes Panther stood there. Finally he spoke, softly, but with a ring of underlying steel to his voice. "You have not greeted me, Wildcat."

With effort, she answered cooly, "Welcome, husband. Your meal is ready if you wish to eat." Still she did not face him. Instead, she picked up a blanket she was sewing for the baby and started to work on it.

Panther sat and took up his bowl. "Have you tended to Shadow?"

"Your horse has been cared for, Panther. Your clothing and paints are laid out for you." Tanya stared blindly at the material in her hands. As the silence lengthened, she asked, "Is there something else you wish me to do for you?"

"Yes," came the immediate, terse reply. "I wish you to look at me when I speak to you."

It was an order, one which she knew she must obey, but she could not mask the anger and hurt as her eyes met his.

Panther held her gaze with his own, his eyes cold and forbidding. "Why do your eyes shoot flaming arrows at me, Wildcat? Your manner is cold, but your eyes are hot with anger. Explain yourself to me."

Her chin went up in defiance. "First tell me this, Panther. Do my enlarging breasts and stomach repel you? Am I so ugly and fat that you no longer feel desire for me? Is this why you come dragging another woman home?" Her voice dripped venom.

Panther's face underwent a series of changes, so unprepared was he for her reply. First it registered confusion, then surprise, and finally anger.

"Do you dare to question me, wife?" His tone sent shivers up Tanya's spine, but she refused to back down. She watched as he set his dinner aside. For long moments they stared at one another.

When next he spoke, his voice was taunting. "She is very beautiful, don't you agree?"

Tanya could no longer hold his gaze. Head bowed, she whispered, "Yes."

"I thought I told you to look at me," he grated through his teeth.

Tanya's head snapped up, but now her eyes were bright with tears.

"Am I the head of this lodge? Do I make the rules and you obey them; without question, or argument, or recrimination?" he went on ruthlessly.

Tanya swallowed, but could not speak beyond the lump in her throat. She merely nodded.

"And if I bring this woman into our lodge, you will accept her, because I wish it." It was more a statement than question, but Tanya responded with a reluctant nod, and the tears she longed to recall rolled down her cheeks.

Panther sighed heavily, and his long, lean fingers reached out to brush the tears from her cheeks. "Oh, Wildcat! What pain you bring upon yourself needlessly. If you had not stung me with your anger, I would not have responded in kind. Where is your faith in our love? Do you hold me in such low esteem that you think I would consider you unlovely when you carry our child within you? I have told you differently. I have told you I need no other woman but you."

He gathered Tanya's shaking body into his warm embrace. "The captive is for Black Kettle, to replace the one he had to trade for Melissa."

All the pent up emotions she'd held at bay broke loose, and Tanya clung to him and sobbed. When at last she'd hiccupped her last, she lay quietly in his arms.

"I'm so sorry, Panther. My emotions run wild these days," she explained. "You were late, and I was so worried. Then I saw her, and she is so slim and beautiful, and I was so jealous I couldn't think straight. I swear I saw red!"

Panther drew slightly away from her so he could see her face. "Don't ever doubt me again, Wildcat," he told her solemnly. "It is an affront to my honor when you do so."

"Never again," she promised.

"Now, clear your face while I dress, and we will go together to present Black Kettle with his new slave."

The smile she bestowed on him warmed his heart to its depths.

When the braves were not raiding, they were hunting, bringing in more meat for the long winter. Then winter set in hard and fast. Almost overnight, the stream froze and the snow came down so hard, driven by a fierce wind, that it was impossible to see more than two feet ahead. Sheltered as the village was by the mountains, it did not get the brunt of the storm, but it was still unlike anything Tanya had experienced in Pennsylvania. Back home, a few inches of drifting snow slowed the city to a crawl, if not to a complete halt. Here the snowfall was measured by feet, not mere inches, and once you were snowbound, it could be spring before you could move about freely again.

The days grew shorter, and the pace less hurried. Once a day Tanya would pick her way carefully over ice and snow to Black Kettle's lodge and visit with her parents. Usually the cougar cubs went along. They were larger now, but no less kittenish. Panther had taken over their training, and was having moderate success but they were still rambunctious little rascals.

Tanya and Melissa whiled away the hours making clothing for their babies. Unlike Tanya, Melissa was miserable, both emotionally and physically. Her pregnancy did not seem to be going well at all. Most of the time she was unable to keep food down, and her back ached constantly. Her skin had a sallow sickly cast to it, and she did not seem to be gaining weight as she should. Tanya worried over her endlessly.

Panther, when he was not in conference with the other warriors in the tribal lodge, spent a lot of his time in their tipi. Melissa was no longer nervous about him, and the three of them spent many peaceful hours together.

Panther set to work making a cradle for his child. Hour after hour he lovingly fashioned the wood, carving elaborate figures on it. He also fashioned the frame of the cradleboard Tanya would strap to her back or her saddle. Tanya covered it with sturdy leather, and then padded it with softer hides, decorating it with beads after Panther had hand-tooled patterns into it. While she sewed tiny clothes moccasins, and blankets, Panther carved miniature toys and rattles. He even made tiny wooden figures dangling from lines over the cradle to amuse the babe. These, in colorful array, would dance and clatter in the breeze, giving the child something to watch and listen to while he was yet too young to hold other toys.

The days were short and usually dreary outside, or too cold to do anything. The wind howled against the sides of the tipi. After the busy summer and fall, the quiet pace of winter did not suit Tanya. About the only thing she truly liked were the longer winter nights, wrapped tightly and warmly in Panther's arms as he demonstrated his love for her night after night.

December came to a close with Tanya and Melissa spending their first Christmas away from their families. Here there were no holiday festivities, with caroling and eggnog and yule log blazing. There were no presents in gaily wrapped paper, no furious shopping and furtive hiding and wrapping of gifts;

no Christmas tree festively decorated and alight with candles. No church services were attended; no holiday dinner, with table groaning under the weight of turkey, dressing, pumpkin and mincemeat pies.

Tanya, in her role as Panther's wife, had been so busy that she would not have known when Christmas Day actually was, had it not been for Melissa. She realized the holiday season was close at hand, but she had fallen into the Indian way of keeping track of time by the moon and the seasons, not days.

Melissa, on the other hand, had religiously marked off the days since their capture on a piece of bark.

"Only seven more days till Christmas," she advised Tanya listlessly one afternoon.

"What did you say?" Melissa suddenly had Tanya's full attention.

"It's only a week until Christmas," Melissa repeated with a deep sigh. "I wonder if everyone is celebrating without us? I suppose they are."

Tanya blinked in surprise, then said thoughtfully, "Yes, I suppose so. Is that why you've been so gloomy lately? I thought it was because you weren't feeling well."

"It's both, I guess. Don't you miss it, Tanya? All the bustling about; all the excitement?" Melissa's eyes filled with tears.

Tanya swallowed hard. "I miss my family. I even miss Julie, as irritating as she could be sometimes." She laughed shakily.

"I wish Indians celebrated Christmas, at least," Melissa complained. "I'd love to have even a small tree to decorate, a cup of eggnog on Christmas Eve, fellowship. . ." her voice trailed off in despair.

Tanya shook her head vigorously, as if to rid herself of the gloomy thoughts and feelings about to take root.

"Best not to think about it, Missy," she advised, "though I'd give a sack of gold for a turkey leg right this minute. Being pregnant certainly does things to one's appetite."

Long into the night, Tanya thought about her conversation with Melissa. She wished she could do something to lift her small friend's spirits, and finally decided on a plan.

The next morning, she presented her idea to Panther. He listened politely as she explained the Christian celebration of Christmas and its traditions. When she asked if they might cut down a small pine tree and bring it into the lodge, he balked. All living things were revered, and should not have their life cycles disturbed unnecessarily, but the pine tree was special beyond this. It was sacred to the Indians, as they believed it housed certain benevolent spirits. He would permit her to decorate a live pine nearby, but not to chop one down. In addition, he promised her a turkey.

For days Tanya secretly made small leather decorations and dyed them in bright colors. She sent Melissa to help Shy Deer for hours on Christmas Eve day. Using some of her precious supply of flour and salt, Tanya made pumpkin pie and a plum bread pudding. She made honey-maple candy and popped corn using honey to make it into popcorn balls. She fried corncakes and baked squash. When Panther arrived with the required turkey, she cleaned it and put it over the fire to roast.

When Melissa returned, Tanya dragged her out to the edge of the village, where she had located a small pine tree perfect for their purpose. With several bemused Cheyenne watching, she and Melissa proceeded to decorate the little tree. Then they stood back to admire their handiwork.

Melissa, her blue eyes brimming with tears, hugged her friend. "Thank you, Tanya! You are the best friend I've ever had, and this is the finest present you could give me this holiday season. Now it feels like Christmas to me."

Tanya returned the hug and smiled. "Merry Christmas, Missy."

She left her friend for a few minutes of privacy near the tree. Later that evening, she, Panther and Missy enjoyed a truly festive dinner together. Tanya swore she'd never been happier.

Two days after Christmas, Melissa got another of her most fervent wishes. She miscarried her child. A little more than halfway through her term, she was too far along to have an easy time of it.

The girls had just finished clearing away the breakfast bowls when Melissa gave a sharp cry and suddenly doubled over in pain, clutching at her stomach. Moving as quickly as possible, Tanya managed to catch her just as her knees gave way. With Panther's help, they eased her onto her pallet. No sooner did they have her settled, than another pain knifed through her. Melissa drew her knees to her chest and moaned.

"Something is wrong, Panther. I think it is the baby." Tanya gave him a worried look. "Perhaps I should go for Root Woman."

Panther shook his head, "No. You stay with her. I'll get Root Woman for you."

Several long minutes later, he was back with the medicine woman. The old lady knelt and examined Melissa. Then she sat back on her heels and directed her words to Panther.

"Your slave is losing her child. She will have a hard time of it. Already she is developing a fever, as her body tries to rid itself of its poisons and the babe. It is possible she may die, for she is slight and has been weakened with carrying the child."

Panther nodded. "Can you help her?"

"I can try to save her life, but the child is lost." Root Woman slid a sidelong glance toward Tanya. "It is not good for your wife to witness this. I will take the girl to the birthing lodge and care for her there."

All that day Tanya waited for word of Melissa. Finally, at dusk Root Woman sent word that the dead child had been expelled from the girl's body. What Panther did not tell Tanya was that the child had been deformed, a grotesque little boy with nothing but stubs for legs. This pitiful thing was the product of Ugly Otter's repeated rapes, beatings, and mistreatment of Melissa, and she was blessed to be rid of it, if she lived to know of it.

Throughout that night and into the next, Melissa barely clung to life. Her fever raged out of control. Her skin burning, her body racked with pain, she was delirious most of the time. It took all Root Woman's skill to pull her through this crisis. More than once Tanya wondered if it wouldn't be a blessing if Melissa would die. She would never be happy here as a slave, and Tanya had done all she could to better the girl's life. She could not ask Panther to set the girl free.

On the third day, Melissa's fever broke, and Root Woman sent word that she would live. The girl slept a restful, curing sleep for three more days, waking only when Root Woman forced broth down her throat. It was three weeks in all before Melissa was recovered fully and returned to Panther's lodge.

* * *

By January, Tanya felt smothered by snow and her own fat. The baby was due in March, but Tanya was sure her stomach would burst by then, so huge was she already.

Being snowbound didn't help much, especially with the biting winds and frigid temperatures that were with them almost daily. One rare, calm sun-sparkling day, Panther decided it would be safe for Tanya to venture out on the snowshoes he had made for her.

Tanya was ecstatic! It felt like years since she'd been able to move about freely or get even limited exercise. As they mushed along, Tanya asked, "Are you sure I won't break through? I'm pretty heavy, you know. I could end up stuck in a drift until the spring thaw."

Panther laughed. "The snowshoes would hold a horse's weight, Wildcat."

"Thanks a lot!" She shot him a dirty look from beneath her lashes.

They stayed out for more than two hours, walking and watching Kit and Kat romp in the snow. Tanya couldn't resist making a snowball and pelting Panther with it. She showed him how to make a snow-angel by lying flat and waving her arms and legs back and forth in the snow. She even talked him into helping her make a snowman. It was a day of fun and laughter, and Tanya slept better that night than she had in weeks.

Panther, in consideration of her condition, was making fewer demands on her at night now. It took all of Tanya's persistent persuasion to convince him he was not harming either her or the baby. Even once he was assured, he was extremely gentle with her, taking his time to arouse her and never fully forgetting his hold on his strength, even in the height of passion. This, more than any words, told her of his great love for her and their child.

Their lives changed in one important way for the better that winter. At a tribal meeting of the warriors, Panther achieved the status of a chief of the Cheyenne nation. After a lengthy review and recitation of his many achievements as a warrior, his astounding number of coup counted, his bravery and natural abilities as a leader, he was elevated to chief by unanimous decision.

Tanya was very proud and happy. Chief Black Kettle was no less pleased, for he had known his nephew would one day be one of their chiefs. Panther deserved the honor, and would execute his responsibilities well.

In turn, this made Tanya's responsibilities heavier. Now that her husband was a chief, there were added duties to perform. Others had often sought his advice before, but they did so more now that Panther's authority was greater. The influx of visitors to their tipi doubled, and it was up to Tanya to see they were offered something to eat and drink. If there was a celebration or festivity of some sort, Tanya had to help organize the preparations and the serving of food. When visitors from other tribes arrived, she had to see to their lodging and comforts, and when the warriors prepared for a raid or a hunt their provisions had to be readied. The welfare and comfort of lesser persons of the tribe had to be seen to, and help offered if need be.

Tanya suddenly found herself with more responsibilities than her condition would allow, and she was very happy when Melissa returned to their lodge, well, and willing to help.

Melissa, for all her problems, was healthier now than Tanya had seen her look in months. She was relieved to be rid of Ugly Otter's baby.

"If I ever have children, I want it to be because I want and will love them, not because they were forced upon me by a brutal man's lust," she told Tanya.

As the weeks went by, Melissa seemed more content, if not happy. She enjoyed Tanya's company and the comforts she was offered in her household. Whether or not she would ever be truly happy after what she had experienced at Ugly Otter's hands, she did not know, but she had started to smile again.

Perhaps it was because they were not so busy and had more time to spend together, but over that frozen winter, love bloomed between Shy Deer and Winter Bear. It was nearly comical to see him almost literally puff up and strut when she was near. Shy Deer in her own quiet way beguiled him endlessly. Her large doe-eyes adored him openly and he worshipped the ground she walked upon. Both found limitless reasons to be in Panther's tipi when the other was present.

Unable to stand it any longer, Winter Bear approached Shy Deer's father, and the marriage was planned for spring. Winter Bear glowed with pride that Shy Deer had accepted him. The rest of the winter, they were like two children with their noses pressed against the windowpane of a candy store, Tanya thought, waiting for the owner to unlock the door.

Early in March, just when Tanya was praying for winter to be over soon, a terrible storm roared down on them. It started with a freezing rain that coated everything in sight with a thick layer of ice. Shelters had to be erected for the horses, and Tanya felt useless as she watched Panther and Winter Bear work in the frigid rain.

Even Melissa lent her hand, bundling up in thick furs to venture out. Tanya, nearly ready to deliver her child, could do no more than prepare warm broth for them, keep the fire going inside the tipi, and dry and warm their clothing.

Behind the rain came the snow, driven by the strongest winds Tanya had ever experienced. Visibility was limited to inches, and drifts twenty feet high and more piled up around them. The weight of the ice caused the lodge poles to creak and groan under the strain, and a couple of tipis actually collapsed as the poles snapped.

One of the tipis that collapsed was the birthing lodge, where all Cheyenne women went to give birth to their children, away from their husbands. An older woman of the tribe tended her, and the new mother remained there until she was fully recovered. Only then did she return to her husband's lodge with her child.

Tanya had regretted this, and felt it was providence that had stepped in just at this time. No sooner had the birthing lodge collapsed, then Tanya's labor started. With everyone bustling about trying to shelter the animals, and prevent other tipis from falling, she said nothing. Quietly she prepared her bed and the baby's. She laid out clothing for her child and herself, set a kettle of water to boil, sterilized a sharp knife, and made sure everything she might need was close at hand. Then she sat down to wait, contentedly stroking her stomach and smiling secretly to herself.

The storm was still raging long after the last of the

daylight had disappeared. The Cheyenne had done all they could to protect their animals and brace their structures against the elements. Now they dragged themselves wearily into their tents to renew their strength and wait out the storm.

Tanya had a warm meal and dry clothing awaiting both Panther and Melissa. She was well into her labor by the time they straggled in. She lay on her fur covered pallet, rubbing her stomach in soothing circular motions, waiting out a contraction.

"Missy, I hate to ask you, but could you serve Panther his meal this evening?" she asked from the corner.

Melissa groaned, but complied readily.

Panther came to the bed and reached for his dry clothes. "Your mother asked about you. She said not to venture out on the ice to visit. She doesn't want you to fall and hurt yourself."

"Is everything pretty well in order now? No one was hurt when the lodges collapsed, were they?" Tanya queried.

Panther sat down next to her, taking the bowl Melissa brought for him. "The tipis that fell cannot be repaired until the storm lets up. Starling had his leg pinned by his lodge pole, but Root Woman has set it and it will heal. No one else was hurt, but several have fallen on the ice. Root Woman has been busy all day setting bones and healing lumps, cuts, and scrapes. You should see the knot on Towering Pine's head. It looks like an antler!"

Tanya, in the grip of another spasm could only grunt an answer.

Panther swung his startled gaze toward her. "Wildcat! How long have you been in labor?"

Tanya panted and tried to catch her breath. As the pain receded, she said on a long sigh, "Most of the day."

"And you said nothing?" He was incredulous.

"You and the others were busy and needed elsewhere, Panther. Women have babies all the time. Don't fret."

"This is *my* baby we are talking about and it is very important to me! My child is arriving into the world and you do not think it necessary to tell me?" he railed.

"Don't scold me now, Panther," she grated out through yet another contraction. "Not . . . now."

Sweat poured down her face as she clenched her teeth and fists against the pain. When it had passed, she continued, "Panther, find something to do, please. You are ruining my concentration. I am trying to bring your son into the world, and it is no easy job!"

Panther's indignation dissolved as he watched her through the contraction. "You must have someone to help you, as you would have had in the birthing lodge. I will go for Root Woman."

Tanya shook her head. "No!" she panted. "It is too late. Stay, or you will miss the birth of your first child. By the time you get to her tipi and back, the deed will be done."

Melissa, who had been standing quietly by all the while, spoke up. "I will help you, Tanya." She wet a cloth and sponged Tanya's face and neck. "Tell me what to do. You are the one who took all the instructions from Root Woman."

Tanya ground her teeth together. "Help me out of this dress. It is soaking with sweat and getting cold."

Melissa and Panther together got the dress off of her and dried her. At Tanya's instruction, they piled robes up behind her back to prop her up. Panther tied knots in two lengths of deerhide and put them in Tanya's clenched hands. The other ends he gave to Melissa, and told Tanya to pull on these as she bore down.

"Scream if you want to, little one," he told her, "if it will make you feel better." His dark eyes were full of love and pity at her suffering.

"Cheyenne women do not scream during childbirth, Panther," she grunted.

"I'm sure some do," he assured her. "Besides, no one will hear you over this howling wind, and I certainly will not tell anyone, nor will Melissa."

Tanya was too far into her pain to hear or understand these last words. The pains had changed suddenly, and now she had an uncontrollable urge to bear down. The pain was constant now, giving her little time to catch her breath.

"My feet keep slipping," she panted a complaint. "Brace my feet."

Propped up from behind, with the rawhide strips to pull on and Panther holding onto her knees and bracing her feet, Tanya strained with her labor. Her stomach constricted in agony, as though a thousand white-hot knives were piercing her.

Between her knees, Panther knelt and hurt for her. He lightly stroked her stomach, trying to ease her misery and murmured quiet encouragements to her, hoping the tone of his voice, if not the words, would help.

Just as Tanya thought she would be torn apart by the pressure and pain, she heard Panther say, "I see the head! Bear down with the next pain!"

Taking a deep breath, Tanya did just that, as Panther helped to guide the baby's body out.

"One more good push," he instructed from below.

Once more she obeyed nature's urgings and heard

Panther exclaim, "It's a boy! We have a son!"

As Tanya caught her wind, Panther cleared the baby's airways, and the child gave a mighty bellow.

Grinning from ear to ear, Panther gently laid his son on Tanya's belly. In awe, she reached down and touched his wet, downy head. Eyes full of wonder, she looked at Panther. "Oh, Panther, he's so beautiful!"

"Handsome," he corrected with a smile.

"Hadn't we better get him cleaned up so he can have his dinner?" Melissa suggested, her eyes suspiciously wet.

Panther cut and tied the cord as if he'd been delivering babies all his life. Then he cleaned the child with warm water and dressed him while Melissa helped Tanya. He left to dispose of the afterbirth after seeing the babe settled at Tanya's breast.

His son was wide awake, cuddled contentedly in Tanya's arms, when he returned. He sat down next to them, where he could see both their faces.

"Aren't all babies supposed to be born with blue eyes?" Tanya questioned. "I thought I heard that somewhere."

"Why?" he asked.

"Because his are gold," she replied. "Look. See for yourself."

Panther leaned forward and gazed into his son's eyes. They were, indeed, gold. "He has his mother's eyes, just as I'd hoped," he said.

"And his father's blue-black hair," Tanya added. "He has the coloring of the panther," she grinned, "moreso than even you do. With this hair and those gold eyes, the Panther's son ought truly to be a hunter of the forest."

Stroking her flushed cheek, Panther said softly, "You have just given me the name for our son."

Tanya's eyes questioned him.

"We shall call him Hunter of the Forest," he told her.

Tanya smiled and sighed tiredly. "I like it. It is a good, strong name, and he will grow strong and tall like his father, whom I love very much."

Panther's lips pressed hers in a brief kiss. "Thank you for my son, Little Wildcat. Now you must rest, for you have worked harder today than any of us."

Tanya's eyes were already closing as she heard him add, "I love you, Little Wildcat—and you, too, Hunter of the Forest."

Chapter 10

HUNTER OF the Forest was a beautiful, healthy baby. Along with his thick mop of black hair, unusual gold eyes, and cherubic face, he had a cheerful personality. He almost never fussed, and rarely had to be stopped from crying. Like all Cheyenne babies, he was quickly taught not to cry aloud. Each time he attempted to do so, Tanya closed his jaws and pinched his nostrils shut, momentarily cutting off his air. In a short time he learned not to cry. Cruel as it seemed, it was a necessary lesson, for a crying infant could be heard for miles, scaring off game and alerting enemies to one's position.

Panther had gone early the next morning to inform Black Kettle and Woman-To-Be-Hereafter of the baby's arrival. Black Kettle was elated to hear of his first grandson's birth, and a celebration was planned for later in the month when the weather would better allow it. Contrary to all tradition, he visited his newly born grandson that same day in Panther's tipi and heartily approved the name Panther had chosen.

Tanya had broken tradition by having her child in her own tipi instead of the birthing tent. Under the circumstances, it could not be helped. Nevertheless, the shaman was now called upon to perform purification rites over Panther and his lodge, especially since Panther had helped deliver his son himself. Only after the shaman had completed his ritual did anyone venture near the tipi, for the old taboos handed down for centuries were not soon laid to rest.

Not many years before, any woman having her monthly flow or still bleeding after giving birth was secluded from the tribe in a special tipi. No warrior could come in contact with her or eat food prepared by her at this time. Only after she stopped bleeding could she resume her normal routine. This was not because a woman was considered unclean at this time, but because she was thought to possess powerful spirits that could adversely affect a warrior's guardian spirit and possibly cause him to be hurt or killed in battle.

These days, because game was sometimes scarce and tribes had to travel so often, this was nearly impossible to adhere to, so the rules had been relaxed. Women having their flow were no longer shunned, but they still could not prepare a warrior's meal, handle his weapons, or lie with their husbands. They still went to the birthing lodge to have their babies, but were allowed to return to their own tipis within days.

Though tired, Tanya recovered quickly. For a first child, her labor had been extraordinarily short and easy. Within hours, her milk came in, and Hunter of the Forest was nursing hungrily at her breasts. By the time the village had recovered from the ice storm, Tanya was back to her regular duties in the lodge.

She and Panther were both privately glad that he had been present for the birth of his son. It was one of the most fantastic experiences of his life, and he wouldn't have missed it for the world. To watch his son's entrance into the world, to aid in it, was worth more than gold to Panther. To see Wildcat's face light up with love and awe as he placed Hunter on her stomach, was a priceless tabloid indelibly imprinted on his soul.

Following the storm, there was a sudden break in the weather. The air turned balmy and held the smell of spring to it. The celebration to honor Hunter's birth was held, and the drums beat out the news; Black Kettle's grandson was born.

Activity picked up around the camp as the Cheyenne were able to move about as they had not since winter had set in. Quickly, the braves organized a hunt, as food supplies were extremely low. While they were gone, the women scoured about for dry firewood and cleaned the winter's collection of debris from their tipis and the camp. From the still frozen earth, they dug roots to supplement their food stores and fished the frigid stream.

Tanya did her share of the work, glad to be out, about, and slim once again. Sometimes she left Hunter with Melissa or Woman-To-Be-Hereafter, but often she bundled him into his cradleboard, swathed in furs, and carried him along on her back. She'd talk softly to him as they walked along, or sing lullabys to entertain him.

Kit and Kat were always underfoot. At first Tanya was fearful the large cubs would harm Hunter, and kept a watchful eye on them. They were about half-grown now and had lost their spots and the rings on their tails. They had exchanged their downy kitten-fuzz for a glowing coat of tawny fur.

From the first, the cats adopted a protective attitude toward Hunter, as though he were one of their brothers. They fought over the space near his cradle, nudging one another out of the way until they could both find room. There they slept, guarding him all night.

They followed when Tanya took Hunter on her walks. If she left him with Melissa or Woman-To-Be-Hereafter, one of the cats would go on with Tanya while the other stayed with Hunter. It was quite a sight to see them padding through the village together. Many a solemn faced Cheyenne had to smile at the picture they created.

The warriors had no sooner returned from their hunt, when a messenger arrived for Black Kettle. It startled Tanya to see a white man in camp for the first time, and she stayed in her lodge until Panther came to explain.

The message was from Major Wynkoop at Fort Larned, Kansas, to inform Black Kettle of a meeting to be held on Pawnee Fork in April, the next moon. General Hancock, newly arrived from the east, wished to meet with the renegade leader of the Northern Cheyenne Dog Soldiers, Roman Nose, and all Cheyenne Chiefs. Hancock and his company, including young George Custer, wished to discuss a new treaty. Major Wynkoop, agent to the Cheyenne and Arapahoe Nations, was arranging the talks.

George Bent, the son of William Bent, and his Cheyenne wife, Owl Woman, was the messenger who had arrived. William Bent had operated the trading post at Bent's Fort, which he later sold to the U.S. government. After that, Bent's Fort had become Fort Lyon, a military fort. Tanya recalled having met William Bent and his second wife, Yellow Woman, when the wagon train had stopped at Fort Lyon.

George Bent, himself a halfbreed, had years before married Black Kettle's niece, Magpie, Panther's half-sister. She had come with him, and Tanya soon discovered why she was called Magpie. The woman never stopped chattering.

Magpie had been married to George Bent at age fourteen. She was now twenty-two, and they had a son, Blue Horse, who had just turned eight, and another who was four.

Tanya thought the woman extremely homely, though very friendly. She could not imagine how Panther's father, White Antelope, could have fathered such a handsome son and such a plain daughter, and she told Panther so as delicately as she could.

Laughing, he told her, "You should have seen her mother! I take after my father, whom everyone thought was very handsome. Magpie resembles her mother, my father's second wife."

"Where is her mother?" Tanya asked.

"She died several years ago."

"And what happened to *your* mother?" she persisted. Until Magpie had arrived, Panther had not talked much of his family, and Tanya had not even been aware he had a half-sister.

"My mother is gone also," he said simply, and from that she assumed Panther's mother, too had died.

"You've never mentioned Magpie. Have you any other brothers or sisters?"

Panther grinned. "Not that I know of; at least none that my father openly claimed as his."

"Panther!" Tanya pretended to be shocked at his words, but she couldn't prevent a smile from escaping as she shook her head at him.

"I think after Father saw what Magpie looked like, he gave up," he joked.

Tanya laughed. "You are terrible, Panther, but I love you."

* * *

Pawnee Fork was roughly 300 miles from where Black Kettle's tribe was now camped. Traveling at a brisk pace, it would take at least half a month to get there, so the tribe packed up and moved out right away. The women were dismayed that they had not had the opportunity to plant their spring vegetables, but Major Wynkoop had sent word that food and blankets would be distributed at the meeting place. Tanya looked forward to a new supply of coffee, flour and salt. The braves hunted along the way and the women gathered berries and roots wherever they stopped to camp.

A third of the way into their voyage, the tribe camped near Fort Lyon. Panther, George Bent, Winter Bear, and some of the other braves went to the fort to trade furs and hides for supplies. Tanya held her breath until they returned safely with their traded goods. She couldn't help wondering if Jeffrey was once again stationed there and if perhaps he and Panther had come face to face, neither knowing of the other.

Under a wave of homesickness, she longed to see her family once more, but she would never jeopardize her life with Panther and her son to do so. She told herself it didn't matter, swallowed her longings for her family and bravely went about her business, reminding herself that she was Cheyenne now. Her family would not understand. They would never accept Panther or Hunter, and Tanya could never give them up. They were her heart, her soul, and her life, and she would die before she would part with them.

When they at last reached Pawnee Fork, a tributary of the Arkansas River, Major Wynkoop rode out from Fort Larned to meet them. Several other tribes had arrived ahead of them, including Roman Nose's band of Dog Soldiers from the North. General Hancock, being new to the area, mistakenly assumed Roman Nose to be a chief, an important chief, and would not hear otherwise. Major Wynkoop tried to tell him that Roman Nose was merely a warrior leading a group of renegade Dog Soldiers on unauthorized raids along the Colorado-Kansas border. He stressed that Black Kettle, a peaceful man, was head chief of the Southern Cheyenne; Dull Knife, the chief of the Dog Soldiers; and Panther, Little Robe, and Little Wolf also important Cheyenne chiefs. Chief Little Raven was also expected with his band of Arapahoe.

Hancock shrugged off Wynkoop's information and advice. He preferred to form his own opinions and enlist his own scouts and advisors. He waited impatiently for the tribes to arrive, expecting them to be grateful and humble that the U.S. government was recognizing them and prepared to treaty with them. He completely ignored the fact that the government meant to steal away more of the Indian land, invade their hunting grounds, and open the territory to settlers, all the while expecting the Indians to calmly accept this, sign away their lands, and remain peaceful.

Black Kettle settled his tribe upstream, away from Roman Nose's band and the main camp of Cheyenne. He was insulted at the snub from General Hancock. Chief Little Raven, when he finally arrived, camped nearby.

While they were awaiting the arrival of the other tribes, Major Wynkoop came often to soothe Black Kettle's injured pride. He brought a few gifts, but most of them would be handed out once the talks were underway.

Black Kettle and Major Wynkoop understood and

respected one another. Their association went back to the time when Major Wynkoop had first come west, when he had been commander of Fort Lyon; before he had been relieved of duty there and replaced by Major Anthony in 1864. Wynkoop had mourned with Black Kettle over the Sand Creek Massacre and the death of White Antelope. He had railed at the government and defended the Cheyenne and Arapahoe.

Wynkoop went out of his way to understand the Indian way of life. He truly liked and respected them. Quite possibly, he was their only true friend among the whites, for he stood up for them time after time. He visited Washington and met with government committees on their behalf, and argued for their rights.

Wynkoop detested the cavalier attitude the government took toward the Indians. They grabbed Indian land with one hand, doling out a handful of worthless trinkets with the other. They initiated treaties that cheated the Indian, then expected him to abide by them while the government broke nearly every one. It saddened him to see peaceful men like Black Kettle sit down in good faith, only to be cheated. He could not blame some of the younger chiefs and braves for becoming angry when they saw the whites breaking their word. He sympathized with their plight, and while he could not condone their raids and war parties, he understood it.

On one of Wynkoop's first visits, he discovered that Black Kettle had an adopted daughter who had married Panther and given him a son. He wondered about the woman they called Wildcat, for he could not recall having seen or heard of her before. His curiosity was such that Panther decided something had to be done about it. Constantly making excuses to Wynkoop to cover Wildcat's absences was likely to make the man suspicious.

All the other white slaves had been hidden whenever Wynkoop or his men were about. Had he not been so curious about her, Tanya would merely have remained out of sight during his visits.

Between them, Panther and Tanya devised a plan. Using Panther's paints and wood dyes, they darkened Tanya's tawny locks. Her skin had tanned almost as dark as Shy Deer's in the last year, but a bit of root dye rubbed into her flesh darkened it further. By leaving her hair loose to shield her face and eyes, her disguise was complete.

The next time Wynkoop arrived, he found Panther, Wildcat, and Hunter in Black Kettle's lodge. Tanya was seated to the rear of the tipi with Woman-To-Be-Hereafter, nursing her son. He greeted her in Cheyenne, and she responded softly in kind. Later, as her mother served Major Wynkoop and Black Kettle their meal, Tanya served Panther, careful to keep her face shielded. With her darkened hair and skin, she looked like any other young Cheyenne woman.

Major Wynkoop spoke to her, nearly causing her to drop the bowl she carried. "You are called Wildcat?"

Keeping her eyes lowered, she answered. "I am called Little Wildcat."

"How did you come to be adopted by Chief Black Kettle?"

Tanya swallowed hard and adlibbed, "He took pity on a girl who had lost her family."

Here Black Kettle cut in, "Truly, I wanted the most beautiful girl in the tribe for my daughter, and jumped at the chance."

Wynkoop chuckled and joked. "Why didn't you take her to wife instead of adopting her?"

Not taking offense, Black Kettle responded, "She already had eyes for Panther, and I am too old and wrinkled to compete with such a handsome, virile young buck."

"You may be long in years, my friend, but your heart is yet young."

At one point in the visit, Wynkoop surprised them all by asking if he might hold Black Kettle's new grandson. Tanya nearly swallowed her tongue, but at Panther's nod, she brought the child forth and laid him in Wynkoop's arms. Luckily, Hunter was asleep, so his eyes remained closed. With his dark complexion and midnight hair, he was obviously an Indian infant. He did not awaken the entire time Wynkoop held him.

Major Wynkoop arrived so frequently and unannounced, that Tanya thought it wiser not to wash the stain from her skin and hair until after the meetings were over and the Cheyenne could move on. As it turned out, this was sooner than anyone expected.

Hancock was ready to start the talks immediately after all the tribes had gathered. He had a treaty to get signed as soon as possible, and wanted to get it sent to Washington quickly. He became agitated with the standard rituals the Indians expected. They were lengthy and involved, and the tribes expected them to be observed as a matter of courtesy before any important matters could be discussed and decided upon.

Hancock, in his impatience, rudely cut the rituals short on the third day. He sent the chiefs back to their tribes, instructing them to advise them of the terms of their treaty to be signed. Giving them two days at most, he told them not to return to Fort Larned at the end of that time. He would come the few miles to their camps and meet them in their own lodges then.

The chiefs were very upset and nervous at this pronouncement. They went back to their people and presented the case for a vote. Black Kettle's tribe decided to ignore the treaty offered them. They were anxious over having Hancock and his troops arrive in their camp. Fearing another deception, and remembering the Sand Creek Massacre, they voted to pack up and flee south before the two days were up. In the middle of the night, under cover of darkness, they fled, taking everything with them. In the light of dawn, the only signs of their camp were a few still smoldering campfires.

The other tribes evidently decided to follow suit, some of them not so quickly, however. Many tribes left their lodges and heavier belongings behind in their rush. Not one Cheyenne or Arapahoe remained when Hancock arrived. So incensed was he by this, that he ordered the villages that still stood burned to the ground. He sent out scouts and small companies to try to locate and overtake the Indians, much to Wynkoop's dismay. General Custer's company spotted what was believed to be Roman Nose's band headed northwest, but could not catch them. No sign of Black Kettle's tribe or any of the others was found except a few scattered campfires and a handful of confusing trails that always seemed to double back on themselves and disappear. They had vanished overnight into thin air.

That spring of 1867, both Northern and Southern Cheyenne banded together to make war on the whites. They raided, hitting settlements and terrorizing settlers all along its course.

As the cavalries lent chase, sent from the forts to

rout the Cheyenne, the tribes split up. In June, the Northern Cheyenne went north of the Arkansas to raid and raise havoc. Black Kettle and Panther, led their people south into Texas territory to a place the whites called Sweetwater, but the Cheyenne had named Bitter Water. They camped on a branch of the north fork of the Red River. With this as their base, they raided in northern Texas, Colorado, and Kansas, rampaging all along the territory south of the Arkansas River. Between them, the Northern and Southern Cheyenne held the entire area in terror that summer.

Far enough south not to be bothered by the soldiers, the Cheyenne women of Black Kettle's tribe felt safe enough to plant their crops. All summer they tended their plants and children under the hot Texas sun.

Early June brought the wedding of Winter Bear and Shy Deer, which had been postponed until now. Between raids, the newly-wedded lovers grabbed every second they could get to be alone together. By summer's end, Shy Deer was already expecting their first child.

Their tribes stayed on at Bitter Water through September, giving the women plenty of time to harvest their crops. Periodically, between raids, the men would organize a hunt, but it was nothing like the hunts they had been on the previous summer. It promised to be a lean winter, unless the weather held.

Hunter grew by leaps and bounds. A sweet-tempered baby, he was constantly smiling and cooing. That summer, as small as he was, Tanya taught him to swim in the shallows of the river. He seemed to do everything at an early age. He was sitting at five months old, and cut two pearly front teeth about the same time. At six months, he was jabbering his very first words, not calling for his mother or father, but for Kit and Kat. By mid September he was crawling, and getting into everything. Tanya swore she had everything imaginable hung from the walls and poles of the tipi out of his reach.

Everything his chubby little hands could grasp went into his mouth, including the cubs' tails. The only time he was still was in his sleep, and Tanya would kneel for ages over his cradle gazing at his cherubic face with its chunky, rosy cheeks and small red bow-shaped mouth. Awake, he played for hours on end with the toys Panther had carved for him, his golden eyes sparkling with delight.

With Panther gone so much that summer, Hunter was Tanya's joy. He never lacked for attention but neither did he seem to become spoiled by it. Black Kettle and Woman-To-Be-Hereafter adored him. Walks-Like-A-Duck and Shy Deer were always willing to take him off of Tanya's hands for a few hours, and Melissa doted on him like a second mother. As much love and affection as he received and gave to the others, Tanya included, when his father came home, Hunter preferred Panther to anyone else.

The summer was hectic. It seemed the men were always gone and Tanya cherished the few times Panther was home. His muscles, always hard and well-honed, were even more so now. He was leaner, having little time to eat properly and being always on the move. If possible, the sun seemed to have bronzed his skin to an even deeper hue.

Lying between his hard thighs each night, Tanya revelled in their stolen moments. Nowadays, they came together with an urgency that bespoke the danger ever-present in their lives. Each time he rode away from her, there was the possibility he would not return.

"I know you must go," she told him, "but I cannot help worrying over your safety."

"I cannot promise to return to you if the spirits wish it otherwise," he answered, softly stroking her hair, "but my heart is with you always."

When Panther was at home, he enjoyed spending time with his wife and son. Each time he returned, Hunter had grown more and learned something new. He applauded his son's achievements as proudly as any father the world over.

The picture Panther took with him on each trip was that of Wildcat nursing his son at her breast. That mental portrait was precious to him. Each time he saw the small dark head nestled tenderly against her, the rosy lips eagerly searching out her nipple, his heart overflowed with love.

Tanya's figure had altered with the birth of their child. Though still slim, her breasts were more full and her hips more rounded. Gone was the girlish maiden's form, and in its place was that of a mature woman.

Since Hunter's birth, though Panther still took time in their lovemaking to arouse her, though he still caressed and fondled her breasts, he never suckled them as he had in the past. This was now his son's pleasure; the source of Hunter's nourishment.

Lying next to him on their pallet, Tanya now guided Panther's head to her breasts, needing to feel his lips upon her. He kissed her breasts, and his tongue reached out to trace the nipple. It puckered immediately at his touch, and tiny drops of milk seeped from it. He tasted the fluid with his tongue, and when he would have backed off, Tanya pressed his mouth to her breast, arching up to meet him.

"Please, Panther," she moaned.

"I would not take my son's meal from him," Panther whispered.

"It will only make the milk come in faster. You will not deprive him," she explained. "Please. I need to feel your lips on me. It has been so long since you have done this, and I starve for you!"

Satisfied that his son would not go hungry, Panther complied readily. Taking her nipple into his mouth, he suckled avidly and the warm, sweet milk flowed into his mouth. Beneath him, he felt Tanya's body tense.

"Am I hurting you?" he murmured against her heated breast.

"Oh no, Panther, It feels glorious! Don't stop."

A few minutes later she was wriggling beneath him, "Make love to me, Panther. You have made me need you so! Make love to me!"

Her breast still sucked tightly between his lips, Panther entered her. As his lips pulled at her nipple, he could feel her body tighten and pull at his manhood.

Within moments her body was exploding around him, and his own passion broke with a force that rocked him to his toes.

Now when he rode off to war with his braves, he carried not only the picture of Hunter at Tanya's breast, but the remembrance of their lovemaking and the taste of her sweet nectar on his tongue.

The last of September brought another messenger from Fort Larned. The man had ridden his horse nearly to death, covering almost 300 miles in seven days. The news he brought was both astounding and depressing. Roman Nose was dead. In intense fighting on Beecher Island a few days prior, Roman Nose and his band of Northern Cheyenne had attacked a specialized company of army scouts. The Cheyenne had won the battle, but Roman Nose had been fatally wounded when he lead his braves into battle, despite the fact that his medicine had been broken when he had eaten food served up by a metal spoon.

Now the army wanted to talk peace with the Cheyenne once more. Major Wynkoop had sent for Black Kettle, knowing if he agreed to come, others would follow. He counted on the fact that Black Kettle wanted peace above all else for his people.

Once again the Cheyenne headed for Fort Larned, Kansas. They arrived in mid-October for the preliminary meetings. All talks went smoothly this time, and a few days later the Medicine Lodge Treaty was signed at a place on the Medicine Lodge Creek. All the Southern Cheyenne, under Black Kettle's pleas for peace, agreed to move south of the Arkansas River and stay there.

Panther understood his uncle's reasons, but could not agree with his decision. Black Kettle wanted peace with the white soldiers. His braves could not hunt while they were busy making war. The tribes needed food and warm clothing for the long winters. Panther could see this, but in staying south of the Arkansas, the Cheyenne were giving up prime hunting land. The buffalo did not have to stay south of the river, but now the Cheyenne could not follow him if he crossed it. It sickened Panther to see the Indian pushed further and further from his lands and given only a few blankets and a little food as payment. It was unjust and it made him angry.

When Panther thought about the entire situation, whites versus Indian, he knew the Indian could not win. The white man would triumph in the end. He had grown up and been educated in their world. He was accepted and had friends and relatives in white society. The white man was greedy and grasping, and there were too many of them. The Indians could fight to the last man, and still there would be more white-eyes than could be counted, and they would always covet the Indian's land. It was a losing battle before it had really started, but these were his people, too, and he would fight with them to the end.

Chapter 11

WITH THE peace that fall came the time for the warriors to hunt. For once it seemed that nature was cooperating. Winter held off her cold and snows until much later that year, and the buffalo and deer were plentiful. Perhaps the tribe would not go hungry after all.

This year they did not go back to their old winter camp, but went further south and camped alongside the mountains in a sheltered valley next to the Cimarron River. After a frenzied, frantic year, Tanya looked forward to an uneventful winter. All she wanted was to snuggle up in her cozy tipi with Panther and Hunter to keep her company.

It was lovely having Panther home again after the harrowing summer. The work of skinning and preparing the hides he brought her seemed lighter than carrying the heavy load of worry she had for months before. Tanya would much rather watch Panther prepare for a hunt than for war.

The sun-warmed days of October lingered on into November. A festive celebration of thanksgiving, honoring the successful hunt and harvest was held, and later still a ceremony full of tradition and ritual to honor their chiefs and warriors for brave deeds. At this occasion, Chief Black Kettle was honored for his peace-making efforts; several chiefs and warriors, including Panther, were honored for their valor in the summer war; and Winter Bear achieved his ranking as chief.

December brought the first snow, but just a few inches to lightly cover the ground. Another Christmas came and went nearly unnoticed, except for the small pine tree Melissa and Tanya decorated on the edge of the village.

January and February brought heavier snow and polar winds with frigid temperatures, but only two major storms. Food supplies dwindled but everyone shared what they had, and no one went really hungry.

The occupants of Panther's lodge stayed content and cozy in their tipi. Melissa, now more of a family member than a servant, had adopted the role of favorite aunt to Hunter. More than ever, Tanya appreciated the extra pair of helping hands, for Hunter had decided to learn to walk. Pulling himself up on his chubby legs, he would wobble and lurch precariously, and Tanya was ever fearful he would topple into the fire.

The rambunctious little rascal entertained them all with his endless antics. He was constantly on the move and usually ended up getting into something he was not supposed to before the day was out. Happy, healthy, and extremely curious, his active mind and body often got him into trouble with his mother. At such times, he would grin his toothy grin at her, look up at her with smiling golden eyes, and do his level best to soften her up. Most of the time he succeeded, but when he did not, he got his bottom whacked.

When Panther saw that Tanya was reaching the limit of her patience, he often bundled Hunter up and took him out with him. They would take Kit and Kat for a walk, see the horses, and visit Winter Bear or Grandfather Black Kettle for a while. By the time they returned, Tanya was usually in better sorts.

Hunter was not a bad baby; he was just a normal, active child. He was not moody or tempermental. Easy to please, he was pleasant and cheerful most of the time. Already Panther and Tanya were giving him lessons in protocol and respect. These were instilled early in all Cheyenne children, as was the necessity for absolute obedience to one's parents. To obey instantly, without question, could well save a child's life one day, and the failure to do so could be fatal in this untamed land.

Each morning Panther would seat Hunter next to himself as he chanted his daily prayers. Even though the child could not understand any of it yet, a pattern was being set for years to come. Both Tanya and Panther would tell him stories and sing songs of nature and Indian lore that had been told to Cheyenne children for countless years. These he could not understand either, but he would sit in Panther's lap and listen to his father's deep voice sound against his ear as he lay against Panther's chest. He would turn large golden eyes up to his father's face and seem fascinated with every word, or he would smile at his mother as she sang to him in her melodic voice.

At this age, Kit and Kat were both his playmates and his horses. The cubs were over a year old now, and about three-quarters their adult size. The poor darlings took a beating from Hunter, but did it gracefully. They never snarled or snapped at the child, but bore his antics with a patient endurance that Tanya secretly admired. Hunter mauled them, chewed on them, pulled their fur, and climbed onto their backs, and they never flicked a whisker, though once in a while Tanya swore she saw them roll their eyes and sigh in tired defeat.

One incident marred a nearly perfect winter. Just after Christmas, Tanya slipped on a patch of ice while out collecting firewood. She fell, hitting her head on a rock, and lay unconscious in the cold for over an hour before Panther found her. For a week she lay with a raging fever and congested chest, rarely regaining consciousness, and then not lucidly. Root Woman, Woman-To-Be-Hereafter, Melissa, and Panther took turns nursing her. All feared for her life, though none voiced the thought aloud.

Panther nearly went crazy with worry. In his worst moments, he cursed himself for ever capturing her in the first place. If she were with her family now, she would have a doctor and modern medicines to make her well. He even considered trying to take her to a town or fort for help, but Winter Bear talked enough sense into him to prevent it.

"She'd never survive the distance on horseback or travois," Winter Bear advised. "Besides, you know most of the medicines doctors give are the same things Root Woman is giving her. Even if she could withstand the journey, don't you think her family would find out? Someone could recognize her, and then where would you be?"

At Panther's thoughtful look, he went on, "You'd end up in jail and most likely be hung. Wildcat would be returned to her family, and Hunter-of-the-Forest would be an orphan. No, cousin, this way is best. Wildcat will pull through this. She has a strong will to survive, and much to live for."

Winter Bear was right. A full week after her accident, Tanya awoke with the dawn. She was weak, thirsty, hungry, and drenched in sweat from her broken fever, but she was awake and lucid. Her head ached abominably and her throat and chest hurt, but she was back in Panther's world again.

Panther was lying next to her, asleep, exhausted from his vigil. Tanya poked him lightly in the ribs, struggling to speak. "Panther," she croaked.

He groaned and stirred lightly.

"Panther."

This time he awoke, his dark eyes flying open to meet hers.

"I'm thirsty," she complained, and they were the sweetest words he'd ever heard.

"Wildcat," he whispered. "You are awake."

Tanya tried to nod and winced at the pain shooting through her head. "I think so," she moaned.

Panther brought her some water, holding the cup to her parched lips. "How do you feel?"

"Awful! I must be alive, because I hurt too much to be dead," she joked lamely.

"Do not joke about such a thing, Wildcat," he admonished gently, his eyes suspiciously wet. "You have been unconscious for a full seven suns, and there were times I was sure you would slip away from us."

Tanya blinked tiredly. "Never, Panther. I love you too much to leave you. You should know that by now."

Tanya slept a lot over the next week, but it was a natural, healing rest. She'd lost weight the week she'd been unconscious and unable to eat, and now she had to work her way up slowly, starting with weak broth. Slowly she regained her strength and health. Her lungs finally cleared, and her throat and head quit hurting. One fact remained. During her illness and recovery period, she'd been unable to nurse Hunter and with no nourishment, her milk dried up. There would be no more breastfeeding.

"What shall we do?" Tanya asked of Panther.

"It is already done," he told her. "Hunter is old enough now to drink from a cup. He has had to learn while you were ill, and is doing fairly well."

"Yes, but he needs his milk yet," she argued.

Panther grinned, "He has it," he told her. "I was too concerned with you to think of it, but Melissa talked to your mother. Woman-To-Be-Hereafter presented the problem to Black Kettle. When no one was found in the village able to nurse him, Black Kettle sent Towering Pine on a raiding mission, and the warrior returned leading a stolen she-goat."

Panther took pleasure in relating the tale to her. "Towering Pine nearly got his rear branches shot off in the process, but he returned unharmed and triumphant."

Tanya chuckled appreciatively. "But, Panther, a goat!"

"Black Kettle thought it was time we had one around to add distinction to the village." He gave her a broad wink. "And don't you dare tell him otherwise."

Tanya gave him a conspiratorial grin. "I wouldn't dream of it."

March brought with it the advent of spring, and several things happening at once. Shy Deer gave birth to a son, and Winter Bear was proud as a peacock. Hunter had his first birthday, and now sported twelve gleaming teeth. Tanya, at age eighteen, found herself expecting Panther's second child. She had been with the tribe for almost two years now, and Panther's wife for a year and a half. It seemed sometimes that she'd always been here, a part of this life; and her first sixteen years seemed a half-forgotten dream.

As soon as travel became possible, the tribe moved

to a place on Crooked Creek for the Sun Dance ceremonies. This year, Tanya was not an outsider any longer. She renewed aquaintances with the children she had met two years previously, and now their mothers were receptive to her. Tanya now had her place in the tribe and a voice in the proceedings, and she enjoyed the responsibilities as well as the comraderie.

It was while the tribes were all gathered for the ceremonies that Rosemary was sold. Actually her master traded her off for a horse. When the tribes split up for the summer hunt, Rosemary went another direction with her new master and tribe.

Of the five girls who had been captured together two years previously Rosemary was the first to leave Black Kettle's tribe. Tanya and Melissa were saddened to see her go, wondering if they would ever see her again. They hoped she would be treated decently.

Of the four remaining women, Tanya and Melissa were faring the best now, but all had accepted their fates, and after two years, even Suellen had given up hope of rescue. Suellen had not crossed swords with Tanya since her beating, though her eyes told Tanya she'd made an enemy for life. Nancy, though treated fairly well, now was pregnant, her baby due in the winter.

As summer approached, Black Kettle's tribe moved south and hunted along the Cimarron and Beaver Rivers, following the buffalo herds through the northern Oklahoma and Texas territories. Peace was tentative at best, for the Northern Cheyenne and Dog Soldiers were once again stirring up trouble with the whites, and vice-versa. War was imminent, and it didn't matter who struck first, white or Indian. The only trouble was, most whites could not tell one Indian from another, and often a perfectly innocent tribe was attributed deeds done by another. After being accused of several attacks they'd had nothing to do with, some Southern Cheyenne entered the conflicts. Even Black Kettle, with all his influence and peaceful intentions, could not prevent Panther and Winter Bear from taking their warriors on a few, scattered raids that season.

Over all, the summer was fairly peaceful. The warriors had a few skirmishes and successful raids, but spent most of their time hunting. War with the whites did not break out full-scale, but the tensions were definitely felt on both sides. Things were gradually building to a head, and Tanya could only pray winter would set in to stop it before things went that far.

Tanya detested having to go through the major part of her last months of pregnancy in the summer. The heat, the stench of the hides and meat, the hard physical labor, and the constant moving about from place to place, were sapping her energy. By the end of September she felt huge. She was an oddity in the village as it was, for most Cheyenne women did not get pregnant so quickly, so often. Perhaps it was something to do with their diets, or the fact that most of them nursed their children longer; but the average Cheyenne woman had two, perhaps three children at most, and there was usually four years or more between their ages. This made Tanya feel like the local fertility symbol. It also made Panther appear extremely virile, which bolstered his ego to no end.

Toward fall, the tribe wandered back into the area where the women had planted their crops. After the harvest and hunting festivities were over, they headed for a new site for the winter. This year, Black Kettle chose a sight some forty miles south of the Antelope Hills on the Washita River.

For five days they had been traveling to reach this area, and Tanya had been feeling worse with each passing day. Now, on the fifth day, she was feeling more terrible with each mile. Since early morning her back had ached abominably, and the horse jarred her spine with each step. Now the pain was spreading around to her stomach, which felt rock-hard and ready to explode. A wave of nausea and dizziness nearly toppled her from her horse and sweat broke out on her forehead. She wished she could lie down, but with her stomach in her way, she could not even lean forward on the mare.

"How much further is it, Missy?" she gasped.

Melissa, who had been eyeing Tanya curiously for the last few miles, answered, "I don't know, Wildcat. Should I ask Panther?"

Tanya bit her lip, "Better yet, bring him to me." She and Melissa had been riding further back behind the warriors.

Within minutes Melissa returned with Panther. One look at her pale, strained face, and he knew. "Your time has come."

Tanya nodded. "Is it far yet?"

"Just a few more miles. Can you make it?"

Tanya laughed ruefully. "I don't know. Is it possible to have a baby on horseback? It is a bit awkward to give birth while sitting on the child's head."

Panther pulled her mare to a halt and reached for Tanya. "Come," he said. "You will ride with me the rest of the way. I will hold you before me in my arms, and you will be able to relax and be more comfortable."

Tanya rode the rest of the way cradled in Panther's arms. After what seemed a century, her pains now coming hard and fast, he said, "We are nearly there. Soon you will be able to lie down."

Tanya tried to joke between clenched teeth. "They'd better get the birthing tent up fast, or I'll have this baby in the open. I'm making a terrible habit of avoiding that birthing lodge, aren't I?"

Panther chuckled, "I wonder if you planned it this way."

The first tipi to go up was the birthing lodge, and Tanya was hustled inside. "This won't take long Panther," she called to him. "Have Melissa keep my meal warm."

Ten minutes later, Tanya delivered a perfectly healthy, howling baby boy. Panther had a second son. Within two hours, displaying a stubborness beyond measure, she carried her newborn son to her own lodge.

To a stunned Panther, she explained, "Root Woman said if I was strong enough to walk through camp to our own tipi, she would let me come home and not keep me in that stupid lodge."

"You are a stubborn woman, Wildcat," he told her, his black eyes glowing, "and I love you for it. Welcome home."

That evening, Black Kettle and Woman-To-Be-Hereafter came to see their new grandson. "My family has grown at an alarming rate since I adopted you, Wildcat," Black Kettle teased her.

Taking the baby in his arms, he unfolded the blanket to view the child. "What is this?" he said, fingering a small red mark on the baby's thigh.

"It is a birthmark," Tanya explained.

"Look here." Black Kettle held the small thigh so all

could see it. "It is in the shape of a bow and arrow. It is the mark of the archer," he suggested.

Panther agreed. "Yes, Uncle. It is plainly a bow drawn with an arrow nocked and ready. As you said, the mark of the archer."

"That is what you should call the child," Black Kettle decided. "His name should be Mark-of-the-Archer."

Hunter-of-the-Forest didn't know quite what to make of his new brother. He certainly took up much of his mother's time and attention. Because of this, Panther took extra pains to pay special attention to Hunter at this time in his young life.

When they had been camped there about two weeks, word came from Fort Larned that the U.S. government, and General Sheridan in particular, had declared war on the Cheyenne and Arapahoe tribes because of all the trouble they had encountered over the summer. These tribes were considered trouble-makers, and the government was out to teach them a lesson. Cavalry troops were on the look-out for them, and any and all rebellious Indians were to be dealt with severely. All previous peace treaties were considered null and void, and if the tribes wished to keep any of their lands at all or receive any government aid, they were to turn themselves over to the U.S. Army and swear oaths of allegiance at once. Any tribe failing to do so would be considered an enemy of the United States.

Black Kettle, upon hearing this, prepared at once to go to the nearest fort and get matters straightened out. His tribe had caused relatively little trouble, and Black Kettle had always been noted for his willingness to maintain peace between his people and the white men. Taking several of his warriors with him, he headed for Fort Cobb, the closest fort to his camp.

Once there, he tried to obtain an agreement of peace for his tribe, but General Hagen, having no word or authorization from his superiors about this, refused to negotiate. He turned Black Kettle away, teling him to return to his people on the Washita and await word there.

Black Kettle returned to camp in the late afternoon to tell his tribe of this discouraging development. Several of his chiefs were uneasy that the army knew the location of their camp, and wanted to move to a new location immediately. Black Kettle refused, saying he had given his word to the army, and he would keep it. A conference was held, and Panther, Winter Bear, and a few other warriors were sent to three other villages further downriver to advise their leaders of the result of Black Kettle's trip and get their opinions on what should be done. They left that evening, though a fierce blizzard had already hit, traveling through deep, blowing snow to reach the other camps. As Black Kettle's encampment was bordered across the river one way by a steep bluff, the couriers had to cross the freezing river twice because of its twists and curves to reach the neighboring villages some ten miles down stream. It took some time to get there, and as it was quite late when they had relayed the messages, they decided to wait and return to Black Kettle's camp the next day.

Tanya was up early the next morning, breastfeeding Mark-of-the-Archer. It was a still, grey dawn typical of winter. The smoke hung heavy and low over the tops of the tipis. Melissa and Hunter slept peacefully beneath their piles of fur. The only sound was the occasional bark of a camp dog. The snow was deep and Tanya wondered how soon Panther would return.

There was no warning before the attack. One minute it was so still Tanya could hear Mark's soft breathing. The next, the air was filled with the sounds of gunfire, whistling bullets, the jangle of metal harnesses and swords, and the screams of the wounded. Shoving Mark roughly aside, Tanya jerked open the tent flap. Everywhere, she saw a sea of blue army uniforms.

Tanya's heart sank as she realized what was happening, and her brain screamed over and over again, "No! No! No! No! No!"

Chapter 12

FOR TIMELESS seconds, Tanya sat motionless, her mind unable to accept what her eyes were seeing. Cheyenne were dashing from their tipis in various stages of dress, some trying to reach their horses, some seeking to escape the barrage of bullets flying into their lodges, others fleeing from already burning tents.

Melissa's terrified screams jerked Tanya back to life. She called Kat to her. "Go get Panther, Kat," she told him, ushering him out of the tipi. "Get Panther!" She watched as the cougar dashed out and quickly disappeared.

Staying as low as she could, Tanya crawled back to Mark and pulled Hunter from his bed. Grabbing the first clothes her hands touched, she dressed mechanically, shoving her knife into her belt and snatching up her bow and quiver. Little good they would do her, outnumbered as they were.

Her mind in a whirl, she ordered Melissa to keep the children quiet and again crept to the tipi entrance to peer out. In the few minutes she had taken, her world had turned into a living hell. In shocked disbelief she watched as soldiers fired upon men, women, and children alike. Racing their horses among the tipis, they trampled anyone in their path. Tanya's mind screamed out in horror as she saw a young child speared through the stomach and tossed into the air on the point of a bayonet. The old, feeble shaman stepped out of his tipi and was immediately trampled. The soldier hauled up on his reins and deliberately rode his horse back and forth over the bleeding body, as Tanya watched, unable to prevent any of it. Swiftly, she got off two arrows, but both fell short of her target.

Across the way, Tanya saw two cavalrymen racing side by side, each with an infant held at arms length. Her heart exploded in her chest as she saw the men fling the babies to the ground, laughing as their tiny skulls shattered like ripe melons.

Her startled gaze caught at the familiar figure of Forest Fern, now heavy with child. She watched in terror as a horseman dashed by, neatly slicing open Forest Fern's bulging stomach with his sword. She fell writhing to the ground, her unborn babe spilling from her stomach. Tanya gagged and turned away.

The gruesome spectacle was only one of many so horrible that Tanya's mind could not tabulate them all. Wave after wave of soldiers poured into the village, Cheyenne bodies were lying everywhere, unbelievably mutilated, some with no heads, others with stomachs ripped open, many with crushed bodies and skulls.

The noise beat at Tanya's ears, as the sights sickened and outraged her. Screams of wounded and dying friends; incessant gunfire; yelling, laughing soldiers; horses; bridles; the clank of swords and bayonets. The attack had come so suddenly. Most Cheyenne had been sleeping; none were prepared.

Some of the warriors, such as Panther and Winter Bear, were away at neighboring camps. More had not made it back from the latest hunt. As Tanya watched, unable to tear her eyes from the holocaust, she saw a handful of warriors making an escape of horseback. They would bring back help; if there was anyone left to rescue. Tanya did not blame the warriors for not staying to fight. By now they were vastly outnumbered, their fellow braves lying slaughtered throughout the camp. They would never willingly desert their people, but their only hope now came in recruiting help.

Hope flared as Tanya recognized Shy Deer and her infant escaping with the warriors. Perhaps there was still a chance she and her sons could do the same. She turned to call for Melissa and found the girl right behind her, gazing dumbfounded at the massacre taking place outside.

"God, Tanya!" Melissa whispered in awe. "I've never seen anything so horrid!"

Tears slipped silently down Tanya's cheeks. "And they call us savages!" she hissed, wanting desperately to vomit.

"Come, get the boys, and let's see if we can escape this madness. If Shy Deer got away, maybe we can too."

The words were no sooner out of her mouth than she heard shooting and shouts near Black Kettle's tipi. Watching, she saw Black Kettle and Woman-To-Be-Hereafter running toward the river, chased by several soldiers on horseback. They almost made it. Just as they stepped into the freezing water, Tanya saw their bodies jerk almost simultaneously, and they fell face-first into the water. Riders trampled their bodies, and after several minutes, Tanya knew they were dead. Turning her head, she saw George Bent standing at gunpoint, gazing stunned at the bloody body of Blue Horse at his feet.

"We'll never make it out of here," Melissa predicted.

"I'm going to try," Tanya told her, fighting a wave of nausea.

"Look!" Melissa cried excitedly. Tanya followed where the girl pointed. At a place near the edge of the melee, Nancy and Suellen stood, flanked by several soldiers. Suellen shook her head, and then Nancy pointed directly to Tanya's tipi.

"Oh, damn!" It was the first English word Melissa had heard Tanya utter in nearly two years.

Melissa was torn between loyalty toward Tanya and a desperate desire for freedom. "What are we going to do?" she asked.

"You do whatever you have to, Missy. This is your chance for rescue. I am going to see that no harm comes to my children . . . or die trying." Tanya gathered her baby to her breast and Hunter tightly against her side. Solemnly she drew her knife and held it ready before her.

Tense seconds ticked by before the lodge flap was jerked aside. Two blood-splattered soldiers burst into the tipi, their swords drawn. Looking about they saw only the two white women and the children and lowered their weapons.

"You girls can come out now. Your friends told us we'd find two more white captives in here. You're lucky she said something before we set fire to the tent."

Tanya didn't move a muscle. She just stood glaring at the men.

One man stepped toward her, his blood-stained hand held out. Kit, who had been silently guarding Tanya, rose to her feet, snarling, her tail lashing.

"Holy shit!" the man cursed as he jumped back. "I

thought it was a damned rug! Call that cat off, lady."

Tanya spoke tersely in Cheyenne and Melissa interpreted, "She said, come any closer and she'll tell the cat to kill you."

The soldiers gaped at Tanya in amazement. "Now wait a minute here. We're here to help you. Don't you understand?"

Another soldier entered the tipi. "What's going on in here, soldier?" he demanded to know. "You were told to collect any prisoners from the tents."

"This one won't leave." The first soldier pointed to Tanya.

The officer turned toward Tanya for the first time. Shock registered on his handsome fair features. "My God! Tanya!" He started toward her, and again Kit snarled. He stopped, unsure of what to do as Tanya stared holes through him.

"You know this woman, lieutenant?" The lieutenant nodded.

"Then maybe you can get her to call off that cat. This other girl says she'll sic him on anyone who comes near."

The lieutenant's gaze shifted to Melissa. "Who are you?"

Melissa bristled at his sharp tone. "I think a better question is, who are you and how do you know Tanya?"

"I'm Lt. Jeffrey Young. I'm Tanya's fiancé."

"I'm Melissa Anderson. I'm her friend."

Tanya spoke for the first time since Jeffrey had entered the tipi. "Tell them to leave, they defile my home," she instructed in Cheyenne.

"She wants you to leave."

Jeffrey was stunned. "What have they done to her?" he whispered, his gaze swivelling from Tanya to

Melissa and back. "Doesn't she recognize me? Tell her to speak English."

Tanya snarled out a guttural reply, and Melissa shifted uncomfortably.

"What did she say?" Jeffrey demanded.

Melissa turned red. "I believe its English equivalent would be 'go to hell.' "

"This is ridiculous." Jeffrey combed his fingers through his blond hair, confused. "Doesn't she realize we're here to rescue her?"

Melissa had started to shake in reaction to the morning's events, but she formed an answer of her own. "Perhaps she doesn't want to be rescued. Maybe she is sickened by your tactics, just as I am. We watched you ride through the village, murdering defenseless women, ripping people apart with your bayonets, smashing babies like toy dolls, splattering guts and brains and blood everywhere!" Her voice rose as her hysteria mounted. "You didn't even know we would be here when you attacked the village. It's pure luck your bullets didn't kill us as they crashed through the tipi. If Tanya hadn't instructed me to stay down and protect the children, I could be dead right now." Melissa choked on her tears and was unable to say more.

It was as if this was the first Jeffrey had been aware of the children. He stared as if they were lepers. "Tell her to give them to Hanes and Billhart. They'll take care of them."

Tanya's eyes shot golden flames as she raised her knife to her chest.

"She'll kill herself before she lets you harm her sons," Melissa warned.

His face white, Jeffrey looked as if he'd been shot in the stomach. "What did you say?" he choked out.

"She'll kill herself and her sons before she'll give them up to you," she repeated. "And I'll help her. We've seen what fine care you give to children!"

"What a bloody mess!" one of the soldier's muttered. "Just shoot the damned cat, grab the brats, and let's get going!" The man drew his pistol.

Jeffrey stared at Tanya. Finally he spoke. "Melissa, explain to her if you can that she must come with us. The corporal will shoot the cat if he has to. There is no need for her to harm herself. If she wants to bring the children," he could not bring himself to admit aloud they were her sons, "she can. No one will take them from her."

To Tanya he said, "There are too many of us for you to fight, Tanya. Can you understand me? I don't know what you've been through to make you this way, but it must have been terrible for you. No one will hurt you. You're safe now. We'll get you back to your family in Pueblo, and things will be better, I promise. They are waiting for you, Tanya. None of us gave up hoping we would find you." His words were soft and hurt, meant to reach her through her shock.

Tanya sighed tiredly. He was right about one thing. There were too many of them for her to fight, and above all else, Panther must find all alive and healthy when he came for them. That Panther would come for them, she had no doubt. "Tell him I will come, but first I must pack a few things for the journey." Tanya refused to speak English.

Melissa related the message, and everyone visibly relaxed.

"We'll wait outside. You have five minutes." The men left.

Tanya packed a leather bag with clothes for herself and the boys. She strapped Mark-of-the-Archer into his cradleboard and bundled him and Hunter into thick furs against the cold. For herself she took the necklace and armbands Black Kettle and Woman-To-Be-Hereafter had given her at her adoption, and the cougar-claw necklaces, both hers and Panthers. She knew the tipi would be fired and everything she wanted must be taken now. Her wristbands she always wore, but she packed the headbands Panther and Shy Deer had made her and her panther-fur purse. In addition, she packed a change of clothes for Panther, and his favorite headbands, thinking he would want them when he rescued her. His weapons and cougar coat he already had with him. Her own hooded wrap she took down from its peg.

Tanya's heart was breaking and her eyes glistened with tears as she looked about her at the tipi that had been her home for two and a half years. There were the hides she'd worked on this past summer, and the furs and the pouches of food. There was the cradle Panther had labored over so lovingly, and the pallet where they had shared so many passionate nights. She had learned to love Panther here in this tipi. It was here Panther had made her a woman, here she had conceived her sons, here she had given birth to Hunter. With one long, last look, she turned her back and followed Melissa outside.

Heads swiveled and stayed to watch as Tanya walked through the village, with Mark in his cradleboard on her back, Hunter on her hip, and Kit at her side. Head held high, she followed Jeffrey through the destruction, stubbornly hiding her revulsion at the sights she passed. Her anger she didn't bother to hide, though it too, showed only in her flashing eyes and flared nostrils.

Jeffrey found a place for her and Missy away from

the others, and posted a guard over them.

"Is he supposed to protect us or prevent us from sneaking away?" Tanya asked snidely, with a sidelong glance at the guard.

Melissa shook her head wearily. "I don't know, Tanya. Both, perhaps."

The soldiers were looting the tipis before burning them. The Indians' simplified way of life lent little of monetary value other than some items of jewelry, but each soldier wanted at least one memento of their victory. Some were satisfied to find handsomely decorated clothing to take home. Tanya wanted to scream out in protest as she saw one sergeant proudly displaying Shy Deer's wedding dress.

Her dismay and anger found new, more warranted fuel soon enough. To her horror, and Missy's, she watched in shock as the crazed, blood-lusting men cut the breasts from the bodies of dead Cheyenne women and the privates from the men. Laughing and waving them about, they told how they would have purses and tobacco pouches made of them.

Melissa turned away and vomited, crying out hysterically, "Oh God, make it stop! Make it stop!"

Tanya envied Melissa the release of emotions. She too, wished she could rant and rave with anger and grief, but at the moment it seemed her body was frozen of all ability to move and feel. Each time she blinked, she thought her body would shatter into sharp, bleeding bits. The muscles of her face were taut as bowstrings and her jaw was clenched so tight her teeth ached.

Part of Tanya's mind seemed to be functioning apart from her body. She saw and understood all that was going on around her. It was as if her mind were painting sharp, detailed portraits of each heinous act her eye beheld. Even as she was revolted by all of it, a safety valve in her brain kept a constant message ticking in her head. "This is a dream! None of this is real! It can't be! I'll go crazy if I know it's real."

Even the sudden appearance of Jeffrey seemed unreal. While once she had prayed for him to rescue her, now all she wanted was for him to go away and take all the other men with him. Any tender feelings she had held for him dissolved in the wake of this monstrous massacre. Vaguely she wondered how many of her friends he had killed. He had come, with others, to murder and pillage and turn her world into a nightmare. She hated him at this moment, and knew she would never forget his participation in this murderous act and never forgive him for parting her from Panther.

Every minute seemed to last a lifetime. Finished with the looting now, the men started throwing everything else they could find into a huge pile in the center of the demolished village. Tipis, furs, hides, food, cooking utensils, clothes, even some bodies were thrown together. Tanya watched silently as the cradle Panther had made was thrown carelessly into the heap.

When there was nothing left to add, the men set fire to it. The flames shot high into the sky, and black smoke darkened the morning sky.

"It's not even midday yet," Tanya muttered inanely. "The world has gone completely crazy in the space of a few hours."

"Yes," Melissa agreed incredulously, "and we're the only ones who know it."

As cold, wet, and snowy as it was outdoors, the heat

of the huge bonfire made it seem like summer. The stench emitted from it was overpowering. Dark clouds of smoke billowed endlessly upward.

It was soon after the fire had been lit that Tanya became aware of a new tension in the air. Several of the men were gesturing excitedly toward the top of the bluff that rose to one side of the encampment. Curious, Tanya rose and walked to where she could see. The guard followed closely, and Tanya clutched her children protectively to her. Kit and Melissa closed rank.

The sight that met her eyes set her heart beating wildly in her chest. Panther!!

There, high atop the cliff, sat a line of mounted warriors. Tanya's sharp eyes picked out Snail, Towering Pine and Winter Bear; but lingered on Panther. Astride his big black stallion, he created an imposing figure, even at this distance.

An intense longing stabbed through her, and Tanya wanted desperately to be able to run to him, however impossible it was to scale the steep cliff. She knew immediately when he had spotted her, though it was impossible from this far to see his features. Holding Mark in her arms, she stationed Hunter in front of her. She wanted Panther to know his sons were alive.

All her movements were deliberate, but deceptively innocent to anyone else watching her. Slowly she eased the hood from her hair and displayed her tawny braids and the headband that circled her head. Crossing her arms over her chest, she touched the wristbands that symbolized her marriage.

Panther, watching from above, spotted Tanya almost immediately. Inwardly, he heaved a silent sigh of relief. All the way from the next village, he had nursed the impossible hope she had survived.

Kat had come bursting into the camp as he and Winter Bear had prepared to leave. The agitated cougar had howled and screamed as Panther had never seen him do before. A chill of disaster danced down his spine; he had followed the cat toward home.

They had met Shy Deer and the warriors halfway, and been told what was happening. Still, they had not been prepared to view such total destruction. It was immediately obvious that they were vastly outnumbered by the soldiers. Panther's eyes narrowed as he caught sight of their leading officer. Even from here he recognized the cocky stance of the yellow-haired General. He had met Gen. Custer at the treaty conferences at Pawnee Fork. He promised himself that someday he would see Custer pay for this massacre.

Panther saw Tanya rise and step forward. He felt her love reach out to him across the distance. Watching, he saw her shift the baby in her arms and place Hunter before her, and knew she was showing him they were well. Without a doubt, he knew she would see that they remained safe until he could rescue them. His heart swelled with pride as he watched her reveal her braids and headband and touch her wristbands. She was telling him she would wait faithfully for him to come to her. His heart heard her gestures as clearly as if she had spoken in his ear.

Solemnly, he returned the gesture, touching his own matching wristbands. To her he was saying, "You are my wife. I will come for you."

Tanya saw Panther touch his wristbands as she had hers, and felt comforted. It was his promise to come for her, and it gave her new strength. Her stubborn jaw tilted out just a bit more as her head came proudly erect. Her spine stiffened and her eyes blazed with newfound courage. It was as if Panther were lending her his strength once again, as he had done the night of her branding. She had made him proud of her that night, and she would not fail him now. She was Cheyenne, and she would not whine and cry before the whites. She was a chief's wife and she would behave as one. She was Little Wildcat, Panther's woman, and they would not break her spirit so easily.

Fired by a new determination, Tanya spun about on her heel and strode through the ruins of the village. Leading Hunter by the hand, she pointed out the atrocities to the toddler, explaining in simple terms what had happened here. The youngster's eyes were huge golden orbs in his solemn face as he listened to his mother's softly spoken words. His small hand trembled in hers, but his steps did not falter. He seemed to understand when his mother told him he must be brave and make his father proud.

Along the way, they came across Ugly Otter's mutilated body. A quiet look of satisfaction passed between Tanya and Melissa. They had already noted that Ugly Otter's wife was among the captives being held by the soldiers. Of all the deaths, Ugly Otter's was the only one Tanya could not bring herself to regret.

At the river's edge, Tanya stopped beside the bodies of Black Kettle and Woman-To-Be-Hereafter. Here she turned and sought out Panther's figure on the bluff.

The warriors were now taunting the soldiers below them, shouting insults and making crude gestures. Tanya recognized it as a ploy to lure some of them up to the bluff, hopefully in numbers the Cheyenne could easily deal with.

When Tanya was sure she had Panther's attention, she drew her knife. Before anyone could stop her, she whacked off her long tawny braids, placing one on each of the bodies of her parents and securing them in their headbands.

Tanya's guard stepped forward to stop her, but Kit snarled a warning at him and he stayed back.

From each of her children, Tanya cut a small lock of hair and added it to hers on the bodies of their grandparents, quietly explaining to Hunter as she did so. In this manner, she told Panther of Black Kettle's death. Then, much to her guard's surprise, she pulled up her sleeves and made long, shallow gashes along each of her forearms, letting her blood fall to mix with that of her parents.

As she reached for Hunter's arm, the man started forward again, with an exclamation. This time Melissa stopped him, a hand on his arm. "Let her be." she told him firmly.

Tanya ignored them both. With her knife, she barely scratched Hunter's arms with the point; just enough to make them bleed, and did the same with Mark. Hunter flinched once, and the baby's face puckered, but neither cried.

Softly, Tanya began the chant for the dead. From a short distance behind her, where the Cheyenne captives had been gathered, she heard more voices add their songs of grief to hers.

"What the hell is going on here?" From the corner of her eye, Tanya saw Jeffrey and the lanky blond general approaching with long strides. The general's face was a mask of fury, and Jeffrey didn't look at all pleased himself. Ignoring them, Tanya went on with the ritual.

"Tell that woman to stop her caterwauling!" the general commanded. "Her wails could wake the dead!"

Melissa drew her petite form to its full height and

stepped in front of him. "That's the obvious idea," she stated firmly, her hands on her hips. "It's a sort of funeral dirge to usher the dead on the proper road to heaven. You have slaughtered nearly the entire population of this village and killed this woman's parents. Now you want to restrict her grief and prevent her from performing traditional ceremonies." Melissa jabbed one slim finger directly into the general's chest and her voice rose. "I'm here to tell you to let her be! Enough is enough!"

Shock registered on the general's face at Melissa's outrage, and his eyes nearly popped. "Here now, little lady!" he blustered. "Who are you to be giving orders to me?"

Melissa stood her ground. "I'm her friend, and I'm not one of your flunky soldiers, so don't try giving orders to me!" she shouted back.

The general's face mottled red. With a long look at Tanya, who was carrying on as if no one was near, he argued, "You can't tell me these two were her parents, girl. I'm not blind! This woman is as white as I am."

"I wouldn't bet my life on that!" Melissa muttered under her breath.

Jeffrey took this opportunity to speak up. "I know this woman, General Custer. Both her parents are waiting for her back in Pueblo. Her name is Tanya Martin, and she and four other ladies were captured two and a half years ago near Fort Lyon. Lord only knows what they had to endure, but Tanya is not herself now."

Custer glared at this young lieutenant. "Whose children are these?" he demanded.

Jeffrey nearly choked on his words. "I've been told they're hers," he answered.

"Is this true?" General Custer directed his question to Melissa.

Melissa met his look defiantly, "Yes, they're hers."

"Some young buck took a shine to her, I gather," Custer sneered.

"Correction," Melissa countered, staring holes into him. "Some young chief took her for his wife, and these two wonderful people adopted her as their daughter." Melissa gestured to Black Kettle and his wife.

Custer looked down his nose at her. "You seem to think highly of these red devils," he challenged.

"Not all of them," Melissa corrected, remembering Ugly Otter and his wife, "but in all the time I've been a captive here, I've never seen them perform such atrocities as you and your men have here today. Tanya was right when she said you were more a savage than any Cheyenne. Civilization doesn't come with fine china and woven clothes, but from a decent, moral heart."

Finished now with her ceremony, Tanya turned to face the general. Her golden eyes full of scorn, she let her gaze travel over him from head to toe, not bothering to cover her distaste for what she saw. Deliberately, she spat upon his boots, and with her head held high, brushed past him, exaggerating her care not to touch his contaminated body. Kit brought up the rear guard, her tail lashing, her obvious disdain matching that of her mistress.

"Son of a bitch!" Custer swore angrily.

Jeffrey, now embarrassed to the extreme, intervened. "Sir, please try to understand what they must have gone through. These savages must have brainwashed them. Somehow. Tanya was such a sweet young thing before. I can't believe the change in her! Once she is safely back in the loving care of her family, I'm sure she'll come out of this." His face registered some of the doubt. "At least I hope so."

"All right, Lieutenant, you've made your point," Custer conceded gruffly. "Just keep those two hellcats out of my hair until I can get them off my hands for good. I don't take kindly to being spit on."

He strode off again, barely hearing Jeffrey's relieved. "Yes, sir."

General Custer had worse problems than Tanya to deal with just now. The warriors were still raising hell on the cliff, and now that idiot Major Elliot and seventeen men under his command had gone chasing after a handful of women and children who were trying to reach the braves. These few Cheyenne had hidden around a bend in the river and were now making their way slowly but gradually through the icy water and around the steep banks to where the warriors were. Several Cheyenne braves had been sent to meet them, and Major Elliot had decided to cut them off.

"Shall we send some men after them, General?" another major asked. "They may be walking into a trap."

"It's their own damn fault if they do." Custer snapped. "I didn't ask the fool to go chasing up there like some hero. I want to get organized and well out of here before nightfall. We can't afford to let our supply train come blustering into the area. We've got to meet them far enough away from here that those redskins don't have any idea of its existence. They'd just love to find that scarcely defended supply train and make off with all our food and ammunition.

Tanya and the others watched as three of the braves

reached the small party of women and children, hauling them up out of the icy water and onto the rocks. It was hard to tell from this distance, but one of the women resembled Walks-Like-A-Duck, and another looked like Magpie carrying her youngest son. Tanya had not come across any bodies she'd thought to be either woman, and she hoped they would both reach safety. Their rescuers were helping them up the steep inclines to higher ground now, and soon they disappeared from sight behind rocks.

A few minutes later, distant gunfire could be heard from beyond that area. A quick review of the cliff told Tanya that Panther was not there. Winter Bear was still in sight, but Panther, Towering Pine, and several others were gone. It was Tanya's guess they had gone to engage Major Elliot's troop in combat.

For several minutes the gunfire sounded, and then all was ominously silent. Tanya watched and waited apprehensively, but Panther and his braves did not reappear on the bluff. After a while Winter Bear and the others left also. Major Elliot never did return, nor did any of his seventeen men.

Tanya settled herself and tended to her sons. A young soldier brought them food. As much as Tanya wanted to throw it in his face, she realized she needed to keep up her strength; to keep her milk flowing for Mark.

Melissa fed Hunter while Tanya breastfed the baby. Jeffrey stopped to check on them, and Tanya noted the revulsion on his face as he saw the child at her breast. She stared hard at him, silently daring him to comment, and he walked off without a word.

Tanya ate what she could and gave the rest to Kit, who would not leave her side to hunt for herself.

Tanya watched with murder in her heart as the only

remaining tipi was dismantled and carried off. General Custer had commandeered Chief Black Kettle's tipi as a personal memento of his victory. He caught Tanya's hate-filled look and seemed to gloat.

In turn, she gave him a look that promised to even the score someday. Her look said, "I am patient; I can wait. My revenge will come someday, and I will see you pay for all of this."

Perhaps he had felt a bit intimidated by her, for later, when he ordered all the Indian ponies shot, he let her pick Wheat out of the herd first. Tanya didn't bother to thank him for letting her have her own horse. For two hours she simmered as Custer's troops systematically destroyed each of the Cheyenne's painstakingly-trained mounts. Hate built its hard shell securely about her heart, and only Panther's return would break through it.

Chaper 13

IT WAS late afternoon when the troops moved out. Major Elliot and his men still had not returned, and no one had been sent to find out what had happened to them. In all, if Elliot and his men were dead, twenty-two soldiers had been killed. A quick tabulation accounted for one hundred and three Cheyenne dead; sixty of these were warriors, the rest women and children. Fifty-three prisoners, mostly women and children and a few elderly Cheyenne men, were taken along on the trip back. This was in addition to the four white women and Tanya's sons. Black Kettle's white slave had been killed in the onslaught; shot in the head by one of her would-be rescuers. Little was said of this of course, as none of the soldiers wished to claim responsibility for her death, accidental though it may have been.

The return trip to Camp Supply was made in four days of hard, forced marching. The terrain was rough as it was, and made nearly impassable by bitter winds, icy temperatures and deep drifts of snow. They met up with the supply train about twelve miles out, and camped a couple of miles further on.

Here Tanya was forced to keep company with Nancy and Suellen in a small tent set up for the four women. Her horse was taken from her, and without it she could not hope to make it back to the Washita with two small boys.

Nancy, seven months into her pregnancy was feeling rotten, but Suellen was back to her natural bitchy self. When she found out that Jeffrey was Tanya's former fiancé, she was incredulous, and commented acidly, "Well, I do declare! Some people can fall face first into a pile of horse manure and come out smelling like a rose! You always seem to land feet first. How do you do it?" she asked snidely.

Tanya smiled and said something in Cheyenne that made Melissa blush and Suellen shriek in anger. Only Kit's low growl kept the redhead from leaping on Tanya.

"If it weren't for that damned cat, I'd scratch your eyes out!"

Tanya replied calmly, "I can always send Kit outside."

Backing down from the challenge, Suellen answered huffily. "Never mind. Why should I lower myself to your level?"

They ate their supper around the campfire for warmth and Tanya was reminded vividly of her first night with Panther. Once again she sat watching as her friends were raped repeatedly, only this time it was Cheyenne women being violated by white men.

Even Melissa flinched at the abuse she witnessed now. "I don't know why I should bother feeling sorry for Ugly Otter's wife, but I do. She was mistreated by Ugly Otter, and now she must endure this as well. I expected to sympathize with some of the others, but not her."

About this time, Suellen sidled up. "Poetic justice, don't you think?" she commented on what was happening.

"What a small mind you have, Suellen," Tanya told her. "You're about three bricks shy of a full load if you can take any pleasure in this."

Jeffrey came up just in time to hear Suellen reply cuttingly, "You deserve to be right along side of them! From the very first you were treated differently from the rest of us. While we ran around dirty and ragged and half-beaten to death, you were clean and clothed and pampered like a princess. I've always wondered why. What did you do for that bronze buck that caused him to treat you so well?" Her voice rose to a strident level. "What special favors did you give him? You must have done something right, or was it just that you enjoyed having him between your legs? Was that the difference?"

Jeffrey's face was white and pinched, a muscle jumping wildly along his jawline as he awaited Tanya's reply.

Her eyes narrow golden slits, nevertheless, she spoke softly, "Your jealousy is showing, Suellen, and green is a very uncomplimentary color on you. It gives your face a ghastly hue."

"What did she say?" Jeffrey asked.

He was ignored as Melissa jumped into the argument. "Tanya is right, Suellen. You are jealous, pure and simple! None of us asked to be kidnapped that day. Of us all, Tanya had the most to lose, except poor Rosemary. Just because Tanya was luckier than we were; just because Panther was more handsome and kind, doesn't give you license to malign her. It wasn't her fault I got stuck with Ugly Otter or you with who you did. She couldn't help any of it."

Suellen laughed hatefully, "Oh, really? Well, how is it she got Black Kettle to adopt her and make her a member of the tribe? Why did Panther marry her? She ran around like royalty while the rest of us were treated like slaves!"

"You hateful bitch!" Melissa spat. "Maybe it's because Tanya worked twice as hard as any of us to learn the language and their ways. What riles you is that Tanya saw a way to improve her lot, and she took it. It's called survival, Suellen. Sometimes, in order to survive, you adjust, and Tanya did just that!" Melissa came up for breath, and then delivered the final insult. "Which bothers you most, Suellen, the fact that Tanya took the chance to improve her position, or that Panther chose her over you?"

Suellen reacted violently, her hand reaching out to slap Melissa across the face.

Immediately Tanya drew her knife. "No, Tanya," Melissa shook her head and smiled triumphantly. "I think Suellen just proved my point. I'm satisfied."

At lunch the second day, Tanya had the opportunity to talk with her half-brother-in-law, George Bent. Perhaps because he was half-white, he was one of the few men taken prisoner instead of being killed. "I'm sorry about Blue Horse," she told him.

George nodded mutely.

"I thought I saw Magpie escape with your youngest son and Walks-Like-A-Duck." George's head came up and hope flared in his eyes. Tanya continued, "They were the last group that escaped downriver just before Major Elliot rode out. I'm almost sure it was her."

George shook his head despondently. "There was much shooting after that," he said.

"Yes," Tanya agreed, "but I think Panther was leading an ambush while the others were helped to safety. There is a good chance they made it. After all, Elliot and his men never returned."

Again George nodded. "You are right, Little Wildcat. There is hope."

"My hope is that Panther can rescue us soon. Lieutenant Young is determined to return me to my family in Pueblo."

"Panther will find you even there," he assured her.

"Let us make a pact," Tanya suggested. "If we are not rescued before we are separated, the first to escape and find the tribe will give word of the other. If I return first, I will tell Magpie what happens to you, if I know. If you make it back first, you must tell Panther where to look for me."

"It is agreed."

Suellen's continual sniping was wearing on Tanya's already frayed nerves. Added to her many griefs, Tanya was now worried about Nancy. The hard traveling was taking its toll on the girl. Tanya recalled how difficult it had been for her the day Mark had been born.

Custer was pushing them hard and Nancy was taking the brunt of it even though she was relegated to a more comfortable position in one of the supply wagons. Nancy was in much discomfort; her stomach as hard as a pumpkin, her back in constant pain. When nausea and stomach cramps added to her complaints, Tanya was sure Nancy was in terrible trouble.

Suellen was a thorn in Tanya's side, Nancy a constant worry, and Jeffrey a growing problem. Convinced by Melissa's arguments against Suellen's vindictive remarks, he felt sure Tanya had been coerced and threatened into accepting the Cheyenne way of life. It was unthinkable that she'd willingly chosen to become Panther's wife and impossible that she might have loved him. Jeffrey much preferred to believe she'd suffered Panther's attentions bravely and borne his children because they'd been forced upon her. He excused Tanya's fierce defense of her sons by attributing to her an overdeveloped motherly urge that was actually admirable under the circumstances he'd invented for her in his mind.

Jeffrey was at Tanya's side every possible moment. While he avoided her children like the plague, he was constantly pestering her. At first he merely chattered, telling her about Pueblo, relating how her parents and sister had moved in with her Aunt Elizabeth and Uncle George. He tried playing on her sympathies by relating how upset her mother and father had been and how they had cried and prayed for her safety, and missed her terribly. Next he attempted to soften her attitude toward him by telling her how devastated he'd been to hear the news; how he'd sworn to move heaven and earth to find her; how heartbroken and angry he'd been.

Tanya endured it all in icy silence, giving him only an occasional glance of disdain. To Melissa she said in Cheyenne, "I wish he would either be still or accompany his sad tale with woeful violin music."

When Jeffrey wanted an interpretation, Melissa said, "Your constant chatter is giving her a headache."

He'd go away for a short time, but in a little while he'd turn up again like a bad penny. He repeated over and over how everyone had missed her and never given up hoping she would be returned to them safely.

Soon his talk took a more amorous turn, and he pelted her with declarations of undying love. He praised her, calling her his brave little darling, until Tanya wanted to choke him. Always he extended his sympathies for the atrocities he was convinced she had endured and bravely hidden from everyone. His understanding attitude grated on Tanya's nerves, not so much because it was undeserved as because it rang false in her ears. Repeatedly he told her it didn't matter to him that Panther had been intimate with her; he was still willing to marry her.

"Condescending bastard!" Tanya muttered. "If he's so willing to forgive and forget, why does he look at Hunter and Mark with murder in his eyes?"

Melissa interpreted this as, "Go find a snowdrift and bury yourself in it, Jeffrey."

Once in a while, Jeffrey's understanding mask would crack, and his anger and frustration would slip through. "Damn it, Tanya," he would shout, "I know you understand every word I've spoken! Quit talking that gibberish and speak English! Stop ignoring me and staring at me as if you'd like nothing better than to slit my throat! And for God's sake, tell that cat to stop growling and licking its lips whenever I come near!"

Truthfully, Tanya's only enjoyment these days came from watching Jeffrey turn white each time Kit twitched a whisker.

Once his anger had cooled, he was right back, trying yet another tactic. "Speak to me, Tanya. You'd feel so much better if you'd let it all out. You need to tell someone who will understand. I'm your friend as well as your fiancé. I won't condemn you, darling, believe me. Get it off your chest. I've got broad shoulders. Cry, scream, do anything except keep it bottled up inside. I'll help you through it, love."

"Of course, Father Young, I'd forgotten confession is good for the soul. I'll bet you're just itching to hear all the gory details," she answered with a sneer in Cheyenne. "I wonder how you'd take it if I described all the passion in glorious, intimate terms. You'd probably have a stroke!"

Melissa rolled her eyes and said, "I don't believe she thinks you could stand up under the strain of hearing about it, Lieutenant."

The third night, Nancy started to bleed, and as Tanya was the only one of the four women who had had a child, she was called to nurse her. If she'd had her tray of herbs, Tanya might have been able to do something for her. All she could do was pack cool, wet clothes between her legs to try to slow the bleeding, and wipe her down in an effort to combat Nancy's rising fever.

By morning Nancy was weak from the loss of blood, and out of her head with the still-raging fever. Tanya traveled with her in the wagon, leaving Melissa to tend to Hunter and Mark. She prayed they would reach Camp Supply in time for the doctor there to save her.

They finally reached Camp Supply in mid-afternoon. General Custer made a big production of his arrival, playing the conquering hero to the hilt. He strutted and preened like a peacock, prancing about on his horse and attracting all the attention he could glean. He proudly displayed his ragged, frozen collection of prisoners, and collected unending praise for rescuing the four white women. (Nothing was said of the death of Black Kettle's prize slave, however.)

Custer took enough time out from his recounting of his glorious victory to get medical attention for Nancy, but help came too late. Two hours later, she died. The doctor confirmed what Tanya had already suspected. The attack, the horrors she'd witnessed, and the hurried pace of the journey back had caused Nancy to miscarry. Had it been that simple, she might have survived it, but there had been added complications.

The baby had been turned wrong, making it impossible for her womb to expel it. The baby had suffocated and Nancy had hemorrhaged. On the very doorstep of freedom, she'd bled to death.

For a solid week they remained at Camp Supply while Custer gathered his accolades. The remaining three women were housed in a larger, more comfortable tent, but a forty room mansion would not have been big enough to contain both Tanya and Suellen. Suellen's bickering and sniping was endless, though Tanya did her level best to ignore her. Finally, Tanya shut her up temporarily by threatening to sew her lips together while she slept. Melissa begged Tanya to do it, regardless.

General Custer was a side-show all on his own. He didn't need anyone else to sing his praises, as he did a fine job of it by himself. He was invariably expounding upon his own glories and expertise each time Tanya saw him. Without deliberately setting out to do so, Tanya became a supreme irritation to him. It seemed everytime he dared comment on rescuing the four young ladies from the clutches of those savages, Tanya would wander by. Just as he'd start to relate how grateful the poor girls were to be liberated from their beastly captors, Tanya would appear silently, and refute his statements with one long murderous stare, frustrating all his efforts to appear the gallant knight. He could cheerfully have throttled her, but that was nothing compared to what she contemplated doing to him if she ever found the chance.

Another area of conflict cropped up shortly after their arrival. It seemed General Custer had a couple of prized pet wolfhounds he doted on. He never traveled far without them, and they were waiting for him when he returned to Camp Supply.

The wolfhounds and Kit took an immediate dislike to one another, and Tanya had to agree with Kit's prejudices. The dogs were rambunctious, noisy, ill-trained, and highly nervous. They were constantly sniffing about Kit's heels, yapping and nipping and generally being a nuisance. Tanya had a hard time keeping Kit in line when they were about.

At long last she'd had enough. Through Melissa, she told Custer to call of his dogs if he cared for them at all. "The next time they come around pestering and taunting Kit, I'm going to turn her loose on them," she warned, "and there won't be enough left to stuff!"

Jeffrey redoubled his efforts to break through her shell, but Tanya presisted in her stubborn refusal to acknowledge him or speak English. It was with relief on her part that they started for Fort Lyon at week's end. Perhaps now his duties would occupy some of his time.

Tanya's main concern was Panther's failure to appear, but she reasoned that he could not attack a fort with so few warriors as he now had. She shelved her impatience and consoled herself with her sons.

The journey to Fort Lyon was slightly less hurried than their last. It was two weeks before the walls of the fort came into sight. No sooner were they inside, than Jeffrey consulted with General Custer. Not usually part of Custer's 7th cavalry, Jeffrey asked permission to return immediately to his post in Pueblo, using the excuse of returning Tanya to her parents in time for Christmas, now just four days away. Anxious to be rid of her, Custer readily agreed, and supplied a contingent of soldiers to accompany them, more to save himself the embarrassment of having the women re-captured again than out of any concern for them.

Since her parents had finally given up and gone on to their destination in California, Suellen had no reason to rush to Pueblo. She opted to spend Christmas at the fort and follow later at a more leisurely pace. There was no love lost on either side as the girls parted company.

As soon as supplies could be replenished, they were on their way again. Tanya took perverse delight in wiping the smirk from Custer's face by departing from him with a secretive smile and a smart salute. She left him with a perplexed frown on his face as he tried to deduce her intentions.

With luck and hard riding Tanya would be spending Christmas this year with her parents. She was starting to feel very apprehensive about it. Part of her anticipated the reunion with joy, and the other part dreaded it. After two and a half years, would they seem like strangers? Had they changed? Tanya had no doubt that she had changed drastically.

How would they react to Hunter and Mark? Tanya knew if they did not accept her sons, she would not want to stay an hour, let alone any length of time until Panther came.

Over the last years, Tanya had often longed to see her parents again. She'd even missed Julie, and all the sisterly fights they'd had. She wondered what they would expect of her. Would they, like Jeffrey, be morbidly curious about her life with the Cheyenne? Would they flood her with their pity and suffocate her with their love and protection? Could they accept her as she was now, or would they expect her to pick up her life where she'd left off, as if she'd never been gone? Would they be embarrassed by her? Above all, could they understand that, though she still loved them, her life was with Panther now; that given the choice, she'd return to him without hesitation?

Tanya pondered these thoughts and more. It had been years since she'd lived in a house, sat at a table or on a chair, ate with a fork, worn cloth dresses. It would seem foreign to her now.

Jeffrey had thrown a fit when he'd seen her eating her food with her fingers. "For God's sake, Tanya," he'd complained, "eat with your fork! You act like one of *them*, you dress like them, and you refuse to utter a word not in their stupid language! You're just being stubborn!"

Melissa, who'd readily reverted to eating with a fork and was looking forward to trading in her deerskin dress for cotton, commented, "Will you stop agitating the poor man, Tanya? He's developing a nervous twitch that's starting to drive me insane."

But Tanya was so firmly entrenched in her Cheyenne ways that she wondered if she could revert once again. Did she even care to try? If she had her way, she would be gone again soon. She much preferred her doeskin clothes now, and she silently vowed never to be laced into a corset again, not on the threat of death! Her moccasins were so comfortable that she cringed at the thought of crimping her feet into hot, tight shoes. Her cropped hair was one thing neither she nor they could do anything about. Melissa had evened it up, and now it curled gently about her head like a soft, tawny cap, barely touching her nape and her ears, feathery wisps framing her face.

While her mouth actually watered for her mother's cooking, a fork seemed as awkward now as chopsticks. She wondered how it would feel to sit on a chair and sleep on a soft bed instead of the ground. The bed would seem too high, she was sure—and empty without Panther next to her in the night.

Her longing for Panther was a physical ache. She longed to hold him, touch him, hear his deep, melodious voice. Her body yearned for his touch, his hard body over hers, his stroking hands arousing her passion, his dark eyes flashing with love and laughter.

Where was he now? How soon could he come for her? How long would it take for him to find her.

Tanya and Melissa had discussed what would happen to Melissa when they reached town. Melissa had never been very enthusiastic about going to California in the first place. Never having met her distant cousin, she was worried about what to expect when she arrived. Now she was doubly doubtful about their reactions to her after having spent the last two and a half years with Indians. Melissa was afraid they would look down upon her as soiled and perhaps treat her as badly as the Cheyenne had. To be a social outcast as well as a poor relation was unthinkable.

Tanya had offered her a home. The two girls had been through thick and thin together and Tanya needed Missy now as much as Melissa needed her. They would weather it out together, come what may. At Melissa's suggestion that perhaps Tanya's parents or her aunt and uncle, at whose home they would be staying, would object, Tanya was firm.

"They'll accept you and like it, or else," she promised. "I dare any of them to try to turn you out, Melissa. You'll always have a home with me, wherever I am. That I promise you."

Midway into their travels, they passed the spot where the wagon train had camped the day the girls had disappeared. Disregarding what the others might think, Tanya stopped her horse in her tracks, then veered Wheat down toward the river. At the exact place where they had bathed, she stopped.

Jeffrey had followed her, telling his men to wait. Melissa, obviously disturbed by bad memories of this place, stayed with the troops.

For long moments, Tanya sat staring into the water, remembering that spring afternoon when her life had changed so drastically. A smile hovered over her lips as she recalled that she had been discussing her upcoming marriage to Jeffrey, when Panther had suddenly swooped down on her and carried her off on his horse. It was almost as if Fate had stepped in to snatch her from Jeffrey's arms and place her in Panther's. Thank goodness it had, or she might never have experienced the one true, passionate love of her life.

Hunter shifted position in front of her on the mare, and Tanya smoothed his silky black hair. How precious he was! Tanya pointed to a spot in the river, directing the youngster's gaze.

"That is the exact spot where I first met your father," she told him softly. "I was bathing in the river when he rode up out of nowhere, and took me away with him on Shadow's back. I thought him very strong and proud and handsome, and he has said I reminded him of a golden-eyed cat, like Kit."

Hunter pointed to his own eyes, so identical to his mother's. "Yes," she agreed, smiling, "you have eyes like Kit, too."

Again she gazed at the river, and a feeling so strong came over her, that she could almost sense Panther's presence beside her, but looking about, she saw no one but Jeffrey.

With a sad sigh, she murmured to her sons, "We must pray to the spirits to guide your father to us soon."

Seeing the sadness on her face, and misunderstanding it, Jeffrey said softly, "Are the memories painful, Tanya?"

Wordlessly, she nodded, not caring if he misinterpreted. The memories of Panther were indeed painful, but not as Jeffrey thought. They were poignant, piercing her heart with an acute longing for Panther and their life together.

"Try not to think about them just now. Soon you will be home, and the memories will fade. We'll all help you if you let us."

Retracing her horse's steps, she contemplated Jeffrey's words. He and her family would probably do their best to make her forget, and if Panther could not come right away, she might fall prey to their sympathy and love, and grow used to the comforts of civilization again, if she were not careful. She knew she must guard against that happening. At all costs, she must not give up hope that Panther would find them, and if he took some time in doing so, she must keep his memory alive inside herself. She must help Hunter to remember his father, and tell even little Mark about him, though he could not understand a word. In doing so, she would hold Panther close to her heart and be comforted in his absence.

Chapter 14

THEY ARRIVED in Pueblo in the early afternoon of Christmas Day. Jeffrey dismissed his troops, and he and the women made their way directly to the Martin house. Wanting to surprise them, he had not sent word ahead.

The family was just sitting down to their Christmas dinner when the interruption came. The maid who answered the door didn't know quite what to think of the bedraggled group standing there with Jeffrey, but she invited him in and told him she would get Mr. Martin.

It was then Kit nudged her way through the door. The poor woman's eyes grew huge in her face, her mouth working desperately, but it was several seconds before any sound came out. When it finally did, her shrill shriek shook the rafters. She fainted dead away just as Tanya's Uncle George entered the hallway.

George Martin took one incredulous look that encompassed them all. He barely had time to ask "What in the world is going on here?" The words were not out of his mouth before he was joined by Tanya's father, whose reaction was much the same.

Zeroing in on Jeffrey, Edward Martin asked, "What on God's green earth is all this about?"

Jeffrey hesitated, then blurted, "Mr. Martin, I've brought your daughter home for Christmas."

By this time, the commotion had attracted the rest of the family. Sarah, Tanya's mother, was standing just behind her husband when Jeffrey made his blunt announcement. She'd been staring dumbfounded at the cougar until his words brought her head up in surprise. Her gaze switched to the fur-wrapped woman with her hand on the cougar's head.

A wisp of honey-colored hair peeking out of the hood, and large golden eyes were the only things to distinguish this woman from an Indian squaw. Across her sun-browned forehead was the strap that supported the bundle on her back, and she carried a raven-haired Indian child on her hip. Flanked by the big cat on one side and a smaller blond woman on the other, she stood silently, a remote, restrained figure.

"Oh, my God!" Sarah exclaimed faintly, clutching her husband's arm as all the color drained from her face.

"Tanya?" Edward still could not quite fathom the fact that this woman was his daughter.

Tanya did not respond, and for several seconds no one said a word.

"Ahem," Jeffrey cleared his throat. "Do you think we might continue this reunion someplace where the ladies might sit down? Tanya and Melissa have traveled a great distance in a short time so that we might arrive today, and Mrs. Martin looks about to faint."

Tanya's Aunt Elizabeth was the first to recover her wits. "Of course, let's go into the parlor. George, you take their wraps, and I'll see if I can revive Sally and get us some tea."

Uncle George eyed Kit warily. "Uh, why don't I let the lieutenant see to their coats. I'll stoke up the fireplace in the parlor." To Jeffrey he said, "Just toss their things across the banister for right now."

The atmosphere was no less strained in the parlor. Julie, who also had yet to utter a word, sat gawking at Tanya, Kit, and the children in turn.

Tanya stood uncertainly, gazing in awe at her aunt's lovely furnishings, unsure of whether to sit or stand. She was outwardly calm, but inside she was quivering with fear, uncertainty, and an intense desire to flee.

Treading softly, as if unwilling to shatter their long-held, fragile dream, Sarah patted the cushion next to herself on the divan. "Come, Tanya. Sit down next to me. Let me look at you."

Tanya crossed the room, and perched uncomfortably on the edge of the cushion. Immediately, she stood again and spoke in Cheyenne to Melissa, who helped her remove the fur-wrapped cradleboard from her back.

Seated once more, she unwrapped the baby, and everyone stared in shock as she lifted the infant from his confining nest.

"Do you want me to take him?" Melissa offered. She spoke in English for the benefit of the others.

Tanya shook her head and smiled slightly for the first time. "No, he needs to eat."

"What did she say, Melissa?" Sarah questioned. Then, as if she'd just recalled her manners, she said, "Oh! Melissa, I'm sorry. I haven't said hello to you. It's nice to see you again."

"Hello, Mrs. Martin. It's good to be back," Melissa reponded.

"Why doesn't she speak English and what is she

doing with that—that animal?" Julie's curiosity finally loosened her tongue.

"The cougar seems to be her pet, and she hasn't spoken a word of English since I found her," Jeffrey answered.

"Oh, dear!" Elizabeth murmured, setting the tea on a small table.

"She'll speak when she's ready," Melissa counseled.

At this point Tanya answered the question that had been uppermost in all their minds. Loosening the drawstring of her tunic, and crooning softly to the baby, she put Mark to her breast. From beneath her lowered lashes, Tanya noted each individual reaction.

Jeffrey, now used to this, merely turned away in disgust.

Sarah's "Oh, dear Lord!" echoed loudly in the still room. Her hands flew to her breast as if to keep her heart from leaping out. Tears flooded her eyes as she stared at the dark head nestled against her daughter's breast.

Aunt Elizabeth nearly dropped the teapot, and it rattled precariously on its tray. Her face registered a series of rapidly changing emotions; first shock, then pity, and finally resignation.

Edward also stared, his face first pale, then mottled, and finally beet red. For a moment Tanya feared he was having a heart attack. Finally he burst out, "Damn! Damn it all! Damn those red savages all to hell!" His clenched fist pounded into the other, emphasizing each distinct word.

Tanya's head jerked up at this, and she clutched Mark to her defensively as Hunter edged even closer to her side.

"Now, Edward, calm down," George advised, his

face solemn and concerned. "It was too much to hope for. She's been with them for two-and-a-half years."

"Are they *both* hers?" Edward choked out.

Jeffrey nodded, miserable. "I'm afraid so."

"Does this mean the wedding is off?" Julie's inane comment drew dumbfounded looks all around.

"I think we can discuss that later, Julie," her mother advised weakly.

"No," Jeffrey interceded, "I've already made it clear to her, and now I want to assure all of you that I will still want to marry Tanya."

Tanya's father leapt from his chair and started to pace angrily. "That's good of you, son, but what about—what are you going to do with—*damn it*!" He could not admit that the two black-haired babies were his daughter's.

Suddenly he stopped pacing and stood glaring down at the children and Tanya. "I won't stand for it, I tell you!" he roared. "Give them away, send them back to the Indians, sell them to Mexican traders, turn them out to starve—anything! Just get rid of them! I won't have some savage's halfbreed bastards underfoot, a constant reminder of a time we'd all like to forget!"

"Edward!" Sarah was astounded at the extent of his anger. This was a side of her husband she rarely saw. Calm, capable Edward rarely raised his voice, let alone lost his temper.

Kit growled low in her throat ready to defend her mistress and her sons, and Edward backed off slightly, though his face was still set and angry.

Tanya's face hardened and her eyes were narrow slits, but she said nothing. Silently, she put the baby back into his cradleboard and bundled him up. Readjusting her tunic, she picked up the baby in one arm and Hunter in the other and started to leave the room.

With a tired sigh, Melissa rose to follow her. "Well, folks," she said, "It's been nice visiting with you."

"Whoa!" Jeffrey stepped into Tanya's path. "Where do you think you are going?"

Tanya spoke one sharp word in Cheyenne.

"Home," Melissa interpreted.

"Wait!" Sarah started toward Tanya. "Wait, darling, please! Try to understand the shock we've all had today. Until an hour ago, we didn't even know whether or not you were still alive—and now this!"

"We'll work it out, Tanya," her Uncle George promised. "Come back and sit down. Your father is upset."

"Your damned right I'm upset!" Edward shouted. "My daughter shows up after nearly three years looking like some Indian squaw, dragging two half-breed kids behind her, and I'm supposed to be *calm*?"

"Be quiet, Edward," Elizabeth ordered, seeing Tanya scowl again at his words. She advanced toward Tanya, watching Kit cautiously. "You are home, Tanya, and what your father overlooked in his tirade is that this is *my* home, not his. I reserve the right to say who goes and who stays. I say you stay; you and your children, and Melissa as well."

As she came closer, Kit snarled. Elizabeth shot the cat an exasperated look. "As for *this* thing," she pointed to Kit, "if you can keep him in line, he can stay; but if he so much as looks like he wants to bite me, I'll turn him into a hearthrug faster than you can blink!"

A reluctant smile tugged at Tanya's lips. Her aunt reached out for the baby, waiting. At last Tanya nodded, and relinquished Mark into her arms.

"Good!" Elizabeth said decisively. "Now that's straightened out, let's get you settled in." Turning to

Julie, she said, "Go find that delinquent nephew of mine and tell him it's past dinner time." At Tanya's questioning look she explained, "My youngest sister's son, Jeremy, is living with us now. He's a twelve-year-old scamp who's never still a minute. Trouble is, he's cute, and he knows it."

"He's a brat!" Julie grouched on her way out. "He and Tanya ought to get along famously!"

A look passed between Tanya and Melissa, and Melissa commented lamely, "Julie hasn't changed much, has she?"

Elizabeth laughed and shook her head, "You can please some of the people some of the time, but Julie—rarely. Now let's leave the problems for later and celebrate Christmas with joyful spirits and profound thanks for the safe return of these two girls," she added solemnly.

"Amen," came the chorused reply.

The next few weeks were an anxious period of adjustment through trial and error, on both sides. Through it all, Tanya had one devoted admirer; young Jeremy. He was truly enthralled with Tanya, and even more so with Kit.

The first opportunity he had to catch her alone, he asked, "Did you really live with the Indians?"

Tanya nodded.

"Are you an Indian now too?"

Again she agreed.

"That's terrific!" he exclaimed, his eyes shining. "Oh, boy," he sighed dreamily. "I sure wish I was one." Then he brightened, "Well, we both have the same Aunt Elizabeth, so that's something anyhow, huh? That sort of makes me related to an Indian I guess, doesn't it?"

Tanya shrugged and grinned at him.

"You sure don't talk much," he commented, "but that's alright. I don't like yakkity girls. I like your cougar, though. What's his name?"

Tanya surprised him with an answer. "Kit."

"Can I pat him?"

The eagerness of Jeremy's face won Tanya over. "Her," she said in English. "Kit's a female."

"Can I?" he repeated.

Tanya called Kit to her. Then she told Jeremy to let Kit smell his hands. He sat down on the floor, his hands extended. Soon Kit was licking his hand, his arms, and his face; and boy and cougar were rolling on the floor, playing. Tanya and Kit had found a friend.

Before he left her that day, Jeremy promised solemnly, "I won't tell anyone you remember English if you don't want me to."

"Not just yet," Tanya agreed.

Jeremy thought about this for a moment, then with remarkable insight, he asked, "Is it because of this Lieutenant Young?"

"Mostly."

Jeremy nodded. "I don't trust him either."

Not everyone was as tolerant as Jeremy, but Tanya did not make it easy for them. Unlike Melissa, who readily reverted to the white world, Tanya repeatedly dug her heels in. She refused to wear shoes or dresses, sticking adamantly to her doeskin clothing and moccasins. Though she sat in chairs and ate with the proper silverware, she would not sleep in a bed. Instead, she slept on a pallet of blankets on the floor. She still refused to speak English, and spent most of her time playing with her sons or gazing longingly out the window.

Edward and Jeffrey had spoken at length the day

after Christmas, and Jeffrey had explained much of what he thought he knew about Tanya.

After Jeffrey had left, Edward talked with Melissa. "Lt. Young says Tanya was married to one of their warriors," he said. "This can't be, can it? What I mean is, he just took her for his captive, didn't he?" He looked so hopeful that Melissa actually started to feel sorry for him.

"No, Mr. Martin," she said as gently as she could. "There was an actual ceremony, and she became his wife. In her eyes, and his, they are married."

"This is preposterous!" he blustered. "Next you'll be telling me she *loves* the savage!"

Melissa deliberately held her temper, knowing how hard this must be for him. "Tanya does love him, and her husband is not a savage. He is a Cheyenne Chieftain, and he is very fair and protective of those he cares for."

"He's an Indian!" Edward argued illogically.

"Yes, he is, but that does not matter to Tanya. He is also proud and strong and handsome. This is what your daughter sees."

Edward's face became mottled as he strove to control his anger. "Tanya is engaged to Jeffrey, and she's lucky he'll still have her. She'll forget the Indian soon enough."

Melissa could hold her tongue no longer. "I really don't see how that is possible, Mr. Martin. Your daughter considers herself married to Panther. She has his sons. You delude yourself if you think Lt. Young stands a snowball's chance in July of ever making Tanya forget Panther. How can a woman be engaged to or marry one man when she is already wed in fact and in her heart to another? Face it, Mr. Martin, don't fight it, or you and your daughter will never have anything between you again but hate and distrust."

"Say what you like, Tanya will get over this Indian," he insisted.

Melissa shook her head at his obstinacy. "We'll see."

Another bone of contention between Tanya and her father were Tanya's sons. Edward still thought it would be best if she'd give them up.

"She'd forget that savage a lot quicker if she didn't have them as constant reminders," he told his wife one night.

"I know," Sarah sighed, "but she loves those children. I don't think she'll ever give them up, no matter what."

"What if they suddenly came up missing?" he suggested.

"That's a horrible, ugly thought, Edward!" Sarah glared at him. "What has come over you?"

Putting his head in his hands, he murmured, "I don't know, Sarah. I just can't stand the thought of our lovely daughter the way she is now."

"Give her time, Edward—but let me tell you this. If anything would ever happen to those children because of you, Tanya would never forgive you. Nor would I, for that matter. You have always been kind and thoughtful and gentle, and those are qualities I've admired in you all these years. I could not live with you knowing you had taken your hurt and anger out on two helpless children."

"What are you going to do?" he cried brokenly.

Sarah sat next to him on the bed and put her arms about him. "I don't know, Edward. Perhaps we start by being thankful we have her back on any terms. She's alive and well and home again, and that is what we were praying for all these past months."

"I'll try," he promised. "If Jeffrey Young can still

want to marry her, knowing Tanya will not give up those boys, I suppose I can put up with it."

"While you're at it, try accepting the idea, not just enduring it," Sarah suggested gently. "Tanya knows you disapprove and she feels my disappointment. Perhaps if we try a little harder to accept what she's become and understand what she's been through, she'll try harder to adapt and adjust to us."

Edward pulled his wife close. "How did you get so wise?" he asked as he kissed her.

"By living with you," she answered, her eyes shining.

But Sarah was having her own set of problems to deal with. While she was relieved and thankful to have Tanya home again, safe and relatively sound, her heart bled with pity each time she looked at her daughter. Here was her beautiful young daughter whose life had held such promise—beautiful, vivacious, intelligent; engaged to a handsome lieutenant, Tanya's future had been bright until her disappearance.

Now it was as if a stranger had taken her place; a silent, solemn ghost who walked, ate, and slept in the same house but existed on a different level from the rest of them. She rarely spoke, and then only in Cheyenne. Where once she had laughed readily, enjoying life to its height, now her face hardly ever revealed what she was feeling. It was as if she wore an inflexible mask; all the features frozen into place. The only time she smiled was when she was playing with her sons.

The children were another matter. While Sarah did not resent them as her husband did, she found it hard to accept them. In her loving heart, she saw them as unfortunate victims of fate. They were innocent babes, not to be blamed for anything that had happened. On the other hand, they stood between Tanya and true happiness.

Sarah felt pity for the children, knowing they would never be fully accepted by society. She felt sympathy for Tanya knowing what her daughter would have to endure to shield her children from slander and prejudice; the pain she would go through in her love for her sons.

That Tanya loved the boys, Sarah did not doubt, and in a way, she understood it. They were Tanya's flesh and blood. They had grown in and been nourished by her body. There was a special bond that could never be broken.

Sarah could not fathom how Tanya could have loved her Cheyenne husband, but Melissa insisted she had. Surely the girl was wrong; mistaken. Surely Tanya had merely submitted to his demands out of necessity and was too proud to admit it. In trying to understand Tanya as she now was, Sarah even entertained the possibility that Tanya felt some sort of commitment to him as the father of her sons.

Was this why she clung to her Indian ways? Jeffrey had even gone so far as to suggest she might try to return to Panther. Until Tanya came to her senses, and threw off this confused state that seemed to have a hold on her, he advised they hide her horse, and make sure none of theirs were available to her. Once she was back to her old self, they might let their guard down.

In her dealings with Tanya, Sarah tried to be understanding, but her expressions of sympathy seemed only to repel her daughter even further. Tanya took offense at her mother's attitude toward herself and her sons, and withdrew behind an impenetrable, invisible barrier of silent pride.

After a week of being inside the house, Tanya felt the walls start to close in on her. Unused to feeling so confined, she took to taking daily walks with Kit. Sometimes Jeremy tagged along, and often Tanya took one of her sons with her.

When first she started going off, her mother or Aunt Elizabeth would make some excuse why she should leave one or the other of the boys at home. On the few occasions when she preferred to take both, Jeffrey or one of the others insisted on accompanying her. It wasn't long before Tanya realized what they were doing. As long as at least one of her sons were left behind, they were assured of her return. Otherwise, they felt obliged to go along. Tanya knew they were doing it out of concern for her. It wasn't that they didn't trust her; it was just that they were unsure of her emotional state and were determined to protect her from herself until she was completely back to normal again. She laughed ruefully to herself over their transparent efforts, but said nothing. Once she was aware of this, however, she voluntarily took only one of her boys along at a time, feeling it easier to give in on this than create more tension needlessly.

Julie despised it when she was drafted to walk with Tanya, and Tanya was well aware of her sister's animosity. Tanya considered it extreme and could not figure out why Julie seemed to hate her. Granted, they had always bickered, as sisters tend to do. There had been the usual rivalry, arguments, fighting and jealousies that siblings are prone to, but Tanya sensed there was something else behind this.

Tanya had missed Julie, and she had thought Julie would have missed her. Jeffrey had led her to believe she had, but now that Tanya was back, Julie surely wasn't acting as if that were the case. Though they'd fought, Tanya had always loved her younger sister, and she'd felt sure Julie returned the sentiment.

Now her sister was becoming as hateful as Suellen. She went out of her way to avoid contact with Tanya and the children. Julie looked down her upturned nose at Tanya, and when they were thrown together, she constantly sniped at Tanya about her Indian attire. She made nasty comments and asked outrageously personal questions about Tanya's life with the Indians. Sarah was constantly having to chastise her about her outspoken curiosity and her offensive attitude.

All this Tanya could abide, if not understand, but Julie's actions around the children were another matter altogether. Julie was always ready to comment on their dark complexions and straight black hair. Though Hunter had Tanya's golden eyes, Julie was quick to point out that Mark, with his dark eyes, had evidently inherited none of his mother's features. She made it clear that she was repelled by them. She cringed if Hunter came anywhere near her, as if he would contaminate her if he touched her lily-white skin. Always, Julie was most spiteful when Edward was present, as if to deliberately fuel his resentment toward Tanya's sons.

Tanya fumed silently, and her own resentment grew as the days went by. Julie's reasons remained a mystery, but Tanya was getting fed up. A major conflict was in the offing if things went on as they were. For herself, Tanya did not care, but her maternal instincts were being aroused to the point of doing battle for her young.

It seemed she had Aunt Liz, Melissa, and Jeremy in her corner. Uncle George and her mother were trying to sit both sides of the fence at the same time. With

Julie, her father, and Jeffrey, Tanya was constantly having to shield her sons from their resentment, animosity, and outright disgust. It was trying, to say the least, especially on top of her constant longing for Panther.

At least Melissa was benefiting from life in the Martin household. She was such a dear, sweet little thing that everyone seemed to want to protect her, even Julie. Her very shyness drew people to her, as well as her natural willingness to help out in any way she could. Even Edward, despite the words they had exchanged, liked the petite blond. He admired her loyalty and her honesty.

As for Aunt Elizabeth, she now had the daughter she had always longed for. For years, she and George had regretted the fact that they could not have children. Their home had seemed so empty until recently. Now they had Jeremy, who had lost his parents in an accident the year before, but much as Elizabeth loved her sister's boy, she had always yearned for a daughter. Melissa filled the vacancy perfectly.

Of all the people in the Martin home, Elizabeth was the stablizing factor. She had the unique talent of being able to see things and people as they were, without all the frills and wrappings. Rarely did she mince words or dither about in confusion. She always seemed to be able to cut through directly to the heart of the matter. Not that she saw everything as either black or white, right or wrong, but she usually saw all the intermediate shades of grey more clearly than others did. As a rule, her instincts were unfailing, and she followed through with the appropriate course of action.

She did this with Tanya. Almost at once, she sized

up the situation and came to terms with it. She alone of Tanya's relatives sensed Tanya's real love for her Cheyenne husband. Instinctively, she knew it ran strong and deep, not relying solely on the bond of their children.

Elizabeth wondered about this man who had captured her niece's heart. Without prejudice, she thought he must be a remarkable person, with strength and character, a man to admire. In her mind, she pictured him as handsome and proud, for she could not imagine Tanya loving a weak-willed man.

As much as Elizabeth liked Jeffrey, she'd had some reservations about Tanya's marriage to him. Realizing his flaws, she'd wondered if Tanya would be truly happy married to Jeffrey. Though he appeared to be a nice young man, intelligent, good-looking, ambitious, Elizabeth also sensed he could be domineering, egotistical and narrow-minded. She worried that he might even be cruel when crossed. As long as things went his way, he would be easy to live with, but Elizabeth wondered what he would be like if Tanya dared to defy him.

As things stood now, Tanya had Jeffrey over a barrel. He had no recourse, under the circumstances, but to wait for Tanya to recover from her traumatic experiences. Elizabeth wondered how long Jeffrey's patience would hold, and what would happen when it finally snapped, as she felt sure it would. She was thankful Tanya was not already wed to him, and hoped Tanya would not knuckle under the pressures of her parents to marry him. It was Tanya's life and her decision, but somehow Elizabeth felt Tanya would resist all attempts to push her into a relationship with Jeffrey again. Tanya had been through too many trials, and she's evidently grown stronger through them. Her love for Panther and her sons would hold her true, both to them and to herself.

Elizabeth did not press Tanya into reforming. She did not harp at her about her dress, or try to get her to speak English, or demand that she sleep in her bed instead of the floor. Calmly, she took it all in stride, as if it were commonplace to sit across the table from a girl in buckskin and headband. Readily accepting Tanya's children into her home, she showed none of the prejudices the others did. She helped Tanya and Melissa look after the babies, feeding and dressing and often playing with them.

Kit she had a harder time accepting, but even they had come to an understanding. The cougar stayed out of Elizabeth's kitchen unless the big cat wanted a wooden spoon bounced off her head. She ate on the back porch, and slept on the floor in Tanya's room, and in order to avoid having her hide nailed to the stable door, she stayed off of Elizabeth's prized furniture. The stable was strictly off limits, as it upset George's horses and milk cows. In return for her good behavior, she was allowed to roam the house and was given choice leftovers, since she rarely left Tanya's side to hunt for herself.

Elizabeth was very patient with Tanya. Her pity was not so strong that it smothered Tanya, as Sarah's did. Her quiet acceptance was a balm to Tanya's tormented spirit, and Tanya found herself seeking out her aunt's company more and more. Tanya would sit for hours listening to Elizabeth speak of commonplace happenings. She and Melissa helped out in the kitchen, aiding Elizabeth in preparing meals, and while Tanya did not contribute to the conversation herself, she would listen to the other two. Their undemanding companionship eased her discontent, and it pleased her to see the fondness developing between her aunt and Melissa.

Tanya had hoped Melissa would be accepted here, but she'd never dreamed Aunt Liz and Uncle George would be so taken with the girl. Aunt Liz was obviously thrilled with her, and kindly Uncle George was developing a distinctly fatherly attitude toward her. He adored his wife, and anyone who could make her so happy immediately earned his gratitude.

Melissa did more than this. In her shy way, she had endeared herself to both of them. Her big blue eyes melted their hearts like warm butter, and before long she had wormed her way into their lives so securely that they could not imagine their home without Melissa in it. Since Jeremy felt the same way, no one was surprised when they asked Melissa to stay permanently.

Melissa reacted with such ecstatic joy that it brought tears to Tanya's eyes. Would she herself ever be as happy again?

Day after lonely day, she waited for Panther. On her treks with Kit, she would walk to the edge of town and gaze longingly into the distance, as if sending her thoughts in his direction would bring him back to her.

As the days turned into weeks and he still did not come, Tanya's worry increased. She did not doubt his love for her and their sons, and she was sure he would come for her if he could. Couldn't he find her? Was he having problems reorganizing the tribe after the massacre? She knew that as chief he had responsibilities to the tribe that outweighed his personal problems. How long would it take before he could leave and come for her? Was the snow and winter weather holding him back?

In mid January she heard through Jeffrey that the

Indian captives had been released to make their way back to their people. George Bent was among them. How Tanya longed to go with them! She consoled herself with the pact she and George Bent had made. He would tell Panther where to find her.

With aching heart, Tanya told herself to be patient a little while longer. Panther would come. Panther would come. Panther *would* come! In the long, dark, loneliness of the night, Tanya repeated this to herself in a litany of hope.

Chapter 15

TANYA HAD been separated from Panther for nearly two months. She ate because she had to, to keep her milk flowing for Mark, but she was getting thinner. The bones of her face were more prominent now, and her clothing hung on her. Her golden eyes seemed too large for her face, with violet shadows beneath them, and her expression was continuously solemn. Her shorn hair was longer now, falling halfway to her shoulders in soft curls. It dismayed Tanya that she could not yet make decent braids out of it.

Of all the strange things to happen to her, Tanya developed a craving for oranges. It had been years since she'd eaten one and now she could not get enough of them. Aunt Elizabeth had bought a crate for the holidays, and had since ordered more, seeing how much Tanya desired them. Pears, apples, and plums would serve in a pinch, but oranges were what she wanted. It was as if her body had done without them for too long, and now was making up for lost time.

What her system could *not* abide was Jeffrey's constant attendance. Tanya avoided him as much as she could, even fleeing to her room to hide if she had advance warning. When he stayed for supper, she requested a tray in her room, or skipped the meal altogether. After this had occurred several times, however, even Aunt Liz put her foot down.

"Tanya, dear, you are much too thin as it is," she told her. "I have to agree with your parents on this. Either you come to the table to eat, Jeffrey or no Jeffrey, or you don't eat. Keep it up long enough, and soon your milk will dry up, or you'll become ill and won't be able to tend to your sons. You have your choice, but you'll get no more trays in your room. You can't hide away up there forever."

From then on, Tanya ate with the family, but she continued to ignore Jeffrey's presence.

This did not stop his attentions toward her, however. At every opportunity he turned up on the Martin doorstep. He'd corner her in the parlor and bombard her with questions, trying to win her confidence and get her to talk to him. He'd join her on her walks, pelting her with declarations of undying love. At times like this, Tanya felt like screaming. Beneath his facade of gentle persuasion and patient understanding, she sensed a falseness. He certainly was putting on a good performance, but her intuition told her not to trust him. Compared to Panther, Jeffrey was shallow and petty. He exuded none of Panther's strength, dignity, or loving gentleness. Jeffrey was petulant, bossy, insanely jealous at times, trigger-tempered, and full of himself: but above all, he was persistent. He followed Tanya like a second shadow, ignoring her silence and the cold shoulder she turned to him.

She endured him with ill-humor. More and more, his attitude sickened her, especially those toward Hunter and Mark. Even while he professed adoration for her, his disgust for her children was plain to see. At first he tried to cover his feelings, but when confronted with the two dark-haired boys so continually, he was unable to mask his contempt.

Finally he stopped trying, telling Tanya, "Surely you understand, darling. If we'd married as we had planned, we'd have boys of our own this age; fair, blond boys that would have been mine to claim proudly."

Tanya gave him a dark look that should have fried him as crisp as morning bacon.

Disregarding her look, he said, "One day we'll have those children, Tanya; you and I. Once we're married, I'll give you a dozen babies of our own and you'll forget the last few terrible years. You'll see the difference then. You'll love our children more, I know, and they'll be *legitimate*. You won't have to be ashamed or embarrassed for them, or feel bound to them merely out of a sense of duty."

He reached out to take her hand, and Tanya drew back as if he had offered her a rattlesnake.

His face darkened in suppressed anger. "Tanya, be reasonable," he remarked stiffly. "We'll be doing things much more intimate than touching hands once we're married."

Tanya's breath released itself in a wordless hiss of anger and disgust. Just the thought of lovemaking with Jeffrey was nauseating. She rose to her feet and started from the parlor.

Angry, and confident that Kit was nowhere around, Jeffrey followed, catching Tanya about the wrist and jerking her back toward him. His face twisted in anger and determination, he said, "I've tried to be patient with you, Tanya, but perhaps that is the wrong way to deal with you. Maybe it's time I showed you who is in charge here and just what you can expect when we get married. That damned cat of yours isn't here to protect you from me this time."

Tanya was incensed. She glared at the hand about her wristband, the band Panther had placed there at their wedding. It was as if Jeffrey's touch was contaminating her marriage to Panther, and her own anger grew. As Jeffrey drew her toward him, intent on pulling her into his embrace, her composure snapped. Her hands flew to his forearm and with a quick twist and accurate leverage, she flipped Jeffrey over her head and onto his back on the floor.

Stunned, he lay blinking in disbelief as she placed one small moccasined foot on his chest. Tanya glared down at him with such an intense look of hatred and superiority that she might as well have spit on him. As she removed her foot and walked sedately from the room, she started to laugh, an evil chuckle that sent chills racing down his spine.

"You'll pay for this, Tanya," he shouted after her. "I'll have my turn!"

Suellen Haverick was now in Pueblo, awaiting the arrival of her parents from California. She was staying with the preacher and his wife, and had been there long enough to spread many tales and malicious rumors about Tanya. The pastor's good wife, whose only sin was a tendency to gossip, had enhanced and enlarged upon Suellen's stories, spreading them throughout the congregation.

Many of the townsfolk had been aware of Tanya's return, some having seen her on her walks. Realizing she had been with the Indians and still dressed and behaved strangely, they were reluctant to approach any of the Martin family, but their curiosity was aroused. Many of the men had dealings with George and Edward in their businesses, and the Martins were a respected family in the community. Wives shopped at Martin's Mercantile and belonged to sewing circles and charity committees with Elizabeth and Sarah. They were well-liked, but that did not stop the gossip.

Some people tried to discount the tales for what they were; malicious gossip. Others wondered how much truth there was to the stories, especially since Tanya was so reclusive. In the month the girl had been home, few had seen her except on her walks, and then she was always accompanied by the huge, frightening animal. She never shopped or attended church services with her family, as Melissa now did. She never attended any teas or social functions with her mother and sister, and the Martin women spoke little about her when asked.

With so much left unexplained, it was no wonder curiosity ran rampant, and Suellen's tales made it worse. Wonder and whisper though they might, most folks were drawn up short by the thought, "It could have been one of our family, but for the grace of God. What if it were our daughter . . . sister . . . *me*?"

The talk reached Tanya's ears, mainly through Julie's tirades, and though she felt sorry for the consternation it caused her family, she had problems of her own. Her whole existence revolved around waiting for Panther. With her family she was silent and withdrawn, but alone in her room, she would break down and weep torrents of tears.

"Why?" she wondered. "Why are you so long in coming, my love? Where are you tonight? Are you thinking of me; yearning for me?" Her heart cried out to him in her anguish.

As the weeks dragged by, she began to worry more and more. Panther was ever in her thoughts and often in her dreams. She would wake in the still of the night thinking she had heard his voice, trembling with longing. Many times she would awaken herself with deep, sorrowful sobs, having dreamed that something terrible had befallen him and he was never coming for her. Her heart would be thundering in her chest, her palms clammy with fear for him, tears coursing down her cheeks.

At such times, she would sit awake for hours, staring out the window. She would clutch her arms about her waist and rock to and fro, keening silently in her sorrow, her heart aching inside her chest.

"Oh, Panther, my love, what am I to do without you? What can be wrong? What is keeping you from me?" By this time, Tanya was sure something was drastically wrong, or Panther would have appeared to take her home.

Looking up at the bright stars, she vowed, "If you cannot come for me, then, I shall find you, my heart. I will find a way to escape with our sons, and I will come to you.

"Feel my love reach out to you; my heart cry out for you; my arms ache to hold you near. I long for the touch of your hands, the sound of your voice, the taste of your lips on mine. Being away from you is killing me slowly. No physical torture can be this cruel! My heart is being torn from my breast and crushed to pieces, and I cannot endure the agony of it. Without you I shall die!"

There were rare moments during her lonely vigil when she would suddenly feel very close to Panther. It was as if his spirit was in the room with her, comforting her. Tanya could almost sense his presence, feel his warmth.

At times words would spring to her mind, almost as if he had whispered into her ear. *Have faith, little one. We will be together again. I love you, Wildcat. I love you, my wife, my heart, my life.*

A warmth would flood her being then, and salty tears blur her vision as she held closely to this illusion; and when it faded she would be left sad but consoled, her strength and faith renewed for a while longer.

Hundreds of miles to the south, Panther was lying on a pallet, fighting for his life. The gaping hole in his shoulder was slow to heal, threatening to putrefy at every turn. Only the avid ministrations of Shy Deer and Walks-Like-A-Duck avoided this. Twice daily they cleaned his wounds, applying salves and dry dressings, praying all the while. This, and Panther's fierce will to live, held his spirit in this world by a slim thread.

Unconscious much of the time, he vaguely recalled the battle with Major Elliot's troop or the bullet that had slammed into his upper chest like a mighty hammer. It had seared into his shoulder like a flaming brand, burning and shredding his flesh, tearing a hole from which his life's blood flowed steadily.

Panther had clung to his horse with the last of his waning senses and Towering Pine led him to safety. He could not know it, but the women and children they'd gone to rescue had been saved and all of Major Elliot's men killed.

Winter Bear had taken charge and led his people to the safety of another tribe. It was a hurried, harsh journey in snow and cold, but they'd made it without further mishap. Through long training Panther clung to Shadow's back even in his unconscious state.

Once safe inside a borrowed tipi, Walks-Like-A-Duck had dug out the bullet buried deep in his shoulder, seared the flesh about the wound, and bound it tightly. Panther had lost much blood and his pulse was nearly nonexistent.

For two long weeks, Panther lay at death's door, never regaining consciousness, barely stirring when his dressing was changed or broth forced between his lips. He lay unknowing and uncaring that his cousin Winter Bear was struggling to provide food and shelter for the devastated tribe. Barely clinging to life, his body and mind were too busy fighting pain and infection to worry over his wife and sons, now traveling further and further from him.

This fact surfaced only after he regained consciousness three weeks after the battle. With little nourishment, he was weak as a kitten and had lost considerable weight. His skin hung on his tall frame, and his dark eyes were sunken into his face. He could barely lift his head.

Under makeshift conditions and with little food following the massacre, Panther's wound began to fester. That the tribe had to move to safer regions did not help. Dragged behind a horse on a travois, Panther suffered the agonies of the damned. Every jolt jarred his shoulder and made pain spear through his body, but he endured it silently, clenching his teeth until it seemed his jaw would crack under the pressure. It was with great relief that he welcomed the grey mist of mindlessness when it came.

No sooner had the tribe settled into a new winter camp, than Panther took a turn for the worse. The rough traveling had caused his wound to reopen. He had lost more blood, which he could ill afford, and his wound was beginning to fester.

For endless days, Walks-Like-A-Duck and Shy Deer labored to save Panther's life. Tirelessly, they cooled his fevered skin, tended his wound, forced fluids and medicinal mixtures into him. Burning with fever, and delirious most of the time, Panther thrashed about so that the women feared he would tear his shoulder wound open yet again. His mind wandered. Time and again he called out for Wildcat, refusing to be calmed by Shy Deer's sympathetic voice.

With Panther's fever came weird dreams. He relived the massacre as Wildcat must have seen it, watching helplessly as his friends and family were slaughtered. He saw Wildcat and his sons taken prisoner by the young blond lieutenant and he raced to rescue them, but suddenly he was afoot in the snow and they were mounted on fast horses. He ran after them until his lungs were on fire and his heart ready to explode in his chest, but he could not catch them. As his legs folded under him, he heard his wife accuse, "You said you'd never let me go, Panther; that nothing would part us . . ."

In another dream, he saw himself as a cougar, tracking his mate. He saw her with their cubs suckling at her belly. He saw her stretching out on the ground before him, sleek and tawny, frolicking, her golden eyes gleaming. They were together in a mountain meadow when they were beset by a pack of wolves. Outnumbered, he fought desperately to save his family, but several wolves launched themselves at him at once, fangs bared, jaws snapping. One wolf sank its teeth deep into his shoulder. As he lay bleeding in the grass, he watched as the wolves herded his family into the forest and out of sight . . .

In another instance he visualized a crowded street in town. As he watched from afar, he saw the same young lieutenant leading Hunter and Mark along behind him, each on a long leash. The scene changed, and he saw the man walking down a street, Wildcat at his side. Her braids were undone and she wore a blue flowered dress and carried a baby in her arms. The couple smiled at one another, and the man reached out and took the blanket from the baby's face. To Panther's dismay, the child was not his son Mark, but a blond-haired baby with the lieutenant's features . . .

Yet again the dream changed and he saw Wildcat looking out from behind the window of a house. Her face was thin, and there were violet shadows beneath her sorrowful golden eyes. Large tears rolled unchecked down her cheeks as she laid her forehead wearily against the glass pane. Her voice choked with sobs, she pleaded, "Please come, Panther. Oh, my love, please rescue us!"

"I'm coming, Wildcat," he answered, but she could not hear him and continued to cry . . .

Time and again he dreamed of Wildcat calling out to him in despair. Always he promised to come to her, telling her of his love, asking her to wait. At times it was so real he could almost touch her hair, and her tears fell like rain upon his heated skin.

Finally the day came when Panther's fever left him, and he could think clearly for the first time in more than a moon. The snow lay deep around the tipi, and an icy wind howled against its sides. Weak, saturated with sweat, he gazed about, half expecting to see Wildcat and his sons. Instead, he saw Walks-Like-A-Duck tending the fire.

He attempted to rise, and a fierce pain shot through his shoulder. Sweat broke out in beads on his brow, and he lay back with a sigh.

"It was true, then," he thought dismally, remembering the massacre. "Chief Black Kettle and Woman-To-Be-Hereafter are dead, along with many more of our tribe. My people are destitute, my wife and sons taken away by soldiers, and I lie here wounded and weak, unable to help even myself, let alone the others."

When he tried to speak, his throat would not work, but finally he croaked out to Walks-Like-A-Duck, "How long since the attack?"

He was shocked to learn five weeks had passed in oblivion. Walks-Like-A-Duck went on to inform him what had happened since. Other tribes had shared their belongings with them, but food and shelter were in short supply. Families were crowded together in tipis. She, Panther, Magpie, and Chief Winter Bear's family were all sharing this one. The tribe was in the north of Texas Territory, and the winter was proving extremely harsh so far. No, they had heard no news of Wildcat's whereabouts, or any of the other captives. At last she told him how seriously he'd been wounded and how close to death he'd come, warning him to conserve his little strength and not tear his wound open again, as it was finally starting to mend.

Flat on his back, warned of the consequences if he tried to move about too soon, Panther had a lot of time to think. Some of the time he spent talking to Winter Bear, discussing the problems facing the tribe. All the time he thought of Wildcat, Hunter and Mark. If it took months of searching, he would find and claim them. Also, he vowed revenge on the white-eyes for ravaging his tribe. Someday he would see them pay with their lives. As soon as he was well, and the tribe re-established, he would set off in search of his wife and sons, but first he must concentrate all his energies on regaining his health and strength.

"Have patience and faith, little one," he called out silently to his Wildcat. "I will come for you, and we will be together again. Wait for me, and remember I love you."

The only good thing that happened during this time was that Tanya's parents were softening toward Hunter and Mark. Her mother could now look at the boys without cringing. The fact that the two little ones were so well-behaved and cute helped.

Mark would lie for hours cooing and smiling. He was a darling, content baby. All Hunter had to do was turn his huge golden eyes on Sarah, and she'd start to melt. He was a handsome miniature of his father, and he could enchant with those eyes of his, and knew it. By nature, he was not a shy child, and once he'd adjusted to the house, he set out to charm everyone in it.

Before long, he had Sarah on the floor playing with him, mostly when no one else was about. Gradually she stopped caring who saw her, and held the children and talked to them at any time. She'd sing lullabies and tell them stories, loving it when Hunter's eyes lit up in delight.

Tanya had wondered how Hunter was picking up so many English words so quickly, and one day, quite by accident, she found out. As she was passing the library on silent feet, she heard her mother's voice and Hunter's delighted giggle. Peeking in, she saw her mother holding him on her lap.

Sarah pointed to Hunter and said in English, "Hunter." Melissa had offered the English translation of the boys' names.

Hunter laughed and repeated the word in his baby way: "Hun-ner."

Smiling, Sarah pointed to herself, and with an emotional crack in her voice, she said softly, "Grand-ma."

"Gran-na," Hunter repeated.

Laughing through her tears, Sarah hugged him to her, "Yes, darling, Granna."

Tanya slipped quietly away, deeply touched by the scene she had just witnessed, and reluctant to disturb the two. Her mouth curved into a poignant smile and one lone tear stole down her face.

Edward was a bit more stubborn; harder to win over. At first, he went out of his way to avoid the children, frowning fiercely when he saw Sarah cuddling them. Hunter, however, was undeterred by his grandfather's gruff manner. He took to toddling after the dour figure, following him like a wobbly little shadow. Whenever Edward would turn and glare at him, Hunter would grin, displaying his new white teeth and the dimples in his chubby baby cheeks. He was truly an irresistible little imp.

Edward did not give in gracefully, nor all at once, but in reluctant stages, and with much grumbling. However, the day arrived when he took Hunter's little tan hand in his much larger one, and from then on, he accepted the boy's company. It was not unusual to see him leading the toddler about, shortening his long strides to accommodate Hunter's.

Tanya would hide a grin to hear her father's gruff voice explaining something or other to the enthralled youngster. She was glad her parents were accepting their grandchildren at last; that they were getting to know one another. This did nothing to delete her desire to return to Panther, however. Besides, Julie was still as hateful as ever, often taking her spite out on Tanya's children, realizing this would hurt Tanya more than anything else she could have done.

A freak February thaw surprised them all with temperatures in the mid-forties for four days running. For the first couple of days, Tanya sat watching the ice and snow slowly melt, wondering if she dared attempt what her heart was urging her to do. She knew that the snow in the mountains and on the open plains would still be deep, but perhaps not impassable. Could she possibly risk her life and that of her sons attempting an escape at this time?

As the thaw stretched through the third day, Tanya made up her mind to try, but she realized she needed help. Jeremy offered the solution when he happened to mention that he knew where Tanya's horse was stabled.

The boy was entirely enthralled with Tanya, and the only one to whom she spoke English. Unlike Julie, Tanya was kind and genuinely interested in the twelve year old. On their walks, she taught him a little of how to recognize animal paw prints and track them. She showed him how to cover his trail and taught him to shoot her bow and arrow. Jeremy thought she was the most interesting person he'd ever met, and was her faithful student and loyal friend. He adored her, and would have done anything she asked. He proved it when Tanya enlisted his aid.

"Could you get my horse for me without anyone noticing, Jeremy?" she asked one day.

"You're going away," he stated solemnly, swallowing a lump in his throat.

"Yes, I must return to my husband and his people," Tanya replied truthfully. "You understand this, don't you? Will you help me?"

Jeremy nodded. "What do you want me to do? When are you going?"

"Tonight, if possible, after everyone else is asleep. I need you to get Wheat for me, and hide him in the woods near the house. No one must guess what I am planning."

"Not even Missy?" he questioned.

"Not until I am gone. I don't want Aunt Elizabeth and Uncle George to feel she has betrayed their trust just when they are starting to love one another. Missy needs their love and deserves a good home."

"What about me?" he queried sadly.

"You, my friend, they have always loved. Besides, you are younger and can be forgiven for your mistakes more readily. Are you willing to risk it? If not, I'll have to do it on my own."

"I'll help," he assured her.

Jeremy performed above and beyond the call of duty. That evening he slipped out unnoticed and stole Tanya's horse for her, bridle, saddle, and all. He hid Wheat in a stand of trees not far from the house. Then he scavenged food and water from the kitchen, tying the sack to Wheat's saddle. He retrieved extra blankets from the house and loaded them onto Wheat's back.

Late that night, Tanya tiptoed down the dark halls of the sleeping house, Mark strapped to her back in his cradleboard, Hunter in her arms. "Thank goodness Cheyenne children are taught not to cry," she thought to herself.

Her knife at her waist, her bow and quiver across her shoulder, she followed Jeremy to where he had hid her horse.

Mounted and ready to leave, Tanya bent to shake Jeremy's hand in solemn farewell. "Thank you, Jeremy. You are a true friend, and I shall tell Panther of your loyalty. We shall both be eternally grateful to you."

"I'll miss you," he gulped.

"Perhaps we'll meet again someday." Then she added, "Don't forget to cover our tracks. I need all the advantages I can get."

"Goodbye," he murmured.

"Goodbye, Jeremy. Please try to explain to the others that my leaving does not mean I do not love them."

"Even Jeffrey?" Jeremy grinned cheekily.

"No, you imp!" Tanya giggled. "*Jeffrey* you can tell to go to the devil!"

"I'll be sure to tell him."

"Not until I've been missed. Cover for me as long as you can."

"I promise. Good luck."

"I'll need all I can get, I'm sure. Goodbye, Jeremy." With that, she was gone, blending into the shadows of the night.

Jeremy carefully obliterated their tracks. Awaking early the next morning, he watched carefully that no one approached Tanya's room. At the appropriate opportunity, he stated that Tanya did not want breakfast and was busy with the boys in her room. He even took Hunter's breakfast upstairs, saying he was going to help feed him, and play with him there. No one questioned him, as he had done it on other occasions.

At noon, Jeffrey arrived in time for lunch. It was then that Jeremy's ploy began to fail. His explanation that Tanya did not want any lunch met with stiff opposition. Told to fetch her, he returned to say she refused to come down.

Edward's patience snapped. He tromped upstairs to have words with his daughter, leaving a quaking Jeremy below. Never had Jeremy wished more that he could make himself invisible, but he bravely awaited the explosion he knew was coming.

Edward returned shortly, his face white and strained. "She's gone! All her things are gone. She's taken the boys with her."

He turned hurt, resentful eyes on Jeremy. "You helped her, didn't you?" For once he did not bellow, but to Jeremy this was worse.

Jeremy gulped and nodded. He got no chance to explain, as everyone began to talk at once.

Sarah began to cry, as did Melissa, and Elizabeth was hard put to soothe her. George sat silently, puffing on his pipe, a concerned frown creasing his brow. Only Julie seemed pleased by the news, a triumphant, satisfied smile on her face, which she quickly hid—but not before Jeremy had witnessed it.

Jeffrey was outraged. Immediately he grabbed Jeremy roughly by the arms, shaking the boy until his teeth rattled. "Damn you!" he shouted. "How dare you interfere! I should break your little neck! Do you know what you've done?"

His irate tirade drew the attention of the others. "Release the boy immediately! Release him, I say!" Sarah flew to Jeremy's defense.

Even as she spoke, Edward was prying Jeffrey's fingers from Jeremy's arms. "It's done! Let him go," he ordered in a defeated tone.

Jeremy stood rooted to the floor, shaken and frightened, but determined to uphold Tanya's right to leave.

Sarah knelt before him, taking his hands in hers, looking up at him with tearful eyes. Her calm, sweet voice trembling, she asked, "Why, Jeremy? Why?"

Biting his lip, Jeremy gathered his courage. "She needed to go," he stated simply. "She told me to tell you her leaving doesn't mean she does not love you. She just had to go."

A sob escaped Sarah's throat as tears streamed down her face.

Glaring up at Jeffrey, hating him more than ever, Jeremy said belligerently, "She told me to tell *you* to go to the devil!"

"Shut up, kid, unless you want me to strip the skin off your backside with my belt," Jeffrey threatened with a growl.

"No one is going to beat anyone," Edward stated authoritatively. "You have no right to administer punishment, at any rate, Jeffrey. That will be up to George and Elizabeth, if they so choose. That is rather beside the point at this stage, don't you think?"

Realizing his mistake, Jeffrey regained his composure with effort. He could ill afford to estrange himself from the Martins now.

"You are right, Edward. Just now we must see to getting Tanya back. I'll get some men together and start out as soon as possible. She's probably headed back to the Washita in hopes of finding the tribe nearby, though we've had no word of where they had relocated. We only know they are no longer there. One of our troops reported back that they had found all of Major Elliot's command dead, and there was evidence the Cheyenne had returned long enough to hold rites for their dead and left again."

Jeffrey glowered down at Jeremy. "I don't suppose

you will tell us when she left so we know how much of a lead she has on us?"

Jeremy remained stubbornly silent.

Edward sighed. "Let the boy alone. Tanya must have left sometime last night. That much we can surmise."

"If we go on the assumption that she left around midnight, she's got a good fourteen hour start on us, if we can leave within an hour," Jeffrey concluded.

"I'm coming with you," Edward stated firmly.

Jeffrey looked startled. The last thing he wanted when he caught up with Tanya was her father at hand. He had a few scores to settle with that little witch!

"That's not necessary, Edward," he argued. "It is going to be rough traveling, and we need to ride fast."

Edward, having glimpsed Jeffrey's trigger-temper, feared for the well-being of his daughter and grandsons if left to Jeffrey's care alone, but he kept his silence.

As soon as Jeffrey left the house, an anxious look passed between Edward and his brother George.

"I don't trust him." George's words echoed Edward's thoughts. "If you want, I will go with you."

"The high and mighty Lieutenant won't like it," Edward predicted. "If we follow along some distance behind, he needn't know. I have a feeling Tanya is going to need us."

George nodded his agreement. "Let's get cracking then. There's no time to waste!"

Blissfully ignorant of the plans the Martin men were forming, Jeffrey strode toward his headquarters, his thoughts vengeful.

"You'll pay for humiliating me in this way, Tanya,"

he promised silently as he went to round up his men. "I'm going to have you for my wife, if it's the last thing I do, and rest assured, there will be no doubt that I am the boss in our household. The gloves are off now, my dear, and I shall teach you a few well-deserved lessons!"

He laughed as he pictured it in his mind. "You might even learn to like my brand of mastery, for master you I fully intend to do, my sweet!"

Chapter 16

THE SNOW on the plains was even deeper than Tanya had expected, and she was making slow progress. A bitterly cold wind was whipping down from the mountains.

Hunter and Mark were bundled in furs and were relatively warm. It was Wheat that Tanya worried about at the moment. The snow was past the mare's knees, and in places, up to her belly. She plowed valiantly through the drifts, trying her best for Tanya and the boys, but many were the times they had to stop when the brave little mare tired.

In three days of travel, they had covered little distance, and Tanya continually looked back over her shoulder for signs of pursuers. It was virtually impossible in snow this deep to cover all their tracks, though Tanya had at first attempted to do so, at least for a few miles out of Pueblo. The backtracking took much precious time, and as soon as she considered it safe to do so, Tanya abandoned the effort. With luck, she had bought a little time by covering the start of her trail and also by cutting across country instead of following the road toward Fort Lyon.

The thaw had discontinued the day after she'd left Pueblo and now, as she neared the Arkansas River, a snowstorm was starting in earnest. Tanya could barely see where they were headed.

When they reached the banks of the Arkansas, Tanya was dismayed to find it swollen and raging from the recent thaw. There was no way she could consider crossing here. She would have to search out a shorter, more shallow span.

Tanya's discouraged sigh was swallowed in the wind. Here was yet another delay. Already she had spent precious time covering tracks, stopping to rest Wheat, and to feed and warm Hunter and Mark. Now this, added to the slow travel in snow and bitter winds. Everything, even nature itself, seemed to be against her desire to be reunited with Panther.

Her gaze traveled the raging river, noting the huge chunks of ice racing along in its current. As she guided Wheat alongside the bank, she realized how hazardous the crossing would be. One misstep, one block of ice, could snap the mare's leg and pitch them all into the icy water. In her desperation to reach Panther, Tanya was courting death every step of the way, taking her children with her. The odds were overwhelmingly against her, and if she'd had the time and energy, she could have cried.

It was late afternoon, now. The sun would be setting soon, and Tanya still had not found a place to cross safely. Then her ears picked up a faint sound on the wind. Throwing back her head, she strained her ears, listening intently, her heart pounding in her chest.

Oh, God! There it was again; the sound of horses; the clink of bridles; the sounds of pursuit! Kit heard it too, and growled low in her throat. A horse whinnied and Tanya clamped a hand on Wheat's nose to discourage her from answering the call.

Visibility was poor, but Tanya knew her pursuers need only follow her trail to find her. Her only hope was to elude them until nightfall or find a way to cross the river and lose them on the other side.

Urgency driving fatigue from her, Tanya kneed Wheat to a faster pace, pushing the weary mare to her limits. Behind her, she heard a triumphant shout, and a cold sweat popped out on her brow. Risking a quick glance behind her, Tanya caught a glimpse of a blue uniform. Her breath caught on a sob as she realized she too had been spotted.

Wheat was winded, breathing heavily now, and Tanya silently admitted to herself the futility of trying to escape capture. Slowing the mare to a walk, within minutes she was surrounded, staring rebelliously into Jeffrey's flushed face.

"You've made a mistake, Tanya, a big mistake, and I'm going to see that you reap the results of your impetuous actions, my love," Jeffrey sneered. "Get off the horse," he ordered sharply. Tanya's eyes darted to the faces of the men surrounding her. Some were openly leering at her; most were tired and sullen.

"Don't look to them for help," Jeffrey advised. "They are under my command and will do as I tell them. Besides, they are none too thrilled at having to come out on this chilly jaunt in the wilderness to retrieve you. Now, get down off the horse, Tanya."

Still she hesitated, and Jeffrey exploded, "Do it! Or I will run my sword through those brats of yours before that cat can twitch a whisker!"

Tanya blanched and dismounted warily.

"We'll camp here for the night," Jeffrey informed his men. "Make a fire and keep an eye on the brats, and if the cougar gives you any trouble, shoot it."

It took about an hour for the men to get the camp set

up for the evening. It was then Jeffrey grabbed Tanya roughly by the arm, directing her toward the edge of the camp.

Kit let out a warning snarl and crouched to leap. "Tell him to back off, Tanya, unless you'd prefer to see him made into a rug."

Seeing no other recourse, Tanya issued commands in Cheyenne, and Kit settled down to guard the children.

"Very wise, my dear," Jeffrey taunted. "Now, come along. We have a few things to settle between us." He gave her a rough shove away from the men.

A few yards out of sight, he pulled her to a halt, swinging her about to face him. "You've made a fool of me for the last time, Tanya. You've made me look ridiculous before my men and the whole of Pueblo, and now, by God, you are going to pay for it!"

Stiff with cold and bundled in fur, Tanya could not answer fast enough to avoid him as he pushed her flat on her back in the deep snow. He followed her down, pinning her with his body and grasping her wrists tightly. Tanya had no opportunity to reach her knife, and try as she might, she could not gain the leverage to throw Jeffrey off of her. The snow, her bulky clothing, and Jeffrey's weight kept her effectively pinned beneath him.

For several minutes Tanya continued to fight him, until she realized her agitated wriggling was arousing him rather than putting him off. Also she was futilely expending what little energy she still possessed. She became still beneath him.

When he lowered his head, intent on kissing her, she turned her head aside and his lips met her cheek instead. Irritated by her gesture of denial, Jeffrey captured both of Tanya's wrists in one hand, and with the other he held her head still. This time his lips met their target, his teeth grinding against her tightly closed lips.

Repulsed and angry, Tanya could not lie quiescent. Her sharp teeth clamped down upon his lower lip until his blood ran with her own upon her tongue.

Incensed beyond measure, Jeffrey shouted an oath, pulling away from her. As she glared up at him, her hatred shining out of her golden eyes, he struck her sharply across the face.

"Don't you ever try that again!" he roared. "You are going to have to mend your ways once we're married, Tanya, or both you and your brats will pay dearly. Obviously, you do not respond to gentle handling, and I've reached the end of my patience with you. I suppose you've gotten used to being treated roughly by your captor, and if that is the only way to get a reaction out of you, so be it."

He reached his hand inside her coat to fondle her breast roughly through her dress. Tanya wriggled in protest and felt the bulge in his breeches along her thigh. Her expressive eyes widened in alarm.

Jeffrey chuckled mirthlessly. "That's right, honey, I want you and seeing as you've already been used by that savage, there is no reason why I should wait, is there?"

He squeezed her breast painfully. "I'll show you what lovemaking is all about, and you'll forget your Indian lover soon enough. When I'm finished with you, you'll be begging for more."

His hand released her breast to yank at her skirts, his breathing heavy as his knee wedged itself between her resisting thighs. His voice was unsteady as he continued, "Don't fret, love. I still intend to marry you, if only to insure that you are mine alone. You may be soiled goods, but by God, you'll be mine!"

Jeffrey fumbled with the buttons on his pants, his knees pressing painfully into her outspread thighs to hold her still. Tanya renewed her efforts to free herself. The thought of Jeffrey taking her after Panther's tender lovemaking sickened her, and her panic grew as Jeffrey started to lower his body to hers. She managed to make Jeffrey lose his balance momentarily with her thrashing as her outraged scream split the air.

Jeffrey slapped her across the face once more. "Shut up!" he growled, "and lie still. You are going to enjoy this as much as I am."

"I doubt that very much." The voice resounding clearly through the snow-muffled air startled them both.

"Let my daughter up, Lieutenant," Edward Martin ordered.

"Do it, Young," George Martin advised firmly when Jeffrey did not move immediately. "If Tanya was your wife, you might have some license here, but since that is not the case, Edward has every right to protect his daughter's virtue. His anger is justified, and if you've harmed her or her sons, he'd be well within his rights to shoot you where you are."

Jeffrey levered himself away from Tanya, facing away from the others as he fastened his pants. With one parting glare at Tanya he stomped back to the camp his men had set up, George hard on his heels.

Tanya scrambled to her feet, accepting her father's extended hand. Pulling her into his arms, Edward hugged her to him.

"Did he harm you?" he asked anxiously.

Tanya merely shook her head for an answer and returned her father's embrace.

"God, Tanya, if he had, I think I'd kill him! If we'd been a few minute later . . ." Edward shuddered to think what would have happened.

He put her away from him, the better to see her face. His fingers traced the vivid marks on her cheek. "He hit you. The lousy bastard hit you!"

Tanya nodded miserably and kissed the fingers stroking her face.

Edward cradled her face between his palms, looking down at his daughter earnestly. "Tanya, darling, we love you. We always will, no matter what. How can I make it up to you for the way I've acted since you've returned? I've been an ass, but put yourself in my place. How can I let my princess, my daughter, leave when she's just returned to us? How can you expect your mother and me to let you go when we grieved over your absence for so long? Come home, Tanya. Will you come home and stay, if only for a while longer?"

Faced with her father's heartfelt plea, Tanya acquiesced with a reluctant nod.

Edward kissed her forehead and heaved a sigh of relief. "Thank you, Tanya. You won't regret it, I promise you. You needn't worry about my accepting Hunter and Mark. I'll proudly claim them as my grandsons, because they are yours, part of you. They are bright, healthy youngsters, and I was a fool to try to deny them. Can you forgive an obstinate old man?"

Once more she nodded, resting her head tiredly against his chest.

"Come," he said. "Let's see how George is managing. Jeffrey Young is sure to be in a foul mood, and I'm none too pleased with him. It's a good thing we decided to follow along behind. He's been acting so strangely lately that I just felt he couldn't be trusted.

"That's another thing, Tanya. After this, you need not feel pressured to marry him. Your mother and I will not force him on you. We'll leave the decision up to you."

They spent the night camped with the soldiers, Tanya and her sons protectively flanked by her father, her uncle, and Kit. The next day they started back toward Pueblo.

Jeffrey was trying desperately to mend his fences with Tanya and her relatives. Shame-faced, he admitted that he'd gotten carried away. He tried to blame it on his anger and the heat of the moment; having just retrieved his runaway fiance. He apologized profusely, promising it would not happen again, and repeating how much he loved Tanya and wanted her for his wife.

None of the Martins accepted Jeffrey's excuses for his behavior, but for the sake of a peaceful journey, they did not argue with him. There would be plenty of time to deal with the problem once they were back in Pueblo. In the meanwhile, they treated him with cool politeness and kept their distance.

Once back in Pueblo, Tanya resumed her life with little change from before. The one exception was that her family was united in their efforts to shield her from Jeffrey's persistent attentions.

Jeremy felt terrible that Tanya had been caught and brought back. "I'm sorry Tanya," he told her with a sad little sigh. "If only I could have kept them from knowing you were gone for a while longer, you might have gotten away."

"No, Jeremy, it's not your fault," Tanya assured him with a smile. "You were a great help."

With a look so hopeful it tugged at Tanya's heart, he asked, "You're not mad at me?"

Tanya shook her head. "How could I be angry with you, my little friend? We tried and failed, but the blame lies with the weather and my impatience, not with you."

"Are you going to try again?"

"No; at least not for a while. Jeffrey will be watching too closely, and I promised my father I would stay for the time being. I must learn to be more patient, it seems."

"Will you still teach me how to be an Indian?" Jeremy's eyes pleaded with her.

"You bet!" Tanya grinned at him, using one of Jeremy's favorite expressions.

Jeremy glowed. "Gee, Tanya, you're the cat's whiskers!"

Tanya burst out laughing. "I'll take that as a compliment, and if I'm the cat's whiskers, *you* must be his grin!"

Though Tanya was on better terms with her parents these days, Julie was as incorrigible as ever. The final spark that set fire to Tanya's temper happened on her third day back. Unexpectedly, she walked into the parlor to find Julie shaking Hunter back and forth, her fingers digging viciously into his little arms, his feet dangling off the floor, and his head snapping to and fro.

Instantly furious, Tanya flew to the defense of her young son. Without thought, she launched herself at her sister, screeching and yanking at Julie's hair until she released Hunter. With a swift glance at the toddler to assure herself he was alright, Tanya pushed her sister roughly away from him.

Julie immediately pushed back, and the fracas was on. Scratching, hissing, pushing, hitting and pulling hair, the two girls went at it tooth and nail. Heedless of the earsplitting clamor they were creating, they screamed at one another, Tanya spouting Cheyenne at the top of her lungs.

"Let me go!" Julie shouted as Tanya yanked on her hair. "It's your brat who needs a good beating! You should see the mess he's made of my crochet thread! *Ouch*!"

A few minutes later, it was, "Stop it, Tanya! *Ouch*! I hate you! Why did you have to come back? Everything was so nice when you were gone!"

Julie's shoe landed a telling blow on Tanya's shin, causing her to grunt in pain. "Ha!" Julie gloated. "That's not half of what I'd like to do to you! I wish the Indians would have killed you or marked you up until you were so ugly, Jeffrey would never have wanted you again. But no, home you come, beautiful as ever, the poor mistreated princess who has to be pampered and coddled and catered to; and Jeffrey is as besotted as ever."

Julie's sleeve gave way with a loud rip as Tanya tugged on it, rapping out a stream of Cheyenne oaths.

"I wish I could get away with saying some of the things I know *you* are saying!" Julie retorted. "I wish Jeffrey could see the way you are behaving now. Maybe then he'd see I'm the better woman; and I don't have half-breed sons to saddle him with. He was starting to come around, beginning to see me as a woman, before you showed up again!" Julie's open hand made a perfect connection with Tanya's bruised cheek.

"Damn it, Julie! I ought to knock your teeth down your throat!" Tanya screamed, unconsciously lapsing into English in her desire to communicate with her sister. For several seconds she'd been trying to tell Julie that she had no interest at all in Jeffrey, but could not get her message across in Cheyenne.

"Try it!" Julie taunted, too angry to realize she'd understood her sister's words.

Instead Tanya yanked out a handful of Julie's abundant hair.

"*Yeouch*!" Julie's eyes filled with tears of pain.

"Are you going to listen to me now, or do I have to snatch you bald first?" Tanya asked grimly.

"Why should I?"

"Because I'm trying to tell you I wouldn't have Jeffrey Young on a silver platter! If you want him so badly, he's yours, with my blessings. I'd be eternally grateful if you'd take the skulking moron off my hands!" Tanya yelled.

"You aren't serious!" Julie stopped dead in astonishment.

"Do I look like I'm joking?" Tanya retorted hotly. "I have a husband! I have two wonderful sons! I never wanted to come back here! What more does it take to convince you that I mean what I say?" Tanya's voice was shrill.

"Truly?" Julie looked as if someone had just offered her a gold mine and she couldn't quite believe her luck. "I thought it was just an act so everyone would feel sorry for you."

"Julie!" Tanya sighed in exasperation. She slumped down onto the sofa, plopping Hunter onto her lap. "I can't help it if Jeffrey still wants me. I've done everything in my power to discourage him."

"You honestly don't love him anymore?" The look on Julie's face was so hopeful it made Tanya's heart ache for her.

"I doubt I ever did. I don't think I honestly knew what love was before I met Panther," Tanya admitted.

Julie's doubt was obvious. "That's your Indian husband? But how can you possibly love a savage, Tanya?"

Tanya's smile was gentle in remembrance. "If you'd ever seen him, you wouldn't need to ask. He is the most marvelous man I've ever known. He's tall and proud and noble, and extremely handsome. Panther is strength and gentleness in the same person. I love him with all my heart and I live only for the day we will be reunited."

Julie was contrite. "I'm sorry Tanya. I didn't mean it when I said I wished you were dead. I missed you, too, and worried about you. It's just that I've come to love Jeffrey, and I was beginning to hope he would learn to care for me. Then you were found and I saw all my hopes and dreams going up in smoke. That is why I've been so hateful. I'm terribly jealous of you, you see," she admitted.

"And you were taking your spite out on my children; two little boys who could not defend themselves?" Tanya reprimanded with a frown.

"Yes," Julie whispered in humiliation, her fair complexion turning a bright red. "I'm sorry, Tanya, but I would have tried *anything* to make Jeffrey think less of you and turn to me. Hunter and Mark were handy, and I was desperate. I used them to try to get him to see that marriage to you would make him unhappy. I also took my anger and frustration out on them unfairly. It's not that I dislike them, Tanya.

Actually I think they're rather sweet, and Hunter is quite handsome."

"He takes after his father," Tanya spoke around the lump in her throat.

"Am I forgiven?" Julie asked hesitantly. "Can we be sisters and friends again?"

Tears blurred Tanya's vision. "Always," she answered, reaching out to accept Julie's outstretched hand. She sat Hunter on the floor and drew her sister into her arms.

For long minutes the two girls embraced and wept on each other's shoulders.

"I missed you so much!" Julie confessed on a sob.

"I missed you too! I love you, Julie."

"Don't flood the rug, girls," Aunt Elizabeth cut in on their private reunion, a broad grin on her face.

Both girls turned to face her, and found Elizabeth, Sarah, and Melissa all standing in the doorway. Sarah was staring in open astonishment at Tanya.

"Julie," Elizabeth went on, "as often as you have aggravated me lately, today you have done wonders. I don't know how you did it, and frankly I don't care, my dear, but you've gotten your sister to speak English, and for that I thank you."

"We heard you clear upstairs," Melissa commented.

Finally able to speak, Sarah added reverently, "I've never heard a sound more beautiful than Tanya screaming at the top of her lungs in English."

Tanya and Julie grinned at one another.

"I do believe this is the first time Mother has been glad to hear us arguing," Julie laughed.

"And probably the last," Tanya added.

That night at the supper table, Edward was in for a surprise. The women had conspired to keep Tanya's decision to speak a secret until then.

Out of the blue, Tanya requested, "Would you pass the butter, please, Papa?"

Edward's jaw dropped in amazement as he stared at his daughter. His hand suspended midway toward the butter dish, he stammered, "What . . . What did you say?"

Tanya smiled saucily. "Would you pass the butter, please, Papa?" Tanya repeated.

"I don't believe it," Edward said softly. "How? When? Why?"

"Who cares?" George laughed delightedly. "Just count your blessings Edward, and for heaven's sake, pass the poor girl the butter!"

From that day on, bit by bit, Tanya started making concessions to her family's way of living. One morning a few days later, she slept past her usual wake-up time, and Sarah went up to check on her. Upon peeking into the bedroom, rather than finding Tanya lying on her usual pallet on the floor, she discovered her daughter sound asleep in the soft bed. Her head was burrowed into the feather pillow and she was snuggled under several quilted comforters.

With a smile, Sarah tiptoed into the smaller adjacent room. There she found Mark gurgling in his cradle and Hunter sitting quietly on his cot playing with his toys. Picking up the baby and taking Hunter by the hand, she led them quietly past their sleeping mother, pulling the door shut behind her.

"Come on boys, let's get you some breakfast," she whispered. "We'll let Mama sleep, shall we?"

Another major change came later in the week, when Sarah presented Tanya with a small pair of cloth trousers and a plaid flannel shirt for Hunter.

"Darling, I realized you wish to raise your sons in your own way, but you can hardly dress the boy in deerskin if it is unavailable to you at this point, and he has long since outgrown the things you arrived with," she explained.

Tanya agreed. "Yes, I've noticed how uncomfortably tight his breeches are, and his shirtsleeves are nearer to his elbows than his wrists."

"Then you don't mind terribly that I've made these clothes for him? I thought he might like having an outfit like Jeremy wears, since he seems to admire him so."

"It's fine, Mother. Thank you for going to all the trouble. It's something I should have done weeks ago, but my mind has been on the other things."

Sarah sighed. "Tanya, dear, how long are you going to wait for him? It's been months. If your—er—husband was coming for you, don't you think he'd have done so by now?"

Tears sprang unbiden to Tanya's eyes, and her chin came up proudly. "He'll come, Mother," she insisted. "He wouldn't desert his wife and sons. Something has delayed him, but I will not give up hope. Panther will come for us. I just have to be patient."

"Well, while you are waiting, couldn't you consent to buying a few dresses for yourself?" Sarah suggested gently. "Your only two garments are stained and worn beyond repair and your uncle's mercantile does not carry a selection of doeskin with which to make more."

Tanya smiled at this. "I suppose it wouldn't hurt. If my son is to be clothed in the typical white manner, I guess I can too."

"It would be more reasonable," Sarah pointed out. "Besides, who knows how long you will have to wait for—uh—Panther. While we accept your right to direct your own life, it would be unfair to make Mark and Hunter bear the brunt of ignorant people's prejudice around town just because you insist on raising them as Cheyenne. They need to fit in, Tanya, and not appear so different from the other children. I don't mean to offend you, but do you understand what I am saying?"

Tanya nodded. "Yes, I do. It is good to know you are not ashamed of us, and I promise to cooperate a little more."

So it was that Tanya found herself attired in lovely new gowns and soft matching slippers, but she adamantly refused to be laced into a stiff corset. Around the house, she still wore her headbands, though her hair, at shoulder length, was still too short to be plaited into respectable braids. When she went out on her solitary walks, she also wore her moccasins, but in public she dressed as the other women did, with one exception. Tanya refused to remove the engraved wristbands Panther had given her on her wedding day under any circumstances. These marked her as Panther's wife as clearly as a wedding ring would have, and she would wear them forever, or until Panther asked her to remove them, a circumstance which Tanya could not imagine occurring.

Hunter preened himself in his new clothes, and Tanya was especially grateful that he was now toilet-trained. Of all people, his Grandpa Edward had taken over this chore, and Tanya hid a smile every time she saw the two of them headed for the outhouse, hand in hand.

Edward had also presented Hunter with a new pair of moccasins he had made himself. Though not as well-made as Tanya would have produced, they were sturdy and the correct size, and Tanya was moved to tears by the gesture.

"It is what he is used to," Edward explained. "I can't see my grandson cramming his feet into hard leather shoes or clumsy boots that might cause blisters and cramp his toes."

February waned into March and stiff winds blustered down from the mountains, rattling windows and bringing the last lingering snows of the winter. Hunter's second birthay was celebrated with much enthusiasm, but with sorrow on Tanya's part as she thought of Panther's absence this year.

The weather did not deter Jeffrey's constant visits. The Martins could not understand how he could fail to see that he was not welcome.

Tanya had no compunctions where he was concerned. Now that she was once more speaking English, she readily told him in no uncertain terms how she felt about him. After her near-rape, at no time did she allow herself to be alone with him, and many times it was Julie who sat through his visits with her.

"I'm glad to see you are finally beginning to act normally, Tanya," he commented, noting her new blue gown. "It will make things much easier when we announce our wedding date."

Tanya's tone was sharp as she answered him. "What must I do to convince you that I am *not* going to marry you, Jeffrey; now or ever? I already have a husband, and I certainly wouldn't have any use for another!"

"I see you are still using that excuse, but it won't hold up in court. Indian ceremonies are not considered legal by the United States government, my dear. Besides, if your alleged husband meant to claim you, wouldn't he have done so by now? Face it, Tanya, the bastard has abandoned you; that, or left you a widow."

Tanya ached to slap the sneer from his face. "Even if that were the case, Lieutenant, you are the last person in the world I would choose as a husband," she grated.

"You were eager enough once before," he pointed out.

"That was before I knew what kind of a person you really are," she rebutted, "and before I knew what real love is."

"You'll change your tune soon enough when you see how few options you have. How many men do you suppose will want you now? You are soiled goods, darling."

"If my choices are you and spinsterhood, I'll choose the latter, thank you."

"Come now, Tanya. Can you truly say that, knowing what it is to share your bed with a man?" Jeffrey's voice was silky, insinuating. "A few more months and you'll be begging me to take you, with or without marriage."

Tanya laughed in his face. "Please Jeffrey, hold your breath until then, and we'll make your funeral arrangements. You'll be doing me a huge favor!"

"You really shouldn't say things like that to me, my love. I might hold a grudge and make you pay for them later," he warned softly.

"Fine!" she snapped. "Then add this to your list. Lieutenant Young, you may go straight, directly to hell and take your lustful twisted mind with you!"

Time and again he returned for more abuse. Sometimes he was calm; at others angry; but he always left frustrated, his ego in tatters, and always he was back again. Nothing Tanya said or did lessened his determination to have her in the end.

Julie could not understand why he persisted in the face of Tanya's blatant rejections.

"I have to admit, Tanya, you are doing your best to get rid of him. Why does he persist in wanting someone who obviously has no use for him? Where is his pride?"

"In the same place as his brains, I suspect," Tanya commented acidly, "and he's evidently mislaid both!"

Julie gave a reluctant chuckle. "Surely he'll give up soon, and perhaps then he'll turn to me for comfort."

Tanya frowned. "Julie, I'm not sure he's right for you, or safe," she added. "I want you to be happy and I don't think Jeffrey is capable of giving you the joy or the gentleness you deserve. I worry that he'd mistreat you."

"Oh, I don't think he'd be that way if he came to love me," Julie disagreed. "You must make him angry with your sharp tongue and your constant refusals."

"I wonder if Jeffrey is capable of loving anyone but himself," Tanya mused. "He's terribly self-centered, has an awful temper—there are times I think he's losing his mind. Only a crazy man would attempt to rape the woman he professes to love. Think about it carefully before you set your heart on him, Julie. I'd hate to see you hurt."

March, having entered like a lion, made an attempt to exit like a lamb. Temperatures were milder, and there was a smell of spring in the air. The snow squalls were less frequent, less fierce, and melted sooner. Spring was finally gaining the upper hand as April brought the Easter season.

With the milder weather, the town came to life. Able to get out and about freely after the long, harsh winter, the women were like prisoners set free. They splurged on new dresses and bonnets and accepted any excuse to show them off. They shopped and visited, arranged teas and luncheons by the score. Social and church committees were in full swing after the winter hiatus.

Urged by her mother, Tanya accepted several invitations to afternoon functions, mostly to silence the gossip stimulated by Suellen's vicious tongue. Still, she went only to the homes of close friends of her mother and aunt, and only in the company of her female relatives. Unwilling to expose her sons to inquisitive stares or catty comments, she rarely took them along.

If nothing else, by entering society, she proved to some of the curious townspeople that she was not an uncouth heathen. Her dress and manners were impeccable. Her speech was soft and genteel, and she was apt to curb indelicate questions and undue curiosity with a frosty demeanor. People soon came to know that while Tanya could be courteous and friendly, she would neither be looked down upon nor divulge information about her life with the Cheyenne.

The only place she could not be convinced to go was to church. Having accepted the Cheyenne religion, Tanya held to her vow to teach her sons the Cheyenne rituals. This she did faithfully, though she was now helping Hunter with his English. She could not see what harm it would do for her children to be bilingual. In fact, she thought it would benefit them in many situations.

As spring progressed, Tanya recalled other springs with Panther, and her heart grew even heavier with worry and longing. She thought lovingly of the first spring when Panther had captured her body and heart. Tears rolled slowly down her cheeks as she remembered her second spring and the birth of Hunter; and the look of pride and wonder on Panther's face as he helped his firstborn son into the world. Last spring they had celebrated Hunter's first birthday together, and Tanya had informed Panther of the advent of a second child.

Poignant memories filled her head and bruised her heart. Would she never again lie next to Panther and feel their hearts beat as one? Would she never hear his voice or see his smile? He had vowed that only death would keep them apart. Surely if he were dead, her heart would have told her. Her very soul cried out to him, "Panther, my love, where are you?"

Chapter 17

THE AFTERNOON was almost balmy as the mid-April sun warmed the tiny glade. Tanya had donned her moccasins and gone to the woods in search of herbs and roots, taking Kit with her. A light breeze played with her tawny locks as they lay shining across her shoulders. Soon her hair would be long enough to braid once more.

Busy digging in the moist earth, Tanya at first ignored the small noises nagging at her brain. Then a feeling of being watched made her tense in alarm. Still stooped, she spun about, her knife held ready, her eyes searching the surrounding trees. Kit, too, had heard the slight movements. The cougar stared intently ahead, her ears perked and listening, her body coiled to spring.

For a few tense seconds nothing moved, and then a tall figure of a man stepped out from behind a tree. He stood in the shadows watching Tanya, saying nothing. He wore dark trousers and shirt, rancher's boots, and had a coat slung across his shoulder. A western hat shaded his face from her view.

Kit snarled a warning. The man said something in a voice too low for Tanya to hear, but Kit evidently heard him. The cougar bounded toward him before Tanya could utter a sound, and to her immense surprise, instead of attacking him, the cat leapt up to rub her head against his chest and lick his chin affectionately with her big wet tongue.

It was then Tanya's heart began a frantic drumbeat in her chest. Her knees went weak, and she stood up on wobbly legs. Her gaze raced over the man's face and form, what little she could see of them, and a thousand butterflies took flight in her stomach as her hopes soared. Tanya's voice cracked as she tried to speak past the lump in her throat. "*Panther*?"

The man stepped forward into the sunlight and Tanya recognized his coat as the cougar-fur jacket she had sewn so lovingly. Her longing eyes traveled to his face, still shaded by his hat, but by now she was sure.

"Oh, Panther!" Her heartfelt cry floated on the breeze. The next thing she knew, without recalling having run to him, Tanya found herself enfolded in his fierce embrace.

"Wildcat," he murmured just before his lips crushed hers. Their kiss carried all the intensity and longing built up through the months of separation.

Tanya's hands crept along his shoulders to find their way into his crisp, sheared hair, her body arching into his in a bid to get closer still, though not a breath of space separated them. Tears of joy flowed down her face, wetting not only her cheeks, but his, adding salt to the nectar of the kiss.

At length, he pulled his mouth reluctantly from hers. "Let me look at you," he breathed. "Let my eyes feast upon your face."

Her own eyes adored his beloved features. "You've grown thinner," she commented breathlessly, "and you've cut your braids."

"So have you," he reminded her. He led her to a fallen log nearby and sat down next to her there.

She lay her head on his chest. "It has been so long, Panther. I worried so!"

"Did you think I would not come?" he asked.

"No. I knew you would come for us, but I worried that you took so long. You said only death would keep us apart, and I wondered if something had happened to you."

Panther nodded. "I was wounded. I came as soon as I could."

At this, Tanya's head flew up and she searched his face apprehensively. "Are you all right now? How badly were you wounded? Who cared for you in my place? When did this happen?"

Panther grinned down at her. "Yes, Woman-of-Many-Questions," he teased, "I am fine, though Shy Deer is convinced only my wish to be with you saved my life. She and Walks-Like-A-Duck nursed me for many weeks. I took a bullet through my shoulder in the last skirmish at the Washita. That alone prevented me from reclaiming you sooner."

"Oh, Panther! Are you *sure* you are all right? It must have been a serious wound to keep you down so long."

"I lost much blood and I still have not regained all my weight, but I am strong and well and here for you now."

He pulled her closer to his side. "How are our sons, Wildcat?"

"They are well," she assured him. "They have grown so much since you've seen them last."

"I am eager to be with them, but first many things must be settled," he told her. "Tell me how things have been for you. You have been staying with your parents?"

Tanya sighed. "Yes. All is well now, but it was a

strange reunion at the beginning. They did not know quite what to think when I arrived with two sons—and Kit! My sister Julie was hateful and my mother pitied me. My father was angry and at first refused to accept Hunter and Mark. They all failed to understand how I could possibly love you."

She paused, and he asked, "Do they accept their grandsons now and the idea of a Cheyenne son-in-law?"

"They all adore the boys. I do not know what they will think of you. They all seemed to believe I would forget you in time, but they are wrong! My love runs too deeply for that, Panther."

"My heart yearned to hear those words from your lips," he told her, rewarding her with a brief hard kiss, then continued, "What has become of Melissa?"

"She lives with us in my aunt and uncle's house. They have adopted her. You would like Aunt Elizabeth. She alone has understood my love for you. Not once did she condemn me for the way I acted upon arriving here. She accepted me as I was and quietly bestowed her love on me."

Panther gave her a thoughtful look. "What did you do to upset them so, besides bring my sons into their home?"

Tanya's chin came up proudly. "When I saw their reactions to me and our sons, I refused to speak anything but Cheyenne, except to Jeremy, my aunt's nephew. He has twelve summers and was quite impressed with Kit and me." Tanya shook her head. "Poor Melissa was left to interpret and do all the explaining. I continued to dress in my deerskins and headbands, I insisted on keeping Kit inside to protect us, I even prepared a pallet on the floor, refusing to sleep in their soft bed. Above all else, I rejected

Jeffrey's declarations of love and had the bad manners to attempt an escape, trying to return to you."

Panther's dark eyes widened at this. "What? When was this?"

"It was two moons past, and Jeffrey caught up to me with a troop of his men. I got only as far as the Arkansas River."

"This Jeffrey," Panther frowned, "is he the man you were promised to before I captured you?"

Tanya nodded. "Yes. He is a lieutenant in the cavalry. He was at Washita with General Custer and found me. At first my family hoped we would marry. Jeffrey still wanted to marry me, but I would not have him. I told them I already had a husband."

"Do they still want you to accept this man?" Panther asked, scowling.

"Jeffrey is still adamant, but my family has seen how crazed he can be and now they shield me from him. My father saved me when Jeffrey tried to rape me after I ran away."

Panther grabbed Tanya by the shoulders, his face stormy. "He *raped* you?"

"No, Panther," Tanya caressed his face between her hands. "He tried and failed. Since then he has apologized, but none of us will listen, except Julie. She is besotted with him and it caused her pain to see how obsessed he is with me. I hope it is a passing infatuation with her, for I fear Jeffrey is not in his right mind half of the time."

"He will never have you, not while I live," Panther vowed passionately, stroking her hair.

"Not under any circumstances," Tanya corrected gently, her golden eyes shining into his. "Oh, Panther, it is heaven to be back in your arms! I missed you so!"

Tanya's hands once more pushed their way into his hair, knocking his hat off. Suddenly a thought occurred to her that she had brushed away until now. Her brow knitted thoughtfully as she inspected his clothing.

"Panther, why are you dressed this way? Where did you get these clothes?"

A shadow seemed to fall over his face as he gazed at her intently. "Tanya, there are things you do not know that I must explain to you." He waited expectantly, trying to gauge her reaction.

It took a few seconds for his words to soak in, and then she exclaimed, "Panther! You spoke to me in English!" Her face registered her shock, her eyes wide in surprise. "How long have you spoken English? I detect no sign of an accent."

"Since I was a child. I grew up speaking Spanish, Cheyenne, and English." Panther's hands tightened on her arms as she tried to pull away from him.

Hurt and angry, Tanya glared at him. "You understood every word I've ever said to you!" she accused. "You let me make a fool of myself! You saw me struggling to communicate my thoughts and feelings, and never let on! You made me falter my way along until I learned Cheyenne!"

Panther nodded calmly. "You needed to learn Cheyenne. In fact, you learned faster because of your need to communicate."

"You could have told me afterward," she insisted.

"I saw no need to until now."

Something in his face made her ask, "Why now?"

"There is more you must hear," he continued seriously. "My father was Chief White Antelope, Black Kettle's brother. This you know. What I have never told you is that my mother is white."

Tanya gasped in surprise, and Panther shushed her with a finger to her lips.

"Actually, she is a Spanish Mexican, captured by my father near Sante Fe. She detested the Cheyenne ways, and though she became my father's wife and they loved one another, after my birth she wished to return to her own people. My father let her go, taking me with her. Now you see why Black Kettle set up such rigid tests for you to prove yourself. He saw how heartbroken my father was to part with his wife and son.

"Raquel and her father, Miguel Valera relocated to Pueblo, where they bought a ranch north of town. No one knew of my heritage, so my grandfather suggested my mother pose as a widow. In a fit of pique at his suggestion, my mother chose the surname of Savage for her married name. She became known as Rachel Savage around Pueblo.

"All my life I was known here as Adam Savage. Not one person knows I spent my summers with my father in the Cheyenne village. They all thought I went to Santa Fe or Mexico to visit relatives, that my father was an Englishman and that I take my coloring from my Spanish background.

"I've been raised and educated as white. I have life-long friends in this town, and everyone knows and respects the Savage name. My mother runs the ranch in my absence, and over the years we've acquired wealth and prestige. I spent a few years attending college back East. Two years before my father's death, I chose to live permanently with the Cheyenne. I prefer their way of life. My mother has spread the tale that I am living in Europe to explain my absence.

"I know you are hurt that I did not tell you these things. At first I saw no reason to. Then, when you became my wife and were expecting my child, I felt that if I told you at that time, you would want me to bring you to your parents. I could not do that, Tanya. I had chosen my life with my father's people, and you had to choose it too, freely and completely, with no regrets and no ties to the past. Later, it did not seem important to tell you. I could not guess that one day we would be separated, or that we would come together again like this."

"You deceived me," she charged, her voice shaking with unshed tears.

"No," he denied promptly. "I was what you believed me to be; what I chose to be. It was important that you accept me as such, and not hope to return to the white world someday. I am A-Panther-Stalks, Cheyenne Chief, and you are my wife, the mother of my sons. Nothing can change that; not all your hurt or your anger. I know it has been a shock to you, but it does not alter our relationship. My love for you is still the same, your heart still calls to mine. If you deny it, you are a liar."

Tanya, fighting her hurt and confusion, said nothing.

"You made vows to me, Tanya; binding vows," he reminded her sternly. "You promised to obey me, to see to my comforts and raise my children, and to follow wherever I go. I am holding you to your words. You are my wife in every sense of the word, and I will never let you go. Both of us have suffered this separation long enough, through no fault of our own. We are together now, as we should be, and it would be foolish to let pride stand in the way of happiness. Are you now going to act as a loving wife should, or are you going to show me how stubborn you can be and hurt us both?"

He smiled down at her tenderly as she considered this. "My arrogance is stronger than your stubbornness, little one. You know I will win in the end, so why not save your energy for better purposes?"

Panther's lips hovered over hers as he finished speaking, teasing at the corners of her mouth until her lips came up to meet his in a kiss of surrender. With a sigh of resignation, her arms encircled his neck as she yielded totally to his sweet persuasion.

"Panther, I do love you," she conceded in a whisper. "I'll always love you."

"Show me," he commanded softly.

There, in the shelter of the glade, they made love after months of agonizing separation. Panther undressed her, slowly exposing every inch of her soft skin.

"I knew there was a reason I dressed you in buckskin. This gown has a thousand buttons." He gave an exasperated chuckle.

Tanya laughed at his expression. "I only gave up my deerskins two months ago, after my attempt to return to you. They were unfit to wear any longer. Besides, my family had fully accepted Hunter and Mark by then, and I also started to speak English then."

"Am I making love to a white woman now?" Panther questioned hesitantly.

Tanya shook her head. "I am what you make me; what you want me to be; your wife and your love."

Her answer satisfied his doubts, and his lips claimed hers in a kiss clearly meant to dominate, to mark her as his alone. Tanya submitted willingly, sensing his need to renew his mastery over her. She revelled in the strength of his arms about her, his lips molding hers, his hands undressing and caressing her.

Following his lead, she helped him shed his

clothing, then stood drinking in the sight of his glorious bronze body. Her fingers traced the still-pink scars of the new wound of his shoulder. Tears blurred her vision as she leaned forward to gently kiss the wound, as if to heal him with her lips, to absorb some of the pain he had endured.

"Don't think of it, my darling," he told her. "Just let me love you as I have longed to for so many months."

He worshipped her with his eyes, his lips, his hands, rediscovering every familiar line of her body. Their fingertips lingered delicately, their senses heightened by abstinence. Her skin tingled beneath his touch, and caught fire as his lips and tongue found sensitive areas so long ignored. Her breasts swelled to fill his palms, and the ache in her belly grew as his mouth teased at her nipples, suckling and nipping gently. Soon she was clutching him to her, begging him to make her wholly his once more.

When he joined his body with hers, Tanya's world exploded in sensual delight. They climbed the mountain of ecstasy together until, at the very summit, lightning struck at her very soul, searing their bodies and hearts. They were complete once more, and Tanya's sigh echoed his own . . .

The lenghtening shadows told Tanya how fast the afternoon had flown. "It is getting late, Panther. We must go. I will be missed."

A look of regret flitted across his handsome face. "Let us get dressed and we will make our plans," he told her.

When they were once again clothed, he drew her to him. "I have given this much thought. I cannot suddenly appear on your doorstep as your husband. My identity as A-Panther-Stalks must remain a secret, especially with the young lieutenant so much in evidence, though he has never seen me close enough to recognize me."

Tanya agreed. "Yes, and there is Suellen to consider. She is still in Pueblo awaiting her parents' arrival from California. We needn't worry about Melissa. She would not divulge your identity, I am sure."

"What about the other women captives?" Panther wondered.

"There are only three of us left; Melissa, myself, and Suellen." Tanya enumerated. "Rosemary was traded to another tribe in the spring, Black Kettle's slave was killed in the attack, and Nancy died at Camp Supply of a miscarriage on the way back."

Panther mulled this over in his mind. "The best thing to do is have you meet me as Adam Savage, but this must be done properly. Your parents must not suspect anything."

Tanya nodded. "What do you suggest?"

"Do you know Judge Kerr and his family? They are some of our closest friends. I grew up with his son, Justin, and my mother and Emily are as close as sisters."

"I have met them." Tanya smiled as she added, "Justin seems to have taken quite an interest in Melissa. He'll probably be hanging about in hopes of furthering his chances with her when we go to tea there tomorrow afternoon."

Panther kissed her hard on the lips, grinning like an overgrown boy. "You have just solved our problems, my brilliant wife," he crowed. "Tomorrow, while you are having tea at the Kerr's, Adam Savage is going to visit his old friend, Justin. Naturally, he will notice the beautiful Tanya Martin with the exquisite golden eyes, and demand an introduction. What do you think?"

"It is perfect!" Tanya agreed with a delighted laugh. Then she sobered, "Except for one thing. We will still be apart from one another. I want to be your wife again."

"Then I shall court you," Panther announced, his dark eyes twinkling. "This time we will have your parents' approval!"

"But it will take so long," she moaned, "and I want to be with you constantly—though it will serve to get Jeffrey Young off my back. With you as my new fiancé, he will have to accept defeat, but I doubt if he will do so gracefully."

"Do not fret, dear heart. Our courtship will proceed at an alarming rate of speed, and I can handle any problems with Lt. Young. Meanwhile, we will arrange hidden trysts to satisfy your burning desires and my own lustful nature," he teased with a lingering kiss. "Now you must go before we are discovered together."

"Wait! You have told me nothing of our friends or where the Cheyenne are now. Where is Kat?"

"Kat is in the village with Walks-Like-A-Duck. The tribe is camped along Medicine Lodge Creek just now, and Winter Bear is chief in my absence. It has been a hard winter for the Cheyenne. We lived huddled together in borrowed tipis, and food was scarce. Circumstances should improve now that spring is here. Already the braves have been out on hunts to replenish food and furs."

Tanya bit her lip in despair at his disclosure. "I worried how you would survive the winter with no shelter or supplies. Even the buffalo ponies were slaughtered."

Her voice quivered as she recalled the massacre

she'd witnessed, and tears raced down her cheeks unchecked. "Never will I forget that day; not if I live to be a hundred! Blood and bodies everywhere! And the screams; Oh, God, the screams!"

Tanya didn't even feel his arms about her as she relived the terror of that day. "Babies with their skulls crushed like melons, bodies without heads or limbs, infants skewered on swords! They cut Forest Fern's stomach open, and her unborn child fell out onto the ground! They shot Black Kettle and Woman-To-Be-Hereafter and trampled their bodies into the river mud, their blood staining the waters!"

Her hysteria mounted as she told him what came next, her voice catching in wrenching sobs. 'The soldiers cut away parts of the dead bodies, mutilating them horribly. They laughed about how they would have tobacco pouches made from the private parts of the men and women. Then they raped the women captives, and I could do nothing to prevent any of it. It was a nightmare! Even now it seems too frightening to have been real!"

"Shush, my darling." Panther held her and stroked her as she cried. "It is over with now. Our people went back and buried our dead, though I remember little of this. Many of our friends died that day, but a fair number survived. Just last month, George Bent and the other released captives caught up with us and brought fresh ponies from his father's ranch. It is from him that I learned where you were. I thought perhaps you were kept with Custer's troops until spring."

"No, Jeffrey brought Melissa and me straight home in time for Christmas. General Custer and I did not see eye to eye, and I think he was heartily relieved to have me off his hands."

Tanya sniffed and blew her nose on the hankie

Panther handed her. "Did Magpie and her youngest son make it to safety?"

"Yes. She and George are together once more, and they have a daughter now. Winter Bear, Snail, and Towering Pine will keep the camp running smoothly. Shy Deer and her child are doing well. She told me to bring you home soon. She misses you. Walks-Like-A-Duck grieves over your absence and pines for Hunter and Mark terribly. I believe she even misses Kit."

Tanya gave one last, lingering shudder and sighed tiredly, leaning heavily against Panther's broad chest.

He stroked her shining hair. "Life goes on, Tanya, and we must make the best of it. We must go on with our lives, keeping our faith, remembering with love those who are gone, and building a future for those who will come after us. We have found one another again, and soon we will be a family once more. I long to see my sons. Will you bring them with you tomorrow to the Kerrs'?"

"If you wish it, Panther. You will hardly recognize them, they have grown so."

"I doubt Hunter will even remember me." Panther's face was momentarily downcast. "And if he does, he must not reveal it."

With one last, prolonged kiss, he set her away from him. "You must go now. I will see you tomorrow."

"It will seem an eternity now that I know you are so near," she said wistfully. "Until tomorrow, husband."

"Until tomorrow," he repeated softly as he watched her disappear into the trees.

Tanya was so excited that evening that she was sure her dinner would not settle properly. It surprised her that none of her family noticed her extreme agitation.

As soon as she could, she dragged Melissa off into a

corner and prepared her for the confrontation the next day. The last thing they needed was for Melissa to betray them in her surprise. Tanya assured the girl that Panther would not drag her back to the Cheyenne camp when he took Tanya and the boys with him. As she had expected, Melissa promised to cooperate and vowed eternal silence and allegiance.

The one cloud on her horizon came when Jeffrey put in an appearance after dinner, but even he could not ruin her happiness entirely. Confident, and full of great expectations of the morrow, she largely ignored his presence. Only when he pressed for her attention, did her temper ignite.

"You look unusually lovely this evening, Tanya. Your cheeks are flushed and your eyes aglow. You look like a woman ready for love," he suggested.

"It is the spring weather, Jeffrey," she stated flatly. "The sun and wind add color to any winter-pale face."

"In spring, a young man's fancy turns to love," he quoted with a satisfied smirk.

"And his mind turns to mush!" she retorted sharply. "Try fishing, Lieutenant. It's less trying on the nervous system."

"I'd rather hook your heart," he replied ardently.

"You haven't the proper bait," she shot back. "There's not a thing about you that tempts me."

Jeffrey smiled tolerantly. "That can change."

"Pigs could grow wings, too," she taunted.

"With time I can make you want me, my sweet," he countered determinedly.

"Oh, go jump in the lake, Jeffrey!" she declared wearily. "Maybe it will cool your ardor. Perhaps it would even deflate your over-sized self-esteem!"

That night, Tanya slept in fits and starts, her mind

and her dreams filled with images of Panther. Finally, toward dawn, she drifted into a light sleep, her lovely lips curved in a satisfied smile as she contemplated the day to come.

Chapter 18

AS SHE sat quietly sipping tea in Emily Kerr's parlor, Tanya nearly shook in anticipation of Panther's arrival. Each time she raised her delicate china cup, she feared she would either drop it or spill tea over her dress.

She had taken particular care with her appearance this afternoon. She wore a cream colored dress with a lace insert in the bodice and loose lacy cuffs that fluttered over her wrists on which, as always, she wore the copper wristbands. Her hair was swept loosely back from her face, and in her ears were the copper earrings Panther had given her before their wedding.

Hunter sat contentedly on his grandmother Sarah's lap and Mark gurgled happily from his cradleboard at Tanya's knees.

Halfway into her second cup of tea, Tanya's heart leaped into her throat as she heard the deep tones of Panther's voice in the hallway. Seconds later, Justin Kerr entered the room, followed by Panther.

Panther was handsomely attired in fawn colored trousers, cream silk shirt, and tobacco brown jacket. His impeccably correct silk cravat was the same shade as his coat, and his expensive brown leather boots were buffed to a fine luster.

As Justin introduced him, he bent to kiss Emily's hand.

"Why, Adam Savage!" she crooned delightedly. "Where have you been off to for so long, and when did you get home?"

"He's been off touring Europe, Mother," Justin supplied.

"I just got back yesterday, and I rushed right over to see your lovely face," Adam said flirtatously. "And now I find myself surrounded by a bevy of beautiful women I've never met before. Had I known Pueblo was attracting such lovely ladies, I'd have returned sooner." His dark eyes and sparkling smile included all the women in the room.

"Oh, my! Forgive my awful manners!" Emily apologized, thoroughly flustered. "Ladies, may I present Adam Savage, Rachel Savage's son. Adam, this is Elizabeth Martin and her sister-in-law Sarah Martin. Their husbands own the mercantile and lumber businesses in town. This," she indicated Melissa, seated next to Elizabeth, "is Miss Melissa Anderson, who lives with the Martins, and these two young ladies are Sarah's daughters, Julie and Tanya."

Adam acknowledged all of them with a slight bow. "And who have we here?" he questioned, stooping down to greet Hunter.

"This is my son, Hunter," Tanya answered softly, her eyes lingering on the two of them, father and son, as Hunter bestowed a toothy grin on Adam.

"He's a handsome boy," Adam commented. "Is this your child also?"

Tanya nodded as Adam bent to chuck Mark under the chin. "My son Mark, Mr. Savage."

"You and your husband are to be congratulated on

such a fine family," Adam complimented. Only Tanya seemed to note the devilish gleam in his dark eyes.

"Thank you," she answered serenely.

Emily gave a small, strangled gasp.

Adam immediately swung his gaze toward her, his brow knitted thoughtfully. "Have I said something wrong, Em?"

"No, no," she assured him hastily.

"Ahem," Justin inserted. "Adam, old friend, Miss Martin spent some years with the Cheyenne—through no fault of her own, you understand. These are her sons by her Cheyenne captor." Justin was extremely uncomfortable at having to explain this in mixed company.

"He was my husband," Tanya corrected immediately, her voice crisp and clear.

"Yes, Tanya dear, so you've said before," Emily commented lamely.

"And did you love him?" Adam pressed, his dark eyes locked with Tanya's.

"Very much, Mr. Savage."

"Well, girls, don't you think we'd better start back home?" Sarah suggested hopefully, anxious to put off further embarrassing questions.

Adam ignored her, concentrating totally on Tanya. "Miss Martin, those are lovely copper bands you have on your wrists. A memento of your days with the Cheyenne?"

"My wedding bands," she admitted, wondering why Panther was asking her these questions in front of the others. What did he think he was doing?

"Are you a widow?" he persisted.

"Not that I am aware of, Mr. Savage. I was rescued quite against my will, and have hopes of being reunited with my husband someday." Tanya's chin rose a fraction. "I find your questions rather personal, sir."

"I beg your pardon, ma'am, but I find your honesty refreshing. Not many women would be willing to reveal a past such as yours, let alone take her sons about with her in public. You have won my admiration. I have never before asked to call on a married lady, but may I have your permission to do so tomorrow?"

Tanya hesitated, not knowing quite how to phrase her reply.

"My daughter does not receive gentlemen callers as yet," Sarah explained in the pause.

"I believe my mother is trying to protect me from your rather forward attitude, sir," Tanya responded. "I must admit I am a bit taken aback myself."

"Again I apologize. Ordinarily my manners do not desert me. My only excuse is that I am stunned by your beauty and charm. If you have doubts, Justin can vouch for my good character. The Kerrs have known me since childhood and will testify to my honesty and integrity."

"Oh, my, yes!" Emily agreed hastily. "Rachel and Adam have lived here for as long as anyone can remember, since Pueblo was little more than a handful of Mormon farms. Their cattle ranch is one of the finest in the state, and a more decent, upstanding family you'll never find. They have won the respect and admiration of everyone in town. Justin and Adam grew up together and were the best of friends until Adam went away. Why, I nearly regard Adam as a second son!"

Tanya's eyes glittered with suppressed laughter. "I wasn't questioning Mr. Savage's integrity, Mrs. Kerr, merely his attitude and intentions."

"Let me assure you they are respectful and honorable, Miss Martin." Adam was having trouble keeping a straight face, but his Cheyenne training held him in good stead.

Tanya decided to let him off the hook. "In that case, you may come for luncheon tomorrow. Is that satisfactory Mother, Aunt Elizabeth?"

"Quite," Elizabeth said decisively.

"Uh, yes, I would suppose so," Sarah stammered.

"Would you care to come also, Justin?" Tanya offered, knowing he would jump at the chance to be with Melissa. "Mr. Savage may feel outnumbered amidst so many females."

"I'd love to," Justin agreed speedily, casting a glance at Melissa.

Julie, who had sat quietly until now, was overjoyed at the thought of someone upsetting Jeffrey's plans for Tanya. "And I always thought teas were a bit boring. It just shows how wrong a person can be sometimes!" she commented.

"My! What a handsome young man!" Elizabeth announced once they were home.

"And well-to-do, if Emily is not stretching the truth," Sarah added thoughtfully. "He didn't seem put off by Tanya's admissions, did he?"

"Quite the opposite I'd say," Melissa contributed with a sly wink at Tanya. "I think he was quite taken with you, Tanya."

"This ought to take the wind out of Jeffrey's sails. I'd say Mr. Savage has come along at a very opportune moment," said Julie.

"Really, Julie!" Sarah admonished. "The man is merely coming to lunch. That does not qualify him as a suitor, though he would be very acceptable as such," she admitted.

"Yes, well, Justine seems to take quite an interest in our little Melissa, in case none of you have noticed." Tanya was glad to turn some of the attention away from herself.

Melissa blushed prettily. "I'd noticed," she admitted shyly. "He's quite nice, don't you agree?"

Tanya smiled. "Yes, Missy, he's very nice."

"It was gracious of you to invite Justin to lunch, Tanya," Elizabeth noted. "Did you do it for Melissa's benefit?"

It was Tanya's turn to blush. "I admit it," she laughed. "I am guilty of matchmaking. I hope you don't mind, Aunt Elizabeth."

Elizabeth chuckled. "Why should I mind? You saved me the trouble of inviting him myself. Besides, I am not entirely innocent of matchmaking myself. I admit I made a mistake pairing you up with Jeffrey, but this Adam Savage seems quite a catch if you ask me. I wouldn't let him slip through the net without looking him over first."

"What do you think of him?" Julie pressed. "And don't hand me that excuse about already having a husband. A bird in the hand is worth two in the bush, you know."

"Julie, I've only just met the man, and I do have a husband as well as two sons to consider," Tanya countered.

"He seemed to like the boys—which is more than I can say for Jeffrey," Elizabeth snorted indignantly.

Sarah agreed. "That is something to keep in mind, Tanya."

"Fine. I'll admit the man impressed me. Now can

we end this conversation for the time being? There is obviously a houseful of matchmakers under this roof, and it could get tiresome after a while."

Tanya had to endure another round of explanations and effusive praise of Adam Savage when her father and uncle appeared for supper.

"I've sold supplies and lumber to the Savages for years, and Emily Kerr was not exaggerating. They are quite well off," George agreed. "Of course, I've only met the son a few times, years ago. He went off to college soon after we arrived here. Good looking young man, as I recall."

"I should say!" Julie avowed.

Edward eyed his eldest daughter thoughtfully. "He must have made quite an impression for Tanya to have invited him to lunch."

"Oh, for heavens sake!" Tanya fumed. "I merely thought it would be a good way to convince Jeffrey of my lack of interest in him," she fabricated.

"It will certainly set him on his ear, all right," Melissa commented, rolling her eyes expressively. "I can hardly wait to see his reaction!"

"What in the world do you suppose Panther—er—Adam was up to yesterday with all those questions, Tanya?" Melissa asked the next day as they polished the dining room furniture. Elizabeth had set everyone, including Jeremy since it was Saturday, to work cleaning the house.

"I have no idea," Tanya replied, "but his conversation certainly took me by surprise, and I intend to ask him about it later. There, the last of the dusting is done. Heavens, Missy! You'd think the President was coming to dine! What's gotten into Aunt Elizabeth? She's got Jeremy shaking rugs, Mother polishing silver, Julie busy in the parlor, and she's been in the kitchen since breakfast preparing the most delicious smelling dishes."

Melissa giggled. "Two of the most eligible bachelors in Pueblo are coming to lunch, and I believe she'd like to marry us off. Perhaps she intends to turn this place into a boarding house and rent out our rooms!" she joked.

Tanya joined in, "If that's the case, she'd better line up a beau for Julie or talk Papa into building his own house."

Melissa suddenly turned serious. "Tanya, I like Justin very much. I suppose I could even fall in love with him, but I'm scared. I don't think I could ever be a real wife to him or anyone."

Tanya crossed to her friend and put her arms about her. "Because of Ugly Otter?"

Melissa nodded. "And the miscarriage. That part of marriage terrifies me!"

"But Missy, you saw how happy Panther and I were, and I know you heard our lovemaking. How could you not, in the same tipi? Lovemaking can be so wonderful, so beautiful, with the person you love. Justin is not a beast like Ugly Otter. He seems to be a fine gentleman, and I'm sure he'd love you tenderly and cherish you all your life."

"What about children?" Melissa persisted.

"Root Woman assured us there was no damage to your body, Melissa. You can conceive again."

Melissa bit her lip in anguish. "I don't think I could stand the pain. The miscarriage almost killed me, and Nancy *did* die."

"Oh, Missy!" Tanya's voice held all the compassion she felt for the girl. "Under the right circumstances, and with proper care, you may never miscarry again. You'll bear lovely children and they will fulfill your life. Childbirth is well worth the pain when you hold that tiny life in your arms; when you see the pride on your husband's face. You were there when Hunter was born. You've seen it all. Don't fear it, Missy. It is the most beautiful, reverent experience for a woman. Don't let fear keep you from the man you love or experiences you'll cherish all your life."

Melissa swallowed hard and nodded. "I'll think about it."

Tanya added one last thought. "Justin knows you were with me those years with the Cheyenne. I'm sure he guesses you had a pretty rough time of it. If he is truly the right man for you, he'll understand and be gentle with you. If things become serious between you, talk to him about it; explain your fears and let him help you."

"A lot depends on Justin," Melissa said.

Tanya agreed, "And a lot depends on how badly you want a life with him and how much you love him."

Seated about the large dining room table were Uncle George, Aunt Elizabeth, Sarah, Edward, Melissa, Jeremy, Julie, Tanya, Hunter in his high chair, and Adam and Justin. The two Martin men had made a point of being home today to meet Adam Savage. Tanya wondered if he felt as if he were under inspection. She certainly felt as if she were on display, rather like a slave on the auction block. At any moment, she expected her father to pry open her mouth and show the others what wonderful teeth she had! She wondered if Melissa felt the same.

"I understand your family owns a cattle ranch north of town," Edward was saying to Adam.

"Yes sir, about twenty miles out."

"But I understand your mother is a widow. Who

runs the ranch while you are gone?" Sarah inquired.

"Mother does," Adam grinned. "She governs the place with an iron hand in a velvet glove, and she has very reliable help. Our foreman has been with us for years, and there are plenty of ranch hands, plus a cook and household help. The place pretty well runs itself, as it has since before my grandfather died."

"Did your father start the ranch?" Elizabeth asked.

"No, my mother and grandfather settled the place when I was a baby. Father never lived there."

"He was gone by then?"

Adam nodded.

"I've heard he was English," George commented. "Do you have relatives in Europe?"

"A few, mostly very distant. My closest relatives are spread out between here and Mexico."

"Are you going to be staying in Pueblo now?" Julio inquired.

"For a while at least," he answered. "There are some things that could hold me here indefinitely." His dark eyes rested deliberately on Tanya as he spoke.

"Do you raise horses, too, Mr. Savage?" Jeremy asked innocently, breaking the spell that seemed to hold the others.

"Some, Jeremy, but mostly cattle. You could come out and ride some weekend if your folks don't mind."

"Could I really?"

"Yes, but I'd like it if you would bring Miss Tanya along to keep me company," Adam grinned.

"Same old Adam," Justin complained comically. "Give him an inch, and he'll try to steal a mile."

Tanya's smile escalated into a laugh. "It is his subtlety that amazes me!" she jibed.

After that, everyone relaxed to enjoy the meal. Laughter and easy conversation replaced the stiffly polite atmosphere that had prevailed earlier. Adam, aided by Justin, charmed everyone with tales of his youth.

When the meal was done, they retired to the parlor for coffee. Hunter toddled up to Adam tugging on his pants leg. Adam automatically lifted his son to his lap, undisturbed as Hunter played with the shiny buttons of his shirt.

"Oh, Mr. Savage, he'll ruin your shirt," Sarah exclaimed. "Let me take him upstairs for a while."

"He's no bother," Adam assured her. "I'm used to children."

Justin looked surprised. "Since when?" he blurted.

Adam's teeth flashed in a grin. "Since the last time I saw you, old friend."

Tanya adored seeing her son snuggled on his father's lap once again. She was surprised that Hunter had gone to him so readily. She couldn't help but wonder if somewhere in his baby's memory he somehow remembered Adam as Panther, even in some small unconscious way.

A crucial moment arrived when Jeremy accidentally let Kit into the house. Kit had been banned for the afternoon. Now she strutted straight up to Adam, licked Hunter playfully, rubbed her head along Adam's thigh, and lay placidly across his feet.

"Well, I'll be!" George declared. "I've never seen her act that way before with a stranger. She usually growls and hisses, and whenever Jeffrey comes by, she'd rather eat him alive than let him near the boys."

"Animals sense whom to be wary of," Adam stated. "I think she knows I'm a friend."

"He's right," Jeremy announced importantly. "Kit has always liked me because I've liked Tanya and the boys from the start. She must trust you, Mr. Savage."

"Now, if I can just convince Miss Tanya as easily," Adam half-joked, raising an eyebrow in Tanya's direction.

"I doubt you'll have me lying quietly at your feet, sir," she teased lightly, her golden eyes shining.

The look he returned told her he might want her at his feet, but never to lie there quietly.

The two young couples, with Julie acting as chaperon, took a walk a short time later.

"Oh, Edward," Sarah sighed as she peeked out between the lace panels at the window, "do you suppose Tanya is finally going to give up her dreams of that Indian husband of hers? This is the first time she's shown any real interest in another man!"

Edward puffed on his pipe and exhaled to watch the smoke drift lazily to the ceiling. "I think Adam Savage has a running start already, Sarah dear. It is all a matter of time, and how stubborn Tanya decides to be. Adam strikes me as a man who knows what he wants and how to get it."

"Since we've already got the house as clean as it's ever going to be, I've invited Adam for Sunday dinner," Tanya announced when she returned.

"Adam now, is it?" Elizabeth noticed wryly. "What happened to 'Mr. Savage' and 'sir'?"

Tanya laughed "I agreed to call him Adam if he'd stop calling me Miss Tanya. It made me feel like an old-maid school teacher!"

"That's not all," Julie tattled. "Tanya even let him hold her hand!"

"You always were a great one for carrying tales!" Tanya accused, not at all carrying off her attempt to look angry.

Julie stuck her tongue out partly. "At least I didn't tell them how he guided you over the path with his hand at your waist!" she confided in a staged whisper.

"Blabbermouth!"

"Oh, go feed your infant son, and don't get yourself upset over little things or next thing you know you'll give Mark colic," Sarah admonished.

"Is that why Julie turned out as she did?" Tanya fired her parting shot as she scampered up the stairs.

"Girls!" Edward muttered to himself.

They had just sat down to their dinner the next day, when there was a knock at the door.

"Anyone care to guess who that might be?" Melissa quipped.

Tanya made a face. "Jeffrey" she groaned. "Oh, dear!"

"Just answer the door, Julie," Edward instructed. "We may as well get this over with."

To Adam he said, "Has Tanya told you about Jeffrey Young?"

Adam smiled wryly. "Her ex-fiancé? Yes."

"Good. I wouldn't want you to walk into this blindly. He's bound to take offense if he thinks you have any interest in Tanya."

"Which I do," Adam answered forthrightly.

Julie led Jeffrey into the dining room. "Look who's come to visit," she announced unnecessarily, steering Jeffrey to the chair next to hers, directly across the table from Tanya and Adam. "I'll get another place setting."

Jeffrey glared at Adam, seated next to Tanya. "I didn't realize you had company. I don't believe we've met."

"Adam Savage; Jeffrey Young," Edward said shortly, without elaborating.

"How like you not to let us know you were coming

before blessing us with your presence," Tanya stated tartly.

"I always come on Sundays," Jeffrey returned defensively.

"We've tried not to notice, Lieutenant," Melissa inserted.

Jeffrey ignored this, thanking Julie as she placed his plate before him. "What brings you to Pueblo, Mr. Savage?" he asked authoritatively.

Adam's lips quirked suspiciously as he hid a grin. "I live here."

Jeffrey frowned. "I've never seen you before."

"I didn't realize census-taking was part of your duties with the Army," George noted dryly.

Jeffrey shot him a quelling look. "It was merely an observation, Mr. Martin. I simply said I'd never noticed Mr. Savage around town."

"Not surprising, since he just returned from an extensive journey in Europe," Julie soothed.

Stretching the truth just a bit, Melissa added, "He's spent the last couple of years with his father's people."

Adam, Tanya and Melissa exchanged a quick look of shared conspiracy.

"Surely you are aware of the Savage ranch, Jeffrey," Sarah enlightened him. "Rachel Savage is quite often in town. Adam is her son."

"I see." Jeffrey took a moment to absorb this information.

Tanya deliberately leaned toward Adam, lightly brushing her breast against his arm, sure that Jeffrey had noted the gesture. "Pass the biscuits, would you please, Adam?" she asked sweetly.

"With pleasure," he smiled.

Hunter chose this moment to demand his dinner, noisily banging his spoon on the tray of his highchair.

Jeffrey glared at him irritably. "Why don't you feed the child before the rest of us are seated, Tanya? He's such a nuisance at the table."

"Cheyenne children are always fed with their mothers," Tanya responded sharply, "after their fathers have eaten."

As she reached for Hunter, Adam ordered quietly, but firmly, "Give him to me, Tanya, and finish your meal."

To everyone's surprise but Melissa's, Tanya obeyed without hesitation, transferring Hunter to Adam's lap.

As Tanya resumed eating, Adam proceeded to feed Hunter from his own plate.

"It amazes me to see how comfortable you are around young children, Mr. Savage," Sarah commented in the lull.

"My people adore children," Adam answered, unperturbed by Jeffrey's sour glare.

"Yet you are an only child," Elizabeth commented. "How sad for your mother. I'm surprised she never remarried. She must have loved your father dearly."

Adam agreed. "With all her heart."

"How admirable," Jeffrey sneered. "There are so many others, such as my sweet Tanya here, who can be so fickle at times." His blue eyes fixed on Tanya. "But that will soon end, will it not, Tanya darling?"

"I wouldn't count on it where you are concerned, Jeffrey. Don't place any wagers along those lines, or you'll lose your bootlaces." Tanya bestowed a falsely sweet smile on him.

Adam managed to look convincingly confused. "Have I missed something here?"

Jeffrey ignored him, concentrating on Tanya. "Once we're married, you'll change your tune, my sweet."

"If that day should ever come, God forbid, I'd expect to hear a funeral dirge in place of wedding bells!"

Edward's voice cut off any comment Jeffrey might have made. "Enough of this bickering! We are trying to enjoy our meal. Sunday is supposed to be a day of peace—though it rarely is around here," he sighed.

Later, having coffee in the parlor, Jeffrey was angered to find himself again outmaneuvered as Adam seated himself next to Tanya on the small sofa.

A short time later, Kit came bounding down the stairs and into the parlor. She stopped once to snarl at Jeffrey, then approached Tanya, gently nudging her leg with her head, and pawing at her arm.

Tanya laughed. "All right, Kit! I'm coming."

To Adam, she explained, "This is her way of telling me that Mark is awake upstairs and needs my attention. If you'll excuse me for a little while, I shall go tend to him."

Jeffrey stood impatiently. "Tanya, I want to speak with you."

On her way out of the room, Tanya swirled to face him. "I hardly think now would be appropriate, Jeffrey. I must feed Mark." Her tone was icy.

Jeffrey's lips thinned in his frustration. "The child is six months old, Tanya. If you'd listen to my advice and put him on a bottle, anyone could perform that chore. You'd be less tied down and have more time for yourself."

Tanya glared at him, her golden eyes flashing. "If your concern were not so self-centered, I'd be touched," she stated acidly.

Turning her attention to Adam, she smiled sweetly. "If you will excuse me, I'll tend to my son."

"I'll wait here for you and we can take a walk when you return," Adam suggested.

Julie grimaced. "Does that mean I have to go along as chaperone?"

"Not at all." Tanya tossed her tawny head. "You can stay and keep Lieutenant Young company. I'm sure Melissa will agree to accompany us if a chaperone is required." With that, she turned and left the room.

Jeffrey caught her in the hall as she returned downstairs. Grabbing her roughly by the arm, he faced her angrily. "I forbid you to go with that man, Tanya!"

Her eyes flashed a warning he ignored. "You are not in a position to order me about, Lieutenant. You are neither my father, nor my husband. Now, let go of my arm, if you please."

"I am your fiancé," he persisted.

"*Ex*-fiancé," Tanya stressed, hissing the words at him. "*Ex*, as in past, passe, finished, done with, gone. I don't want you, I don't need you, and I'm heartily sick of you!"

Jeffrey's grip tightened painfully on her arm. "You're mine, Tanya!" he bellowed. "I won't let an Indian husband stand in my way, and I'll be damned if I'll step aside for the likes of Adam Savage!"

Tanya's furious look matched his. "You'll undoubtedly be damned any way you care to view it, Jeffrey, but I'll rule my own life, thank you, and you have no part in my plans for my future. Now kindly take your hand from my arm."

"I'd strongly advise you to do as the lady requests, Lieutenant."

Jeffrey's head swivelled to find Adam lounging indolently in the doorway, his arms crossed over his chest. As relaxed as he seemed, Tanya could sense Adam's fury, muscles tensed to spring at any moment.

Kit stood at his side, ready to attack if given the order.

Cursing beneath his breath, Jeffrey released Tanya's arm.

Adam commanded, "Come here, Tanya."

Immediately she crossed to stand in the shelter of his embrace, as his arm encircled her shoulder. "You see, Young," Adam pointed out deliberately, "the lady is with me." His dark eyes dared Jeffrey to make a move.

With a muttered oath, Jeffrey slammed out of the house, banging the door heavily behind him.

"I could have handled him," Tanya murmured softly into Adam's shirt.

"You shouldn't have to," he replied evenly. "You are mine to protect, and I thoroughly enjoyed doing so just now. I have a few scores to settle with Lieutenant Young, but the time is not right just yet. Someday, someday."

Julie, thoroughly upset by Jeffrey's abrupt departure, took refuge in her room. That left only Melissa to accompany Adam and Tanya on their walk.

"Melissa, you won't be hurt if we ask you to disappear for a while, will you?" Adam asked once they were on their way. "Take Kit for a walk, pick some flowers, talk to the birds; just don't come back for at least half an hour."

"Or longer," Tanya added, her eyes twinkling merrily.

Melissa pretended to be insulted. "Well!" she huffed, pointing her small nose to the sky. "I can tell when I'm not wanted. You don't have to knock me over the head with a brick to get a point across."

"Which is more than I can say for some people, mainly one Lieutenant Jeffrey Young," Tanya grumbled testily.

"Shall I stand guard?" Melissa offered with a grin.

"Somehow I don't think you'll want surprise guests breaking in on your—*activities*."

Adam laughed. "For someone as timid as you are sometimes, Melissa, you can be very astute. Just give a whistle if someone comes along. We won't be far."

Melissa blushed and giggled. "I think you should know that I never could learn to whistle," she confessed.

Tanya rolled her eyes heavenward. "Then just send Kit to alert us. We wouldn't want to offend your sensibilities."

Tanya stretched her nude body full length on the moist grass, watching as Adam removed his clothes. The sunlight dappling through new leaves shone on her skin, and her golden eyes glowed with expectation.

"Hurry, Panther," she pleaded, holding out her arms to him. "I need you so much!"

He came into her arms, wrapping himself about her. "You must remember to call me Adam, my love, at least for a while," he reminded as his lips found the soft skin of her neck.

"Mmmm," her answer was lost as his touch carried her into a world of sensual pleasure. Time became meaningless as they teased and tempted one another with heated caresses. Her hands clutched at the muscles of his shoulders, his back, his thighs, as he led her along the paths of love. His lips did not miss one square inch of her feverish body as he rediscovered her delight.

"Love me, my darling. Love me," she whimpered, her desires flaring beyond all limits.

"Be patient, my greedy kitten," he murmured with a soft chuckle. He guided her hands and lips to aching areas of is own body, and she gladly gave back all the pleasures he bestowed upon her.

Finally, both of them ablaze with desire, he plunged into her, silencing her cries of delight with his lips. Every nerve responding in unison with his, she met him move for move, following as he led her ever higher on the spiraling staircase of ecstasy. Unconsciously she scored his back with her fingernails as her passions shattered in a violent cataclysm that triggered his own devastating explosion of rapture.

Replete, she lay serenely snuggled in his arms. "I could search the world over and never find another love such as ours," she purred, her head pillowed on his chest. "I was lost without you, Panther."

"Adam," he corrected gently, then answered her thoughts. "That is because we are only whole when we are together. Our souls are united for all eternity, and our love will live long past the time when our bodies turn to dust."

Chapter 19

THE ENTIRE next week, everywhere Tanya went, Adam was sure to turn up. When she went to tea at someone's home, if Adam could find a legitimate excuse for dropping in at the same time, he did so. If not, he invariably showed up in time to escort her home.

She and Julie spent part of one day helping George inventory his stock of ladies' apparel at the mercantile, and Adam came in, decided he had nothing better to do, and spent the afternoon helping them. Not that he was all that much help, but they had a few hilarious hours watching him sort through everything from bonnets to ladies' undergarments.

Tanya saw another side of Panther that she'd barely glimpsed before. He had a fantastic sense of humor that often reduced her to helpless giggles. He had a remarkable head for business, displaying a sharp intelligence that rivalled that of any Eastern lawyer or businessman Tanya had ever met. Also, he displayed a disturbing knowledge of women and what they liked, and enough charm to lure bees away from honey.

One day he caught up with Tanya and her mother just as they'd started shopping. For hours he patiently escorted them from store to store, waiting as they tried on bonnets, dresses and shoes. He offered sound advice on colors and fabrics, gallantly volunteered to carry their purchases, and treated them to tea in a small restaurant when they were done. By the end of the day, Sarah was completely won over. To her he seemed a saint and Sir Galahad rolled into one, and she told Tanya point-blank that she'd be a fool to turn him down if he offered marriage.

Twice that week Tanya invited Adam to the house for dinner. It warmed her heart to see him playing with Hunter and Mark. Though Mark was only an infant, he responded to Adam with instant rapport. Whenever Adam would pick him up, he'd laugh and coo, his black eyes sparkling. It was Adam who discovered Mark's first tooth breaking through. His gentleness and affection for the children drew the approval of the entire family.

It was blatantly obvious to all that Adam was courting Tanya. He made no secret of it, taking every opportunity to hold her hand or put his arm about her in front of the others. He complimented her extravagantly, made her laugh more than she had in months, and centered his attention solely on her. He was courteous, gallant, thoughtful, and for the most part, respectful.

He presented her with flowers, and made her blush when he told her she outshone them. He brought her chocolates, brushing off her hesitancy by telling her he'd missed being here at Easter to give them to her.

Though she yearned to speed the courtship along, Tanya knew that to appear too eager would make people wonder. After months of professing her undying love for her Cheyenne husband, she had to go slowly at first.

For Adam's part, he deliberately held things at an even pace, proceeding with what he was sure was acceptable behavior. He did not want to offend Tanya's parents and upset all his and Tanya's plans. Still, every few days he would arrange to meet with Tanya privately, mostly with Melissa's aid.

Justin Kerr was also becoming a frequent visitor at the Martin house. He lived only a few doors down the street, and was brilliant at inventing excuses to drop by. Should his mother's hens happen to lay an extra dozen eggs that day, Justin would naturally offer them to Elizabeth Martin first, and then stay to chat with Melissa. As a budding young lawyer, he offered his legal services to George and Edward and talked them into making new wills. This required several trips to the Martin home, of course. And when invited to stay to dinner on these occasions, he'd accept.

Justin and Adam saw more of each other coming and going from the Martin home than they did anywhere else, even though Adam was staying at the Kerr's while he was in town. Though Adam admitted to Justin that he was courting Tanya, he did not tell his friend all. Justin knew that he was serious about Tanya, but he hadn't the slightest inkling of Adam's secret identity nor the fact that Adam was actually Tanya's long-lost Cheyenne husband. Though he saw Adam's genuine enjoyment with Hunter and Mark, it never dawned on him that Adam was their father. The only thing Justin knew was that Adam had his heart set on marrying Tanya Martin, and that Jeffrey Young was still making a pest of himself.

"What is Lieutenant Young's problem?" Justin asked Melissa one day. "Can't he see Tanya is not interested in him?"

"He sees only himself," Melissa explained. "He's so self-centered it is sickening! He refuses to believe any woman could not want him."

"For God's sake, why not?" Justin asked, shaking his head in disbelief.

"It is rather complicated, Justin. You see, Jeffrey was Tanya's fiancé at the time she was captured by the Cheyenne. She was coming here to marry him."

Justin nodded.

"Jeffrey was with Custer's troops when they attacked the Cheyenne village. He was one of the first to spot Tanya and me, and he was delighted to find her alive. But he was not so overjoyed to discover she had an Indian husband and two sons. Also, he failed to understand why she did not view him as her savior and fling herself into his arms."

"Which she did not, because of her love for her husband," Justin suggested.

"Partly," Melissa continued. "Two and a half years is a long time, Justin, and a lot can happen to alter your life. Not only did Tanya love Panther, but she discovered that what she had felt for Jeffrey was not love at all, but only girlish infatuation. Besides, she'd found a new and better life with the Cheyenne, one that suited her perfectly. That is the primary reason Tanya fared so much better than the rest of us. She adapted to the Cheyenne life so readily; totally and willingly. Of course, it helped that Panther treated her so well."

"He did?" Justin found this hard to believe.

"He adored her," Melissa avowed fervently. "He loved her every bit as much as she did him. It was a beautiful thing to behold."

Justin needed to know more; anything that might help his friend Adam win Tanya where Jeffrey had failed. "Is that the entire reason Tanya rejected Jeffrey?"

Melissa shook her head. "Not entirely. Tanya saw

how Jeffrey reacted to Hunter and Mark. He resents and dislikes them because they are halfbreeds, and she knows it. Tanya will not have her sons rejected or made to feel like second-rate citizens. She is proud of them and their father."

"I can understand that."

"Also, Tanya had become a part of the tribe long before the attack came. Chief Black Kettle and his wife had adopted her as their daughter before she married Panther."

"Whew!" Justin whistled. "I didn't know that."

"Few people do. The day of the attack, Tanya saw her adopted parents killed by the white soldiers. She watched as they were shot in the back and then trampled by horses." Melissa shuddered. "We watched together as a nightmare unfolded before our eyes. In all my time with the Cheyenne, I have never seen such heinous acts as the soldiers performed that day. Prisoners were raped, and everything in the village—tipis, dogs, people and horses—were killed and then burned. Few escaped or survived, and nothing was left to be salvaged. The attack came before dawn, while everyone was sleeping, and by noon the village was completely destroyed."

Justin was dumbfounded. "My God! I've never heard of such things! That's certainly not the story the military circulated."

Melissa scowled. "That doesn't surprise me! It wouldn't surprise Tanya, either. She despises what they did, and I can't blame her. As much as I hated living with the tribe, and as thankful as I am to be back, I can never condone what I saw that day. Neither can Tanya, and she knows Jeffrey is not completely blameless. He was there, and undoubtedly contributed his fair share in the massacre that took place. I doubt whether Tanya can ever forgive him that. In her eyes, he is a murderer."

"I can't say I blame her," Justin responded thoughtfully. "Tell me something, Melissa. You've said Tanya loved her husband, and I've heard her say the same thing. Do you think Adam stands a chance with her? He's a very good friend, and I'd hate to see him hurt."

"I'd say his chances are quite good," Melissa assured him gently. "Tanya needs some love in her life. It has been five months since the attack."

"Yes, but what if her husband somehow manages to come for her? Wouldn't she go with him?"

Melissa gave a small laugh. "You are worrying unnecessarily, I promise you. If he has not come for her by now, he never will." And that was the complete and utter truth.

The last week in April brought balmy, sunny days that sent everyone into fits of spring fever. Tanya yearned to ride across the open land, and when Adam suggested just this, she complained, "I'd like nothing better, Adam, and I'd prefer to ride Wheat, but after my escape attempt, Jeffrey took him from me."

Anger flared dangerously in Adam's dark eyes. "You shall have your mare back again, my darling, I promise you."

That very day, Adam spoke with Tanya's father privately. "Edward, I understand Lt. Young has confiscated Tanya's mare."

Edward blinked in surprise. "Yes, I guess he did. I'd forgotten all about it. I didn't say anything at the time, since it seemed a good way to prevent Tanya from trying to leave again."

"She'd like the horse returned now," Adam stated.

Edward's brow furrowed. "I don't know if that's really a good idea yet, Adam."

"What you mean is, you are not sure you trust Tanya not to attempt to run off again," Adam interpreted.

Edward flushed uncomfortably, but argued, "I'd think you'd concur with that, Adam. I thought you were interested in my daughter. It would be to your advantage, too, if she were not tempted to return to her Cheyenne husband."

Adam smiled. "I don't think there's much chance of that now. In any case, if we have to hold Tanya here by force, it is not much of a victory for us, is it? I'd like to take Tanya riding, and since you are her father, you can demand that Jeffrey return her mare."

"You seem awfully sure," Edward commented, eyeing Adam speculatively. "I'd hate to see Tanya run away just when she seems to be adapting to our way of life again."

"Trust me, Edward—and trust Tanya."

Edward sighed. "All right, Adam. I'll talk to Jeffrey this afternoon. I just wish I could be as confident as you are."

True to his word, Edward talked to Jeffrey, and at supper that evening, he told Tanya and Adam that he'd had no success. "That young pup refused to release the horse to me!" he bellowed. "He's handing me some cock-and-bull story about its now belonging to the U.S. Army, part of property confiscated in the raid at Washita!"

"That's a lie!" Tanya exclaimed. "Before they shot the other horses, General Custer offered me my choice of mounts. When Melissa pointed out that Wheat was my horse, there was no objection. Everyone knew the mare was mine!"

"Calm down, Tanya," Adam advised. "I'll get your mare for you. In fact, I'll see to it right after dinner. Jeffrey Young is in for a rude awakening."

At his quietly determined tone, Tanya became aware of his anger. "I'm coming with you, Adam," she declared.

Adam grinned. "You sound alarmed. Are you afraid I'll hurt him?"

"No, dear sir," Tanya assured him with an innocent, wide-eyed look that didn't fool him at all. "I'm afraid you'll *kill* him! What good will you be to me swinging from the end of a rope?"

Adam pulled the buggy up at the corral the cavalry had erected near their Pueblo headquarters. There was no actual fort in Pueblo, but the Army kept a post in town to defend the residents if need be. Next to the corral was a stable and a small office. It was to this office Adam headed, a determined glint in his onyx eyes, Tanya scurrying along beside him.

A young private sat behind a desk just inside the door. To Tanya's dismay, she recognized him as one of the men who had accompanied Jeffrey on his trek to intercept her flight in February.

Apparently surprised by her sudden appearance, he jumped to his feet, almost toppling his chair in his haste. "Oh, Miss Martin! Are you looking for the lieutenant?"

"Not particularly, Private. I've come to claim my horse," Tanya replied decisively. "Would you be so kind as to bring her to me? I noticed she's just outside in the corral."

The private's face turned red and he blurted, "No,

ma'am, I can't do that. Lieutenant Young has given orders."

At this point Adam stepped into the conversation. "Private, the mare is Miss Martin's private property. Her father is in agreement, and there is no reason the lady should be denied her horse."

"I'm sorry, sir," the private blustered, "but Lieutenant Young would have my hide if I let the horse go against his orders."

The words were no sooner out of his mouth when the door swung open to admit Jeffrey. "What's the problem here, Private?" he asked, as if he didn't already know. His cool blue eyes skimmed over Adam, obviously dismissing him, and zeroed in on Tanya.

"I want my horse, Jeffrey," she told him bluntly in a no-nonsense tone.

Jeffrey smiled tightly and shook his head. "No, darling, that's quite impossible. As I informed your father, the horse is now Army property." His tone implied he was speaking either to an ignorant child or a moron.

Tanya glared at him. "That's nonsense, Jeffrey, and you know it. Wheat has belonged to me for years, and General Custer let me take her. Besides, as was pointed out when the Cheyenne ponies were slaughtered, an Indian-trained horse is of absolutely no earthly use to the cavalry."

Jeffrey gave a short, nasty laugh. "No, Tanya, it's your word against mine."

"Not quite," Adam cut in sharply. "You see, Young," he continued, his dark eyes spearing Jeffrey, "Melissa was there when Panther gave Tanya the mare. She was there when Custer allowed Tanya to cut her horse out from the others. I've already discussed this with Justin Kerr, who is willing to act as Tanya's attorney in this matter. If necessary, we'll call the sheriff in." One dark eyebrow lifted as he delivered his final point. "Stealing horses is frowned on here, Young. Horsethieves are often hung before they ever come to trial."

Jeffrey colored, but tried to hold his ground. "The sheriff has no voice in military matters, Mr. Savage," he snapped.

Adam shrugged. "Explain that to St. Peter after word gets around town that you are a common horse-thief."

"Are you threatening me?" Jeffrey exclaimed.

Ignoring him, Adam directed Tanya, "Go get your horse, Tanya."

As Tanya stepped toward the door, Jeffrey moved to stop her. Adam put himself between Jeffrey and the door, effectively blocking him. The young private stood where he was, shuffling uncertainly.

"Don't forget your saddle and bridle," Adam reminded as Tanya slipped into the darkening evening. His dark eyes never left Jeffrey's flushed face.

"Any more objections, Lieutenant?" he asked.

Jeffrey eyed his opponent, anger making his blue gaze shimmer. "You've been getting pretty high and mighty lately, Savage, pushing your nose into other people's concerns," he snarled.

Adam returned his gaze with a warning look of his own. "Anything that concerns Tanya Martin is my business, Young. Remember that!"

From outside, Tanya called, "I'm ready, Adam."

"My lady calls." Adam grinned wickedly at Jeffrey's furious expression and turned toward the door.

"Later, Savage," he heard Jeffrey growl.

"Anytime you choose," Adam shot back over his shoulder.

A few seconds later, the sounds of the horses and buggy leaving the yard echoed through the open door. "Someday I'll break you apart, Adam Savage," Jeffrey muttered under his breath. "That's a promise!" Hands clenched into tight fists at his sides, he stamped out of the small office, leaving the befuddled private to heave a sigh of intense relief.

Now that Tanya had her mare at her disposal, she and Adam dispensed with the buggy much of the time, preferring to gallop the fields and wooded trails on horseback. Despite her mother's scandalized objections, Tanya refused to ride sidesaddle. Instead, she donned a split riding skirt and rode astride, as a few of the rancher's daughters were starting to do these days. Still, once in a while, in deference to Melissa and Julie, she would accompany them in the buggy, fully arrayed in frills and bows and lady-like graces.

One repercussion to having recovered her mare was immediately apparent. In addition to the tension Tanya perceived in her parents as they waited to see if Tanya would take advantage of the situation and run, Tanya noticed that she was under additional surveillance from Jeffrey and company. Tanya pointed this out to Adam.

"I'd noticed," he confirmed wryly.

Tanya sighed in exasperation. "I feel like a bug in a bottle!" she complained. "Every time I step out of the house, I feel eyes boring into my back! I went out to the stable the other night and nearly ran headlong into one of Jeffrey's subordinates." She gave Adam a long, searching look. "This could seriously impair our love-life, you know."

Adam smiled, his eyes twinkling knowingly. "We'll find a way around it, I'm sure. Any Cheyenne woman worth her salt should easily be able to elude a few dull-witted soldiers."

"I'll admit I had a good teacher, but your absolute confidence in your own charm annoys me, Adam," she pouted prettily.

Adam laughed in delight at her wounded expression. "I know you too well, my love." He nibbled teasingly at her lower lip. "You pout very prettily, Tanya, darling," he said as she shivered at his touch. "It's an invitation no man could resist."

Tanya often did manage to sneak off undetected to meet Adam. However, the added tension and fear of discovery was telling in their lovemaking. While it added an element of forbidden excitement that enhanced their ardor, they felt hurried, often rushing into their union without preliminaries. Tanya yearned for the time they could be together all night, taking time to discover and arouse one another, pacing their passion to their needs.

Tanya complained of this to Adam, offering an alternative. "If I can sneak out of the house, surely you could slip in just as easily. Truly, Adam, making love hurriedly on the damp, cold grass is not my idea of comfort. It would be so much nicer to take advantage of that lovely soft mattress and the downy comforters on my bed." Her golden eyes glinted up at his in the moonlight.

A mischievous look lit up his bronze face. "Are you suggesting I sneak into your room and make love to you right under your father's nose?"

"Yes, why not?" Tanya wanted to know. "After all, you *are* my husband."

Adam's chuckle reverberated in her ear. "One good reason why not is that you make altogether too much noise when aroused, my Little Wildcat. You yowl like a feline in heat, whinny louder than your mare, and hoot like an owl!"

Tanya gasped in mock indignation, and poked a pointed finger at his chest. "Might I point out that I'm not the only one, Mr. Savage? My sounds are nothing compared to yours. You grunt as loudly as a rutting stag, groan with the force of a falling tree, and there are times I'd swear I've heard you out-howl a coyote!"

"Woman, there you have it," Adam admitted through his laughter. "Besides, I'd be willing to bet your bedsprings creak atrociously. With all that racket, how could we possibly manage to avoid getting caught? Your father would be storming into the room with his shotgun before we knew it."

Tanya's eyes shone with delight, and Adam could almost see her mind working feverishly. "What's going on inside that head of yours?" he wanted to know.

"Well," she said with a devilish smile, "you said you wanted a short engagement. That would certainly speed things up and put Jeffrey out of the picture at the same time."

"I said I wanted a *short* engagement, not a dangerous one," Adam corrected, shaking his head. "I don't intend to damage either my reputation or yours. Certainly I don't need to offend your family at this point, not to mention how distressed my own mother would be. I would like to at least introduce the two of you before our engagement is public knowledge."

"I suppose you are right," Tanya agreed reluctantly. Then she sighed. "Still, it was an exciting idea."

Adam grinned, and his teeth flashed white against his dark face. "Oh, absolutely!" he said. "I can see the *Herald's* headlines now: 'SHOTGUN WEDDING HELD IN DARK OF NIGHT'. The following story would read, 'A surprise wedding was held last night in the Martin household. The bride's family turned out in force, decked out in their finest firearms. The precipitous ceremony was held immediately following the discovery of Mr. Adam Savage (the groom) and Miss Tanya Martin (the bride) caught in intimate embarrassment amid the rumpled bedcovers of the latter's bed.' "

Tanya tried unsuccessfuly to stifle the giggles that rose as Adam continued. " 'The ceremony, though hurried, was festive. Mr. Savage, held captive by his bride's beauty—and also by her uncle, Mr. George Martin—stood nervously to the left of Judge Kerr. Attired in robe and slippers, Miss Martin's sister, Julie, preceded her down the stairs. The mother of the bride yawned regally in nightwear and rag curlers, while Elizabeth Martin, the bride's aunt, played the wedding march, her face alight with Dr. Daniel's face cream (guaranteed to prevent age lines and wrinkles).' "

By now Tanya was howling with laughter, her face hidden in Adam's chest to absorb the sound.

Adam chuckled along with her and went on. " 'Edward Martin escorted his daughter. The shackles were barely visible beneath the flowing sleeves of his nightshirt. Like most brides, Miss Martin's face was aglow—in fact, it was a brilliant shade of bright pink that perfectly matched her filmy negligee. She carried a matching feather duster as a unique bouquet.

" 'Miss Melissa Anderson, acting as bridesmaid and witness, had to be nudged awake several times in order for the ceremony to proceed, but she didn't seem to mind greatly. Young Jeremy, official ringbearer, was noted pulling up his underwear only twice. Judge Kerr, dragged from a sound sleep, and still wearing his nightcap, got off to a slow start. Whether it was his spectacles or the fact that the book from which he read the ceremony was upside-down was never determined, but the start of the ritual sounded strangely like gibberish until he got the hang of it. It should be noted that the groom was lacking only his underwear, shoes, and stockings!' "

"Stop, Adam—hic—please!" Tanya pleaded between hiccups, clutching her aching ribs.

"Oh, but don't you want to hear how it ends?" he teased. " 'In lieu of a wedding band, the groom placed a shiny brass ring on the bride's ring finger—the parlor curtains are now missing but one. At the end of the rites, the bride (with her father's help) placed a matching ring through Mr. Savage's nose. Coffee and cocoa were served immediately afterward to those who were still awake. Miss Martin's sons slept through the proceedings, and will awaken to a fine surprise this morning. The honeymoon was omitted, as it had been held in anticipation of the actual wedding. Best wishes to the newlyweds and any little bundles that may arrive slightly shy of the accepted nine months after the wedding.' "

Weak with laughter, Tanya clung to Adam's shoulders, her tears dripping down his neck. "You crazy fool!" she hiccupped. "Are you trying to kill me with laughter? I've never laughed so hard in my life!"

"You wouldn't be laughing if it actually happened that way, my love, and neither would I," said Adam seriously.

Tanya nodded and wiped the tears from her cheeks.

"In other words, sir knight, you decline to join me in my bed."

Adam bent to kiss a lingering tear from her spiked lashes. "For the time being, yes," he answered softly. "Soon, Tanya. I hope to arrange to take you out to the ranch to meet my mother. Maybe there we can find more time and peace of mind—and privacy."

Tanya bit her lip in a sudden attack of anxiety. "Does your mother know about us—*all* about us?" she qualified.

"Yes," Adam admitted. "She is the one person besides Melissa who does know the truth. Who would better understand than she, who lived with the Cheyenne? She too loved a Cheyenne chief and bore his son. She knows what you have gone through; what you are feeling now."

Tanya's eyes searched his. "She truly understands?"

"Without doubt. She is anxious to meet the woman who finally won her son's heart. Already she loves you, and wants to hold her grandsons close to her."

The next day, Adam accompanied Tanya, Julie, and their mother on a shopping expedition. The entire day was delightful and lighthearted, with a final stop at the mercantile to advise Edward of his indebtedness.

As they were leaving the mercantile, Tanya glanced up to see Suellen and Mrs. Wright, the preacher's wife, directly across the street, staring intently at them. For just a moment, Tanya froze, feeling her heart lodge in her throat. As quickly, she recovered, realizing Suellen's intent to approach them.

Jabbing an elbow sharply into Adam's ribs, she reached for the packages he was about to load into the buggy.

His startled "Oof!" was covered as she brightly

exclaimed, "Oh, Adam! Haven't you forgotten your appointment with Justin? As long as you are so near, why don't you run in and see him now? We can manage from here. We'll see you for supper," she babbled.

One look at her pale face and over-bright eyes made Adam immediately wary. His dark gaze scanned the area, quickly noting the source of Tanya's distress.

"You are quite right, darling," he agreed quickly. "Thank you for reminding me. If I hurry, I can catch him in time." He kissed her lightly on the cheek and hurried off in the direction of Justin's office, his long strides carrying him swiftly away from Suellen's sharp eyes.

"It is so fortunate you reminded him," Sarah commented distractedly, taking the packages from Tanya's outstretched arms. "What does he need to see Justin about?"

"Some business about the ranch, I suppose," Tanya invented breathlessly.

"My goodness, Mother!" Julie exclaimed in amazement. "Do you realize Adam just called Tanya 'darling'?"

Sarah's head snapped up in surprise. "Oh, my!" A satisfied smile lit up her face. "He did, didn't he?"

Just then Suellen and Mrs. Wright appeared next to the buggy. "Hello, Sarah dear," Mrs. Wright sang out in her high-pitched voice. "How nice to run into you! Is this your daughter we've heard so much about?"

A slight frown marred Sarah's features, but she answered smoothly, "Of course. Tanya, may I present Rev. Wright's wife, Ruth."

Tanya nodded respectfully, but said nothing.

"We haven't seen you in church, Tanya," Suellen

commented casually, but the venom in her tone rang out clearly to Tanya's ears.

"How observant of you, Suellen. Are you quite sure you have time to listen to the sermon and count heads at the same time?" Tanya's tone was honey-sweet, though her words were sharp.

Julie choked on her laughter as Mrs. Wright interceded. "Now, girls." Turning to Sarah, she asked, "Who was that devastatingly handsome man we saw handing you into the buggy mere seconds before we arrived? I would have adored meeting him!" Her small rotund body fairly quivered with nosiness.

"Oh," Sarah waved a hand dismissively while Tanya silently applauded her, "That was just Adam."

"Adam?" Suellen pressed.

"Adam Savage, Tanya's new beau," Julie added, as if the information were unimportant.

"Rachel Savage's son?" Mrs. Wright inquired.

"That's right," Julie confirmed.

"Oh, dear!" Ruth wailed. "I wish I could have met him—though he's a Catholic like his mother, I suppose," she added.

"I would assume so, Ruth. Not that it makes a jot of difference," Sarah assured her, bristling.

"Well, not to some, especially as wealthy as the Savages are reported to be," Mrs. Wright said.

Tanya' noticed that Suellen was suddenly green with envy. Not only had Tanya effectively survived Suellen's gossip, but was now being actively pursued by a handsome, wealthy young rancher.

"Are you no longer pining for your dear, missing husband, Tanya?" she asked cattily.

Tanya faced her squarely. "Actually, no, Suellen. How thoughtful of you to be so concerned."

"That's rather fickle of you, isn't it? What will your Cheyenne lover think of that, I wonder, if he ever comes for you?"

"Why don't you let me worry about that, and turn your poor overworked brain to other matters?" Tanya suggested in a kindly voice that contrasted wholly with her urge to strangle the redhead.

"Speaking of waiting for someone," Sarah inserted, "When do you expect your parents to come for you, Suellen?"

"Not for a couple of months, at least. No one can get word to them until the snow clears from the mountain passes. They'll know I'm in good hands with Rev. and Mrs. Wright, and I'm sure they'll come as soon as they can. I can't wait to shake the dust of Colorado from my feet permanently!" she declared.

"Neither can we!" Tanya echoed beneath her breath.

Suellen frowned. "By the way, how is Lt. Young taking your defection now that your interests lie in another direction?"

"He'll survive, I'm sure," Julie assured her with a stony glare.

Suellen persisted, "And how does your new suitor like your two children—or haven't you told him about them yet?"

"So sorry to disappoint you, Suellen," Tanya cooed, "but Adam *adores* my sons."

Thoroughly frustrated by now, Suellen looked as if a thundercloud had settled over her head. "It never ceases to amaze me how some people constantly reap rewards they don't deserve!" she muttered.

"So true," Tanya added, staring intently at Suellen's angry face. "Some folks just never seem to get what's coming to them, do they?"

"Amen!" Mrs. Wright declared, blissfully unaware of Tanya's true meaning. "Well, it's been nice chatting with you, but Suellen and I have some charity work to get on with."

"That would be an interesting change of pace for you, Suellen," Tanya said as she climbed into the buggy and took up the reins. "At any rate, it will keep you off the streets." With that, she flicked the reins, raised a hand in farewell, and drove off.

Chapter 20

"TANYA IS in the back parlor." Melissa's voice floated back to where Tanya sat nursing Mark. For just a moment she tensed, ready to grab the small blanket near her and throw it over her exposed shoulder and breast. Then she relaxed as she heard Adam's deep voice in the hall.

Adam stopped in the doorway, his eyes taking in the scene before him. Tanya sat proudly, her golden eyes glowing up at him as she held Mark's dark head to her breast. Her lips parted in a slight smile, that revealed her pearly teeth as she and Adam shared this precious, intimate moment for the first time in six months. No words were needed between them, for their eyes expressed more eloquently than words the emotions each felt.

Adam's eyes caressed her face, her breast, his small son suckling contentedly, and returned once more to meet Tanya's flaming gaze. Without false modesty, Tanya accepted his avid look, his unspoken praise, his silent expression of pride and love. Her own look told him how proud she was to be his wife, his woman, the mother of his children.

Adam crossed directly to her and sat down next to her on the divan. A slight shaking of his hand betrayed the depth of his emotions as he reached out, caressing first a lock of her flowing tawny hair. His long fingers then trailed along her shoulder, lightly brushing the top of her breast before coming to rest on the downy black hair of his son.

For long minutes they sat surrounded in their love, letting their hearts drink deeply of this rare moment together. Their eyes locked above Mark's head, and slowly Adam's mouth decended toward hers. Their lips touched almost reverently at first, as if loathe to break the spell they were under. Then, as Tanya leaned toward him, parting her lips beneath his, the kiss deepened, becoming filled with passion as Adam exerted his magical mastery over her mouth and his tongue searched out its hidden secrets.

Finally he drew back and looked deeply into her passion-glazed eyes. "Never was there a woman such as you," he whispered. "You are my sun, my moon, and all the stars; you are my entire world, my whole existence."

Tanya's heart leapt into her eyes. "Oh, Adam! If I am these things, it is because you make it so! I was created for you, and I exist only to love you and to be loved by you."

As voices from another part of the house reached their ears. Adam shifted reluctantly to a more respectable distance from her, but remained on the divan. "You didn't say how your meeting with Suellen went the other afternoon."

Tanya gave an indignant sniff. "She was her usual, hateful self, and Rev. Wright's wife is one of the nosiest busy-bodies I've met lately."

"So I've heard. It is fortunate you spotted them in time for me to retreat gracefully, but I hated leaving you in the lurch."

"It was a bit close for comfort," Tanya replied with

a shiver. "When I think what Suellen might have done if she'd recognized you!"

"Hopefully she'll be gone before too long," Adam offered in consolation. "Then we won't have to worry about running into her unexpectedly."

"She'll be here for at least a couple of months yet," Tanya informed him with a frown. "Luckily, the good Reverend and his wife don't move in the same social circles as we do. They tend to mingle with the more religiously dedicated of their flock. Those who drink or smoke or go to grand parties in fine attire are not held in high regard, not to mention those who enjoy dancing and playing cards!"

Adam's black eyes sparkled. "Fortunately for us," he chuckled, "that means we are less likely to encounter Suellen at any of the gatherings we attend."

"Yes, and I'm sure Suellen resents that fact. She was used to being in the thick of things back East, since her father is a prominent lawyer. I'll bet she wishes she was staying with anyone other than the prudish preacher. I've heard he runs a strict household."

Adam's eyebrows raised in amusement. "Feeling sorry for Suellen, are you?" he teased.

"Not a bit!" Tanya assured him with a smile.

Just then Sarah came gliding into the parlor, glancing about distractedly. "Tanya, do you have any idea where I've left my sewing scissors? I can't seem to find them any—Oh, my word!" Sarah's eyes grew huge, and her mouth hung open momentarily as she realized that her daughter was entertaining Adam while she nursed Mark.

Elizabeth, passing by the door, stuck her head in curiously. "What's all the fuss about, Sarah?"

Struck dumb, Sarah could do no more than point at Tanya in dismay.

Elizabeth's gaze veered from Sarah to Tanya, who serenely continued to feed her son, and on to Adam, who seemed completely unruffled by the entire episode.

With obvious effort, Sarah found her tongue. "Tanya Martin! Have you no sense of decorum? How can you calmly sit there exposing yourself like that! If you have no concern for yourself, you can at least think of Adam! He's probably too polite to tell you you're embarrassing him!"

"Oh, posh!" Elizabeth spouted on a burst of laughter. At Sarah's incredulous look, she said, "Adam has grown up on a ranch, Sarah. All his life he's been around animals feeding and mating and birthing. It's nothing new to him, I'm certain."

"Yes, but . . ." Sarah began.

"But nothing," Elizabeth interupted, to both Tanya and Adam's delight. "It's quite natural, and nothing to be upset over. I doubt that Adam is shocked. Besides, at his age I'd be willing to bet he's seen a good deal more of a woman's body than that. If he hasn't, there's something wrong with him!"

Adam's guffaw blended with Tanya's choked laughter.

"I still say it's indelicate." Sarah's censuring look included all three of them.

"*I* say it's between the two of them and none of our business," Elizabeth said pointedly. "They are both adults."

Doubt flickered over Sarah's face as she looked from Adam to Tanya.

"It's quite all right, Mrs. Martin," Adam assured her in his quiet, calming voice. "I'm not in the least embarrassed. As Elizabeth said, it is a natural and beautiful fact of life, a mother nurturing her young."

"You're quite sure?" Sarah questioned, her anxiety quieting somewhat.

"We're quite sure, Mother," Tanya added softly. "Adam and I are very comfortable with one another."

Anything else she might have said was cut off as Jeffrey's angry words resounded just beyond the door. "I'll find her myself then, Miss Anderson!" Mere seconds later, he stomped into the room, followed by a flustered Melissa.

"I'm sorry, Tanya," Melissa said breathlessly, her cheeks blazing as she viewed the others gathered in the room.

Jeffrey gaped in irate astonishment at the cozy domestic picture Tanya, Adam, and Mark presented. "Good God, Tanya!" he exclaimed. "What is going on here?"

Tanya took the small blanket Adam extended to her and tossed it over her shoulder, shielding her breast from Jeffrey's view. With an exasperated sigh, Tanya glared at Jeffrey. "It's an exhibition, Jeffrey! Didn't you buy your ticket at the door?"

"That's not funny, Tanya!" he retorted.

"Indeed it's not," she agreed heatedly. "Neither is having someone force themselves into your home unannounced and uninvited!"

"I wanted to see you," he said curtly.

"I believe you've seen more than was intended already," Adam remarked cooly.

Jeffrey glared at Adam, his blue eyes alight with naked hatred. His gaze switched to Tanya, then on to Sarah. "Mrs. Martin, surely you do not condone this disgusting display before a stranger!"

Sarah's chin went up at least three notches. "Adam is *not* a stranger, Lieutenant," she answered stiffly.

"Furthermore, there is nothing disgusting about a mother nursing her child."

"Bravo!" Elizabeth whispered softly.

Jeffrey glared at her. "Still, it is better done in private," he insisted.

"It *was* private before you barged in," Tanya pointed out.

His jaw clenched tightly, he ground out, "Tanya, I need to speak with you."

"Speak, then," she commanded.

"Alone."

"I think not."

Jeffrey took one threatening step in her direction, and Adam rose to stand in front of Tanya. "Young, you've overstayed your welcome. The lady does not wish to talk to you."

Jeffrey's fair complexion turned bright red in his anger. Fists doubled, he shook them at Adam. "One of these days, Savage, you'll cross me once too often, and I'll forget I'm an officer and a gentleman."

"Well, remember it for now and show yourself out," Elizabeth advised firmly. "And the next time, wait to be invited in before pushing your way into my home. This is my home, not an Army barracks, Jeffrey Young!" Elizabeth stood up to him like a ruffled banty hen, staring him down.

With a muffled oath, Jeffrey strode from the room. The violent slamming of the front door told of his angry exit.

"That man means trouble," Sarah predicted dourly, and no one ventured to disagree with her.

Adam spoke to Tanya's parents, getting their permission for Tanya to visit his ranch and meet his mother. Of course, Julie was to go along, and not entirely for appearances. Everyone was concerned with Julie's continued infatuation with Jeffrey, and it was decided a few days away from him would do her good. Melissa volunteered to go along and watch Hunter and Mark, so naturally, Justin invited himself for a visit at the same time.

"Are you sure your mother won't mind?" Tanya asked as the last of the bags were loaded into the buggy. "We look like an invading army!"

"Mother is so anxious to meet you and the boys that you could bring the devil himself along, and she wouldn't object," Adam assured her.

Justin and Jeremy accompanied Melissa and Julie in the buggy, but Tanya elected to ride Wheat. In her split riding skirt, with Mark strapped into his cradleboard and hanging from the pommel, she rode beside Adam. It was almost like old times; she with Mark, and Adam holding Hunter before him. Tanya's eyes sparkled with delight as Wheat sidled up to Shadow with a playful whinny. Adam's laughter blended with Tanya's in a moment of pure contentment.

The sun was setting behind the purpling mountains as they drew up before the Spanish-style ranch house. Through the lengthening shadows, Tanya caught a glimpse of barns, stables, and outbuildings beyond the main house. Then Adam was guiding his guests through a wide, gated archway, into an outer courtyard, and up to the front entrance of the house.

No sooner had the wheels of the buggy ground to a halt, than the heavy oak door opened, and a tall, slim, raven-haired woman appeared. For just a moment she stood framed in the shadowed doorway. Then her feet carried her swiftly toward Adam, a wistful smile on her otherwise serene face. On tiptoe, she kissed her son lightly on the cheek, but her arms reached out for Hunter.

"We've been watching for you." Her slightly accented voice was directed to all of them, but her eager dark eyes were devouring the boy in her arms. Tears glistened momentarily as she clutched Hunter tightly to her, resting her cheek tenderly atop his dark head.

The next minute, she seemed to recover herself, and turned to her guests. "Welcome," she said with a bright smile. "*Mi casa es su casa*, as my people say. My house is your house. Come inside where we can be comfortable. You must be tired, and supper will be ready soon."

She led the way into the house. "José will see to your luggage and the horses."

They entered into a wide, dark hallway, and almost immediately into a large, comfortable room to the left. "This is the *sala*, the main living room," she explained. "Please, be seated, and I will have Juanita bring refreshments. Adam, see to a drink for yourself and Justin."

Adam grinned at his usually refined mother, who was now so obviously ruffled. "*Si, mamacita*, but first let me make the introductions. That young man, whom you so promptly pirated from me, is Hunter, and this young lad in the cradleboard is Mark." He indicated the baby in Tanya's arms. "This beautiful young woman is the lady I've told you so much about, Miss Tanya Martin. Tanya, may I present my mother, Raquela Adama Maria de Valera Savage, or Rachel, as she is commonly called in these parts."

Tanya nodded politely to her mother-in-law. "*Senora*, it is an honor to meet you."

Large black eyes smiled back at her. "It is an honor to have you in my home," Rachel replied, though her eyes said much more than her words as she studied Tanya and Mark warmly.

"This lovely lady is Tanya's sister, Julie," Adam continued, "and the other is Miss Melissa Anderson, Tanya's best friend."

Rachel acknowledged each with a welcoming nod.

"Justin you know, but Jeremy is relatively new to Pueblo. He is Elizabeth Martin's nephew, her sister's son. He lives with the Martin's now, and I've promised to teach him how to ride while he is here."

"Hello, Jeremy," Rachel greeted him. "So you want to learn to ride. You could choose no better instructor than my son, you know."

"Yes, Ma'am," Jeremy replied politely.

Rachel laughed at his solemn face. "I am Rachel to all of you, for we shall be great friends, I am sure. I am only 'ma'am' to strangers, and *La Señora* to the ranch hands and servants."

She clapped her hands decisively. "Now, you shall all make yourselves comfortable, and I will consult with Juanita about refreshments. If you wish to wash or change, Adam will show you to your rooms."

Aside to Adam, she said, "I have put Tanya and the babies in the room next to yours, since it has the most space. Melissa and Julie will share the one next to mine, if that is acceptable. Justin is next to them in the smaller room, and Jeremy may choose whether he wishes to sleep in the house or in the bunkhouse with the hands."

Jeremy's face lit up in delighted amazement. "Oh!

Can I really sleep in the bunkhouse?" he squealed.

Adam grinned at him. "Of course, if you want to."

"Oh, I do! I do!" Jeremy nearly jumped for joy.

Tanya was in for an agreeable surprise of her own when she viewed her room. Not only was it spacious and beautifully decorated, with a cot for Hunter and a railed bed for Mark, but it adjoined Adam's room through a connecting door.

"You see, my love," Adam pointed out with a glint in his dark eyes, "my mother is discreetly letting us know of her approval by giving you this room."

Tanya looked back at him in amazement. "She certainly seems very understanding, under the circumstances."

Adam nodded, suddenly sober. "My mother considers us married, Tanya, as she always considered her marriage to my father valid and binding. That is why she's never remarried, not for lack of opportunity. Now that she is free to do so, she may accept one of her suitors one day."

"She is still a very beautiful woman," Tanya commented. "No wonder your father coveted her."

Adam grinned down at her. "We Cheyenne have an eye for beautiful captives. We thrive on subduing them and making them bow to all our lustful wishes."

Tanya's golden eyes twinkled mischieviously. "You *do* have a way about you," she agreed with a smile that promised further delights later. "You can refresh my memory later, but perhaps we should join the others before we are missed."

At supper that evening, there was another stranger at the table; a tall, good-looking young man who greeted Adam with a brotherly hug, a brilliant white smile, and a rapid stream of Spanish.

"*Como está*, Roberto?" Adam said with a laugh. Introductions were made, and it was discovered that Roberto was one of Adam's cousins. He had come up from Santa Fe for a visit several months before, and stayed to help Rachel with the ranch. He'd been out on spring roundup when Adam had returned, and this was the first time the cousins had seen one another in years.

His dark eyes flashing, Roberto openly admired the female guests. "Ah, Adam! Home so recently, and already you have collected the best Pueblo has to offer!"

He bowed low and kissed each of their hands in turn. "Such beauties! Surely you can spare one for me, cousin!"

Adam laughed. "That depends on the lady, Roberto, but the choice is more limited than it seems. Justin may take offense if you work your wicked Latin wiles on Melissa, and I would have no compunction about murdering you if you so much as look twice at Tanya. Therefore, you will have to try your excessive charms on Julie and see how you fare."

Never breaking stride, Roberto turned smoothly to Julie, his teeth flashing in a devilish smile. "But, cousin, you have just offered me the choicest of morsels, and I am a starving man!"

Julie's brow creased in a frown. Jerking her hand from his, she snapped, "Nobody has offered you anything, sir! I'm not to be picked up like—like some item at a church bazaar!"

Roberto's eyes widened along with his smile. "Ah, *señorita*, but I love a challenge! It will be interesting to match wits with such a spirited woman, and to see how long it will take before you fall into my arms like a ripe summer peach!"

"My goodness!" Julie exclaimed as the others struggled to smother their laughter. "You will wait an eternity before I throw myself at the likes of you!" She stamped her foot in exasperation.

Far from being discouraged, Roberto threw his dark head back and laughed heartily. "We will see, my little spitfire! We will see."

All in all, it promised to be an interesting visit for everyone.

Late that night, after everyone had gone to bed, Tanya checked on her sleeping sons. Then, guided by the moonlight filtering in through the windows, she slipped quietly into Adam's bedroom.

Adam heard her before she ever touched the door-knob. He'd lain awake, listening to her every movement in the room next to his, anticipating her arrival.

Now, he watched as she approached his bed, moving like a wraith as the moonlight caught the gossamer threads of her white nightgown and turned them to silver. Her hair was loose, lying in soft waves across her shoulders.

"You look like an angel," he said softly, catching her hand and pulling her down beside him on the bed. His fingers caught at the hem of her gown until his hand rested on her bare thigh. There he traced the panther-shaped scar, now three years old but still visible. "But you have the devil's own brand on you."

"Then I must be a fallen angel, for I am a willing slave who adores her master," Tanya whispered as her lips found his and clung.

For only a moment, Adam let her control the kiss. Then his own lips claimed dominance over hers, staking their claim and parting them beneath his insistance. His tongue traced their shape and slid smoothly past her sharp, even teeth into the moist cavern of her mouth. Her own tongue darted up to duel with his, and he caught it softly between his teeth, sucking sensuously, causing her breath to quicken.

Her hand reached out to caress the muscled wall of his chest and continued onward, exploring each scar and rib with her seeking fingertips. His lips at last relinquished hers, only to travel a path across her jaw to her ear. Shivers raced across her skin, raising gooseflesh even as a flame ignited within.

As his lips nuzzled their way into the baby-soft skin of her neck, the hand on her thigh caressed its way upward to the curve of her hip, his thumb searching out the ridge of her hipbone and the hollow of her stomach.

Tanya moaned as his mouth left her shoulder to find a breast through the cloth of her gown. Her breast swelled at his touch, and she arched toward him as if to an unspoken command. His teeth found her nipple, his tongue laving the fabric across its sensitive tip. Tanya felt the heat building inside her, her muscles tensing in anticipation as she threaded her fingers into his dark hair and gloried in his touch.

"Panther! Adam!" she whimpered.

Bracing her half over him, Adam whisked the gown over her head. "We never had this problem to contend with in our tipi," he murmured as his mouth reclaimed its now naked prize. His teeth once more caught a nipple, and his tongue teased it mercilessly. Tanya gasped in delight as flames of desire raced through her. Again she drew in a sharp breath and clutched him closer as his hand feathered a path up her inner thigh and found the moist warmth between her legs. There his fingers lingered over her most sensitive pleasure points until she squirmed and whimpered beneath him.

Her fingers seemed to have a mind of their own, for even as he brought her untold pleasure, she caressed and fondled him, urging his body to join hers in the age-old dance of love.

Not until he had brought her to wondrous heights, her body quivering, her muscles still contracting about his seeking fingers, did he move over her. His own body screaming for release, he entered her welcoming warmth, feeling her envelop him in her velvet sheath. Gritting his teeth, he willed his body to go slowly, savoring each glorious sensation. In slow, easy movements he stroked her upward along the slopes of passion, until at last his body took control. Her nails scored his back as his hands gripped her hips and held her to him. More and more swiftly he plunged into her pliant body, leading her with him until they both careened over the edge of eternity. His mind barely registered her teeth biting into his shoulder as she stifled her cries of ecstasy, his own deep moans muffled in her hair. Sweat-drenched and replete, they drifted contentedly off to sleep, Tanya's head snuggled securely on his shoulder, Adam's leg thrown possessively across hers.

Tanya awoke to Cheyenne love words whispered in her ear, followed by a series of kisses planted along her spine. She opened her eyes to realize it was still dark; her inner clock told her she'd slept only a couple of hours.

"Mmn," she sighed, cuddling closer to the heat his body radiated. "This is nice."

"About time you woke up, lazybones," Adam teased. "I thought maybe I'd have to resort to tickling your feet the way the cubs used to."

"What do you want?" Tanya giggled past a yawn.

"Guess."

"A snack? A glass of milk?" she offered with an impish grin.

"I'll have the snack if you are on the menu."

"Hungry devil, aren't you?"

"Absolutely starving!" He nibbled on her neck to prove his point, then made love to her with infinite thoroughness, driving Tanya mindless with desire before he finally satisfied her consuming need for him.

More than once that night he woke her, sometimes taking her gently, sometimes urgently, but always with love.

"It's been so long since I've had you to myself like this, to hold and love and touch all through the night," he whispered.

"Too long," Tanya agreed, then teased, "but it seems you are trying to make up for it all in one night. I'll never be able to walk properly tomorrow. What will I say if someone notices?"

Adam laughed. "At least you have an excuse! You can blame it on the long ride out here. What excuse I will give, I can't imagine!"

"An extraordinarily long ride of another sort?" Tanya suggested provocatively.

"Shocking, Miss Martin! Truly shocking!" He gave a fair imitation of Ruth Wright, reducing Tanya to a state of giggles.

At breakfast the next morning, the dark shadows beneath their eyes caused comments.

"Tanya, are you ill?" Julie inquired solicitously. "You look as if you didn't sleep a wink last night."

Tanya nearly choked on her toast. "Strange bed," she muttered shortly.

Roberto smiled wryly. "That is understandable, but why does Adam look so tired as well?"

"All that thrashing about in the next room," he offered between bites.

"I'm sure I'll settle in soon, Adam," Tanya assured

him. "I'd feel guilty thinking I was causing you to lose precious sleep." She smiled demurely.

Rachel gave her guests a tour of the house, which was spacious, elegant, practical, and homey all combined, with the distinct Spanish flavor of a busy working ranch. In contrast to the Martin home, the rooms were large and airy, the furniture sturdy and built to accommodate the larger male frame. The color schemes were bold and bright, blending Indian and Spanish cultures, and there was little of the frilly, dainty effect that Aunt Elizabeth preferred.

Tanya loved it, and felt very much at home immediately. Also, she felt comfortable with Rachel. Unlike many other mothers-in-law, Rachel did not display any resentment toward the woman who had captured her son's heart. If anything, she seemed relieved and grateful that Adam had found a woman capable of sharing all aspects of his unusual life. From her own sad experience, Rachel knew it took a special kind of woman, strong and adaptable, to stand up under the pressures of the Cheyenne life. She had not been able to cope, and had brought sorrow upon herself and White Antelope whom she had dearly loved. Tanya seemed to thrive in any atmosphere, and Rachel admired her ability to do so, for it boded well for their future together.

Rachel adored her grandsons. Right from the start, she took over their care, helping to dress and feed them, taking them with her about the house and yard. She brought them out to the stables and showed them the horses. Together they explored the barnyard, feeding the chickens and ducks, visiting the corrals, viewing the cattle.

At first Tanya feared she would spoil them, but Rachel did not hesitate to be firm when the situation warranted. She strictly forbade the inquisitive Hunter to visit the stables, barns, or cattle pens alone, stressing the dangers.

Another dimension was added to Hunter's life while at the ranch. Rachel began teaching him a few words of Spanish to add to his growing vocabulary. Also, while allowed certain freedoms, he encountered his first responsibilities. It was his duty to see that Kit did not eat Rachel's chickens or ducks, or venture near the cattle. He was to alert an adult if Kit got out of line. While Rachel accepted Kit's presence graciously, she didn't quite trust her to ignore her natural urge to hunt, realizing what a temptation the cattle and fowl offered. She made it quite clear to all that they were to keep an eye on the sleek cat, and that she wouldn't hesitate to put a bullet-crease across Kit's tail if she decided to develop a taste for beef or feathers. It was only due to Adam's rigid training and Kit's willing obedience that trouble was avoided in that area. The minute Tanya or Adam issued a command, Kit complied readily. The cat seemed to sense that she was walking a fine line, and certain things would not be tolerated here that may have been permissible in the wilds. She contented herself with trailing after Tanya and Adam, or guarding the boys.

Watching her one day, Tanya commented, "I think she misses Kat."

"Probably," Adam agreed, "but with luck she'll see him again in a few months."

"Will we be going back soon after we're married here?" Tanya wanted to know, a hopeful look on her face.

Adam watched her face carefully as he questioned, "Do you really want to go back? Will you be satisfied with that way of life now that you have been back to civilization and reunited with your family; now that you realize I have the option of staying here and running the ranch or picking up my Cheyenne identity?"

Tanya gazed up at him tenderly. "Adam, I love you. Whatever makes you happy also makes me happy. I know your heart lies with the Cheyenne, and I understand. Wherever you go, I will follow and be content. I was happy with the Cheyenne and I'll gladly return with you. It is a hard life, yes, but an honest and good one, and every day I miss it more. I miss my friends. I miss having something productive to keep my hands and mind occupied." She snuggled closer to him. "No longer am I content with the sedentary, frivolous manner in which I was raised, where ladies spend most of their time shopping, tatting useless, pretty bits of lace, and attending teas. There are more important things to life than deciding which gown and slippers to wear, how to arrange one's hair, and watching every word or action for fear of causing gossip. I feel stifled in Pueblo after the freedom of the plains, as if the very air is tainted! I feel restricted, like an eagle with a broken wing, who can only sit and dream of flying, and remember with a sad heart what it was like to soar."

Adam shook his head in wonder. "You amaze me, little one. Black Kettle was right when he said you have the heart of a Cheyenne. Your thoughts and your words are more Cheyenne than white, even now. You make me yearn to forget all our plans, to disregard your family's feelings, and carry you and my sons away with me this very minute. My heart sings with gladness that you feel as you do, that your wishes match mine so exactly. We are truly well-mated, Little Wildcat."

"It was inevitable that I belong to you, Panther," she replied softly, her golden eyes glowing with love. "It was written in the stars and blown on the winds that we would meet and fall in love. Now tell me when we can return to our people and live as we both desire."

"As soon after we are married as we can possibly arrange to do so," he promised. "I cannot imagine telling your family the truth, so we must make it look as if we wish to reside elsewhere for the time being. Perhaps they will not be too hurt if we promise to return for visits at decent intervals so they can see the children."

Tanya nodded. "Yes, perhaps during Christmas holidays and the like."

"They will be disappointed," he warned.

"They'll learn to live with it," she assured him. "At least it won't be the way it was before, when they worried so about me. They never knew if they would see me again. This time they'll know I'll be back."

"That's not altogether true, Tanya," Adam disagreed. "The life we live is full of perils, and there are no guarantees from day to day. Danger could befall us at any time. You know this as well as I."

"You are right, but our days on this earth are listed in the heavens and when our time is up we will be called away. That day could be tomorrow for any of us. It could happen anywhere; here, in Pueblo, or on the plains, and nothing could prevent it. I might step in front of a carriage on a busy street, or die peacefully in my sleep in my feathered bed. It matters not where we are when it happens. If we stayed here, tragedy could still befall us. We cannot hope to prevent the inevitable; to stem the tide of fate."

Adam smiled. "How wise you have become in the ways of life, my woman."

"I have learned well from your people; *our* people," she corrected. "They have taught me much about patience and mystery, and the futility of trying to fight against things over which I have no power."

"You have much power over me," he breathed, as his lips touched hers, "yet you do not fight me."

"That is because you have greater power over me," she responded on a whisper. "You hold my heart forever captive."

Chapter 21

TANYA THOROUGHLY enjoyed every minute of her ten-day stay at the ranch, though there were a couple of disturbing moments. Being with Adam during the day and enclosed in his warm embrace each night, was heavenly. Here, there was no one constantly peering over her shoulder to make sure she was behaving properly, and it was relaxing to be free of Jeffrey's irritating presence and sudden appearances.

Julie had little time to oversee her sister's behavior, for she had her hands full fending off a very determined Roberto. Undaunted by Julie's rejections and sharp tongue, he delighted in teasing her, laughing heartily when he roused her temper.

"Ah, my prickly little cactus," he chuckled. "When are you going to pull in your sharp needles?"

"Never!" Julie assured him adamantly, her lower lip protruding in a pout.

"Do you know how alluring you are when you are angry, my pet?" Roberto asked with a broad grin, his white teeth flashing. "Your lips beg to be kissed, especially that lower one you are constantly thrusting at me. I believe you are teasing me to arouse my desire even more."

Julie stamped her foot angrily. "How conceited you

are! How many times do I have to tell you that I'm interested in another man? Have you no pride?"

Robert's dark eyes gleamed. "Pride has nothing to do with it. Is this other man your lover?"

"Of course not! What kind of woman do you take me for?" Julie exclaimed.

Roberto's smile widened. "Are you betrothed to him?" he persisted.

Julie hesitated a fraction too long before she replied, "No, not yet."

"Then there is no reason why I should cease to pursue you, is there, my dove?"

Before Julie fully realized his intentions, Roberto swept her into his embrace, his dark eyes searing hers for just a second before his mouth came down to cut off her surprised exclamation. His warm lips claimed hers as if to set his seal forever on her soul. While it was not the gently seeking kiss she'd often dreamed would be her first, neither was it brutal. Roberto was merely staking his claim to her in a most definite, undeniable manner.

Even as she strained against the hand that held her head still, Julie fell prey to the wonder of the moment. His warm, firm lips upon hers were conjuring up feelings she'd never dreamed possible. Though her mind shrieked warnings and resisted his dominant force, her body began to melt under his expert touch.

At last she ceased to pull away from him, her hands feathering across the fabric of his shirt, feeling the rapid beat of his heart beneath her palm. At the urging of his hand on the small of her back, she leaned against him, letting him support her weight as her knees buckled. Tingles raced up her spine as his hand splayed itself across her back.

By the time he released her, she was limp with a desire she'd never imagined before. His dark eyes studied her soft features, her dazed blue-green eyes, her kiss-swollen lips.

"Now I have an idea what you will look like after I've made love to you; all soft and dreamy, your hair spread out across my chest," he whispered softly.

Reality jolted through her like a spear as she realized what she had done; what he had made her do. Her face flamed as she recalled how she had responded to him, and she stiffened with injured pride and pushed herself hastily out of his arms, frowning with disapproval of both herself and him.

"You will *never* make love to me, Roberto! This was just a temporary lapse on my part. You took me by surprise. It won't happen again." She delivered her message across her shoulder as she stalked haughtily away from him.

"Run, little rabbit, run!" His laughter followed her as his humor reasserted itself. "Just make sure you don't run in circles, for the fox will catch you yet, and what a dainty morsel you will make!"

"I'll poison myself before I let you touch me again!" Julie shot back.

He merely laughed the harder. "The fur is already starting to fly!" he taunted. "You have lost—you just don't know it yet!"

It was mid-May in the Colorado hills, and the fresh spring breezes seemed to be affecting all of nature. The countryside had shed its white winter coat for a new one of vibrant green. Wildflowers were in abundance, showering the rolling hills with every color conceivable. The willow trees, the first to produce their leaves, spread their long fronds gracefully to the ground, creating shady bowers along the riverbanks.

The call of spring brought life to its fullest crest. It instilled the urge to mate in all creation. Small animals darted about with renewed zest, and the bees searched out the nectar in the fragrant flowers. New life abounded in the form of newborn calves and colts. Baby chicks and ducks waddled awkwardly behind proud mothers, peeping and quacking uncertainly as they struggled to keep up on wobbly legs.

Jeremy particularly favored the colts, darting about on their long, spindly legs. "They sure stick close to their mothers," he commented to Adam. "Are they afraid they'll get lost?"

Adam laughed and draped an arm over the boy's shoulder. "There is not much chance of that. Their mothers would find them soon enough. The foals just don't want to be far from their next meal, that's all."

"They sure look funny with that fuzzy hair and those short, wispy tails," Jeremy grinned in delight. "Looks like someone put part of a broom on their backsides!"

Just before bedtime one evening, Jeremy burst into the house, bubbling over with excitement. "Tanya! Adam! Come quick! There's a mare in the barn about to foal. José sent me to tell you." He spun about, retracing his steps toward the door at a lope. "He says I can watch if I'm quiet!" The back door slammed shut behind him.

Tanya and Adam exchanged an amused look with Rachel.

"*Qué torbellino*!" Rachel declared with a chuckle. "What a whirlwind!"

"He's all boy," Adam grinned in agreement. "Surely you haven't forgotten what Justin and I were like at his age."

"*Dios mio*! How could I? What one of you could not think up to get into, the other one would. You were terrors!"

Justin faked an offended stance. "Why, Rachel! Adam and I were angels!"

Rachel skewered him with a skeptical look. "*Si*! The only thing supporting your lopsided halos were your devilish little horns!"

Melissa's giggle was contagious. "Please tell us more, Rachel," Tanya begged. "This could prove very interesting." She slid a sidelong glance at Adam.

"Never mind," he told her, helping her to her feet. "Jeremy is waiting. You can exchange sordid tales with Mother later."

Jeremy was awed by the miracle of the foal's birth. Never had he witnessed anything to compare with it. He sat quietly mesmerized by the heaving sides of the mare, watching as José and Adam soothed and aided her. His breathless exclamations upon the final arrival of the fuzzy, wet newborn foal brought tears to Tanya's eyes. Jeremy's smothered giggles as the spindly-legged babe tried out its legs for the first time brought chuckles all around. His marvelous, wide-eyed delight infected them all.

Across Jeremy's head, Adam's glowing ebony eyes held Tanya's, and she knew he was recalling the night Hunter was born. For long minutes, they silently shared the memory of that magical moment when Adam had helped his firstborn into the world and held him in his hands.

"I love you," he mouthed soundlessly.

"I know," she mimed back, her eyes misting once more. Without so much as a touch, they were wrapped in the warmth of their love.

As promised, Adam patiently taught Jeremy how to ride, selecting a gentle mount for him. Part of each morning was set aside for Jeremy's lessons, and often Tanya watched, recalling how Adam had taught her in a similarly patient yet entirely different manner. Here, Adam was teaching Jeremy to ride his first horse, instilling fundamentals of a fairly routine measure. In the Cheyenne village, he had taught Tanya, who already knew how to ride a horse in the usual fashion, how to ride as an Indian brave should.

Sometimes, while Adam was occupied with Jeremy, Tanya would chat privately with Rachel. The more the two women got to know one another, the closer they became.

"I wish you'd had the chance to know Adam's father," Rachel told her. "He was a fine man."

"If Adam is anything like White Antelope, I am sure I missed meeting a wonderful person."

Rachel smiled wanly. "It helped and it hurt at the same time to see Adam grow up to be so like White Antelope, not only in looks, but in attitude. I loved White Antelope, even after we parted, and I grieved for him then and when he died."

Her face took on a wistful expression. "I've often wondered what would have happened if I'd stayed with the Cheyenne. I suppose in time White Antelope would have come to hate me for not accepting his ways. It was better this way, perhaps, after all. At least I have provided my son with an education, and the option of living as a white man someday if he chooses." A long sigh escaped her lips.

Tanya touched Rachel's hand briefly. "I've been told White Antelope loved you until the day he died. He grieved as you did at being parted, but it gave him great joy that you shared your son with him. He did not resent you because you could not conform to his way of life."

"Thank you," Rachel murmured, her eyes soft with memories. "That is kind of you, especially since Adam has told me how dearly you had to pay for my mistakes."

"I don't understand what you mean." Tanya frowned thoughtfully.

Rachel explained, "Adam told me what rigid tests Black Kettle set up for you before you could become Adam's wife. I thought you might resent me, for it was because of me that Black Kettle did not want Adam to marry a white captive. It appalls me to think of what you endured, and yet you met Black Kettle's standards. Knowing how hard it must have been, I admire your courage and stamina."

Tanya shrugged. "It was not an easy goal to attain, and I had to work harder at it than I ever have for anything else, but it made me strong and gave me pride in myself. It also made me realize that I can survive anything—but the loss of Adam and his love."

"My son tells me you like the Indian way of life." Rachel shook her head in wonderment. "I loathed it so thoroughly that I can't imagine how you could possibly enjoy it."

Tanya smiled. "I love the simplicity and freedom of Cheyenne ways. There is a basic, raw-boned honesty—a thing is either right or wrong. Everything hinges upon basic needs; food, shelter, clothing, families. Everyone pulls together for the good of the tribe, sharing and caring for one another, putting individual needs aside. Petty squabbles and back-biting are less noticeable than elsewhere in the so-called civilized world. There is less time for it, and more important things to worry about."

"But Tanya dear, it's so *primitive!*" Rachel shuddered. "I'll never forget how shocked I was. No snug homes with cheery fireplaces; china, silverware, or utensils. I was astounded to see people actually eating with their fingers and children running about naked. I yearned for a soft bed, a comfortable chair, a real bath with scented soap! My fingers bled from scraping hides and working bone needles through tough leather. The sight of buffalo or deerhide sickened me, and I longed for the feel of silk and satin, or even muslin! And when I discovered I was pregnant with Adam, it frightened me that there were no doctors for hundreds of miles, nor anyone with whom I was close to comfort me. Most of all, I missed my family. Everything was so strange to me there; the language, the people, the entire way of life. When I married White Antelope, they merely tolerated me. I prayed for rescue even after I came to love my husband. He and Adam were the only bright spots in my existence." She sighed. "I hated the cruelty and the bloodshed. It made my blood run cold to see the warriors in their warpaint and hear their horrid chants. I detested the food, the clothes, the land, the people; literally everything about the village!"

Tanya laughed ruefully. "It doesn't sound as if much has changed in the last quarter of a century. Life among the Cheyenne is still pretty much as you described it then. The hard work was satisfying to me once my muscles were accustomed to it. It was music to my ears to awaken to the sound of Panther—er—Adam chanting his morning prayers, and the day I discovered I was carrying his child was one of the happiest in my memory."

Tanya's eyes rested on Rachel's face, willing her to understand. She held out her arms, revealing her wristbands. "These are the only wedding bands I need, and the other jewelry I treasure is all Cheyenne.

"As with you, the Cheyenne did not like me at first, but I won their respect and I proved myself worthy of their friendship. Now there are many I grieve for, and others I yearn to see again. Once I'd proven myself to be as capable as any brave, they willingly accepted me as one of their own; Black Kettle's adopted daughter, and the bride of A-Panther-Stalks."

Rachel studied her thoughtfully, then asked, "What about your sons, Tanya? Is that the life you want for them?"

Tanya answered without hesitation. "Yes. It is what Adam wishes, too. Our sons will grow up strong and brave, proud and loyal, with good values. They will have a religious belief that is natural and pure in its basis. They will have a knowledge of nature that no classroom could instill in them. When Adam decides the time is right, we will see they are educated in the proper white schools. Meanwhile, they will be learning three languages from childhood, and all else that Adam and I can teach them of both cultures."

"Didn't you miss your family?"

Tanya nodded. "Yes, and I will miss them again when we return to the village. Adam has suggested that we tell my parents we wish to live elsewhere for awhile, or that we are traveling. We will return for visits as often as we can so all of you can see your grandsons."

"I hope so," Rachel said with a sigh. Then she gave

Tanya a little smile. "Now, Tanya, please tell me one thing you do *not* like about Cheyenne life so I do not feel so inadequate!"

Tanya thought a second, then grimaced. "I do not like scalps, especially those I am forced to take myself. They are grotesque! Thank goodness Adam understands this, and except for those rare occasions when I am required to wear them, they hang abandoned on our lodge pole."

Rachel shuddered. "I don't blame you! Brrr!"

"I try not to think of it," Tanya admitted, "as I prefer not to think of the massacre at Washita."

"It is better to think of the good times," Rachel advised.

Tanya smiled. "I have treasured memories of love and laughter with Adam. When he first discovered I loved him, he looked so victorious, and he was so proud and handsome on our wedding night. I still miss his braids," she confided. "The look on his face the night we first talked about our unborn child was beautiful; and the night Hunter was born, all wet and warm and new, Adam's eyes glowed with the wonder of it. He is a magnificent man, a marvelous husband, and a wonderful father. You should be very proud of your son, Rachel."

"I am," the older woman confessed softly, "and I am proud that he chose you for his wife. You are a unique and special woman."

Tanya shook her head. "No, Rachel, I am merely a woman deeply in love with her husband."

Tanya spent many hours riding over the ranch with Adam. Sometimes, if they were only going a short distance, Jeremy went with them. What Jeremy lacked in ability he made up in determination. He enjoyed his new accomplishment so thoroughly that his exuberance spilled over onto the others.

More often, Tanya and Adam rode out alone. Tanya learned the boundaries and lay of the land that comprised the ranch. Under Adam's tutelage, she began to grasp a basic knowledge of how a cattle ranch was operated. It was much more complicated than she's first thought, and her admiration for Rachel grew as she realized the responsibility her mother-in-law shouldered. It was no easy undertaking to run the ranch so smoothly in Adam's absence.

As they stopped their mounts on a knoll, watching the cattle grazing placidly below them, Adam turned to Tanya. "You like it here," he said. It was more a statement than a question.

"Yes," Tanya concurred. "It is beautiful. Your mother does a spectacular job."

His hand directed her gaze in an arc about them. "This, too, is my heritage," he said with a heavy sigh. "It was not an easy decision to join my father's people. All my life I've been pulled in two separate directions."

"Your Cheyenne blood must have had the stronger pull," Tanya said.

Adam smiled down at her. "Yes, but someday I will have to come back and take up my responsibilities here. My mother will not be able to handle it alone forever, and then I will have to take over. There will come a day when I put aside my personal preferences to do what I must as my mother's only child."

"We'll cross that bridge when we come to it," Tanya said. "As you say, you are the only son both of your mother and your father, and I know your responsibilities weigh heavily on you. You can only give your best, Adam, and I will help you in any way I can."

"Tell me about Melissa," Justin requested of Tanya. They were standing outside the corral watching Adam give Jeremy his riding lesson.

Tanya slid him a sidelong glance. "What exactly do you want to know, Justin?"

He sighed, running his fingers through his hair. "Something, anything that will help me break down the barriers she has erected. I love her, and I think she loves me, but every time I suggest anything remotely connected with marriage, she backs off as if I'd slapped her. I simply don't know what to do."

Tanya leaned her arms on the fence rail and thought for a moment before speaking. "Missy did not have an easy time of it with the Cheyenne, Justin."

"I didn't think she had," he countered.

"No," Tanya went on, "but I don't think you realize how bad it truly was, and I'm not sure how much I should tell you; how much Melissa would want you to hear."

"But you know why she holds me off; you know what her fears are," Justin suggested hopefully.

Tany nodded. "First you have to understand that of the five of us captured together, I was the most fortunate. It was pure luck that the kindest, most considerate of men claimed me."

Here she stopped to gather her thoughts. "Go on, please,' Justin pleaded.

"We were all frightened nearly to death, not knowing what to expect at first," she recalled. "Melissa was the youngest, barely fourteen; and she drew the ugliest, most vile of all the Cheyenne who happened along that day. Ugly Otter was a beast!

When he had had his pleasure with Melissa, he tried to rape me." Tanya shuddered at the memory. "I fought him, and Panther pulled him off me before he succeeded, but not before I'd bitten off part of Ugly Otter's ear. Of all of us, Melissa fared the worst. Ugly Otter's wife was nearly as cruel as he was, and she took out her spite on Melissa at every opportunity. After a long, hard day's work, Melissa had to look forward to meeting Ugly Otter's savage demands each night. As if that were not enough, he took added delight in loaning her out to other warriors in the tribe."

"Enough!" Justin choked, his face twisted in pain and anger.

"No!" Tanya answered, her golden eyes blazing. "You insisted on knowing, and now you shall hear it all! If you think it is hard to hear, try living through it, as Missy has done! She was so young and delicate that I feared for her life. As my wedding gift from Black Kettle, I begged him to buy Melissa from Ugly Otter before his cruelty killed her. She became our servant, and Panther and I saw to it she was clothed and fed and clean. It took a long time to convince her that Panther would not beat or rape her, but finally she stopped flinching each time Panther entered our tipi."

Here Justin interrupted, "Did your husband have her too?"

Tanya shook her head. "No. It was within his right to do so, but he did not. He was thoroughly appalled at Missy's condition when she came to us, and soon it was certain she was pregnant, most likely with Ugly Otter's child."

Justin groaned in wordless agony, and braced himself for the rest of the tale.

"Because of her weakened condition, she miscarried the child halfway through her term. It was a merciful end to a disastrous situation. She almost lost her life in the process. She was deathly ill for a long time, and only the constant care of the medicine woman pulled her through."

By now, all the color had fled from Justin's face.

"Someday," Tanya concluded softly, "she may recover enough to marry and have more children, but she will never fully forget the terrors she went through. Physically, there is no lasting damage, but emotionally and mentally Melissa is still very bruised. She has endured abuse and terror that might have killed her or left her mentally crippled, but she has survived, and I pray she will recover fully one day and be able to live a normal life."

"The poor child," Justin murmured, still in shock.

"She doesn't need your pity, Justin," Tanya told him. "She needs your help and understanding. She needs someone to cherish her with gentle patience; someone to protect her from all the inquisitive gossip-mongers who profess concern and only succeed in re-opening already raw wounds. She needs time to regain the pride and self-respect that have been stripped from her along with her confidence in herself. She needs your love."

"She has it," he assured her, his eyes gentle. "I'll help her any way she'll let me, but I don't know where to start."

"I sincerely hope you mean that, Justin. Too many of the proper citizens of Pueblo would be repelled by what I have told you. Many would shun her and hold her somehow responsible for that which she had no control over."

He nodded in understanding. "I know, but I'll gladly protect her from those who would hurt her. If she'll marry me, I'll adore her all my life."

Tanya, convinced of his sincerity, touched his arm gently. "In her mind Melissa knows you are not like Ugly Otter, but she fears the physical side of marriage and the pain of childbirth, even though she helped me the night Hunter was born, and she's seen how happy I was with Panther. With time and patience you can convince her, Justin. She loves you, I am sure. If only she can conquer her fears, you'll be very happy together."

He nodded. "Thank you for explaining everything to me, Tanya. At least now I know what it is she fears, and why. I will go very slowly and gently with her. I'll make her see she can trust me."

"I hope so," Tanya replied, "for both your sakes. She has so much love to give, and she deserves so much more than life has dealt her so far. Fill her world with love and joy, and I'll be forever in your debt, Justin."

"I'd give her the stars if she asked for them," he said solemnly.

Chapter 22

THEY HAD been at the ranch for a week, when one morning a young dark-haired girl rode up. Tanya and Adam were in the barn, showing Hunter the new foal. They heard the girl shout at one of the men, asking where Adam was.

Minutes later, she raced headlong into the barn, stopping only long enough to let her eyes adjust to the gloom. Spotting Adam, she ran to him, throwing herself into his arms.

"Oh, Adam! You're home!" she squealed. "It seems like forever since I've seen you."

She drew back a bit and eyed him balefully through soulful brown eyes. "You've been gone for over *three years*," she scolded. "I've had a dreadful time keeping Stuart Hammond at bay all this time, but I waited for you just as I promised."

Tanya, who had been standing to one side, could not decide whether to be perturbed by this forward, dark-haired beauty or amused at the disconcerted look on Adam's face. Obviously, he was completely surprised by her sudden appearance.

"What the . . ." he started, then his eyes widened in startled recognition. "Pru? Little Prudence Barnes?" he questioned. "Heavens, Cricket! How you've grown!"

The girl's face glowed. "Of course, silly! I'm sixteen now, and we can be married. When I asked you before, you said I'd have to grow up a bit."

Tanya barely stifled a giggle at the dumbfounded look Adam could not hide.

Before he had a chance to say anything, Prudence pushed back from him and twirled about gaily, showing off her faultless figure. "There!" she announced pertly. "You can see I'm all grown up now."

"You certainly are," Adam concurred, a smile twitching at his lips, "but Cricket. . ."

"That's another thing," Prudence interrupted. "Once we're married, you've got to stop calling me that—except in private, of course. It's much too juvenile to suit me. Why have you always called me that?"

"Probably because you're always chirping about, interrupting when someone is trying to talk to you, and rattling on constantly," he stated dryly.

Temporarily taken aback, Prudence frowned. "Oh," she murmured. "Yes, well, I'll have to learn not to do that, I guess."

Tanya cocked an eyebrow in Adam's direction, her lips curved in an amused smile. At his wordless plea for help, she gave him a look that clearly said he was on his own.

Prudence caught his glance, and followed it, finally noticing Tanya and Hunter for the first time. "Oh, hello!" she said, not in the least embarrassed to find that someone had witnessed her bold behavior. "Who are you? Is that your little boy? He's a cute tyke."

Tanya smiled, debating which question to answer first. "Thank you. Yes, he's my son. I'm Tanya Martin."

Prudence's eyes widened. "I've heard of you, I think. Aren't you one of the women who lived with the Indians for a while?" she asked bluntly.

"Word travels fast," Tanya commented.

Prudence shrugged. "It's a small town. I've watched for you at church since we've finally dug out from all the snow and can get to town."

"I haven't gone."

"I wondered what you'd look like. Everyone is curious about you," Prudence admitted guilelessly. "Were you really married to an Indian?"

"Yes."

"You look different than I thought you would." Prudence surveyed Tanya with an assessing gaze.

Tanya didn't know whether to be offended or amused. "What did you think I'd look like?" she asked curiously.

"Kind of haggard, I guess; skinny, bedraggled, beaten."

"Humbled? Pitiful?" Tanya suggested further, her golden eyes twinkling with suppressed mirth.

Prudence nodded. "Was it really awful? Did he beat you?"

"Once," Tanya admitted, her gaze sliding to meet Adam's.

Prudence considered this a moment. "Only once? What did you do?"

"I tried to escape."

"Did you ever try again?"

"No."

"I suppose you soon learned to do things his way," Prudence decided.

Adam's guffaw echoed in the large barn.

"Mostly," Tanya answered, sending Adam a quick glare.

"What are you doing here?" Prudence wanted to know.

"Visiting Adam."

"I wanted her to meet Mother," Adam inserted.

"Why?" Prudence's brows wrinkled in a considering frown.

Adam sighed. "Well, Cricket, you see, I hadn't realized you were serious about waiting for me. I thought you'd have led some young swain to the altar long ago. When I met Tanya, I decided she's the woman I wanted."

A heavy silence followed his words. Finally, with the resilience of youth, Prudence sighed. "Drat! Well, I guess that will make Stu happy. He's been after me to marry him for the last eight months, and Mom is definitely pushing me in his directiion. She's even quit spying on us when we're on the porch swing after dark, and she's constantly making all his favorite foods and inviting him to dinner."

"That explains how he feels, and how your mother feels, but how do *you* feel about him?" Tanya queried gently. For some reason, she could not resent the vicacious brunette.

"Oh, Stu is great! He's good-looking, hard-working, and he adores me. There is nothing at all wrong with him, you see, it's just that I had my sights set on Adam since I was in diapers." Prudence dimpled impishly. "Stu won't know what hit him when I finally accept his proposal!"

"He's a very lucky young man," Adam conceded.

"Sure he is," Prudence agreed with a grin, "and I'll make certain he doesn't forget it, either!"

"No use crying over spilled milk, as Mom would say," Prudence said cheerfully. "I've got my life to get on with, and you'll have Tanya to console you. I hope you'll be happy."

"Thank you. Just one favor, Cricket," Adam suggested. "We haven't had the chance to tell Tanya's family of our decision yet, so keep this to yourself until we announce it, will you?"

"Sure!" Prudence grinned delightedly. "What are friends for? Besides, this way I can let Stu think he's won me over fair and square, and he won't feel he's getting me on the rebound. He'll be strutting like a barnyard rooster!"

"Since Adam is home for once in time for his birthday, I've been considering having a fiesta in his honor," Rachel mused one afternoon. "Do you think your parents would like to come, Tanya?" They were alone in the kitchen.

Tanya looked up in surprise. "Goodness! I've just realized I don't even know when his birthday is!"

Rachel smiled sadly and shook her head in instant understanding. "Yes, there are more important things to worry over with the Cheyenne, such as surviving for yet another year."

"When is Adam's birthday?"

"Actually, it is next Monday, but I thought Saturday evening would be a good time to celebrate. What do you think? I know it would be short notice for some people, but it would be so nice if we could manage it."

"It is a lovely idea. I'm sure Mother and Dad will come if they can."

"I'll send a rider into town tomorrow morning with invitations," Rachel decided.

"Is it to be a surprise?" Tanya asked.

Rachel laughed. "Oh, no! I won't chance that

again! When Adam was nine, I gave him a surprise party, and everyone showed up except him. He was off fishing, and didn't turn up until the guests were ready to leave.

"Explain something to me, Tanya," Rachel said, changing the subject entirely. "What is the problem with this Lt. Young Adam has told me about? Why don't your parents tell him point-blank not to come around any longer? Do they fear him?"

"It is very complicated, Rachel. You see, I was engaged to Jeffrey when Adam captured me. I was on my way to Pueblo to marry him. He waited for me for two and a half years. He consoled my family and grieved with them over my disappearance. He organized search parties to look for me, and he was with General Custer when I was finally found. My parents are indebted to him, not only for bringing me home, but for his support during my absence. When it became obvious I did not want to resume our former relationship, they felt sorry for him. At first they felt I should be grateful he still wanted me."

"And now?" Rachel prompted.

"Now they realize what a mistake it would have been for me to marry Jeffrey. He has shown his true colors since I've been back. He has become obsessed with the idea of having me, to the point where I truly feel the man is demented. His persistence is amazing, but aggravating. I've treated him abominably. I've been rude and hateful and outright cruel, but he's bound and determined I shall be his. He even went so far as to try to rape me when he caught up with me in February, when I tried to escape."

Rachel gasped. "Does Adam know this?"

"Yes, and he also knows my father arrived in time to prevent it, thank heavens. Since then, my family has protected me from him, and they were thrilled when I showed such an interest in Adam.

"The trouble is, I think my parents still feel an obligation toward Jeffrey. Not only that, but he does head the cavalry unit in charge of protecting Pueblo. He has a lot of authority for such a young man, and he's ambitious enough to use it to its fullest extent. He has a vicious temper when crossed, and he could and would make a lot of trouble if pushed too far."

"I see," Rachel said thoughtfully. "They feel they have to cater to him to some extent, whether they wish to or not."

"If that were not enough," Tanya elaborated, "Julie became enamored of him while I was gone, hoping he would turn his attentions toward her. She was quite distressed when I returned, and it wasn't until I convinced her that I wanted nothing to do with Jeffrey that she and I could be friends once more. She's thrilled that Adam is on the scene now. My parents are having fits over her infatuation with him. That is part of the reason she came with me to the ranch. They thought it would be helpful for her to have a change of scene and be away from him for a while."

Rachel looked confused. "But the lieutenant does not return her feelings, so what is the problem?"

"I think they fear that if Jeffrey ever does give up on me, he will then decide on Julie. Besides which, Julie is nearly as stubborn as I am when she wants something."

"So is Roberto," Rachel chuckled. "It will be interesting to see who is the more stubborn of the two. Who will win, do you suppose?"

Tanya laughed. "My money is on Roberto!"

* * *

Roberto was, indeed, relentless in his pursuit of Julie. "Come riding with me, my dove," he wheedled.

"You know I prefer to ride in the carriage," Julie responded tartly.

"If you are afraid of the horse, I'll carry you before me on mine," he offered with a cheeky grin. "There is a lovely bend of the river not far from here that is very pretty and private."

"It is not the horse I fear, and what you are suggesting is extremely improper," she huffed.

"One would think you do not trust me. I have the greatest respect for you, *querida*."

Julie glared at him. "I trust you about as far as I could pick you up and throw you."

Roberto clutched his chest in feigned agony. "You wound me with such words!" he declared. "Don't you know how much I adore you?"

Julie snorted at this. "In a pig's eye! You only want me because you can't have me. You are a born flirt, Roberto!"

Rather than being offended, he answered jauntily, "I have told you before, I can and will have you. You simply must resign yourself to this fact, *chica*. How can you go on resisting me when I have so much to offer?"

Julie rolled her eyes heavenward in exasperation. "Oh, yes, I can see it all now! Where will we live, Mr. Cowhand? In the bunkhouse? In a lineshack? Mother will be so pleased when she comes to dinner!" she scoffed.

Roberto gave her a startled look and burst out laughing. "So! You think because I am working with *Tía Raquela* that I am a poor relation! No, my pet, you are mistaken. I am merely helping her as a favor."

He let Julie digest this for a moment, then added,

"At the risk of having you decide to marry me for my money, I must tell you I am a rich man. My father owns a fine home and much land in Santa Fe, which I, as the eldest son, will inherit one day." He gave her an elegant bow. "Now, I will leave you to think on this more by yourself. Consider carefully, Julie, all that you will forfeit by rejecting me. I am young, rich, healthy and charming—and I will give you such beautiful children!"

"You will *not* give me children!" she shouted at his retreating back when she finally found her tongue.

"Dozens!" he retorted, laughing as he walked away.

A door slammed in the next room, rousing Tanya from a deep sleep. She shifted positions, seeking the warmth of Adam's body. A hand clamped gently over her mouth just as she heard Julie call her name.

Tanya's eyes flew open to meet Adam's. He motioned for her to stay quiet, and when he was sure she was awake enough to understand, he slipped noiselessly from the bed. He'd just slipped the bolt on the connecting door when the knob jiggled.

Tanya grimaced as she realized how close they had come to being discovered by her sister. Usually she locked her bedroom door when she retired, but last night she had forgotten.

A moment later, the door shut again, and Julie's voice was heard in the hallway. It faded as she retreated toward the kitchen.

"What on earth is she doing up so early?" Adam whispered.

Tanya shook her head as she stumbled out of bed. "I don't know, but I'd better get dressed."

"First, lock your door," he advised. "That was too close for comfort."

Tanya did just that. Then, once dressed, she unlocked the door and crept quietly out her window, telling Hunter she would be right back. As she rounded the outside corner of the kitchen, she encountered her sister.

"Good morning, Julie," she said calmly. "You certainly are up earlier than usual. What's the occasion?"

"Where have you been? I was looking for you," Julie asked petulantly.

"Fine, thank you, so nice of you to inquire," Tanya joked at her sister's lack of greeting. "I've been for a short walk."

"Sorry," Julie grumbled. "It is just that I couldn't sleep, and I thought I could talk with you."

"What's wrong?"

"Oh, Tanya! I'm so confused! Roberto is driving me crazy!"

Tanya had to smile. "He *is* rather persistent, isn't he?"

"That hardly begins to describe it! He insists that he will win me over, and now that I know he is not without means, it scares me."

"Why should it? You wouldn't marry a man for his riches, would you?"

"No, but it certainly helps. What I mean to say is, it makes him an acceptable suitor. He's not a penniless beggar."

"I fail to see how his wealth or lack of it would cause you concern, unless, of course, you are attracted to him."

"That's just it," Julie complained. "I've been in love with Jeffrey for years, and now I feel this unreasonable attraction for Roberto. He's very handsome, and he simply oozes charm! I don't *want* to want him; I want Jeffrey! But Roberto is wearing down my resistance, and I don't like it one bit! It is all so confusing! I thought I knew what I wanted, and now I'm not sure. What do I do, Tanya?"

"Have you told Roberto how you feel?"

"Good heavens, no!" Julie exclaimed. "He's altogether too sure of himself as it is!"

"Julie, I'm afraid I can't be much help to you. This is one problem you have to solve on your own. Just one word of advice, dear; follow your heart. No matter what your logic tells you, listen to what your heart is saying. Only then can you be sure you are doing the right thing."

Julie was chewing on her bottom lip. "I suppose so. Now all I need is to figure out what my heart is trying to tell me. It seems to be talking in a foreign language these days."

Taking advantage of the few odd moments not spent with Adam each day, Tanya set to work making his birthday gift. From Rachel she obtained a length of cured, tanned cowhide, which she worked into a belt. In addition, she made a new sheath for his knife, decorating both with colorful Cheyenne designs.

The days sped by, filled with love and peace and a warm feeling of family togetherness. Most days the warm spring sunshine kissed the land awake after its long winter sleep. Once in a while, a gentle spring rain would keep them indoors, or occasionally a thunderstorm.

One Thursday morning they awoke to dull grey skies and rain-laden clouds that raced before a brisk wind. Lightning speared the sky, illuminating the heavens with its brilliant light at increasing intervals, while thunder rattled the windowpanes.

Tanya wandered from window to window restlessly, unable to settle down to any task for longer than a few minutes.

Adam came to stand beside her, watching the rain lash against the windows. Leaning closer, he whispered, "Meet me in the barn in fifteen minutes. There is a waterproof poncho on the hook by the kitchen door."

Tanya nodded.

A quarter of an hour later, she dashed into the dark barn, throwing off the wet raingear. Immediately she was enveloped by warm arms, pulled tightly against a broad, muscular chest.

"Your face is all shiny with rain," Adam murmured as he kissed the drops away, licking at them with his tongue.

On tiptoe, she feathered her fingers through his midnight-dark hair. "Your hair is soaked."

His lips left her cheek to find her mouth in a long, drugging kiss that seemed to draw her soul out of her body into his. Her lips trembled when the warmth of his finally released them.

"Come," he said, leading her toward the ladder to the loft high above. They climbed to the upper level, warm and sweet with the smell of clean hay.

The rain drummed down on the roof with a steady beat, joined by the thunder, but in the dry loft they stood in a private, cozy world of their own.

Adam broke the twine of a couple of nearby bales, and spread the loose hay into a pile, creating a sweet, if prickly, mattress.

Tanya giggled as he pulled her down onto it with him. "We've never made love in a hayloft before."

Adam smiled broadly, his white teeth flashing. "What? Do you mean to tell me a lusty wench like you has never been for a roll in the hay?"

Tanya threw him a coy look and smiled. "Why, sir, surely you jest!" Then she snuggled her lithe body close against his. "You know you are my only lover. Now you may instruct me in the fine art of lovemaking in a loft."

"It will be my pleasure." His nimble fingers were already making short work of the buttons on her dress. He slid the bodice down to her waist, his lips following along the curve of her neck and shoulder, and coming to rest along the slope of her breast, guarded by the lace of her chemise.

"Too many clothes," he muttered thickly, his voice gravelly with desire. Under his impatient fingers, the chemise also found its way down her body.

Once her arms were unrestricted, Tanya helped Adam to divest himself of his own clothing, her hands caressing his skin with smooth strokes.

The hay poked and scratched at her tender flesh, but Tanya was beyond noticing, her mind and body consumed by the raging fires Adam was stoking in her. His lips traversed the length of her, his hands soothing and creating havoc simultaneously. The husky tones of his voice murmuring words of love in the dim loft caressed her thirsting soul.

She reached out to him, touching him in all the well-known places guaranteed to arouse him; stroking, nipping, kissing. She surrounded him with her love and her body. When he came into her, she locked him tightly in her embrace, searing him with her heat, her body melting into his.

His expert lovemaking sent her careening into another sphere, on a collision course with the stars, and she carried him with her to the heights of glory. He held her trembling on the brink of ecstasy until their passions at last exploded in a brilliant starburst.

Over and over again she sighed out his name, their mutual cries of fulfillment masked by the rumbling thunder overhead.

Weak with love, she slowly opened her eyes to see his face above hers, illuminated in the white light of the storm. His ebony eyes were soft with sated passion. "My Wildcat," he whispered, his lips tenderly claiming the love-swollen contours of hers.

Her lips trembled against his. "My Panther, my love," she sighed.

At the supper table that evening Tanya still had that look of a well and truly loved woman about her; her lips were still slightly swollen from his demanding kisses and there was a glow to her face, a glitter to her golden eyes.

Melissa and Rachel paid little attention, knowing full well what brought the added glow, and Julie, never having experienced such things, gave it no thought. Roberto, however, took note right away, and his curious glances passed back and forth between Adam and Tanya throughout the meal. At one point, he leaned over and whispered a quiet question to Justin. Justin shrugged nonchalantly, saying nothing, but every so often afterward, his contemplative gaze rested on his friend's face or Tanya's.

Later, Justin got Melissa aside. "Tanya hasn't said anything to you about what is going on between herself and Adam, has she?"

"No, why?" Melissa asked.

"Roberto has some crazy notion they've been—well—making love," he said hesitantly, "and I think he may be right."

"It is none of our business what they do together," Melissa countered smoothly.

Justin looked at her in surprise. "No, but I thought

Adam was more of a gentleman than to take advantage of a lady, and regardless of what she's been through, I consider Tanya a lady."

"It doesn't concern us," Melissa repeated.

Justin looked puzzled. "That is a strange attitude for you to take, Melissa, considering the way you hold me at arm's length. You surprise me."

Melissa shrugged. "I'm not so small-minded that I would stoop to condemning my friends for what they feel is right. My ideas may differ from theirs, but that does not necessarily make either of us right or wrong. Nothing is ever altogether black or white in this world, Justin. If nothing else, I've learned to be more tolerant of others these past years."

Justin looked down on the petite blonde he'd come to love so much and shook his head. "Will I ever come to understand you?"

Melissa gave him an enigmatic smile. "You never can tell."

The day of the fiesta was hectic with last-minute preparations. The beef had been cooking slowly on outside spits for hours, and the house was filled with the spicy aroma of other foods being prepared. Dozens of pies, cakes, and confectionery delights lined the sideboards in the kitchen and dining room.

Tables were being erected outside, and lanterns strung for the evening's festivities. Extra rooms had been prepared for guests who would be staying over, as the festivities would no doubt last into the early hours of the morning.

Late afternoon brought the arrival of the Martin family. Eager to relate all his new accomplishments, Jeremy was the first to greet them, almost before the wheels of the buggy had stopped turning.

Tanya gave the flowers she was arranging one last adjustment, and nodded in satisfaction. "They'll do," she said to herself as she went to welcome her parents. On her way to the door, she scooped Mark up from his spot on the floor. "Come on, little spider," she told him. "Let's go see Grandma and Grandpa."

Julie and Melissa were already outside, and Rachel was welcoming her guests. Just as Tanya was about to step forward, Adam came striding around the corner of the house, Hunter riding proudly atop his shoulders.

As Adam's long-legged stride carried him swiftly to Tanya's side, Mark spied him. With a delighted coo and a wide, four-tooth grin, he threw his arms open. It was pure coincidence that he chose the one moment of pure silence to call out, "Da-da! Da-da!"

Shocked to her toes by her son's first words, Tanya felt the blood rush to her face. To his credit, Adam did not break stride; neither did his face show undue surprise. Upon reaching Tanya, he ruffled Mark's hair, put his arm about Tanya's waist, and said calmly, "Smart boy! He's talking earlier than most, isn't he?"

Tanya gulped and nodded, noting the shocked looks on both her mother's and father's faces. Then she suddenly burst out laughing. "I never expected his first words to be in English!" she exclaimed. "What a surprise!"

Rachel laughed. "He's a *pícaro*, a little rascal! Last week he cut a tooth on the rung of my best rocker, which I shall cherish all the more, and crawled into the pantry to hide. What next, I ask you?"

At last Tanya's father ventured a comment. "Well, at least you have to admire his taste, if not his discretion," he said on a chuckle. "He knows a good man when he sees one."

"I cannot help but agree with you, sir," Rachel concurred as everyone laughed.

"Now all we have to do is see if the mother is as smart as her son," Roberto suggested with a sly wink in Tanya's direction that set her blushing anew.

"She is." Adam smiled cryptically and led the group indoors, his arm snugly about Tanya's waist.

Friends and neighbors from miles around came to celebrate Adam's birthday. The house and yards were overflowing with laughter and gaiety. Everyone from Judge Kerr to the lowliest ranch hand was having a grand time. Mountains of food disappeared like magic, to be replaced by more from the kitchen, and the supply of liquor seemed endless. A few of the more talented in attendance took turns providing the music, and the soft sound of guitars wafted on the night air, often accompanied by the haunting tones of a harmonica. As everyone became caught up in the gala atmosphere of the evening, more of them joined in the singing and dancing.

Adam was very relaxed and congenial in his role as host, and somehow, as the evening progressed, Rachel managed inconspicuously to shift the role of hostess from her own shoulders to Tanya's. With Tanya constantly at his side, often with his hand resting possessively on her shoulder or the curve of her waist, Adam wordlessly conveyed the distinct message that Tanya was his.

Tanya met many new people as well as renewing acquaintances with several she'd met previously. She knew Judge Kerr and his wife Emily, of course. Prudence Barnes was there with her family and Stuart Hammond. The young couple looked very happy, and Tanya was fairly certain that Prudence had broken the good news to him already.

Dr. Emmet Jones, a distinguished gentleman in his mid-fifties, was there, as well as the town sheriff, Tom Middleton. From what little Tanya overheard, Sheriff Middleton was none too pleased with the interference of the military in his town. It seemed the cavalry was stepping on the good sheriff's toes, as well as his jurisdiction, in their zeal to help protect the citizens of Pueblo. Particularly offensive was one Lt. Young, who seemed to think his authority came from God himself, and far outweighed the sheriff's.

From her parents, Tanya discovered that Jeffrey had been as riled as a bear with a sore paw since the day she'd left Pueblo with Adam. The only reason he hadn't found time to come out to the ranch himself was that he'd been kept constantly busy with the influx of wagon trains now passing through Pueblo heading west.

"They are just starting to reach here from the east, and the town is booming," Edward stated. "That is why Elizabeth and George could not come. Someone had to keep the mercantile open for business."

As the evening progressed, Tanya noted that while Justin devoted himself to Melissa, Roberto was employing a reverse tactic. He flirted and danced with nearly every pretty girl present, and his strategy appeared to be working. Julie could not seem to keep her eyes from him for long, and with each new woman she saw on his arm, her frown grew. Tanya knew her sister well enough to recognize that the bright gleam in Julie's blue-green eyes was less excitement than out-and-out jealousy.

Other than a few obligatory turns with other partners, Adam and Tanya reserved their dances for one another. She politely but firmly refused offers by a number of other men, and they soon got the message. Even the women took note of how often Tanya and Adam circled the floor together, and how intimately he held her.

Her cheek resting on his shoulder as they drifted dreamily to the music, she whispered, "Adam, you are holding me much closer than is proper, my darling. People have started to talk."

"They are just jealous," he assured her, his breath fanning her hair.

"Of you or me?"

"Both, I imagine!"

Later, seated beside him at one of the tables with Rachel and her parents, the topic arose again.

"Tanya, dear," Sarah began. "At the risk of sounding critical, I must point out that your conduct this evening is causing comment. The gossips are having a heyday!"

Tanya smiled wryly. "Mother, that is hardly something new where I am concerned. I am sure half of the people I met tonight expected me to appear in buckskin, a tomahawk in my hand!"

"Don't be facetious, daughter," Edward said curtly. "Your mother is right. It is our responsibility to see that your reputation suffers no more abuse than it already has."

"Not for long," Adam drawled nonchalantly, taking a sip of his drink.

Edward's head snapped about. "What was that?"

"She won't be your responsibility for long, Edward," Adam elaborated. "With your permission, I'd like your daughter's hand in marriage."

Even though she herself was unprepared for Adam's bold pronouncement, Tanya was amused by the stunned looks on her parents' faces. She'd never seen her mother's mouth hanging open like that, or her father at a loss for words.

"Tanya has already agreed to be my bride, and I intend to adopt the boys, of course," Adam went on calmly, as if discussing nothing more important than the weather.

Tanya wondered if her father had been rendered permanently speechless. Finally he cleared his throat several times and stammered, "I—yes—of course." He shook his head as if to clear it. "You certainly caught me unaware!"

Sarah's hand fluttered uncertaintly to her throat. "This is rather soon, isn't it?" Her voice wavered suspiciously.

A devilish twinkle lit Tanya's eyes. "Do you disapprove then, Mama?"

"Gracious, no!" Sarah responded with improper haste, then blushed to the roots of her hair. "I just want you to be certain," she amended.

"I've never been one to take long to decide what I want," Adam explained, "and I want Tanya. I take it we have your blessing then?"

Sarah and Edward exchanged a quick glance. "Yes," they chorused.

Rachel beamed. "You are perfect for one another. I am so happy for you, and so excited! Please let me help you plan for your wedding, Tanya." Her dark eyes sought those of her son's and lingered lovingly. "Adam is my only child, and so I have no daughter to fuss over at her wedding."

"Of course you must help," Sarah insisted kindly, obviously moved by Rachel's plea. "Elizabeth and I will have our hands full, no doubt." Already her mind was busily spinning plans. "We will have to organize a formal engagement party . . ."

Adam leaned forward. "Excuse me, Mrs. Martin, but you'd better plan fast, for now that Tanya is to be my wife, I find myself anxious. In just a few moments I am going to quell all the whispers and rumors by announcing our engagement here and now."

Rachel, used to her son's split-second decisions, smiled indulgently as Sarah sputtered, "But—but . . ."

She patted the other woman's hand in a gesture of comfort. "Now, Sarah, it will work out fine. We can have the engagement party in a few weeks."

"They'd better be short weeks then, Mother," Adam instructed. "Tanya and I want to be married by the first of July at the latest."

Sarah gasped. "My dear boy! We can't possibly have everything ready by then! That is only four—five weeks away!"

"Why drag it out?" Tanya asked, her eyes dancing merrily. "Let's get him to the altar quickly, before he changes his mind!"

"*Tanya*!" Sarah was scandalized.

Tanya, Adam, and Rachel burst out laughing, and Edward joined them. "Tanya has a point, Sarah," he chuckled. "Lord knows when we'll have another opportunity like this!"

Chapter 23

IT WAS the wee hours of the morning before the party broke up and everyone straggled off to bed. Due to the number of guests staying over, Melissa had volunteered to bunk in with Tanya to make more room.

No sooner had they locked the door and put out the light than Tanya tiptoed toward Adam's room. "Mark should sleep through the night, but if he wakes and needs to be fed, call me," she whispered to Melissa.

"All right," Melissa mumbled in response, already burrowing her head into her pillow. "G'night."

Thinking Melissa was nearly asleep, Tanya left the connecting door open a crack, the better to hear the boys if Melissa slept too deeply.

Adam was waiting for her. As she stepped into a path of moonlight next to the bed, he spoke softly. "The price of admittance into my bed is the forfeiture of that concealing nightgown you are wearing."

Tanya laughed. "Getting rather bossy now that our engagement has been publicly announced, aren't you?" Her voice was muffled as she pulled the offending garment over her head and slid into bed beside him.

"I think I deserve extra consideration since this may be one of the last opportunities we have to be alone for weeks," he countered. "Your mother will be keeping you busy in town with fittings and plans and invitations, and there is no guarantee we can schedule another visit to the ranch between now and the wedding."

"True," she murmured, her lips finding the hollow in his throat.

He gathered her close, enjoying the feel of her silken skin against the rougher texture of his, burying his hands and his face in her fragrant hair. Inhaling deeply, he sighed, "I've been wanting to do this all evening. You smell of lilacs and you feel like warm satin. It has driven me to distraction to hold you so close and not be able to kiss you or touch you as I wanted to."

His lips feathered across her forehead, her temple, her cheekbone. "You are so beautiful, Tanya. You are a magnificent witch! You've had me under your spell since the first moment I saw you."

His lips remained elusive as she sought them with her own. "The moonlight has gone to your head," she responded softly.

Again she tried to capture his mouth, but he was intent on a path from her neck to her shoulder, nipping lightly at the sensitive flesh. She moaned in delight, tipping her head back to allow him better access. Shivers of sensual pleasure danced through her. Her slender fingers wound their way into his ebony locks.

Adam chuckled. "Like that, do you?"

"Mmm-hmm," she sighed languidly, then caught her breath as his fingertips brushed lightly up and down her sides.

With her hands to his head, she guided his mouth toward hers, eager for the kisses she craved. But instead of the fulfilling kiss she so desired, he held her off, nibbling his way all along the outer edges of her mouth; teasing the contours with his tongue, his teeth, his warm breath, until her lips were trembling for the full weight of his.

"Kiss me, Adam. Kiss me," she pleaded.

When he complied, it was all she could ask and more. His mouth took command of hers, molding, searing, a promise of delights to come. His tongue sought entry, and her lips parted gladly to allow it to slide smoothly between her teeth. Their breath mingled as their tongues began a mating dance of their own, twisting, tangling, tasting.

Tanya felt the familiar fires of passion licking along her veins, heating her blood. Her body strained to make closer contact with his, her hands stroking the contours of his shoulders, urging him nearer.

Adam's skillful fingers teased along her ribcage, edging ever nearer to her aching breasts. As they neared their goal, he lightly traced the outer curves, and for the briefest of moments, she felt his work-roughened palms brush their pouting tips.

A frustrated moan of pure agony escaped her lips as his hands failed to claim their prize. His deep chuckle told her he was deliberately taunting her. "Damn it, darling!" she breathed, wrenching her mouth from his. "Stop teasing me!"

"Tell me what you want, my pet," he directed huskily.

"Touch me." Her hands guided his to her throbbing breasts. "Fondle me. Let me feel your hands and mouth on my breasts."

"Tell me how it makes you feel, my love, when I caress your breasts and tease the nipples with my tongue. What goes on inside of you?"

Just inside the next room, Melissa was in the process of closing the door to shut out the sounds of their lovemaking. She paused with her hand on the doorknob as she heard Adam's words. Even as she felt her stomach lurch in revulsion, curiosity stayed her hand. Heat flushed her cheeks as she eavesdropped on this most intimate of scenes. She knew she should leave, but her feet seemed rooted to the floor.

For months now she had been experiencing unfamiliar twinges of response toward Justin. The few times she had allowed him to kiss her, a previously unknown flutter erupted in her stomach, and her breath had shortened magically. The one time he had gently cupped her breast, her nipple had risen immediately, and when his thumb had brushed tentatively across it, a shaft of emotion had speared through her, frightening her with its intensity. She had backed away in confusion and shame, unable to understand her traitorous body.

From Ugly Otter she had learned the pain and degradation of physical union with a man. While living with Tanya and Adam in their tipi, she came to realize that some people found pleasure in it, though she could not understand why. With Justin, she was now experiencing for the first time the emotional side of love between a man and a woman. Her heart was opening in response to his, but her mind was sending mixed signals. She had not expected her body to respond to his touch; she had anticipted disgust. Her mind and better judgment told her she should be repelled and ashamed, even as her lips thrilled to his.

Never had she linked the ideas of emotional and physical love together in her mind. To her thinking, the two were separate and distinct, one hateful, the other ethereal. Now, as she stood in the dark listening to the murmurings in the next room, she readjusted her thinking. The two types of love did, indeed, belong together.

As she heard Tanya's heartfelt responses and Adam's corresponding words of love and praise, she at last realized that where the heart was involved, the act of love brought no shame. Where tenderness existed, no pain could intrude. Without love, the act of mating was just animalistic rutting, with no regard for human emotion; but with love, it was the ultimate expression of the heart and soul.

Tears streamed unheeded down Melissa's cheeks. She'd never understood what Tanya had tried to tell her before, because she had not known Justin or come to love him. Now, for the first time, she saw clearly that the love she and Justin felt for one another would not be sullied by the union of their bodies. Justin was kind and gentle, and the love they shared would reflect that.

Quietly Melissa shut the door and tiptoed back to bed. An immense sigh shuddered through her body, bringing with it a blessed release of all the emotional upheaval she'd been coping with lately. She drifted into a peaceful sleep, knowing she should be ashamed of listening to Tanya and Adam's lovemaking, but grateful that her curiosity had led her to the resolution of her problem. At last she was free to love Justin as he deserved.

"I love it when you touch my breasts," Tanya whispered as Adam's mouth claimed a nipple. His teeth grazed the sensitive tip, and his tongue laved it. "It sends sparks clear through me, and every nerve in my body comes alive. A lake of lava forms in the center of my being and spreads its heat outward, and I feel a tightening and an ache between my thighs."

Her shy words of explanation sent a surge of love and pride through him, and he doubled his ministrations, determined to give her all the pleasure he could.

Wanting to return the favors he was bestowing, her eager hands traversed his body. Her fingers traced each bone and sinew within her reach, each muscle of his chest and back and arms. Her palms caressed; her fingers kneaded. Her lips and tongue sought out the sensual arena of his ear, her teeth nipping at the lobe and eliciting a shiver of passion from him.

Long fingernails skimmed along his ribcage and tantalized each ridge of his spine, extracting a groan of arousal. Her hands drew languid designs on his naked flesh as she reveled in the feel of his skin beneath her touch. The salty taste of him was on her tongue as she rained tiny bites across his shoulder, then soothed them with kisses.

"You are destroying my self control with that magic mouth of yours, my darling," he warned her. His method of retaliation took her breath away. As his mouth reclaimed hers, one of his hands resumed its teasing on her breast. The other ventured on, charting a lazy course along the plane of her stomach, stopping to delve into her navel, journeying along the curve of her hip. As his fingers traced tiny circles up the inside of her thigh, she tensed in expectation, her body arching up to seek his touch.

A muffled exclamation of sheer bliss escaped her lips as his fingers at last sought and probed her most secret, sensual valley of desire. All coherent thought fled as his fingers worked their sweet torture.

His mouth retreated from hers to take the route of his fingers. Every bone in her body was melting. "You're a devil, Adam Savage," she moaned shakily. "A sweet, sweet devil!"

He swirled his tongue along her inner thigh and grinned. "You are no angel yourself, my pet. Your body is heavenly enough, but your responses are as hot as hell itself."

His tongue took up the torment of his fingers. Ripples of rapture swamped her senses as she quivered to his touch. "Adam, Adam," she breathed. "Please, Adam!"

"Not quite yet, my greedy Wildcat," he growled as he nipped and nibbled his way back up her feverish body.

Her hand slid down his back to clutch at his buttocks, urging him wordlessly to quench her need for him. When he ignored her request and continued to feast upon her flesh, licking and biting, her fingers slipped about to enclose his pulsing shaft. With silken strokes she teased and tantalized him in turn, knowing she was pushing him to the limits of his endurance.

"You're a wanton witch! An enchantress!" he groaned in agonized desire.

"Satisfy me," she whispered. "I'm on fire for you!"

Looping her legs over his arms, his hands cupping her buttocks, he brought her up to meet his thrust. Her body, moist and ready, welcomed him eagerly. A sigh quivered through her at his deep penetration.

"You are like warm honey; as sleek as satin," he murmured, as he savored the feel of her about him. His sure strokes soon changed that first feeling of gratification to one of building need. With each thrust the yearning grew, intensifying into a raging inferno that engulfed them both in a savage ecstasy.

Tanya writhed beneath him, straining with the effort to blend their bodies and souls. Their union was wild and wonderful; their bodies hot and slick, laboring in perfect unison, seeking that sweet pure moment of total rapture. Then they were slipping into a swirling abyss of bright lights and brilliant colors; clinging, twirling round and round, weightless and free in awesome exultation.

It was a long time before Tanya recovered enough to speak. In a voice quavering with emotion, she whispered, "You make me faint with the wonders of your love, my darling. Do you know how much I love you?"

Adam kissed the tears from the corners of her luminous golden eyes. "Enough to steal the heart from my body and give it back again, stronger and more powerful than ever. You make me invincible with the force of your love."

Two days later, Tanya found herself back in Pueblo, up to her armpits in wedding arrangements. It took some tall talking, but she finally convinced her mother that it was ridiculous to try to plan an engagement party and a wedding so close together.

"I fail to see what all the rush is, anyway," Sarah complained. "You only get married once, and it should be as near to perfect as possible. That means weeks of planning and management to make it the most memorable day in your life."

"July first, Mother," Tanya reiterated. She left the room thinking to herself, "Only married once? Not in this case! I wonder which wedding anniversary Adam and I are going to observe?"

To reconcile the differences between her Protestant background and Adam's Catholic ties on his mother's side, they decided to have Judge Kerr marry them. Melissa was to be the maid of honor, and Julie the only other bridesmaid. Justin, as Adam's best friend, was to be best man, with Roberto also in attendance. Judge Kerr had offered his home for the ceremony and Emily had agreed to play the organ. With these details quickly arranged, Tanya could not believe the state of turmoil that still reigned in the Martin household.

"I wish I'd never agreed to all this," she lamented to Adam. "That shotgun wedding you described is looking better and better all the time. Mother is in a constant dither. She is arranging to have a photographer come from Denver, and she's changed the menu for the reception four times in the last three days! If she's not fussing over fittings, she's worrying that we'll have a dry spell and all the flowers will die before the wedding!"

She eyed Adam balefully, noting that he was struggling to keep from laughing. "Go ahead! Laugh, you big lout! Wait until she gets hold of *you*! We three girls feel like pincushions! We're black and blue from being poked and prodded and measured from our teeth to our toes! Worst of all, Mother insists on an adequate trousseau, which you and I know I won't be here to wear, and there is no way I can tell her that all her efforts are a waste."

Their engagement became official in Sarah's estimation when Adam presented Tanya with a stunning marquis diamond engagement ring. The stone had been his grandmother's, and he'd had a local goldsmith reset it. This same artisan was now busily fashioning a unique wedding band for Tanya, at Adam's request. It was to be a surprise, and Adam was very secretive about it.

As if Tanya did not have enough to cope with now, there was Jeffrey Young to deal with once more.

Luckily, it was a few days before he was aware that she had returned. But inevitably, the day came when Jeffrey heard of Tanya's engagement to Adam, and there was no putting off the ensuing confrontation. He came rushing over to the house one afternoon a week after her return. Forcing his way past Sarah and Melissa, he stormed into the dining room where Tanya was setting the table. He strode up to her, grabbing her roughly by the arms.

"Is it true?" he shouted.

Tanya eyed him levelly. "Is what true, Lieutenant Young?" she asked in a cool tone.

His grip on her arms tightened as his wild blue eyes glared down at her. "The whole town is buzzing with the news that you are engaged to Adam Savage. Is it true?"

"Quite true." She held his gaze steadily.

His face became contorted with rage and pain, and he let out a roar as he shook her. "No! I won't let you!"

Even knowing how cruel and self-centered he was, Tanya felt a momentary twinge of pity for him. Regardless of how beastly and aggravating Jeffrey had been, he was now in genuine agony, and Tanya had inflicted the wound.

Compassion colored her voice as she tried to reason with him. "Jeffrey, I've told you for months now that it was over between us. You should have listened to me. Now I am going to marry Adam, and it is time you accept this."

The look on his face was frightening in its ferocity. "Never!" he shouted. "You're mine! You'll never belong to anyone else!"

Realizing she wasn't getting through to him in his demented state, Tanya switched tactics. Leaning against him and relaxing her body, she waited until she felt his grip on her arms loosen. Then she jerked free. Stepping back, she retrieved her knife from the sheath at her belt and screamed for Kit.

Julie and Sarah stood petrified in the doorway. Melissa watched silently, chewing her lip in agitation as she waited for Tanya's next move.

Holding Jeffrey at bay with her weapon, she glared at him. "Get out!" she growled. "Get out before I slit you from gullet to gizzard and feed you to Kit!"

As if on cue, the huge cat glided into the room and sidled up to her mistress, teeth bared in a snarl at Jeffrey.

Some semblance of sanity returned to him, and Jeffrey blinked and backed off, his arms outstretched to Tanya in supplication. "Tanya, honey, I'm sorry if I was rough with you, but you've got to listen to me. I can't let you throw yourself away on that man. Think of all we mean to one another; all we've gone through to be together!"

At this point, Julie, who'd been under a strain of her own lately, ran to Jeffrey. Tugging at his arm, she cried, "Stop it, Jeffrey! Can't you see she doesn't want you? Why do you degrade yourself like this? Can't you see what it is doing to you?"

Incensed, Jeffrey flung her away from him, his hand slamming into her cheekbone in the process. "Get away from me, you bitch!" he raged.

With a shriek, Julie landed in a heap at her mother's feet, hurt and frightened.

Kit gave a snarl of warning, but Jeffrey took no notice as he sneered down at Julie. "You don't look quite so proud now, do you? But then, you never had much pride to begin with. Do you think I didn't notice how you've chased after me all this time?" He shook his head, his eyes gleaming oddly. "I'd have had to be blind not to see how you've thrown yourself at me!" His face twisted cruelly. "I could have had you anytime!" he announced brutally, "but how could I want you when it was Tanya I was after? Even used, she's the better prize."

"Jeffrey, that's enough!" Tanya cut in sharply. "I'll not have you abusing my sister, either physically or with cutting words!"

"But she's been asking for it for months," he said pointedly. "She pictures herself as my wife when she has none of the qualities necessary to be the wife of a cavalry officer. She's spoiled and pampered and used to getting everything she wants. She hasn't the stamina to withstand the rigors of life in the military—but you do." His eyes blazed at Tanya. "You have the strength, and you don't whine or faint or give up when the going gets rough. With you by my side, I could become a general!"

Tanya laughed cynically. "You're perfect too, Jeffrey! Perfectly insane!" At his enraged look, she flashed her knife at him. "Now get out of here before my blade finds its way between your ribs into your rotten heart, if you have one!" Kit snarled again, adding emphasis to her words.

With one last, hate-filled glare, Jeffrey turned on his heel. "You'll regret this, Tanya," he warned. "All you high-and-mighty Martins are going to regret this! One day you'll come crawling to me!"

Almost as an afterthought, he directed one last cutting remark to the weeping girl on the floor. "Cheer up, Julie. All may not be lost. If your sister actually does throw caution to the winds and marry this fool rancher, I may take you as my paramour. Lord knows, you've offered yourself to me often enough! You'd be an impossible wife, but perhaps you'd make a decent mistress."

Elizabeth was appalled when she arrived home from shopping to see Julie's cheek all red and swollen. Her reaction was mild compared to that of the men, for there was no way to hide the injury.

"He should be hanged!" Edward ranted. "First he tries to rape Tanya, and now he hits Julie. The man is mad!"

"Hanging is too good for him," George insisted.

"I wanted to kill him so badly," Tanya avowed softly, her eyes seeking Adam's. "You'll never know how close I came to planting my knife in his black heart!"

"You'd have been jailed for murder if you had," Adam pointed out.

Tanya nodded. "I know. That's the only thing that stopped me!"

Elizabeth let out a snort of disgust. "This is a fine kettle of fish! The Almighty Lieutenant Young can march in here and manhandle us all he wants, and we can't do a thing about it because he has an army behind him!"

"Can't Sheriff Middleton arrest him?" Sarah suggested.

Adam frowned and shook his head. "Not over this," he said. "Young would just claim it was an accident that Julie was hurt."

"I should have shot him when we caught him trying to force himself on Tanya," Edward fumed.

"And gotten ourselves killed for it," George added. "His men wouldn't have waited for explanations."

"What are we to do?" Melissa asked. "Julie is scared to death to leave the house, and who's to say when Jeffrey will take a notion to come around again for one of his delightful 'social chats'!"

Julie had been hysterical nearly all afternoon. Now she sat quietly next to her mother, saying little. A tremor shook her every so often, but the weariness that often follows shock had set in.

Adam gave her a sympathetic look. "I have a suggestion, if Julie agrees."

Julie looked up questioningly.

"My mother is coming into town this weekend. Julie can go back to the ranch with her. She will look after you, Julie," he promised, "and Roberto will be there to protect you. Would that suit you?"

Julie nodded solemnly. "Yes," she croaked, "but what about Tanya?"

"I'll look after Tanya. We'll be busy preparing for our wedding, and I'll practically be camped on the doorstep, I imagine. When she's not with me, she'll be with your father or uncle, and when they are at work, Justin or I will be here."

When Tanya and Adam had a moment alone together, Tanya confessed, "You can't imagine the tortures I've fantasized about putting Jeffrey through since this afternoon."

Adam's black eyes burned into hers. "Yes, I can. I have been having the same thoughts," he admitted gravely, "but you are forgetting one of the most important lessons you learned as a Cheyenne—patience. When the apple is ripe, it falls from the tree. When the time is right, we will deal with the young lieutenant. The circumstances must be in our favor. We do not want the law breathing down our necks. We will wait, and the time will come."

* * *

Julie left as planned with Rachel after the weekend. If nothing else, it would let her have more time with Roberto, and for this Tanya was grateful. Now that Julie saw Jeffrey in the proper perspective, perhaps she'd see what a truly magnificent man Roberto was.

The rest of the family went on with plans for Tanya's wedding. The guest list was decided upon, and the invitations written and sent out. Rachel had undertaken the task of seeing that Julie's dress was finished in time, while Elizabeth and Sarah worked on their own and Melissa's.

Tanya's wedding gown as well as the goodly number of additional dresses that made up her trousseau was being sewn by a local seamstress. There were numerous trips for fittings, in addition to visits to the milliner and cobbler for matching hats, accessories, and shoes. Swatches of material were constantly being exchanged, discussed, and mislaid until Tanya thought she would lose her mind.

"It will soon be over," Adam soothed.

"Thank goodness!" Tanya retorted, rubbing her throbbing temples. "If Mother changes her mind over one more color or fabric, I swear I'll get married in a gunny sack out of spite!"

In the midst of all this, Melissa came up with a few surprises of her own. One evening shortly after Julie's departure, she and Justin found themselves alone on the porch.

"There is more to this wedding business than I'd thought," Justin commented conversationally.

Melissa nodded. "I don't think if I got married I'd want all this fuss and planning. I'm a very private person." She watched Justin's reaction as he digested this. His face became very thoughtful.

Finally he ventured, "How would you have it, Missy?"

Melissa hid a smile. Justin was being so cautious, avoiding pressing her about their own relationship these days. "After all I've been through, I'd want a quiet ceremony with just family and a few close friends, I think; something a lot less formal. Does that appeal to you?"

Justin eyed her carefully, his face hopeful, yet cautious. "Are you talking about us, Missy? You and I?"

She looked up at him demurely from beneath lowered lashes, but her answer was far from shy. "Justin," she sighed, "it's a terrible shame when a girl has to ask the man she loves to marry her! Are you going to accept or not?"

For one long minute Justin stared at her in shock, trying to decide if he'd heard her correctly. "Yes!" he blurted, before he was conscious of even opening his mouth.

Melissa laughed, delighted at both his open-mouthed reaction and his answer. "Good! Then it's settled!"

At last Justin recovered his senses. With a small but exuberant whoop of joy, he leaped from the swing, pulling her up with him. His eyes shining, he twirled her around, then pulled her into his embrace. "Oh, Missy! Missy!" He hugged her tightly, kissing the top of her head.

Then he put her slightly away from him, frowning down at her in concern. "You're sure? You won't change your mind?" His eyes searched her face.

Putting her palms to his face and pulling him down to her, she assured him, "I'm positive." Bringing her lips just below his, she whispered, "Aren't you supposed to kiss me now, or am I supposed to kiss *you* since I did the proposing?"

It really didn't matter, for once their lips touched, it was difficult to determine just who kissed whom.

Not wanting to infringe on Tanya's wedding, Melissa was reluctant to announce their news, but Justin had no such reservations. With a directness that was inherent in him, he took charge. After announcing their intentions to his parents and the Martins, the assorted relations sat down to a family planning session. Adhering to Melissa's wishes, the arrangements were kept simple. They were to be wed a week after Tanya and Adam, and Judge Kerr would again perform the ceremony. Tanya and Adam would stand up with them. A few flowers, a bridal bouquet, and a new gown were sufficient for Melissa's needs, with an intimate family dinner to honor the occasion afterward.

Jeffrey made a few additional attempts to see Tanya, and finally retreated, though not with good grace. The Martins simply did not answer the door when Jeffrey came to call. He left notes for Tanya, which she promptly destroyed. Whenever he caught sight of her about town, she was always in Adam's company. Finally he gave up—or so they thought at first.

Then, with the wedding only a couple of weeks away, strange things began to occur. The first was dramatic, and nearly fatal. After supper one evening, Tanya and Adam went for a stroll. They were walking along one of their favorite paths in the woods behind the house, chatting amiably and stopping every so often to exchange a kiss or two. The lovers were totally wrapped up in one another, unaware of much around them.

On impulse, Adam reached down to pluck a wildflower for Tanya's hair. At that exact moment, a bullet whizzed over his head, slamming into a tree a few feet away. With lightning reflexes, Adam jerked Tanya down with him, rolling quickly behind a tree.

Drawing his own gun, Adam waited. When he heard nothing, and no more bullets came their way, he edged out to take a look. No one was about. Judging where the shot was fired from, they found fresh footprints in the soft earth, but the unknown assailant had fled.

"Jeffrey," Tanya claimed with certainty.

"Or one of his faithful henchmen," Adam concurred readily, "but we have no proof."

"He's changing tactics." Tanya ground her teeth together in agitation. "Now he's playing the cowardly sneak! That's just his style!"

"It certainly appears he wants to see you widowed before you're wed. We'll have to be alert. I should have heard him, but I had my mind on other things."

"So did I," Tanya admitted. "I thought he had given up. I should have known better."

When they related the experience to the others, Melissa added a new bit of information to be considered. "You know, it may not mean a thing, but lately I've heard a lot of gossip concerning Suellen and Jeffrey."

"What about them?" Tanya asked.

"Nothing special, just that they have been spending a lot of time together lately."

"They deserve one another," Tanya pronounced with a grimace. "They are two of a kind."

Melissa persisted. "Yes, but I hear that they are closer than two peas in a pod. Don't you think that is odd?"

Adam shook his head. "What is odd about it? They have a lot in common. Both have the disposition of a snake. Each would love to see me eliminated; Jeffrey because he covets Tanya, and Suellen because she so despises Tanya that anything that causes her grief makes Suellen glad."

Glancing at her parents, Tanya said cryptically, "So far Suellen has not seen Adam close up, and she knows nothing about him, which is all to the good. I'll be ever so grateful when her parents come for her."

"Well," Elizabeth piped up, "the parson's wife told Emily Kerr that they expect Suellen's parents any time now, within a few weeks at the most."

"Yes," Sarah added, "and from what I hear, Ruth will be glad to be rid of her. Now that the novelty has worn off, even she is sick of Suellen's harping."

At the weekend, Rachel, Julie, and Roberto came to town. With them they brought a disturbing bit of news. Someone had attempted to set fire to the barn and stables a few nights earlier.

"Luckily, José was tending a sick colt when he heard someone skulking about," Roberto explained. "He grabbed the shotgun by the door and got off a shot at whoever it was. The shot alerted the rest of us, and we all went running.

"The culprits fled before much damage was done. José found a lit torch near the corner of the stable and stamped it out, and the roof of the barn was on fire in one place, but it was quickly extinguished."

"Did you see who it was?" Adam asked.

"No," Rachel told him. "It was too dark. All we know is there were about half a dozen men." Her brow furrowed as she recalled something else. "It is funny, but Pedro said he thought the man he saw was wearing an outfit similar to a cavalry uniform."

* * *

The sheriff received an unexpected invitation to dinner. Afterward, over brandy in the library, the men explained briefly what had been going on. A short history of the situation between Tanya and Jeffrey brought the problem into focus. Added to that, the near-rape, Jeffrey's crazed obsession with Tanya, and the more recent problem with Julie gave weight to their tale. Last, they told him about the attempt on Adam's life and the fire at the ranch.

"I don't doubt anything you've said, but without proof, there is little I can do," Tom Middleton explained regretfully. "He's wily, that one. So far he's stayed just inside of the law."

"We know that, Tom," Adam assured him. "We just wanted you to be aware of what is going on. The man is demented. There is no telling what he is capable of trying, or what he's liable to do next."

Tom shook his head in dismay and understanding. "I'll keep an eye peeled, and I'd advise you to do the same."

"Roberto has posted guards at the ranch until I say otherwise."

Drawing deeply on his cigar, Middleton expelled a cloud of smoke. "That lieutenant has been nothing but trouble since he set foot in Pueblo," he growled. "Got big ideas, he does. Thinks that uniform makes him some kind of big cheese." The sheriff laughed tersely. "Somebody ought to tell him a cheese has holes! That gold bar on his shoulder isn't going to protect him from flying bullets or flaming arrows. I can't condone outright murder, and I shouldn't even be saying this, but the fella that gets rid of Lieutenant Young for good will be doing the town a great favor."

* * *

Everything was peaceful until two days before the wedding. All the arrangements had been made. The bridal gown was ready, and the dresses for the bridesmaids and mothers. The flowers had not died off; everyone was healthy, if nervous; and what food could be prepared ahead of time was done.

The girls were upstairs trying on their gowns yet one more time. Adam and Justin were going over some papers in the library. George and Edward had escaped to work, and Elizabeth was puttering about in the kitchen. Jeremy had gone off to play and Sarah, Kit, and the boys were in the backyard while Sarah tended to the laundry drying on the lines.

Suddenly Sarah's screams pierced the air, easily carried to the ears of those in the house through the open windows.

Papers flew everywhere as Adam and Justin bolted from the study, nearly bowling Elizabeth over in a rush for the back door. Melissa jumped, Julie shrieked, and Tanya ripped the entire side seam out of her gown as she jerked it on over her head. Three sets of feet raced down the stairs.

Dashing out the door, Tanya stumbled to a halt near her mother. She watched in confusion as Adam and Justin ran from the yard. "What is going on?"

"Where are Adam and Justin going?" Melissa questioned.

Sarah, little Mark clutched in her arms, leaned against Tanya for support. Hunter was safely ensconced in the folds of Elizabeth's voluminous skirts. "I think someone tried to kidnap the boys," Sarah sobbed. "I just left them for a second to bring in a basket of dry clothes. When I stepped back to the door, Kit was raising all sorts of Cain!" She stopped a second to catch her breath. "When I ran out to see what was wrong, I saw someone hiding in the trees at the edge of the yard. That's when I screamed. The man started to run, and then I saw another man running with him."

"Adam and Justin are trying to catch them," Elizabeth finished for her.

"Oh, God!" Tanya gasped in stunned disbelief. "Who?" Her gaze swiveled to her mother's.

Sarah nodded and gulped. "Blue uniforms," she confirmed.

Justin and Adam were soon back emptyhanded. "They got away."

"Damn him!" Tanya ranted, close to tears. "Damn him to hell! I can understand why he'd try to shoot you, Adam. I can even see how burning your ranch ties in. In his twisted mind, if your livelihood were wiped out and your fortune reduced, he probably thinks I wouldn't marry you. But this is too much! To abduct my sons! What would that gain him? What good would it do him?"

Adam gathered her trembling form into his arms. "Blackmail, my love," he explained. "I suppose he would have used them as bait to get you to marry him instead."

Tanya sighed exhaustedly. "When will it all end?" she asked. "When will he finally stop?"

"Perhaps once we're married, Tanya. Two more days, darling. Hold on a bit longer. We'll make it."

"And two weeks from now you'll be gone from here," Melissa comforted. Tanya and Adam had told everyone that as soon as Justin and Melissa were married, they would be leaving. Adam wished to show Tanya and the boys what Europe was like. Only

Rachel and Melissa knew that Tanya and Adam were actually going back to the Cheyenne.

"I can't say I'll be sorry," Tanya claimed. At Sarah's hurt look, she said, "I'm sorry, Mother, but Jeffrey has made my life a nightmare. I pray each night that he'll get transferred to Africa or die of a fever, or accidentally poison himself!"

"Maybe he'll go out on patrol and get himself scalped," Adam suggested quietly, sharing a secret smile with Tanya. "We can always hope."

Chapter 24

THE FIRST day of July dawned bright and sunny. The sky was a brilliant cloudless blue, the perfect backdrop for the mountains that stood out in relief against it. Just a hint of a breeze kept the sun from being too hot, and the humidity was blessedly low. Had she ordered the day specially, Tanya could not have had a more perfect wedding day.

The ceremony was scheduled for eleven o'clock, in the Judge's gardens since the day was so fine. Afterward, there would be a luncheon and celebration, leaving the newlyweds plenty of time for their trip to the ranch, where they would spend a couple of days by themselves. They would return to town for the Fourth of July festivities, and stay for Melissa and Justin's wedding a few days later. The time would be spent making final preparations for their journey.

This morning, the Martin household was in chaos, but Tanya was strangely calm. This, she reasoned to herself, was probably because she had considered herself married to Adam for nearly three years now. She had no reason for the usual pre-nuptual jitters, wondering if she was about to make a mistake.

Sarah was flitting about like a demented butterfly. She sent poor Jeremy on so many errands to the Kerrs' to check on last-minute details, that Tanya swore he would have a permanent path worn through the neighbors' yards.

At last they were all ready a good half-hour ahead of time. Tanya thought Hunter looked so handsome in his little miniature suit, a small replica of his father. He stood proudly next to his grandmother, his black hair gleaming and in place for once. Elizabeth was taking charge of Mark, who at eight months was too active to be content for long in any one place. Dressed in his first set of kneepants, he would view the ceremony from Elizabeth's lap. Tears of pride stung Tanya's eyes as she looked at the two fine sons Adam had given her.

Tanya checked her reflection in the mirror one last time. Her ivory gown with its long, lacy sleeves and embroidered lace bodice was perfection. The copper wristbands, which Tanya refused to dispense with even for this one day, barely showed through the tight cuffs at her wrists. Her tawny hair had been drawn up and back on both sides, and secured with ivory clasps borrowed from her Aunt Elizabeth. The back of her hair fell in gleaming waves past her shoulders, partially hidden by the bridal veil.

The gown was new; the hair clasps borrowed. Hidden in her bodice was an old lace handkerchief of her great-grandmother's, and beneath her skirts she wore a blue garter on her thigh. Sarah had insisted on making Tanya put a brand new penny in her shoe to complete the old adage for luck. It went without saying that Adam had been forbidden to glimpse his bride before the wedding.

Hearing the opening chords that were her cue, Tanya picked up her bridal bouquet of delicate yellow and white rosebuds and went to stand beside her father at the bottom of the stairs. They watched Julie make her way down the petal-strewn garden aisle on Roberto's arm. Next, Melissa and Justin traversed the path they would again walk the following week. Then, her hand firmly upon her father's supporting arm, Tanya made her way serenely and regally toward Adam, who waited with glowing dark eyes before Judge Kerr.

Many thoughts raced through Tanya's mind as her father led her down the aisle. There stood Adam, once again waiting to claim his bride. He was superbly handsome in his suit and brocade vest, yet Tanya could not help but compare this Adam with the tall, bronze warrior in elaborately fringed and decorated buckskin who had claimed her as his bride in a Cheyenne ceremony. In all honesty, Tanya privately preferred him as Panther and considered the tribal rites more beautiful.

This time, Edward gave her to her husband. Short years before, Chief Black Kettle had performed this honor. Before, the tribal shaman had administered the vows that Judge Kerr would recite today. Tears blurred her vision momentarily as Tanya thought of those wonderful people so brutally killed in the massacre, and she sent a silent prayer skyward in their memory.

Tanya came out of her reverie as her father placed her hand in Adam's. Together they faced the judge as he began the traditional ceremony.

"Dearly beloved, we are gathered here today in the sight of God and in the presence of these witnesses to unite this man and this woman in the bonds of Holy Matrimony . . ."

Part of her mind listened to the solemn words, while with another she was acutely conscious of Adam's presence beside her. The clasp of his hand about hers was calm and sure, warm and comforting. The scent of his spicy cologne blended with the sweeter fragrance of the flowers and her own perfume. His silent strength and pride bolstered her own.

As her ears attuned themselves to the ritual words of the service, she heard the judge saying, "If there be any man here who can show just cause why these two should not be joined in wedlock, let him now speak, or forevermore hold his peace."

In spite of the fact that Jeffrey had not been invited and she was sure he had not come, Tanya felt a brief spasm of fear flash through her. Adam's hand tightened about hers as her fear communicated itself to him, and the moment passed with no objections forthcoming.

Now Judge Kerr was saying to Adam, "Adam Savage, do you take this woman to be your lawfully wedded wife, to live together from this day forth; to love, to comfort, to honor and keep her, in sickness and in health, keeping thee only unto her for as long as ye both shall live?"

Adam's rich, deep voice avowed clearly, "I do."

Turning to Tanya, the judge repeated, "Do you, Tanya Martin, take this man to be your lawfully wedded husband, to live together from this day forth; to love, to comfort, to honor and obey him, in sickness and in health, keeping thee only unto him as long as ye both shall live?"

"I do," she intoned softly.

Then Adam was facing her and saying, "I, Adam, take thee, Tanya, to be my wedded wife," and Tanya was vowing, "I, Tanya, take thee, Adam, to be my wedded husband." Together they repeated solemnly, "To have and to hold from this day forward, for better, for worse; for richer, for poorer; in sickness and in health; to love and to cherish till death do us part; in accordance to God's Holy Ordinance; and therefore do I pledge thee my troth."

Adam's hand released hers as Justin handed him the ring. As if in a trance, remembering this same exact moment in a previous ceremony, Tanya watched as Adam slipped the gold band on her ring finger. His fingers slipped upward to clasp themselves about the hidden copper bands on her wrists, and she knew he was remembering also and renewing his pledge as he said, "In token and pledge of our deep and abiding love, with this ring I thee wed."

The judge's voice droned on as Tanya and Adam shared this private moment of poignant remembrance. They were brought back to reality as the judge announced, ". . . I now pronounce you man and wife. You may kiss your bride."

His eyes aglow, Adam bent his head to claim her lips. The ceremony concluded, the guests gathered about to congratulate them, to kiss the bride, and to offer best wishes for a happy future.

To save time, gifts had been sent on to the ranch, to be opened and acknowledged later. Also, slightly irregularly, Tanya had elected to toss her bouquet and garter prior to the luncheon, so that she and Adam could slip away unannounced at their earliest convenience.

As soon as the initial clamor had settled, Tanya and Adam went indoors and climbed partway up the open staircase. A cluster of hopeful, eager maidens gathered below as Tanya turned her back and flipped her bouquet over her shoulder. The shrieks and giggles were earsplitting, as everyone clamored to see who had caught the coveted prize. Knowing Melissa's wedding was scheduled for the following week, it was expected she might catch it, since tradition said the girl who caught it would be the next to wed. To everyone's surprise, it was Julie who stood staring at the roses in her hands, a strange expression on her pretty face.

A short, playful scuffle ensued as Adam wrested the coveted garter from his bride's thigh amidst cheerful calls of encouragement from the waiting bachelors below, and blushes and giggles from the girls.

Holding it high above his head and laughing, he called out, "What am I bid for this blue beribboned treasure?"

Hoots of laughter filled the room below.

"A dollar!" one enthusiastic young man offered.

His friend standing next to him elbowed him sharply in the ribs. "One measly dollar?" he jeered. "I'll give you two!"

"Three!"

Blushing and laughing at the same time, Tanya made a wild grab for the garter and missed.

"Tsk, tsk, my dear," Adam grinned, whisking it out of her reach. "You are infringing on my rights as bridegroom."

"You are supposed to *throw* it, not auction it off," she instructed, trying to sound offended.

"Too common," he decided authoritatively. "We need to spice up the game a bit." Turning to his avid audience, he instructed, "Let the bidding continue! I have three dollars!"

"Four!"

"Five!"

"You keep the garter and I'll take the bride!" one brave fool joked.

Adam laughed and shook his head. "Not on your

life, Harry! I've more than five dollars invested in her already!"

The bidding went to twelve dollars. "I have twelve dollars. Do I hear more?" Adam called, twirling the garter on his finger. "Twelve once; twelve twice . . ."

At the last moment, Roberto stepped forward. "I'll top that," he claimed. With a flip of his wrist, he tossed a gold coin into the air in Adam's direction. As Adam reached out to catch it, Roberto bounded up the stairs and snatched the garter from him.

Adam chuckled as he palmed the coin. "Sold! To the man with the twenty-dollar goldpiece!" Everyone guffawed as Adam slapped Roberto on the back and said, "Wear it in good health, cousin!"

Roberto colored to the roots of his hair. He gave Adam a silly grin, but said nothing.

Glancing down, Tanya caught sight of her sister and wondered why Julie looked so awfully pale.

A short while later, as she and Adam were mingling with the guests and preparing to sit down to the luncheon, Judge Kerr motioned them to his side. "I need to talk to you in my study," he advised them, leading the way.

He ushered them into his study, where a red-faced Roberto and a very pale Julie stood waiting. Rachel was pacing the floor.

"What is going on?" Adam inquired.

Judge Kerr cleared his throat. "Julie and Roberto have asked me to marry them."

Tanya's face lit up. "That is fantastic!" she exclaimed. "When? Do Mother and Papa know?"

Julie raised pleading eyes in her direction, her chin trembling. "Oh, Tanya!" she wailed. "I don't know how to tell them!"

Tanya frowned. "I don't understand."

"I'm beginning to," Adam said. "Let me guess. You want to get married now, the sooner the better. Right?"

"Yes," Roberto admitted, his chin jutting out defensively.

Tanya's mouth made a round O.

"Yes, *oh*!" Rachel commented as she watched. "I'm so mad I could hop! What do I say to your parents? They placed Julie in my care, and *this* snake," she gestured angrily toward Roberto, "was supposed to protect her. He certainly guarded her more closely than any of us considered, and he protected all but her virtue, which he promptly relieved her of!"

Julie was in tears by now, and Roberto stood stiffly at her side, his hands clenched into tight fists.

"Oh, Julie!" Tanya laughed softly, crossing swiftly to enfold the embarrassed girl in her arms. "It's not the end of the world! You are not the first couple to consummate the marriage before the ceremony, and you surely won't be the last!"

"I'm sorry!" Julie blubbered. "I've ruined your wedding day!"

"Hardly!" Tanya said. "Now, let's see what we can figure out. You are only seventeen, so our parents will have to consent, but under the circumstances, I think they'll agree."

Her gaze took in the entire group. "The judge is here, the flowers are fresh, the photographer is waiting, and we are all in our finery. The guests and champagne await. All we have to do is break the news to Mother and Papa."

"You certainly have cut the problem down to size," Adam commented dryly, chuckling at Roberto's stunned expression.

"Oh! We couldn't impose on your special day!" Julie complained. "Besides, how would we explain such a sudden decision to all those people?"

Tanya snorted. "You'll raise eyebrows whether you marry today or four days from now. At least this way we can say we suddenly decided to have a double ceremony, especially since Adam and I would probably not be able to return from Europe for some time, and I would not want to miss my only sister's wedding. It will save Mother a lot of time and trouble, and Papa the expense of a second wedding. Besides, lots of sisters do it. Years from now we'll all celebrate our anniversaries together."

"That is very generous of you, Tanya, to offer to share your day with us," Roberto ventured. "I only hope Adam shares your sentiments." He eyed his cousin speculatively.

Adam spread his palms wide and shrugged. "If Tanya is willing, so am I."

"Just one thing." The seriousness of Tanya's tone brought them all to attention. "Is this what both of you truly want? Do you love one another? Will you be happy together?"

"Oh, yes!" Julie swore.

Roberto was more articulate. "I have loved your sister since we first met. I will do everything in my power to make her happy."

"Judge," Tanya announced. "You'd better find our parents."

When the judge left, Tanya drew Julie aside, handing her a hankie to wipe her eyes. "How did all this come about? I thought you weren't sure of your feelings for Roberto."

Julie sniffed and looked abashed. "That is not entirely true. It is just that Roberto makes me so mad sometimes, and I didn't know how much I cared for him under all my anger. Then, when Jeffrey said all those terrible things, it completely shattered my image of him and made me realize how lucky I was to find someone who loved me as much as Roberto does.

"Jeffrey was so horrid, and it scared me so badly; and Roberto was so kind and gentle. He was only holding me and comforting me, and the next thing we knew things . . . got out of hand."

"It's all right," Tanya assured her, "but how much of this do you want Mother and Papa to know?"

Julie cringed. "As little as possible," she whispered.

"Then you'd better dry your eyes and look a good deal happier," Tanya suggested.

Tanya took charge. Calmly, sensibly, she presented the case to their bewildered parents, avoiding any comment that would cause them to suspect the actual reason behind their impulsive decision. Tanya saw no sense in causing them grief or getting them upset if it could be avoided.

Adam explained to Judge Kerr privately while Tanya and Julie were talking to their parents. It took a lot of convincing, but the girls' pleadings and Roberto's heartfelt declaration of undying love combined with the confusion of the day finally won them over.

A short fifteen minutes later, the guests were reconvened in the garden, and Judge Kerr gave the agreed-upon explanation. Carrying her sister's bouquet, with Julie's ruby birthstone ring in lieu of an actual wedding band, the two lovers were duly married.

Finally, after much delay, the luncheon was served. Several toasts to the happy couples later, no one cared that the same bouquet had been thrown twice or that the chicken was a little tough from being held over so long. The photographer was slightly harried at all the delay, as were the hired musicians, but they would be paid extra for their trouble.

After leading the first dance, Tanya and Adam sneaked away to change into their riding attire. Their sons were to stay in town with the Martins and Tanya had sent clothes ahead to the ranch, so they were ready and eager to be on their way.

"I wonder if we'll be expected to share our honeymoon with Julie and Roberto, too?" Adam mused in mock dismay.

"Well, we spent our first one with Melissa in the same tipi," Tanya pointed out. "At least they won't be in the same bedroom with us."

"They'll sleep in the barn first!" Adam promised. "I intend to have you all to myself for the next few days."

"This room seems strangely familiar," Tanya joked on their wedding night as they lay in Adam's bed.

"So does the lady in my bed," Adam countered.

Tanya gazed at him in mock indignation. "I should certainly hope so, Adam Savage!"

Adam chuckled. "Well, it would help if you would stop changing identities on me. Do you realize that to date I've made love to you as my slave, my squaw, as Miss Tanya Martin, as my fiancee, and now finally as Mrs. Adam Savage?"

Tanya grinned. "Mrs. Adam Savage. Tanya Savage." She rolled the words off her tongue, then nodded. "Yes, I like that. It has a nice ring to it, don't you think?"

"Absolutely," Adam agreed. "And speaking of rings, you haven't said how you like your wedding band."

Tanya's face glowed as she gazed at the gold band

on her finger. "Oh, Adam! It's gorgeous! I never expected anything so absolutely unique!" Inlaid into the surface of the solid gold were bands of copper and silver, criss-crossing in an Indian pattern.

"I wanted something that would symbolize both ways of life. It was designed especially for you."

Tanya leaned to kiss him. "Thank you. I love it. I love you!"

That kiss of thanks escalated into a night of love-making both torrid and tender. Adam alternated easily from white rancher to Cheyenne chief, and Tanya followed his lead. Today he had taken her for his bride in a traditional ceremony, making her lawfully his in the eyes of all the world; but in their hearts and minds they had been man and wife since that Cheyenne wedding nearly three years ago.

Tonight Adam was both husband and bridegroom, white and Indian, gentle and demanding by turns. Tanya matched his moods, glad that she was not the trembling virgin she should have been on this, her wedding night. Her hands sought his body readily, knowledgeably, and she revelled in his ardent love-making.

It was a time of renewal for them, renewing honored vows and repledging their lives and love to one another. In the privacy of their dimly lit room, Tanya surrendered anew to his dominance, and to the masterful savage she had come to associate with his role as Panther.

Knowing their privacy would be respected, they let themselves relax into old familiar patterns. Once more Tanya thrilled to the sound of his resonant voice whispering Cheyenne love words in her ear. She slipped as easily back into her role as Wildcat as Adam resumed the identity of Panther. He led and she followed, he commanded and she joyfully submitted, anticipating the wondrous rewards her obedience would reap.

Throughout the night they explored that wonderland of ecstasy reserved for lovers. Adam's hands and lips unerringly found each sensitive spot on her body, and Tanya responded sensuously to his erotic touch, returning the pleasure with an intensive foray of her own, her fingertips gliding over his heated skin; seeking, stroking. For each whimper of delight he brought forth from her, she elicited a deep groan of pleasure from him.

When Tanya lay weak and trembling in his embrace, his strong arms gathered her close to his pounding heart. When she cried out at the height of her passion, his voice blended with hers. Together they scaled the heights of ecstasy, coming out of the clouds into a land of sunlight and air so pure it was almost painful to breathe. Then, spellbound by the rapture they had shared, they lay clinging to one another; breath mingling, limbs entwined, hearts forever welded in an inseparable bond.

For two days, they secluded themselves from the rest of the world.

Julie and Roberto did, indeed, show up at the ranch, but they made themselves as scarce as did Adam and Tanya. Rachel would have had more company with ghosts in the house. She barely knew they were around. Meals were taken behind locked doors, and the dirty dishes left in the hall to be taken back to the kitchen.

After Rachel's initial annoyance with Roberto had cooled, and since everything had worked out so well, she could not stay angry at him. She even agreed to help him explain his sudden marriage to his parents in Santa Fe.

The little time Tanya and Adam did not spend making love, sleeping or eating, they used to make plans for their return trip to the Cheyenne village. They compiled lists of supplies and food they would need, and decided what needed to be done before they left.

It was then Adam presented Tanya with her wedding gift. Tanya gasped in delight as he unrolled a blanket to reveal a beautifully worked and decorated doeskin dress. Her golden eyes were huge and sparkling with tears as she reverently stroked the soft material. "Oh, Panther," she sighed.

Pulling out a pair of moccasins to complete the outfit, he smiled at her near-speechless delight. "Shy Deer and Walks-Like-A-Duck made these for your return. They insisted that what little you might have salvaged from our tipi would be in tatters by now, and they were sure you would not wish to return to the village in a white woman's clothing."

Clutching the dress to her, and rubbing her cheek against the soft hide, she nodded. "They are right, but I never expected this. With all the travail of rebuilding the village and staving off starvation, I am amazed that they would take what little time and energy they could spare to make garments for me. Their thoughtfulness moves me to tears."

"You are their sister," he said simply.

"I also have something for you," she told him, rummaging through the small bag she had packed. "I had forgotten it until now."

She handed him a slim box about a foot long. Inside, he found a gleaming new hunting knife. His dark eyes lit up as he lifted it from the box and inspected the fine craftsmanship. The blade was of the finest tempered steel, honed to a razor-sharp edge. The handle was solid oak, elaborately carved and buffed to a sheen that bespoke long hours of work and pride. It lay perfectly balanced on his fingertips, and when he wrapped his fingers about the handle, the grip fit his hand exactly.

The look on his face was reward enough for Tanya, his words of thanks but a bonus. "Thank you, Little Wildcat," he murmured, his eyes shining into hers. "It is a fine knife." In those few words, he voiced his immense pride that his woman had bestowed on him such a special gift.

Late in the afternoon of the third day, Tanya and Adam finally emerged from their honeymoon seclusion and set about making final preparations for their journey. They planned to leave immediately following Melissa and Justin's wedding. Ostensibly, they would be heading back to the ranch to pick up their heavier trunks and baggage and go on from there. In reality, they would go only a few miles out of town, then veer off in the direction of the Cheyenne village.

Before daybreak, July Fourth, they all left the ranch in order to reach Pueblo by noon. Tanya cared little about the town celebration, but she was eager to see her sons, and to spend these last few days with her family.

She felt a twinge of guilt when her parents greeted her after her brief absence as if she'd been gone for months. They also greeted Julie in like manner, however, and Tanya was doubly glad that Julie and Roberto would be staying in Pueblo for a while.

The house was once more in a flurry over wedding plans, this time Melissa's.

"I just can't believe both my babies are married," Sarah bemoaned. Casting a sorrowful glance at Tanya, she continued. "And I don't see why Adam has to carry you away from us so soon. Why, we've just begun to know our grandsons, and now that you are going, they probably won't even remember us by the time we get to see them again."

Tanya sighed. "Now, Mother, we'll be back periodically for visits. We've told you that."

"Yes, but it's not the same as having you near, and you know it. It makes especially little sense when you consider that Adam has a ranch a few hours from town that he could content himself with instead."

"You'll have Julie," Tanya pointed out.

Sarah pouted. "For how long, I wonder, before Roberto decides to go home to Santa Fe, taking her with him?"

Tanya shrugged. "At least Melissa and Justin will be close, and you have Aunt Elizabeth and Uncle George and Jeremy. And if that is not enough, maybe you and Papa will decide to move to Santa Fe to be closer to Julie. After all, Santa Fe is not that far away."

"Oh, I guess it's not," Sarah conceded with a grumble, "but I still wish you and Adam would settle here soon."

"We will eventually, I'm sure. It's just a matter of time," Tanya fibbed.

By shortly after noon, the entire town was a madhouse. The Martins, Savages, and Justin watched the parade from the Martins' front porch. Afterward, they joined the crowds in the streets, viewing the different displays that had been erected, and tasting the various foods along the way. While Sarah and Elizabeth gravitated toward the quilts and pickles, the younger couples sought other entertainment. In their wanderings, they found an artist making charcoal portraits. On impulse, Adam suggested that he, Tanya and their sons each sit for a separate sketch. "Someday we will have our portraits done in oils, to hang in the library at the ranch with my mother's," he promised. "But for now, let's get these done and let Mother frame them." The sketches turned out beautifully, and Julie, Roberto, Melissa, and Justin all decided to have one done of themselves.

After a cursory tour of all the exhibits and games, they all gathered for the cake raffle and community picnic on a tree-shaded lot near the church. A small creek ran close by, and Jeremy eagerly joined a fishing contest after stuffing himself with as much food as he could possibly handle.

All through the day, and especially during the picnic, Tanya was uncomfortably aware that Suellen was undoubtedly at the festivities, and that they could run into her at any moment. As the day progressed, a feeling of unease hung over her like a cloud of doom, growing gradually. Adam tried to reassure her, telling her she was worrying needlessly, but nothing he said made Tanya feel any better, and she could not shake her conviction of impending disaster.

Tanya begged Adam to be as inconspicuous as possible, but it was nearly impossible for him to do, with so many of his friends urging him to participate in various events. He ended up riding Shadow in the horserace down the main streets, coming in second. Then he entered the turkey shoot.

When Tanya complained that all the competitive events were either for children or men, he talked the other entrants in a knife-throwing contest into allowing Tanya to try her hand. Reluctant at first to admit her, they had no recourse when Adam chided them for their fear that a woman could beat them at their own game. Their taunts and guffaws soon changed to amazement when Tanya walked off with first prize, a brand new knife almost as good as the one she'd bought Adam.

The town had set up a small rodeo with several events, and Adam and Roberto participated in calf-roping, which Roberto won; bronc busting; and stunt riding, in which the rider had to exhibit his talents and maneuverability on horseback. Tanya was not surprised that Adam won this hands down.

It was nearly suppertime when they all decided they'd better try to find Jeremy and the elder Martins. With a day so full of excitement and activity, Hunter and Mark were exhausted.

They'd just left the rodeo area, headed toward home, when Sheriff Middleton came loping up, a grim look on his face. Without a word, the sheriff plucked Hunter out of Adam's arms, handing him to Melissa. Then, to their utter amazement, and before anyone could guess what he was about to do, he hauled back and hit Adam with a sharp right to the chin.

As Adam staggered backward, stunned by the unexpected blow, Sheriff Middleton hissed, "Hit me, damn it! Hit me back!"

When Adam hesitated, shaking his head to clear it, sure his hearing had been damaged, the sheriff hit him again, this time with a fist to the stomach. Reflex took over, and Adam swung back automatically, landing a telling blow to the sheriff's midriff.

"You're under arrest, Savage!" the sheriff grunted.

Chapter 25

ABOUT THE same moment, Tanya saw Suellen and Jeffrey hurriedly fighting their way through the crowd toward them.

Middleton drew his gun, leveling it at Adam. "Don't argue; just do as I say, and I'll explain later," he growled, nudging Adam with the gun. "You know the way to the jailhouse. Now let's get going!"

A look of total confusion on his face, Adam started to argue, as did Justin and Roberto, but Tanya took one long look at the sheriff and caught his quick, worried glance over his shoulder at the advancing lieutenant. Grabbing Adam's arm, she tugged him toward the jail, sure that regardless of how it might appear, Middleton was doing his best to help them. Something was afoot, and it had to do with Suellen and Jeffrey.

Pulling Adam along as fast as she could, with Middleton right behind, Tanya entered the jail about ten seconds before Suellen and Jeffrey. Adam was sure he'd never seen Tom Middleton move so fast as he shoved him into a cell, slammed the door and locked it. The sheriff pocketed the keys and strode to his desk, quickly jotting something down in his log.

"This man is under arrest!" Jeffrey shouted as he stormed into the office, Suellen close behind.

"Yeah, I know," Middleton drawled.

This abrupt announcement took some of the wind out of Jeffrey's sails, causing a look of confusion to cross his face momentarily. "I am arresting Adam Savage in the name of the United States Army!" he proclaimed with loud authority.

"Well now, sonny, you'll just have to wait in line. This man is my prisoner right now, and possession is nine-tenths of the law."

"What have you charged him with?" Jeffrey demanded.

"I might ask you the same thing," the sheriff countered. "What are *your* charges against him?"

Jeffrey looked disconcerted. "I—uh—I'm not sure what the exact charges will be," he blustered, "but I have a witness here who will swear that Adam Savage and the Cheyenne chief known as A-Panther-Stalks are one and the same person!"

Sheriff Middleton stared at Jeffrey as if the lieutenant had just sprouted three heads. Then, after the first shock began to fade, he started to laugh, great rolling belly-laughs that seemed to come clear from his toes and shook his entire frame.

After several minutes and much effort, he managed to get hold of himself. "That's a good one, Lieutenant!" he chortled. "Best laugh I've had in ages!"

Jeffrey glared at him, his face red with suppressed rage. "I'm not joking," he said through clenched teeth.

"I know, and that makes it twice as funny!" Middleton chuckled.

Suellen decided it was time she put in her two cents' worth. "Sir!" she said tartly, spearing the sheriff with her direct gaze. "I was with Tanya Martin in the Cheyenne village all those months, and that man," she pointed to Adam who was lounging indolently against the bars, "is her husband."

Sheriff Middleton smiled benignly at her, as if placating an infant. "Of course he is," he agreed. "I was at their wedding just last Saturday."

Suellen stamped her foot in exasperation. "No, you fool!" she huffed. "He's her *Indian* husband, Panther!"

Middleton cocked an eyebrow at her. "Sure he is, miss! And I'm George Washington. Now, just who might you be?"

Ready to spit nails by now, Suellen let out a small shriek, then tried to calm herself. "I am Suellen Haverick. I was captured in the same raid as Tanya, and I know what I am talking about! Adam Savage is Panther!"

"Well, now, even if he was, that's not a crime," Middleton said firmly.

At this, Jeffrey intervened. "But it *is* a crime to kidnap women and use them as slaves and whores. Also, this tribe has been particularly noted as troublemakers and has been active in unlawful attacks against settlers and the U.S Military."

Tanya could hold her tongue no longer. "And just what do you call the massacre at Washita if not an unwarranted attack?" she spat out. "Those people were peacefully minding their own business, and within hours a tranquil village was turned into a bloody, burning ruin!"

Jeffrey glared blue daggers at her. "That was a military coup."

Tanya snorted in disgust. "Is it standard military policy to murder women and children and old people? It was an absolute bloodbath, and you and I both know it!"

"Ahem," Tom Middleton cleared his throat loudly. "That is not the question here, Mrs. Savage. Miss Haverick and the lieutenant are claiming that Adam is your Cheyenne husband. What do you have to say to this?"

Tanya gave Jeffrey and Suellen a killing look. "I'd say Suellen has been out in the sun too long!" she retorted sharply. "Of course, the poor dear *did* have a rough time of it with the Cheyenne. One can't really blame her if she's not quite right in the head!"

A look of rage contorted Suellen's features, and Jeffrey looked as demented as Tanya knew he actually was.

"That's a lie!" Suellen shrieked. She leveled a finger at Melissa. "Melissa knows! She was there, too!"

The sheriff sighed and rolled his eyes heavenward. "What is this, a reunion?" Turning to Melissa, he said, "Okay, Miss Anderson, can you shed some light on the situation?"

Melissa turned her huge cornflower-blue eyes on the sheriff, the very picture of innocence. "Tanya must be right, sir. Suellen could be a bit addled. I know for a fact that Suellen despises Tanya and would do anything to get revenge on her."

Suellen choked on her anger and could not manage to get a word out at the moment. The sheriff nodded in silent understanding of Melissa's statement.

Jeffrey, however, had no trouble finding his voice. "I know what you are trying to do here, but it won't work. Miss Haverick is in full control of her faculties, and I intend to prove she is telling the truth!"

"Adam, what do you have to say to all this?" Middleton asked. "We haven't heard a word from you."

Adam leaned an elbow on one of the bars and

surveyed them all with a lazy smile. "Frankly, Tom, I'm stunned almost speechless. You and Justin here have known me since I was in diapers. If anyone knows me, you do."

"I've never heard anything so ridiculous in my life!" Justin added. "Adam and I grew up together! Everyone knows Rachel Savage, and a lot of folks remember when she and her father moved here from Santa Fe when Adam was just a baby. We all know her husband was English, and that her people are Spanish. I fail to see how anyone could claim he was Cheyenne, let alone a chief!"

Roberto now took up the cudgels. "Adam is my cousin, and I too have known him all my life. What you say is too ludicrous to give credence to. It is absurd!"

Middleton exhaled a cloud of cigar smoke. "There you have it, Lieutenant. Justin is right. Most of the population of Pueblo have watched Adam grow up under their noses. I'd say you don't stand a snowball's chance in Hell of bringing such far-fetched charges against him, let alone making them stick."

Jeffrey eyed them all malevolently, his blue eyes shooting flames. "We'll just see about that!" he threatened. "I've sent a runner to Ft. Lyon for authorization to bring him up on charges before a military court, where you have no authority. It is purely a military matter, and you know how General Custer and General Hancock feel about Indians."

"You have to prove I *am* one, first," Adam pointed out.

Jeffrey sneered at him, his eyes narrowed with hate. "That shouldn't be too hard in a court of cavalrymen just itching to string up a 'dirty Injun'. Then too, there are others besides Suellen who know what this Panther looks like. I'm sure Major Wynkoop, the Indian agent to the Cheyenne, could easily identify him."

Only sheer willpower enabled Tanya to keep her face from showing the shock this last statement brought with it. She was never so thankful for the rigid training Panther had drilled into her. She was also thankful that Melissa was facing away from Jeffrey and Suellen just then, and had somehow managed to stifle her involuntary gasp before anyone noticed. Adam's face revealed nothing.

Middleton frowned and rubbed a hand along his cheek. "I thought Wynkoop was back in Washington raising a ruckus over the Washita massacre."

"He was, the fool, for all the good it will do him," Jeffrey replied, "but we expect his return any day now. In the meanwhile, I intend to keep an eye on Mr. Savage here and file the proper charges against him."

"Like I said, the line forms behind me, and even if you had authorization today to arrest him, you'd have to wait until I'm done with him."

Jeffrey nodded stiffly. "Just as long as I know where to find him—and believe me, Sheriff, I'll be watching closely. I intend to post my own guards around your jail to make sure he doesn't suddenly disappear."

"You just keep your men outside my jailhouse and out from under foot. I won't abide having my office overrun and my routine upset by a passle of greenhorn know-it-alls." Middleton snapped. "Now get out of my office. I've got better things to do than talk nonsense all day."

"I'll be back!" Jeffrey barked the warning over his shoulder as he left, shepherding an indignant Suellen before him.

For long seconds after he'd gone, no one spoke.

They just looked at the door and each other. Not until Melissa let out a long-held breath was the spell broken.

"Adam," Tanya began, turning a worried face to his.

Through the bars, he reached out a hand to stroke her cheek, his dark eyes burning into hers. "Later," he said gently.

In a louder voice, he directed his attention to Sheriff Middleton. "I believe you have something to explain to me, Tom."

A wide grin split Middleton's face. "Wondered when you'd think of that. I should apologize, but fact is, I did you a favor."

Adam groaned. "Tom, if your idea of favors is slugging someone when they least expect it, save them for someone else in the future."

"Well, you didn't do my bread-basket a lot of good either." Tom rubbed a broad hand across his stomach and grimaced. "You pack quite a wallop."

"What was that all about?" Julie asked, thoroughly bewildered.

"It was the best I could come up with on the spur of the moment," the sheriff explained. "I happened to stumble on those two just as the Haverick girl was babbling about Adam being a Cheyenne Indian. The lieutenant was lapping up every word like a cat at a bowl of cream. I tell you, he got a real dangerous look to him, all excited and hateful, with those blue eyes of his gleaming wild-like. One look was enough to tell me he was off his rocker and bound to cause some kind of trouble. Then I heard him say she'd just given him all the proof he needed—the perfect reason to arrest you, the excuse he's been looking for to see you hang.

"I didn't wait much longer, except to hear him ask if

she knew where you were now. When she said she'd last seen you at the rodeo corral, I took off to find you before they could."

"But why did you have to arrest Adam?" Melissa asked. "Why couldn't you just warn him, or tell Jeffrey to back off? This whole thing is insane!"

"It does seem a little extreme, Tom," Justin put in.

Middleton gave Justin an incredulous look tinged with mild annoyance. "Son, for a lawyer you sure can be dense sometimes! Use your common sense. If Young had latched on to Adam first, his authority would override mine, and none of us could have done a thing about it, not even the judge. It would have been a military matter then, with trumped-up charges, few witnesses, and a biased jury, with a military trial and execution so quick it would be over before it started. It wouldn't matter that both the girl and the lieutenant are crazy as bedbugs. It would be their word against Adam's—if he were even allowed to tell his side of it—and none of us would have been permitted to testify in his behalf if I read the lieutenant right.

"It's a lot different here than back East, where they can drag a trial out forever. Here we are dealing with a bunch of glory-seeking cavalrymen eager to prove themselves superior to the savages, while they jump at their own shadows. Some of their commanding officers are so fresh from the East they don't know a lance from a toothpick. They don't know a Sioux from a Comanche, and couldn't care less. As long as they make themselves look good, get an advance in rank, and get out of here with their scalps, it doesn't matter what they have to do or how they do it. I've seen some of these jackasses bragging about how brave they are in battle and showing off scalps I know damned well came off a child or squaw instead of a warrior."

Middleton sighed and shook his head in disgust. "Now, I ain't saying I have a lot of kind feelings for the Indians, but a cavalry full of greenhorn soldiers and glory-hunting officers ain't much better. Seasoned officers who know anything about the Indians are as rare as bird's teeth, and those like Lieutenant Young stir up more trouble than they are worth.

"What I am trying to tell you is this. Right now the troubles with the tribes are starting up heavy again, and it would be a feather in Young's cap if he could claim to have caught a Cheyenne chief. Feelings are running high, and the military is out for every coup they can grab. They'd love to make an example of someone, and I'd hate it to be you, Adam. It wouldn't matter that it was all a cock-and-bull story. It wouldn't matter that half this town has known you all your life and would be up in arms defending you. One glimpse of possible fame and honor, and the military would hang President Grant himself without a proper trial or defense! They'd most likely arrest you, try you, and hang you so fast it would be over before you could do anything about it."

Roberto had wandered to the front windows of the sheriff's office. "Lieutenant Young didn't waste any time posting his guards," he observed. "They are out there already. What do we do now?"

"We have to figure a way to sneak Adam out of town before Young gets the authorization from his superiors to arrest him," Middleton said. "You were going to take a trip anyway, so at least it won't upset your plans much. In the meantime, you'll remain my 'prisoner'."

"Oh, dear!" Tanya murmured in frustration. "While Jeffrey runs around creating havoc, Adam must sit here like a treed raccoon. It isn't fair!"

"Don't you fret, Mrs. Savage," Middleton said with gruff kindness. "We'll think of something."

"I hope it includes tearing Suellen's hair out and slicing Jeffrey's black heart into tiny pieces," she suggested with a vengeance. "I could kill them both with my bare hands right now and feel no remorse whatsoever!"

"Tanya." The tone of command in Adam's voice brought her back into control. "Take the boys home. They are tired and hungry." She nodded wordlessly.

"Justin, explain what has happened to my mother and the Martins, and also to your father. See if he has any suggestions."

"Of course, Adam."

"Roberto, I put you in charge of looking after Tanya and the boys, if you will. Jeffrey's main objective is to have Tanya for his own. He is as mad as a rabid dog, and just as unpredictable, so take great care."

"I will guard them with my life," he vowed.

"Okay, now," Middleton directed, clearing his throat. "All of you clear out of here so Adam and I can think. I've had about all the excitement I can put up with for one day."

Tanya took two steps, then turned back to Adam, unshed tears glistening in her golden eyes. "I'll get you out of here, Adam, I swear it! And someday I'll see Jeffrey pay for all his treachery." That said, she left, head held high and proud.

It didn't particularly surprise Tanya to find guards posted not only outside the jail, but around the Martin house. Even with Adam in jail, Jeffrey was making sure Tanya did not flee.

Justin explained everything briefly to Tanya's family, then went home to speak to Rachel and his own father.

Edward was outraged. The others were stunned. While Tanya sat silently seething, cursing and condemning Jeffrey, Edward ranted and raged, openly venting his ire.

After a supper was served for which no one had any appetite, Tanya put her sons to bed. Soon thereafter, Judge Kerr, Justin, and Rachel showed up, and everyone gathered in the parlor to discuss this unexpected turn of events.

"The sheriff suggested we find a way to sneak Adam out of town without Lieutenant Young knowing about it," Roberto stated, "before the lieutenant can get authorization from Ft. Lyon."

"What if we can't?" Rachel asked, her brown eyes huge with worry. "What if they arrest Adam? Tom can't keep him in his custody indefinitely."

"It is Lieutenant Young's word and Suellen's against ours," George said. "Even as anxious as the military is to get revenge on the tribes, surely they will see how ridiculous this incident is. Besides, we can point out that Jeffrey is obsessed with Tanya and Suellen is full of spite toward her."

"Will we be able to voice any opinions at all in a military matter?" Justin questioned uncertainly. "Tom seemed to think once they get Adam into their clutches, it will be a closed military procedure."

Judge Kerr frowned. "I'm afraid he's right. That could be disastrous. I've also heard General Custer is back in Ft. Lyon, regrouping."

Tanya groaned. "Jeffrey was with his troop when they raided the village at Washita, and the two of them seem to have similar attitudes. According to Custer, the only good Indian is a dead one."

Melissa nodded dispiritedly. "Yes, and Jeffrey said they would be trying to locate Major Wynkoop to identify Panther." A look of intense concern passed between Melissa, Tanya, and Rachel, the only ones in the room who knew the whole truth.

Judge Kerr noted the look that passed between the women and his frown deepened. "That shouldn't cause a problem, should it?" he asked. "As far as I know, Wynkoop has always worked in the best interest of the Indians. Besides, he should be able to positively confirm that Adam is not a Cheyenne. He could be the answer to our prayers." His gaze traveled from one ghost-white face to the other, sensing the dismay in each. "Well, won't he?" he pressed.

When none of the three confirmed this, his expression became definitely apprehensive. "Rachel, Tanya, Melissa," he directed gruffly, "may we meet privately in the library to discuss something of vital importance that has just occurred to me?" At their reluctant nods, he added, "Justin, you should probably come too."

Once in the library, he rounded on them. "All right! I get the undeniable impression that there is something important that you have failed to tell me, some secret the three of you share, and I'm beginning to think there may be some truth to these allegations after all. Am I correct?" His level gaze focused on Rachel's face, waiting.

At last she nodded miserably. "Yes, Garfield. It is true." Her voice broke on a sob, and she hid her face in her hands, weeping.

Justin was incredulous. "How can that be? Adam and I have grown up together. I've known him all his life!"

"Not quite," Judge Kerr was quick to point out. "Rachel, her father, and her son came to Pueblo when Adam was a babe. We all accepted without question the explanation that Rachel's dead husband was an Englishman. It was a lie then, Rachel?" His tone was gentle, but insistent.

Rachel let out a shaky sigh and raised her head to face him. "Yes, it was a lie. Adam's father was the Cheyenne chief White Antelope. After he returned me to my family, my father brought Adam and me to Pueblo to avoid gossip. Each summer, when you all thought Adam went to my family in Santa Fe, he went to stay with his father in their village. He grew up learning two separate ways of life, and five years ago he chose to live with his Cheyenne family for good—or at least until I could no longer manage the ranch myself. I tried to understand, though I resented it. It is his destiny; the Cheyenne blood flows in his veins."

"Dear God!" Justin exclaimed softly. "Then Suellen is right? He *is* a Cheyenne chief and Tanya's husband, Panther?" His accusing gaze darted from Tanya to his own sweet, deceiving fiancée.

Melissa nodded silently, her big blue eyes begging Justin to forgive her.

Tanya was less reluctant, her valiant pride coming to the fore. "Yes, Adam and Panther are one and the same, and Hunter and Mark are our sons. Did you really believe I could claim to love my husband and fall so readily into a stranger's arms?"

"Who else knows?" Judge Kerr asked.

"No one. Suellen, Melissa and I are the only captives left from the raid. And Major Wynkoop will if he sees Adam."

"What about Roberto or any of your other relatives?" he asked Rachel.

She shook her head. "Only my father knew. We told none of the family."

"Perhaps we should inform Roberto now. Will he

help us, do you think, or will he turn against us?" With this statement, Justin announced his allegiance to his lifelong friend.

"He'll help."

"We probably should inform your family, too," Judge Kerr told Tanya. "They have a right to know. How will they react, Tanya? Will they betray Adam?" Evidently, Judge Kerr was also willing to aid his friends of many years.

"I don't know," Tanya responded. "I suppose we'll have to chance it, and hope they'll understand. They've come to know Adam. They like and respect him. The fact that he is part Cheyenne should not change things."

"It shouldn't, but it might," Judge Kerr warned dourly. "Justin and I have known Adam a lot longer. This comes as a shock to us, but we know Adam is a good man, with respectable values. Being Cheyenne does not alter the decent man we know Adam to be."

"Perhaps you should be the one to point this out to my family," Tanya suggested. "It is not easy to explain when your heart leads your head. They will expect me to defend Adam because of my love for him, but you would do so out of respect for a man you know and trust."

Predictably, Edward had a fit at first, Sarah nearly swooned, and Julie was torn between indignation and loyalty to her new husband and Tanya. Roberto readily accepted this news about his cousin and offered his help. George merely nodded and lit his pipe, and Elizabeth smiled as if to say, "I should have known." Jeremy was elated, and had to be sworn to secrecy, though he would have liked nothing better than to be able to brag to all his friends.

After their initial reactions, Sarah quickly became resigned to it, even rather glad that Hunter and Mark would be raised by their real father and that Tanya was reunited with her true love. With some help from Judge Kerr and Rachel, Edward finally accepted it more calmly, realizing that the Adam he had come to admire was a worthy man, whether white, Indian, or both.

United in their efforts to save Adam, they now had the task of devising a plan. Weary and emotionally drained, they finally gave up for the evening, deciding they'd think better when they were more rested.

The next morning, Tanya still had not come up with a workable plan, but her mind was working better. Regardless of all else, there were still certain things that could be done. Now that her family was aware that Adam and Tanya would be returning to the Cheyenne camp, there was no need for the pretense of packing for a long European voyage. Instead, Tanya readied appropriate clothing for herself, Adam, and their sons. She packaged dried fruits and meats, filled canteens, and packed the necessary tools and other items they would require in their flight.

With sharp-eyed guards watching, Tanya wondered how they could spirit the horses out of Uncle George's stables and away to a more accessible place. When she happened to spy a can of whitewash intended for the back porch, she devised a method. Enlisting Jeremy's aid, she set to work. Knowing her presence in the stable for long would draw the guards' attention, it was decided Jeremy would be sent to clean the stalls—supposedly, at any rate. Under Tanya's direction, he painted three white socks and a blaze down the face of Adam's midnight-black stallion. Then, with walnut stain, he darkened the buckskin's coat until Wheat was a solid gleaming brown.

The last part of the scheme was the trickiest. Once darkness fell, Rachel and Justin left their own mounts in the stable and rode out of the yard astride the disguised Wheat and Shadow. Luckily, the guards noticed nothing amiss in the dim light, intent only on properly identifying the riders. Rachel and Justin then stabled the horses at the Kerrs', where they could be retrieved without notice.

With the horses and essentials ready and waiting, all that remained was to somehow manage to get Tanya, Mark, and Hunter away from their diligent guards and slip Adam under the noses of his, no easy matter, especially with Jeffrey dogging Tanya's every step. Roberto escorted her to the jail that first morning to speak with Adam. After she explained to him what they were doing, they then discussed possible ways to help him escape, but nothing sounded reasonable. Meanwhile, Judge Kerr was using his influence with high officials in the territory, to no avail. No one seemed to have the authority needed to intercede or influence military affairs.

Upon leaving the jail, Jeffrey approached them. Tanya felt Roberto stiffen at her side, prepared to defend her, and grateful as she was, she didn't want him to give Jeffrey an excuse to arrest him too. She decided the best course was to ignore Jeffrey, if possible.

With head held high and shoulders straight, she stared past him, walking slowly but steadily toward home. Undeterred, Jeffrey kept pace with her. With a nasty leer, which she saw from the corner of her eye, he taunted, "Thought you'd gotten away with it, didn't you, Tanya love? Well, thanks to Suellen, the tables are turned."

"Go away, Jeffrey," she hissed.

"Tanya darling, you'd do better to be nice to me. The life of someone dear to you will soon be in my hands. What happens to him depends entirely on you."

That stopped her short, and she swung about to face him. "Perhaps you'd better explain to me exactly what that comment means!"

He spread his hands out in a gesture of innocence, his face a false mask of sincerity. "It is as simple as this, Tanya. If you could manage to have your marriage annulled and marry me before Savage's trial is over, I could no doubt arrange to have him set free. If not, he'll assuredly hang, and you will be a widow. Either way, you will soon be mine again. Of course, I won't accept his sons in the bargain. You'll have to get rid of them."

Her eyes shot deadly golden daggers at him. "I'll *never* belong to you, Jeffrey. Never! If you weren't insane, you'd have realized that by now. You are quite mad, you know. If I didn't hate you so much, I could actually feel sorry for you."

"You bitch!" he exploded, grabbing her roughly by the arms. "You'll regret those words! I'll see you pay for each and every insult you've subjected me to!" In rhythm with his words, he shook her like a rag doll, stopping only when he felt the barrel of Roberto's pistol in his ribs. "Take your filthy hands off my cousin's wife!" Roberto ordered.

Jeffrey released her then with a look of contempt at Roberto. "If you shoot me, you won't get five feet before you are arrested."

Roberto smiled evilly, his teeth flashing in his dark face, his eyes snapping fire. "That may be, but you'll already be dead by then, your blood seeping its way into Hell." His soft, slow words held the weight of a sacred oath.

Jeffrey backed off. "Think about what I have said, Tanya. Your time is running out. And don't try anything. I have you all under close surveillance, even your brats. If I see anything suspicious, it won't be hard to make you regret it. Your sons will be the first to pay, and then your Indian lover." He turned on his heel and stalked off.

Roberto and Tanya shared a worried look. "I think we need next to find a way to get your sons to safety," said Roberto. "Even with Kit guarding them, I feel uneasy."

"So do I," Tanya concurred. "His mind is so twisted, it is impossible to follow the line of his thoughts."

It was Rachel who came up with an idea to protect her grandsons. That very day she sent Roberto back out to the ranch, and by midnight he had returned to town again.

The early morning sun glistened on Tanya's hair as she stepped lightly off the front steps, a huge basket balanced carefully in her arms.

"Sorry, ma'am, but I have to know what's in that basket you're carrying," one of the guards said, stopping her.

She glared at him, but halted. "In case you are unaware of it, there is a wedding planned in two days," she said stiffly. "I am taking these pies to Emily Kerr in preparation for it."

The soldier lifted a corner of the checkered cloth and sniffed appreciatively at the fresh-baked aroma escaping. "Apple and blueberry," he sighed. "Sure smells good." With that, he let her pass, watching to make sure she entered the Kerr home.

A short while later, he watched as she made the return trip. As she passed him, he caught sight of a couple of eggs peeping out from under the cloth. "Careful going up those steps, ma'am," he cautioned politely. "Those eggs look about to tumble."

She nodded wordlessly. Tanya passed Justin and Roberto at the door. They were lugging a good-sized trunk between them. "What are you doing with that?" she called after them.

Justin grinned ruefully. "This is just a small portion of Melissa's wordly goods," he joked. "I'll be hobbling down the aisle after a few trips like this!"

The guards laughed with him. "Marryin' is hard work," one offered with a wink.

One more delivery was made to the Martin household that morning. Elizabeth pulled the wagon to a halt at the front gate, a huge box balanced on the seat beside her. Julie and Melissa came running out of the house. Melissa reached the wagon first, tearing the top off of the box. With a squeal of delight, she reached in and pulled out a lovely yellow gown, twirling about joyously, the gown held out before her. "Oh! It's lovely, Elizabeth! Is the rest of my trousseau in there! Did she get it all done?"

Elizabeth smiled indulgently, her sharp eyes noting the silly grins on the faces of the guards. "Every stitch," she promised. "But, dear heart, I really think you should examine the contents in a more private place. Help me take these things inside."

Between them, Julie and Melissa carted the box indoors, and Elizabeth pulled the wagon around back.

Inside, several anxious people heaved a collective sigh of relief as they helped a small, dark-haired boy from the box.

"Hello, *hola*, Pepito," Roberto said in greeting.

"You were as quiet as a *ratoncito*, a little mouse."

The boy grinned, his small white teeth flashing in his olive face. "Is Felipe here?"

"Yes, he arrived in a basket of eggs this morning. He is taking a nap now."

Pepito nodded. "He's still a baby. I don't take naps anymore," he stated importantly.

Rachel came bustling into the room. "Oh good! I was hoping he had arrived safely," she said upon seeing Pepito. "It was good of Anna and Selena to loan us their children for a few days."

Turning to Tanya, she said, "Hunter and Mark are having a lovely holiday with Emily Kerr. She is already spoiling them outrageously." She added gently, "Do not fret, Tanya. They will be safe there, and it will not be for long."

"It is best this way," Sarah offered. "Now when you are ready to leave, the boys will be waiting. In the meanwhile, Pepito and Felipe can easily pass for Hunter and Mark at a distance, and Jeffrey will be none the wiser."

"I know," Tanya agreed, "but Jeffrey was right about one thing. Time is running out quickly. We must devise a plan to rescue Adam!"

Chapter 26

IT WAS Melissa who inadvertently came up with the best plan. Not without risks, it still had a good chance for success. Besides, it was their only hope.

Late in the afternoon on the eighth of July, a party of twelve adults and three children, all elegantly attired in their wedding finery, trooped past the guards and into Sheriff Middleton's jail.

Short minutes later, Jeffrey burst in behind them, a look of thunderous anger on his face. "What is going on here?" he demanded.

Tom Middleton bristled. "Look, you belligerent bigmouth, I don't answer to anybody in my jail! You just wag your tail on out of here! This is a private party."

"Yes!" Julie piped in. "If Melissa wanted you at her wedding, she'd have invited you."

"*Wedding*!" Jeffrey exclaimed. "You're holding a wedding in a jail?"

"That's about the size of it," Judge Kerr said. "Melissa and Justin insisted that Adam and Tanya be present at the ceremony, and this was the only way we could see to arrange it."

"Got some problem with that?" Middleton drawled. "If you do, that's too bad, 'cause this is my jail and I say it's fine."

Jeffrey gave them all a look of contempt. "Go ahead with your stupid wedding. Just remember, I have my men watching you. They'll see that no unauthorized person leaves here." His blue eyes leveled their gaze on Adam, still securely behind bars.

The words of the solemn ceremony carried easily through the open windows to the guards. So, too, did the sounds of congratulations and toasts to the new bride and groom.

The sight of the photographer lugging his bulky camera toward the jail brought the guards to attention. They stood uncertainly as the guests filed out to stand in front of the jail, the setting sun casting a golden glow on their faces. They jerked to full alert as Sheriff Middleton exited the building with Adam in tow.

"Halt!" a fat sergeant ordered.

"Oh, pipe down!" Middleton said gruffly. "And don't get all riled. This man is still my prisoner, and I'll make sure he doesn't wander off just yet."

"What's he doing out here?" the sergeant demanded.

"What's it look like?" the sheriff retorted. "Even you should know you can't take a picture indoors, and these folks want their wedding picture taken with their best man and their matron of honor." He led Adam to stand next to Justin. "Now, smile pretty and don't make a move in the wrong direction," he admonished Adam, "cause I've got you covered, and so do these guards of the lieutenant's." For emphasis, he drew his gun and pointed it at Adam.

The photographer lined everyone up and prepared to snap the picture, fussing constantly about the waning daylight. "Will you gentlemen kindly step out of the way?" he directed the guards. "I'm sure the wedding party will object to having you in the finished photograph."

The guards frowned and tightened their grips on their weapons, but obliged reluctantly. Their eyes never left Adam for a moment, alert in case he would try to make a break for freedom. They didn't take a relaxed breath until Adam had been herded back into the jail and was safely behind bars once more.

The wedding party continued in the jail, and a small but noisy celebration ensued. After a while, the guards were content that the prisoner, having made no attempt to escape when the photographs were taken, had lost his only opportunity to do so. They quickly reverted to their casual watchfulness, careful only in noting anyone who approached the jail.

The celebration seemed destined to go on forever. It was fully dark by the time the bride and groom dashed out of the jailhouse door, surrounded by laughing relatives and pelted with rice.

The tired guards came momentarily alert again as they stood next to the rest of the wedding party, watching the newlyweds make their way hurriedly in the direction of the Judge's residence. Their sharp eyes took note of the creamy yellow gown and lacy veil the bride had worn, and the brown and tan suit of the groom. One quick glance inside the jail confirmed that the prisoner was still there.

Adam's back was to them as he hoisted a drink in toast to his friends. He was joined again by the others, his tall form in white shirt and dark trousers soon hidden as they crowded into the small room. The guards caught a flash of peach-colored skirts somewhere in the center of the confusion, and were content to know that Tanya was still there, as well as her two dark-haired sons.

It was another two hours before Lieutenant Young came striding up, accompanied by a major. "This is Major Wynkoop," he said. "I have the authorization for arrest here, signed by General Custer. Now let's see the sheriff put me off." He turned to his sergeant. "Is everything all right? I see the party is still going on. Has anyone left?"

"Just the bride and groom," the sergeant answered. "The rest are still in there."

Jeffrey entered the jail with a flourish, a devious gleam in his blue eyes. He strode up to Sheriff Middleton and slapped the papers into his hands. "I have orders here from General Custer to arrest Adam Savage in the name of the United States Army. I have also brought Major Wynkoop to confirm his identity as that of the Cheyenne chief, A-Panther-Stalks."

The sheriff smiled slyly back at him. "Well now, Lieutenant, that might have held some weight if you'd have arrived sooner. As it stands, there is no one here for you to arrest, and until you arrest him, no formal charges can be administered. Ain't that right, Judge?"

"Quite correct, Sheriff," the Judge intoned.

Jeffrey nearly had a stroke on the spot. "What do you mean!" he roared, pushing his way past the others to the jail cell. His eyes swept the small crowd, failing to find either Adam or Tanya; instead he saw a serenely smiling Melissa attired in Tanya's peach gown.

"Where is he? Where is Tanya?" he screamed.

"Gone."

His feverish gaze searched out the two small boys. "*Gone*?" he echoed. "Well, they can't have gone far without their sons." He strode toward the boys. "They'll be back to get these two, and when they do, I'll have them."

Roberto stepped into his path. "Look again, Lieutenant. These children are not Tanya's sons. They are two boys my aunt is looking after for their parents."

Jeffrey's face registered yet another shock as he realized the truth of Roberto's statement. He let out a roar of frustrated rage and turned on the sheriff. "I'll have your badge for this! You've let my prisoner escape!"

Tom Middleton's hand rested on his holstered gun. "He wasn't *your* prisoner, Young. He was mine," he reminded him.

"What about the charges you had against him?" Jeffrey tried to collect his thoughts.

"I dropped them."

"What were they?" Major Wynkoop spoke quietly for the first time.

"Assaulting an officer of the law," Middleton responded, "but the attack was provoked, so I decided to drop charges and release him."

"How convenient! And just as I was about to take him into custody!" Jeffrey ranted.

"I don't have to catch your prisoners for you, nor hold them neither," Middleton said shortly. "Do your own dirty work! You want him? Go catch him! But don't expect any help from me. Everyone knows you're as crazy as a loon and out to get your grubby hands on Adam's bride. If it weren't for that, you wouldn't bother making up such ridiculous charges and far-fetched tales about someone we've known and respected for more than twenty years."

Wynkoop's eyebrows went up at this. "You say Adam Savage has lived here all these years?"

"Yep, and the whole town knows he ain't no Indian."

"Suellen Haverick says differently, and so do I," Jeffrey insisted furiously.

"Suellen Haverick is as crazy as you are," Melissa put in.

"I'm going after them! I'm going to catch them and prove that you are wrong; and you, Major Wynkoop, are coming with me!" Jeffrey bellowed.

Dawn filtered like a grey mist through the trees as Wildcat and Panther wended their way deeper into the foothills. It was good to be in the mountains once more; good to breathe the pure, pine-scented air.

Mark slept peacefully in his cradleboard, suspended from the pommel of Tanya's saddle, while Hunter rode before his father.

It had been a long ride, though they had traveled as swiftly as possible in the dark. Tanya swore Panther had the eyesight of his namesake as he brought them safely through the night, Kit loping happily alongside.

They made a short stop for a cold breakfast and to change into more suitable clothing, and were quickly on their way again. Now Tanya wore her beloved doeskin dress, headband and moccasins. The boys and Panther wore only breechcloths and moccasins. Tanya's hair had at last reached a proper length for decent braids, and although Panther now looked more familiar in his headband and feathers, she missed his long, dark braids. If it weren't for the fact that Jeffrey and his band were surely somewhere on the backtrail she would have been completely content at that moment.

They traveled all day with barely a stop to water the horses, heading steadily into the mountains. Shortly after dark, they had to rest. The horses were ready to drop, Mark was wriggling in his restraining cradle board, and Hunter was drooping wearily in Panther's arms. Tanya, unused to such vigorous activity after many months in Pueblo, was a mass of aching muscles, especially those surrounding her weary posterior.

Panther laughed as he watched her slide awkwardly from Wheat's back. "You'll be stiff and sore tomorrow," he predicted.

"I already am," she answered with a grimace.

The night's sleep seemed much too short, and long before dawn, they were on their way again. "Why are we headed into the mountains, husband?" Tanya asked, already reverting comfortably to the Cheyenne language. "Is the tribe not already following the buffalo on the plains?"

"Yes." His dark eyes roved over her appreciatively, delighted that she was his Little Wildcat once again. "But we dare not lead those who follow to our village. When we have lost them in the mountains, we will turn our feet toward the plains." The Cheyenne words flowed easily from his tongue, and Tanya rejoiced to hear them intoned in his deep, rich voice.

Tired as they were, Tanya hated having to camp the second evening. Some sixth sense told her that Jeffrey was closing in. She could practically feel his hot breath on the back of her neck. Panther must have sensed it too, for once again he ordered no fire be built for cooking. Had it been only Tanya and Panther, they could have easily outdistanced their pursuers, but with their sons along, traveling was slower. The pace was necessarily easier, and the numerous stops took precious time they could ill afford.

They were preparing to depart their camp on the third morning. Tanya was loading the last of their belongings behind her saddle when her ears suddenly picked up the sounds of fast-moving horses closing in.

Her frightened gaze swung swiftly to Panther.

His eyes were searching the rocky terrain, seeking shelter for his family. Pointing to a collection of huge boulders near the edge of their camp, he instructed, "There! That is the best spot."

Before his words were finished, Tanya had Mark in her arms and her weapons collected, and was headed in the direction he had pointed out. Panther, too, made sure his weapons were at hand. Scooping Hunter off the ground, he slapped each horse on the rump, sending them trotting into the trees. Then he followed Tanya.

Shots rang out, ricocheting sharply off the rocks as Panther made a final leap for cover. He drew his pistol and fired, letting his enemies know he was as well armed as they and prepared to defend his family. At least they would be wary of approaching too closely too soon.

Jeffrey's insanely triumphant laughter bounced up to them. "We have you trapped, Savage. Give up!"

Panther disdained to answer this taunt. He barely glanced at Tanya as she informed him in a tight whisper, "Major Wynkoop is with them."

From the corner of his eye, he saw her nock an arrow into her bow. Peering around the edge of a boulder, he counted eight men, including Jeffrey and Wynkoop. They were all on the far side of the small clearing, concealing themselves behind rocks and trees.

"Send Tanya to me, and we'll let you and your sons go free," Jeffrey called out.

"Does he honestly think we'll believe that?" Tanya muttered.

"I'll kill her myself before I turn her over to you," Panther shouted back in English.

He barely heard Jeffrey's snort of disbelief and Wynkoop's low warning. "If he truly is a Cheyenne, he will kill her first," the major advised. "It is their way."

"Come to me, Tanya," Jeffrey shouted. "I'll protect you."

"Go to hell!" she yelled in reply.

Panther shot her a humorous look completely at odds with the gravity of the situation. She returned his look with a grin and a saucy wink.

Enraged and embarrassed that she would taunt him before his men, Jeffrey lost all control over his temper, and with it his better judgment. He galloped his gelding into the clearing, charging for the rocks where Tanya and Panther were hiding.

He had reached the edge of the lower boulders, and Panther's finger was tightening on the trigger, when Jeffrey's horse suddenly shied. Its ears laid back, and its eyes rolling white with fright, the gelding reared up on its hind legs. Totally unprepared for this, Jeffrey made a mad grab for the pommel and missed. His feet failed to find the stirrups they'd slipped from. With a strangled cry, he tumbled to the ground.

Tanya could hear the snap of bone from where she sat. Peeking between the boulders, she saw the twisted angle of one leg, firmly wedged in the rocks. Her mouth flew open in surprise as she heard almost simultaneously the angry hiss and ominous rattling of several rattlesnakes. Jeffrey's horse had bolted with good reason, and in the process had thrown him into a nest of rattlers!

Jeffrey's screams of fright and agony had nothing to do with his broken leg. Between shrieks of pain came pleas for help. "Help me! Help me! Oh, God! Someone get them off me!"

For anyone else, Tanya would have felt pity, but the thought pounding in her brain as she watched Jeffrey flail at the writhing snakes was that it was a fitting ending for him. He had the slithering disposition of a viper, and for months she had endured his particular brand of venom, one almost equal to that of the snakes. It seemed poetic justice that he would enter the portals of Hell with the lethal poison of the rattlesnakes mingling with his own tainted blood.

Within seconds, Jeffrey had succumbed to unconsciousness. Even as Major Wynkoop, next highest in rank, stepped into the open, a white flag of truce tied to a stick, it was too late to save him.

"Let us help him!" he called as he came forward.

"He is beyond help, but you are welcome to his body," Panther answered.

Several others came forward when it was clear that Panther did not intend to shoot. One young cavalryman, obviously newly arrived from the East, took one look and promptly vomited. In order to retrieve Jeffrey's body, it was necessary to first eliminate the snakes. A volley of shots rang out, reverberating off the hills and echoing back to double the deafening din.

As they carried the body away, Panther positioned himself atop a large boulder, boldly displaying himself. Tanya climbed up to stand beside him. Together they stood, proudly facing the enemy.

The soldiers stood staring at them, wondering at the arrogant warrior and his defiant tawny-haired wife with the strange golden eyes. Major Wynkoop broke the silence. "We'll leave you in peace, to go on your way," he said calmly, meeting Panther's gaze squarely.

Panther nodded wordlessly, and the major went on, "We will return to town and bear witness to the fact that Lieutenant Young was out of his mind and that you were in no way responsible for his death. I personally will testify that I have seen the man, Adam Savage, and that he cannot be A-Panther-Stalks."

"But, Major," one young soldier interrupted, "how can you say that when the man stands before you dressed as an Indian?"

Wynkoop's searing gaze lanced through the speaker. "I have met A-Panther-Stalks," he stated loudly. "I have sat in his tipi and eaten of his food. I have seen his wife and she has dark hair. I have held his son, and he is not white. Even if this man were A-Panther-Stalks, no charges have been filed, and we have no authority to arrest him. Lieutenant Young had no valid reason for chasing him, other than his insane lust for another man's wife. He acted solely on the accusations of a vindictive woman, who obviously lied to cause another woman pain. I have it on good faith from the sheriff and Judge Kerr that Adam Savage is a respected citizen of Pueblo who has lived there all his life. Do we accept the word of one scorned woman and a demented man over that of an entire town?"

"No, but . . ." the soldier began again.

Wynkoop interjected angrily, pointing to Adam and Tanya, "It is not a crime to dress in buckskin, damn it! Neither is it a crime to prefer life as an Indian! I say this is *not* A-Panther-Stalks, and I am the one who should know! Now, I repeat, we will leave this family to go their way in peace."

"Yes, sir."

"Do I hear any objections?" Wynkoop pressed.

The men exchanged glances among themselves. "No, sir!" they all answered.

Then one soldier ventured a further opinion. "We all know Lieutenant Young was crazy. We all saw how he hounded the young lady here. Some of us were even in his troop last February when he chased after her when she tried to go back to the Indians, and he tried to—er—attack her person." He glanced shame-faced at Tanya. "I'm real sorry, ma'am, for all the trouble he put you through, and for being any part of it. All of us," his gesture included his fellow soldiers, "were just following orders." The others nodded in agreement.

Tanya accepted the apology. As she went to round up their horses, Wynkoop and Panther had a private word together.

"Why do you say I cannot be A-Panther-Stalks?" Panther asked in Cheyenne.

Wynkoop chuckled, his eyes twinkling merrily. "Why, everyone who's met him knows that A-Panther-Stalks has long black braids. I can't honestly say I'd recognize him without them."

Panther returned Wynkoop's grin and offered his hand. "Farewell, friend."

"Farewell."

The soldiers rode off, taking Jeffrey's body with them, and Panther and Tanya mounted their horses with their sons.

Tanya, her face aglow with love, her golden eyes glistening with joyous tears, held her husband's dark gaze. "Let us go home, Panther, my husband," she said softly.

"Yes." His own dark features mirrored the emotion of hers, his heart speaking more clearly than his words. "Let us go home, to where the Wildcat runs free and A Panther Stalks the land."

Passionate tales by one of the country's most cherished historical romance writers...

CATHERINE HART

Leisure's Leading Lady of Love

____2661-9 **ASHES & ECSTASY**	$4.50US/$5.50CAN
____2791-7 **FIRE AND ICE**	$4.50US/$5.50CAN
____2600-7 **FOREVER GOLD**	$4.50US/$5.50CAN
____2732-1 **NIGHT FLAME**	$4.50US/$5.50CAN
____2792-5 **SATIN AND STEEL**	$4.50US/$5.50CAN
____2822-0 **SILKEN SAVAGE**	$4.50US/$5.50CAN
____2863-8 **SUMMER STORM**	$4.50US/$5.50CAN

LEISURE BOOKS
ATTN: Customer Service Dept.
276 5th Avenue, New York, NY 10001

Please send me the book(s) checked above. I have enclosed $ ________
Add $1.25 for shipping and handling for the first book; $ .30 for each book thereafter. No cash, stamps, or C.O.D.s. All orders shipped within 6 weeks. Canadian orders please add $1.00 extra postage.

Name ______________________

Address ______________________

City ____________ State ________ Zip ________

Canadian orders must be paid in U.S. dollars payable through a New York banking facility. ☐ Please send a free catalogue.

WINNER OF THE GOLDEN HEART AWARD!

By Patricia Gaffney

Exquisitely beautiful, fiery Katherine McGregor had no qualms about posing as a doxy — if the charade would strike a blow against the hated English. But her certainty turned to confusion when she was captured and confronted by the infuriating Major James Burke. Now her very life depended on her ability to convince the arrogant English officer that she was a common strumpet, not a Scottish spy. Skillfully, Burke uncovered her secrets, even as he aroused her senses, claiming there was just one way she could prove herself a tart...But how could she give him her yearning body, when she feared he would take her tender heart as well?

_______2721-6 $3.95US/$4.95CAN

LEISURE BOOKS
ATTN: Customer Service Dept.
276 5th Avenue, New York, NY 10001

Please send me the book(s) checked above. I have enclosed $ ________
Add $1.25 for shipping and handling for the first book; $ .30 for each book thereafter. No cash, stamps, or C.O.D.s. All orders shipped within 6 weeks. Canadian orders please add $1.00 extra postage.

Name ____

Address ____

City _____________________ State __________ Zip __________

Canadian orders must be paid in U.S. dollars payable through a New York banking facility. ☐ Please send a free catalogue.

Bold historical romance set in the great Outback. Brimming with passion and bursting with exotic delights!

For a female convict like flame-haired Casey O'Cain, New South Wales was a living nightmare. Exquisitely beautiful, utterly helpless, she was expected to cater to her master's every whim. And from the first, arrogant, handsome Dare Penrod made it clear what he wanted of her. Casey knew she should fight him with every breath in her body, but her heart told her he could make a paradise of this wilderness for her. His callused hands took rights she should never have granted, his warm lips whispered of pleasures she had never known, and his hard body promised a love she would never relinquish.

____2755-0 $3.95

LEISURE BOOKS
ATTN: Customer Service Dept.
276 5th Avenue, New York, NY 10001

Please send me the book(s) checked above. I have enclosed $ ________
Add $1.25 for shipping and handling for the first book; $ .30 for each book thereafter. No cash, stamps, or C.O.D.s. All orders shipped within 6 weeks. Canadian orders please add $1.00 extra postage.

Name ________________________

Address ________________________

City ____________ State ______ Zip ______

Canadian orders must be paid in U.S. dollars payable through a New York banking facility. ☐ Please send a free catalogue.